The Secret Mother

Victoria Delderfield

"Full of vibrant scenes of the realities of Chinese life, Victoria Delderfield's debut novel explores the complexities of growing up in a different culture with sensitivity and heart."
Deborah Swift

The Secret Mother

Victoria Delderfield

Hookline Books

Published by Hookline Books
Bookline & Thinker Ltd
#231, 405 King's Road
London SW10 0BB
Tel: 0845 116 1476
www.hooklinebooks.com

A CIP catalogue for this book is available from the British Library.

This book is a work of fiction. Names, characters, places and
incidents are either a product of the author's imagination or are
used fictitiously.
ISBN: 9780993287442

Cover design by Jessie Barlow
Printed and bound by Lightning Source UK

In loving memory of Cynthia, my nan

Then the king said, "Bring me a sword." So they brought a sword for the king. He then gave an order: "Cut the living child in two and give half to one and half to the other."

The woman whose son was alive was deeply moved out of love for her son and said to the king, "Please, my lord, give her the living baby! Don't kill him!"

1 Kings 3 v24-26

Falling leaves return to their roots.
Chinese Proverb

Blood

He hangs it by the ankles, its blue hands splayed, the small kidney-shape of its body crowned with my blood. I open my arms, but the *yīshēng* shakes his head.

"Look away, you hear? Look away." He plunges my baby head first into a waiting bucket of water.

Pain roars in my haunches. I push hard, my womb emptying like a blanket thrown into the air. Between my legs...so much blood.

"Stop pushing, another one's coming," he bawls and discards the limp newborn beside the bucket. He pulls at the second head – half in, half out – and it slips from me, screaming.

A girl.

He grabs a knife from his work block and hacks at the knotty cord that binds her to me. I snatch her. Rock, rock, rock...

"Sshhh, little one."

Her lips quiver. Birth has rippled the puddle of her features; a child that has lived ten lives already.

"Here, take her as well." He picks my firstborn from the mat and thrusts her onto me. She seems almost to be choking. I tap her back and she spews up water. Her chest heaves with life. How neatly she is packed in skin!

But the *yīshēng* returns. In his hand, a syringe. "Straight to the brain. They won't feel a thing," he says.

My heels dig into the mat. "Get away from us!" I seize some rags and the envelope containing Manager He's money. "I'll kill you, I swear. Get away from my babies."

"Women here never keep their babies."

I smell his empty breath and gag. His laugh is sour. I scramble to my feet and stagger towards the door, the cords still swinging from inside.

He catches me by the shoulder, ripping my birth gown and pins me to the wall. The liquid in his syringe drips over my babies. I try to push him off.

"What the hell was He-Chuan thinking? Sending me a mad woman? Those little maggots don't stand a chance. The placenta's still inside. It has double *qi*. I must have it! Now give me the

1

money. Give me – the killing money." He squeezes my wrists until I drop the envelope.

I knee him with all my strength and the *yīshēng* crumples, spewing the bucket across the floor.

"Come back," he groans.

But I am already half way down the wooden staircase that leads to the back door. Outside, the clinic's sign clacks on its hinges, rain runs down the alley.

"You'll never survive," he cries from an upstairs window. "You'll all be dead by dawn." His pallid, scale-marked face is yellow in the streetlight; a gloating man in the moon.

I swaddle my babies and lurch into the rain. A few of the streetlights blink and flicker. The night sky grumbles.

Where to?

I claw my way to the end of the alley where a flooded street opens out in front of me – Shengli Road. The rain bites my face. My firstborn gnaws at the night air, wailing. She is pale, barely there. I put my face to hers. Maybe he is right, maybe we won't survive?

Be brave, little ones. For Mama.

Then suddenly I see him up ahead, in the deserted street. A solitary figure. His head is cocked low, shoulders hunched, collar up. He runs and walks, stops, then runs again. He peers at me through the rain as if looking at the ghost of some long-dead relative. I turn tail. He lopes after me, with a briefcase for a makeshift umbrella.

The pain is searing, far worse than my period cramps. *Got to hold on tight, got to protect...* Suddenly a doorway. I slump onto its hard ledge. Rock, rock, rock my babies.

Hong ching-ting...

Ching ching ting...

Shui shang ching ching ting...

Feel drowsy. Singing or dreaming or drowning, it is all the same. The man with the briefcase is pulling on my arm.

"Get up, get up!" He shouts something about a hospital. *Hospital. Hospital. Hospital.* The whites of his eyes are like halos.

"Leave me alone," I mutter.

"I'll not leave you," he says. Then that word *hospital* again.

I cannot fight.

"It's Yifan. Don't you recognise me?"

"What?"

He hunkers in the doorway. The rain hisses and dances along the guttering, slanting into rivulets across his back, his hair, his face. His fingers press against my neck. He stares at the crimson puddle on the doorstep.

"We don't have long. Can you make it to the square?"

In the distance, lasers jitter over the Uprising Monument. As the colours change, so do my thoughts – as mechanical as the factory line. I expect to hear the klaxon. The sooty rain tastes bitter. Blue neon shop signs blink.

"I want to tell you a story," Yifan garbles, "about double happiness – do you remember it? The student gets sick on the way to his finals. A herbalist and his daughter look after him. The girl is beautiful – they fall in love. She writes down half a couplet..."

Yifan clutches my arm to steady me. My mind wanders around his story, only half understanding.

"The student comes top in the exam. The Emperor is delighted and sets a greater challenge. He writes down half a couplet for the student to complete. Straight away, he knows what to write: the words of his true love."

Yifan's voice is in the faraway. I hear the beginnings and ends of his sentences. I glimpse two babies wrapped in a bundle and wonder who they belong to? Where am I going with this man? He is telling me about his marriage. He is a student, a minister in the Emperor's court. Or is that the student?

"…And that's why we put *happiness* couplets on the door at Spring Festival," says Yifan.

I double over in pain. "Why?"

It is the last thing I remember saying to the man with halo eyes.

Nancy barely noticed the faint pulse of an ambulance as it turned uphill towards the Fairweather Golf Club. The first she knew about the accident was when a receptionist tapped her on the shoulder.

"Excuse me, Mrs Milne. I'm sorry to interrupt your celebrations, but I need you to come with me, there's been an accident."

"Accident? What kind of accident?"

"The Chinese lady that was here earlier – she's been hit, by a car."

May had been in the garden. Her mood strange, morose and yet excitable, garbling about Jen and what a talented student she was, how she could go far if she wanted to pursue her Chinese. But Nancy knew that already.

"Mrs Milne, she's in the ambulance now. She's asking for you."

Jen hurried to her side, "Shit, Mum, you'd better go."

"I've been looking for you – where's Stuart?"

"Mrs Milne, I think you ought to come straight away."

"She's right, Mum. Should I come too?"

Jen's cheeks were flushed with...guilt! It was that darn boy again.

"Mrs Milne, please, if you don't come now..."

"Alright. Alright."

The ambulance was parked further down the golf club driveway, past the poplar trees. The back door was open, she could see two paramedics: one putting a splint on May's leg, another holding an oxygen mask in place.

"May!"

"Are you Mrs Milne?"

She nodded.

"Get in, love."

Nancy perched on the fold-down chair inside the ambulance and watched as the paramedic gave May an injection.

She groaned, her face drained of colour, her head held rigid by a neck brace.

"Don't worry, this will help take the edge off her pain." She turned to Nancy. "She's had a nasty bump to her head. We think her leg's fractured. We're taking her to A & E, they'll see to her properly."

A graze on May's forehead was studded with grit. Her eyes were open, but unfocused. She mumbled in Chinese.

"I'm here, don't worry, you're going to be fine," said Nancy. "We'll get you to hospital." She searched for May's hand beneath the blue emergency blanket.

"Best not touch her, love," said the male paramedic.

The ambulance pulled away, siren warping. Through the darkened glass of the ambulance doors Nancy saw her twins, Ricki and Jen, and some of the guests on the driveway, looking like characters from a Cluedo set. She scanned the crowd for Iain, but the faces of friends and family grew blurry. Her daughters' birthday ruined. Her sixtieth too!

It felt unreal – grown-up – to be in the ambulance as the paramedics talked in that *everything is going to be alright* voice. The same voice people used the day her mother walked into the sea and didn't come out alive. A memory of the emergency crew wrapping her mother's water-logged body like a FedEx package made Nancy feel light-headed. She gnawed at her thumb nail from its wick.

May croaked from beneath her oxygen mask. Something that sounded like "case".

Nancy didn't dare lean in too close. "What is it, May? What do you want?"

"*Keys*," she said again, more clearly. "Take keys."

The paramedic reached into her overalls and handed Nancy a set of house keys that belonged to May. "If you could let her relatives know? Are you in contact?"

May had talked about her family, about her fiancé – what was his name? Yifan? "Her family are all in China. I'll search for an address book, there's bound to be one at her place."

The paramedic checked May's oxygen mask. "That would be best."

May held out a hand. "Please, forgive me Mrs Milne," she said weakly.

"Ssshh, now. Save your strength. We're nearly there," Nancy replied.

"That's right, keep breathing steady. You're doing really well," said the female paramedic.

At Hope Hospital, Nancy waited in the foyer and sipped on a cup of weak vending machine coffee. It tasted empty and burnt her lips.

Two and a half hours had passed since the nurses wheeled May through the swing doors at the end of the corridor. She wished Iain were there; he would be worried. As she rummaged in her handbag for her mobile, a nurse called out her name.

"That's me," said Nancy.

"Would you like to come with me?" The nurse looked reassuringly robust, yet spoke softly. "My name's Alison, I'm one of the team taking care of May. I understand you're her next of kin?"

"Friend, actually. She teaches my daughter."

Alison ushered her into a nearby room. "It's more private in here."

This wasn't good: the Family Room, Kleenex on the coffee table, a hush that went on for centuries. Nancy's lips throbbed where she'd burnt them on the coffee.

"She's dead, isn't she?"

Alison sat down tentatively as if she might hurt the chair. "No. But I'm afraid she is very poorly... May sustained a severe injury to her head and bleeding into her brain, which is causing the pressure in her skull to increase."

"Oh God."

"We've done some CT and MRI scans that show widespread swelling and nerve damage."

"What does that mean?"

"It means we're taking her up to theatre now for an operation to try and relieve some of the pressure."

"Can I see her?"

"I'm afraid the medical team need to be alone with her."

"But she needs me – please..."

"She's in good hands, Mrs Milne. The doctors are doing everything they can."

"How long will it take?"

"It could be some time. The best thing would be for you to go home and get some rest. We'll contact you as soon as she's out of theatre."

Nancy couldn't believe it. A few hours ago, May was explaining how to make Chinese wantons to a bunch of their friends at the buffet table. Now her brain was swelling out of her skull. How could she tell that to May's fiancé? And where was the fucking driver who'd done it?

"Will she be alright?"

The nurse gave a non-committal smile. "We'll let you know as soon as there's any news. I know it's hard, but try not to worry."

The black cab smelt sickly and Nancy covered her nose with a silk scarf.

"D'you say Burden Road, love?"

"No, Burton. Ninety-two *Burton* Road."

"Sorry, it's your accent, couldn't quite catch it. Which part are you from? The Big Apple?"

"Long Island."

She wiped away the condensation, enough to see out. She'd never been to May's house. May always insisted on coming to theirs for Jen's Chinese lessons. Nancy closed her eyes and imagined floating in a clear lagoon, as Michael her T'ai Chi instructor had taught her. She breathed in through her nose and, as she exhaled, visualised cooling down from an anxious red to orange, yellow, pale green and eventually blue, but not blue like the ocean. The air flowed out through the ends of her fingertips.

Slow and steady, slow and steady.

When she opened her eyes, there was a ramshackle end-terrace with metal bars over the ground floor windows. The frames were rotten, and one window was covered in sheets of faded newspaper. A skull had been graffitied on the front wall. Nancy checked the house number. Perhaps the cab driver had the wrong street? She wavered by the door, and then rang the bell.

An ancient eye peered through the jamb.

"What do you want?"

"I'm a friend of May's."

"She's not in."

"I know. She's been in an accident. She was taken to hospital this afternoon. The paramedics gave me her keys." She held them up for the woman to see. "I just need to collect some of May's belongings."

There was a pause before the old woman slipped the latch. "Better come in then."

The house smelled of cigarette smoke, there was also the lingering, fusty odour of dry rot. One corner of the hallway was taken up with a cheap motel reception desk where a vase of red plastic roses gathered dust. *Who Wants to Be a Millionaire* blared from an open door.

The woman stood barring the way to the stairs. "Upstairs on your left," she said, "May's number six."

"I won't be long; I just need her fiancé's telephone number."

"Fiancé? I didn't know she had a fella."

Nancy edged past her.

7

"Don't go making a din up there. I can't afford any complaints."

The staircase was steep. Nancy's hands shook as she fumbled May's key into the stiff lock. She put a knee against the door and gave a firm push. Something on the other side prevented it from opening fully. She crouched in the dark and dislodged a shoe. It was black and petite and fitted perfectly into her hand.

Inside the room was a spartan ten feet by ten. The pink lampshade gave off a garish glow and the air felt grubby. Saliva, skin, semen... it was easy to imagine the residue of previous occupants soaked into the bed and carpet; their hair and toe nails lurking beneath the fringes of the candlewick quilt. Instinctively, Nancy wiped her hands on her skirt. Surely May wouldn't sleep here? But May's clothes hung on the wardrobe door, her slippers sat neatly paired at the end of the bed, her notebook lay open on the scuffed desk.

Brayn food, it said in the left hand margin. Nancy leafed through.

British loving animals

Thick as pig shit

Rat arsd

Rabbiting on

Barking!

Ducky (Mrs Eva)

Raining is dogs and cats - or is it cats and dogs???

Not good idea mention dog food in England. British thinking cruelty to animals in China :(RSPCA like police for dogs & cats.

She placed it back on the desk, as carefully as if it were May's fractured skull, then turned to the task in hand: Yifan's number.

Inside the top drawer of May's desk were a Collins Dictionary and some biros, a ruler, calculator, some receipts from ASDA and what seemed to be a high school certificate with a photo of a startled looking May pinned to the top corner. The next drawer down was crammed with teaching materials: a GCSE Mandarin syllabus, past exam papers, Post-it notes spidery with May's erratic writing. She came across one of Jen's essays entitled *Me and My Family*, followed by her Chinese translation. Nancy skimmed it for mention of Jen's adoption, then slipped it into her handbag to read later.

Another drawer was full of old photographs. She recognised May from the distinctive sickle-shaped scar on her cheekbone. Her features used to be more angular and her rough-cut fringe looked androgynous. May hugged two of her girlfriends. It was night time, a funfair. A ferris wheel loomed in the background. The Chinese loved that sort of thing; she remembered riding one like it in Nanchang. *Tallest in the world!* Iain thought it would help take their mind off the waiting – waiting for news of their babies.

Nancy flopped onto the foot of the soft bed, it absorbed her without resistance. Something sharp dug into her backside. She lifted the edge of the quilt. May had tucked her sheet in tightly at the corners, like a hospital bed. Beneath the quilt, was a wooden figurine, small enough to fit in Nancy's palm. A young waitress at The Bluewater Hotel had given the twins one just like it. She said it would bring them happiness, some sort of Chinese talisman. The waitress had been quite a fusspot, cooing in Chinese as they ate breakfast, even offering to take care of the twins while Iain and Nancy napped. Nancy kept the figurine and later made it into a necklace, fearing the twins might choke on it. Turning it over in her hand, Nancy wondered how to break the news to Yifan.

You don't know me but...

I'm so sorry, Yifan. May's been in an accident...

The only place left to search for his number was the closet. It smelled musty, like a long vacant holiday home.

May didn't own many clothes: the few dresses she wore for teaching, jeans and a neat pile of sweaters folded on the top shelf. There was nothing glamorous or sexy, nothing bold or unruly – only what was necessary. May didn't wear hats, or keep outfits that didn't fit her; there were no flowery smocks or tie-dye, no high heels or power suits – apart from an old skirt and blazer which looked a decade out of date. She hadn't imagined May to live so frugally.

A tin box was her last hope; tucked at the bottom of the closet, behind a mud-crusted pair of trainers, its lid emblazoned with a Chinese logo.

She paused, then opened the lid.

A photograph of Jen on the beach in Nice! Nancy had spent the best part of a week searching for this photo, hoping to stitch it into a memory quilt for her daughters' sixteenth birthday. What was May doing with it? As she lifted it to the light, Nancy uncovered photos of Jen riding her bike. Jen on summer camp in the Lake District. Jen in the school play. Jen eating ice-cream under the plum tree. She flicked faster through. Every single one was of her daughter. And not only Jen. There were photographs of Ricki on family holidays, birthdays, days out...What the hell were they doing in May's closet? The rational part of Nancy said they had something to do with Jen's studies. A project on the family. Yes, Jen's essay was on that very subject.

"Stop being a ninny," Nancy said out loud.

But why had Jen never asked to take the photographs? She knew they were Nancy's treasured possessions. And why hadn't May mentioned them? It was practically the twins' entire childhood.

She knelt amongst the scattered pictures of her girls and held one up to the garish light. Immediately, she wished she hadn't. It was the photograph of the twins in the People's Park hours after their arrival. In the original, Nancy and Iain's faces were like sunshine – delighted to be parents after years of waiting. But someone had cut them out, leaving two holes, two dismembered bodies.

She stumbled to the sink, fearing she might wretch.

Did May know about the mutilated photograph lurking in the bottom of her closet? No – no – she couldn't believe it of her. It must have found its way there by mistake. But how could a whole album find its way into someone else's closet by accident?

What if...Oh God...what if May was a psychopath? A pervert? A child molester? She'd been coming to the house every week to teach Jen. What if she'd been preening her in secret or...

Nancy lunged towards the desk, flung open the middle drawer and scrutinised the photograph of the ferris wheel. She'd missed it at first: a sign in bold neon letters, *Welcome to Nanchang*, suspended across the centre of the wheel. May had lived there – Nanchang – the very place her daughters were abandoned. Why, in all the years they'd known each other, had May never mentioned that fact?

She stood in the centre of May's small, dingy bedsit, sweat rings seeping through the underarms of her silk blouse. That's when the feeling started – beginning in Nancy's guts and rising. Six years...six years! May had taught Jen Mandarin; six years she'd fetched tureens of Chinese food to the house, treating Jen with respect, admiration, encouragement. All along...lies.

Nancy gaped around her in panic.

Could it really be May's fingerprints over her precious babies? May's Chinese blood pumping in their veins? Her Chinese hair on their heads? Her Chinese eyes staring Nancy in the face every day? Mocking her.

Yes, answered her intuition.

Why else would she steal photographs from the twins' adoption album, or take such an interest in their lives? Or lie about

10

never having been to Nanchang? May was no child molester. She was only five feet nothing in her faded, raggedy heels.

Nancy laughed in horrified hysteria. She had always dreaded this moment. The twins' past pouncing up on her, devouring the bonds she'd worked so hard to make, the Milne family unit. May the birth mother, the tummy mummy – the person she never wanted to meet.

The sound of her mobile made Nancy jump. Her hand shook so badly she could hardly pick up.

"Nancy?"

"Iain. What do you want?"

"Where are you?"

"May's place."

"Are you with anyone?"

"No."

"Are you sitting down?"

"Look, Iain, now is not a good time. Phone back later can't you?" Nancy fumbled to disconnect the call.

"Wait," said Iain, his voice flat and inert.

"What?"

"It's…"

"What is it?"

"It's May, darling. You'd better get over here."

Wooden figurines

A different kind of girl to the one I was back then – a girl like
Cousin Zhi – might have seen it coming. A different kind of mother
to my own, a kind and gentle mother, might have warned me
childhood was about to end.

Yes, sixteen is an important age for young women like Jen
and Ricki. I attend their dreadful birthday party to mark their
passing into womanhood, their shedding of years; but my arms
come burdened by the past, as well as gifts. Sixteen is an age I
cannot easily forget.

I was swilling out the skillet in the yard when I caught sight of
Father, making his way home through the rice fields. His head was
bowed as if listening to his own whispers. He was early and there
were no other workers to share his flask of tea or cigarettes. He
bustled past, his cheeks reddened by the wind.

"Don't stand like a gatepost, Mai Ling, come inside and help
your mother. Everything must go to plan."

I wanted to ask Mother about the plan, but she was busy
chopping half moons of garlic. A fresh pot of smoked pork and
spices rested on the side. The plan likely concerned Cousin Zhi,
who was due to arrive home for Spring Festival. She worked at a
car factory in the city and had grown used to luxuries. My parents
were keen not to lose face in front of her or Auntie.

I took my place beside Mother and began peeling the ginger.
The work was harder when I couldn't feel my fingers and I nicked
my fingertip with the knife. A sliver of blood rose up instantly. I
brought it to my mouth, a small pleasure in the taste. My belly
growled with hunger. Outside, the pig scratched the earth for
something more nutritious than stones and frosted mud.

The sound of their voices in the yard caused Father to leap up
from the table and hurry to the door. There on our doorstep stood
the town's most prestigious coffin maker, Gao Quifang and his
wife, both empty-handed, bringing only the cold winter draft into
our home. It was to be a short visit.

Father bowed and ushered the Quifangs through our dark,
smoke-blackened kitchen to the fireside, where three stools had

been arranged. I wiped my hands on my trousers and followed Mother, who carried a bowl of dates and peanut candies. The room seemed suddenly too small for us all and I wondered if we still owed them for Grandmother's funeral.

Mr Quifang's skin was pallid, his eyes serious. I remembered how gently he'd laid Grandmother out, arranging her white burial robes so as to disguise the thinness of her frame. The same couldn't be said of his son and apprentice, Li Quifang, who teased the old women of the village by pretending to be their husbands back form the dead.

Father instructed me to sit next to Madam Quifang who squinted in my direction and then kicked the chicken pecking by her feet until it flapped away.

"Is this the girl?" she asked abruptly.

Father bowed again. "Yes, Madam, this is our daughter Mai Ling."

"She looks reasonably fed and not altogether ugly, a little unfinished, but is she strong?"

"Yes, very strong; she works with my wife."

"So you can cook?" asked Mr Quifang.

I was unsure whether or not to speak. Father had not yet introduced us.

"She cooks well and knows many local dishes; she can also grow vegetables and understands how to care for animals," Mother said, proffering candies.

Mr Quifang took one and rolled it slowly, thoughtfully, around his mouth.

"Well I hope the pig I can smell cooking is better than the skeletal beast you have squealing outside," declared Madam Quifang.

I began to fidget with a loose thread on my cuff. Father filled some cups of baijiu.

"A toast! Let's make a toast to warm us."

"I'm afraid that my wife does not drink."

"Surely a little on such an important day?"

"No."

"But it is so cold out there," added Mother.

"No."

"Perhaps you would prefer wine?" Father fussed.

"I am allergic to both baijiu and wine."

"Please – do not ask my wife again."

I gulped back the fragrant, honeyed liquor and hoped they would soon go. Mother had laid out our finest bowls – the hand-

13

painted ones with blue jasmine flowers along the inner rim. They had belonged to Grandmother, who kept them hidden in the ground during the Cultural Revolution.

"Your wife should not have gone to so much effort," said Mr Quifang.

Madam Quifang shuffled her stool closer to mine, so that our knees brushed.

"We cannot stay long, winter is a very busy time. Besides, we have not come for a banquet." She nodded in my direction. "Girl, I will start with your feet; take off your boots."

Mother gave a solemn, approving nod.

"Come now," said Madam Quifang, "no need for shyness, it is important we make doubly sure."

A sudden wind brayed at the door as if *Nian*, the beast, had come early. I unlaced my boots and removed the newly darned socks. My toes were the colour of frosted violets and I recoiled as her icy fingers prodded the bones in my outstretched foot.

"Hm, as I feared."

"What is it?" Mother asked.

Madam Quifang stiffened. "The girl's feet are broad. A narrow foot shows wealth, a broad foot is... I cannot allow a peasant's foot to rest under my table. I'm sorry husband, but our family doors must be of equal size."

She sat up quickly and jerked my head to one side so that I yelped. "Here, look at this nose! How can I trust my wealth to a girl with such a nose?"

Mother stooped to tend the fire. "But Madam Quifang, you're overlooking something important." She nudged a large log in the grate with the poker. "Surely the matchmaker told you?"

Madam Quifang let go of my chin and I felt the blood return. "Told me what?"

"About my daughter's forehead; see for yourself how high her brow is, how good she is at hard labour? Surely this is what's required of a daughter-in-law?"

Daughter-in-law!

"Stand up, girl, I can't inspect you sitting down."

My legs felt weak. Madam Quifang clapped her hands across my apron and pawed at the place where babies grow – the place Mother called an 'infant's palace'. Recoiling, I realised she was assessing its proportion to my hips; my potential to produce a grandson.

The soup bubbled noisily on the stove – wild garlic and ginger. It reminded me of the woods above the farm where I liked to play with Little Brother. It was four o'clock, he was late home from school – where was he? I wanted to give him the family of figurines I had finished that morning. Had he been instructed to stay away?

Mr Quifang signalled for his wife to stop. "Child, I want you to answer me this: what is your opinion of marriage?"

What was I supposed to say? My daydreams of falling in love were the fairytale my life could never be.

Mother's hand pecked behind my back for the correct answer.

"An affectionate couple cannot live together to the end of their lives," I blurted.

"Do you mean to say that a man and wife should not be affectionate?" said Mr Quifang.

I nodded unconvincingly.

Madam Quifang clapped. "It is a wise child that knows marriage is a duty."

"Our daughter has been raised correctly," said Father.

"She will bring your family honour," praised Mother.

As they talked I withdrew to the sink with the empty baijiu cups and stared into the thickening snow.

Mr Quifang followed, wanting a light for his cigarette. "I see some of the logs are set aside," he said. "Why is this?"

I lit his cigarette from the stove and passed it to him. "I save the smaller logs for Spring Festival," I said.

"For fuel?"

"No. Little Brother and I make figurines. I make up stories for him."

"Stories about dutiful marriages?"

I slipped my hand inside my pocket and clenched the figurines. I wouldn't let him take them away.

Mr Quifang's tobacco smelt rich and smooth compared to Father's. "Child, my son needs a sincere and loving wife if he's to become an honourable man. So many girls have left to work in the city. They know nothing of its dangers, nor do they understand they will be tricked into brothels and never heard of again. You are one of the wise girls to have stayed home, and we do not want a bare branch on the Quifang family tree."

I shuddered. What would it be like marrying a coffin maker? I imagined Li Quifang's hands would smell of embalming fluid as he touched me, the smell of rotting flowers. A tight bud of desperation formed in my throat.

Madam Quifang unfolded a large sheet of paper over Grandmother's bowls on the table. "It is time to consult the

15

astrology chart – let us see what *Gaotang* says of the union," she said.

My name was scrawled next to Li Quifang's. The matchmaker's calligraphy was rushed and had smudged.

Madam Quifang ran a neat, clean finger down the chart. "Let's see…here we have it… the Goddess of Love predicts the marriage should fall after the Spring Festival, on the second day of the second month in the lunar year and not a moment later. It is all here. She is to come to me."

Mother nodded.

"It is so," said Father.

"Mai Ling?" said Mr Quifang. "Do you accept the will of your mother and father, the will of my son and of our family?"

"Speak child," said Madam Quifang. "To marry my son is the greatest opportunity of your life."

But I could no more speak than marry their awful son. I pushed past Madam Quifang and rushed out of the kitchen, brimming with tears.

Outside, the sky was a shiver of ivory. I ran past the old sow tethered miserably to her post, her husband dead in the deep pit upstairs, and down the frozen path which led out of the gate. *No, no, no* my heart beat out. The astrology chart is wrong; the matchmaker is a silly crow. I could never love Li Quifang or live in a house of souls. I would run to the woods where the garlic grows and when I reached the clearing – keep on running.

The red envelope

Benny's motorbike headlights flickered through the black palings of the trees.

Cousin Zhi hugged herself. "About bloody time."

It was well after midnight. We'd been waiting in the lane for more than an hour. Sharp air needled my ears. I shifted my weight from foot to foot, wriggled my toes. The ground was hard with frost. I checked the farm in case a light came on and Mother charged out to find me wriggling away from my destiny. She was always the first to rise; at five o'clock her sock-feet would tramp downstairs to make Father's flask of tea. She'd notice straight away: I was missing from my *k'ang*.

However, the longer we waited in the freezing cold, the more I thought: running away stinks, marrying Li Quifang (and his mother) wasn't so bad. I would be free from the boring chores on the farm and the drudgery of housework. My husband, Li Quifang, would inherit his father's wealth and I could have new clothes and a comfy bed. Then I remembered the time I saw Li Quifang tormenting a chicken by tying its legs as he prodded it with a stick all the way to school. I did not want to be his chicken.

Benny's engine growled. "What are you waiting for, babe? Climb on."

And there was no more time for thinking. I perched behind Zhi and slipped my hands into the pockets of her leather jacket. Her hair whistled in my face as we sped through the dark valley, so fast it felt like holding the corners of the wind.

I was travelling light: my newly carved wooden figurines, a few jumpers and clothes. I wore everything I owned in layers. My feet bulged with woollen socks, some stolen from Mother.

By dawn, the station was rammed with students and workers returning to the city after Spring Festival. Most were in their late teens and early twenties. By thirty a girl was too old for the factory, Zhi said. Around every corner I saw Li Quifang and his mother, but of course they were not there; no-one from the valley would make an insane train journey to the city at this time of year, unless it was to work.

Zhi gave Benny a lingering kiss and we squeezed through a horde of men. Someone grabbed me by the arm and I spun round, my coat zipper caught in the electric fan heater he carried. The men sniggered and I pulled free. I clutched Zhi's hand until we were safely inside the station foyer where the air was humid and the high glass dome dripped like a peasant's brow. At least seven rows of people queued at the ticket booths, many stooped hunch-backed, burdened with cubes of clothing, portable radios and rucksacks. One man bore a yoke of vacuum cleaners across his shoulders.

"You have got the money I gave you, haven't you Cousin?" said Zhi as we joined the queue.

I felt in my coat pocket for the *hongbao*. Three nights had passed since we lay side by side in my too-small *k'ang* on New Year's Eve and she'd given me three hundred yuan! More money than I'd held in my life. With it, I was free from the arranged marriage to Li Quifang. I had barely slept with that red envelope inside my pillowcase and Zhi's promises in my ear.

"Hey, Zhi!" A loud whistle echoed through the crowds.

"Fatty! How you doing?"

I peered over to where a thin woman with dark skin bobbed above the crowds, lifted like a champion wrestler.

"You're not the only one going up in the world Zhi!" She laughed throatily and disappeared into the crowd.

Zhi's accent had changed since working in the city; her bold, thick lips refined by pearly pink lipstick, her eyebrows, now plucked thin, looked surprised to find themselves so high above her eyes. Her eye shadow shimmered in the washed-out winter light. Money had made her brand new. I wanted it to make me new too.

Up ahead, green guards infiltrated the lines and held people back. A tannoy crackled in the dome.

"Passengers waiting to validate a ticket must wait in line. Any passenger without a valid ticket must leave the foyer immediately. No passenger will be allowed to buy tickets for today's travel."

"Now what?"

"They do this every time," Zhi said.

"But I've not got a ticket."

A uniformed guard passed down our line. Several of the passengers fell away. We shifted closer to the barrier. I clutched the red envelope. For a moment, I wished to be home, hiding in my *k'ang*. I could forget about the city, the bustle and friends, the factory and wages Zhi bragged about. It wasn't too late to beg forgiveness.

A whistle blew. The queues broke down. The foyer echoed with shouts. A swathe of guards tightened in; a man with vacuum cleaners was dragged to one side along with many others. I felt someone yank my arm.

"Quick," said Zhi, dragging me out of the chaos. "Now's our chance."

We ran towards the barrier. Where Zhi darted, I followed, dodging sideways through the crowds. The air was cooler, and I felt a gust whip across my face. I heard the low thrum of the train's engine. Zhi dropped her rucksack.

"Leave it," she shouted, shinning her way up the barrier. "Take my hand."

"I'm not tall enough. I don't have the strength."

"Yes you do, little wimp."

A voice called out from the crowd. A young man in a suit pointed at us. "They've not paid! Stop them! They're getting away!"

"Mai Ling, hurry up, I can't hold you."

I was almost to the top when Zhi pulled me over by the hood of my coat. I landed hard and ran, limping, onto the platform. Zhi was already on the train, beckoning me. I held out my hand and she hauled me into the cram of squashed faces and limbs.

"Mind your back," said a young woman as the door swung shut like a coffin lid.

A whistle blew. The train spat out steam and shunted. I lurched into a stranger's armpit. Zhi was nowhere to be seen as the train crept away from Hunan – and everything familiar.

To my left swayed a man with ratted, greasy hair and dandruff dusted across the shoulder pads of his black suit jacket. To my right, a woman sighed and ground her teeth, which set me on edge. We lurched as the train picked up speed, clattering forwards.

One-and-two-and-three-and-

I counted five minutes before shifting the weight off my sore ankle. There was no air and sweat pooled at the base of my spine. When we reached the fourth or fifth stop, the man with the dandruff got off and I left my place by the door. Half the space was taken up with piles of suitcases and bundles of washing. Eventually, I spotted Zhi in the gangway of the next carriage.

"You look pale, Cousin. Here, chew this." Zhi unwrapped a silver stick of foil and held out something I'd never seen before. "It's called *Wrigley's*. Don't swallow, otherwise it'll get twisted around your heart." Her eyes glinted.

The air was cooler in the carriage. Night had thinned into a pale band across the distant hills and a winter breeze from an open window tickled my face. I let my shoulders relax. Nearby, two studious-looking boys played rummy. The one closest was about to win. He had inquisitive, deep-set eyes that reminded me of Father's. I wondered which village he was from.

Zhi chomped her gum. "We'll have to buy you some new gear, Mai Mai, you can't turn up for an interview looking like a greasy hat – even though you are."

I reached into my coat for the red envelope, excited about the shops and the idea of my own salary. My plan was to send enough of my wages back to Mother and Father to buy their forgiveness and lift them from shame.

"What's the matter?" asked Zhi.

"It's the envelope, Cousin. I had it in my hand a minute ago… I…"

"Mai Ling?"

My ankles gave way, my knees buckled and the train became blackness.

When I came round, an old man was staring down his nose at me. I'd fainted on his copy of the *Sanxiang City Daily.*

Zhi knelt by my side. "Give her room to breathe."

"This girl isn't fit to travel," grimaced the man.

"Don't be so hard, this is her first time by train," said Zhi.

He shook out his paper and shuffled up.

I held onto the bench and pulled myself in beside him, apologising.

"How many fingers?" Zhi waved three in front of my nose. "Now watch this." She moved her index finger in a pendulum. "*Tsk!* Your temperature's not good. You need to drink more."

The studious boy coughed. "Excuse me. I have a flask of green tea, if your friend would like some?"

"Really? Give it here will you?" said Zhi.

He produced a cup from his knapsack and began to pour some of the steaming tea. The movement of the train unsteadied his hand and the liquid spilled onto his shirt sleeve. He fumbled for a handkerchief and hurriedly dabbed it away without a fuss.

"Here, this should help re-hydrate her," he said.

Our hands touched momentarily. He was quite handsome; his nose stately; his eyes gentle. His presence was like a shady tree on a hot day and I sipped the tea, feeling shy.

"Give her some more," said Zhi.

"Are you sure you're alright?" he asked. "You still seem disorientated."

"I'm not sure, it must be the heat."

"One minute we were talking about shopping, then all of a sudden - *zoumph!* You went out cold," said Zhi. "You'd better not go fainting on me at work; I don't want you mucking up the orders."

I smiled at the kind boy, feeling inadequate at the sight of so many textbooks bulging from his knapsack.

"Do you like reading?" he asked.

"Very much," I lied, ashamed to have left school at twelve.

"I'm studying medicine. Do you work in the city?"

"She's an engineer," interrupted Zhi.

The old man next to me tapped his cap. "She ought to take better care of her brains then."

"She's a rising star of the Forwood Motor Corporation in Nanchang. She's working on their new 4x4."

"You don't look…"

"Appearances are deceptive, my friend," said Zhi and fluttered her heavy eyelashes like a songbird fluttering its feathers.

I pinched her leg – an engineer! I struggled to work the plough. I didn't like the way she flirted with him either.

"I'm also heading for Nanchang. My name's Yifan. Perhaps our paths will cross there?"

Another crowd of passengers poured into the carriage and we moved on, for fear of the ticket inspector. I lost sight of Yifan behind a couple of young businessmen, who joked loudly about getting drunk over Spring Festival. We squeezed past the two suits and a woman carrying a television on her hip. Zhi stumbled over a pair of shoes, where a man lay asleep beneath the seats. "Move it!" she said and bunched him.

I spent the rest of the six hour journey squeezed into a space of about twelve inches, surrounded on all sides by bags, boxes and steaming passengers. My body soon ached with a pain I'd not thought possible. Unable to get to the toilet, I soiled myself.

Wedged beside me, Cousin fell in and out of sleep. She muttered the word *Manager* as her head rolled against my shoulder, buffeted by the rattle of the train. I pictured my family at home in the kitchen: Mother furious at the stove, Father staring at his boots wondering how he lost his obedient daughter. By now, Little Brother would be eating breakfast – his lip trembling because there was no Big Sister to play figurines in the yard. I swallowed hard at my guilt. Could I run away from them? Did I have the guts to see it through and make a new life in the city?

"You'll easily find a job," Zhi had said. "You don't have to live like our grandmother and her mother's grandmother." She made it sound so easy. She promised my family would forgive me. "As soon as your wages brush their palms, you'll be their daughter again. They'll love you even more because they don't have to bow and scrape to the Quifangs. You can earn four times as much as they do in a year." We had been curled beneath my blanket on New Year's Eve, firecrackers shattering the night sky. She had watched my eyes light up the dark at the sight of so much money inside the red envelope – money that could free me from my fate.

But did she really know our family? Or care about the old ways? Listening to Zhi talk, there was no past, no sense of 'our work', 'our history', 'our family,' it was only 'me, me, me' – and always in the future. All she knew about was the city and even that could be one of her tall tales. Maybe Nanchang only existed in the sky? I had the sudden urge to fling myself from the train.

Tucked inside the sleeve of my jumper, were two of the four figurines I had carved over Spring Festival. I had taken the parents and left Little Brother with the children. They were my confidants, my reminder of home and would be called *Nie*, secret. I wriggled Mr and Mrs Nie free. Their faces looked disgruntled. Their quiet smiles had vanished in the train's dim light. Were they upset to be escaping so fast and so far from Hunan? Should I turn back and go home, to my family – Li Quifang's family, the funeral parlour?

Stop now. Go back. Stop now. Go back.

I strained to hear their warning. Through the window, I could just make out the slow ache of a new day cutting through the city haze.

It was the silence of the place that got to her, made her wonder if she was the last one alive on earth and where she existed in the cosmos – how she, Nancy Milne, aged sixty, fitted into it all – and what separated her from the other side? If May, or any of the silent bodies in Hope Hospital's Intensive Care Unit, could deteriorate so easily, fall from consciousness in an instant, might she be next? And then who would look after her girls? Her girls, her precious twins, by law and by right – not the birth mother's - not May's. She'd given up her rights the day she abandoned them on the steps of Nanchang's Welfare Institute.

Nancy perched on the edge of a plastic chair and waited to be called from the numb safety of the ICU reception. Her eyes returned frequently to a pile of leaflets on bereavement counselling left discreetly on a table. The silence stretched unbroken, except for the coaxing voice of a nurse breezing in her ear.

"Mr and Mrs Milne, it's this way when you're ready."

Her hand reached for Iain's and they followed the nurse down the corridor. A familiar knot tightened in the back of her neck. Nancy pushed away the memory of the hospital where her mom died.

The nurse paused in front of a hand-gel dispenser. "Before you go in, I should say May is hooked up to monitors, and a ventilator. It might look like a lot of wires. Her head is also misshaped after surgery…"

Her voice faded into the background as Nancy remembered the stolen photos stashed in May's closet.

The nurse's bleeper vibrated and she excused herself.

"Nancy, are you sure you want to do this?"

No.

"I'd like to be alone with her, just for a while."

Iain squeezed her hand. "If you're sure…she's your friend. I'll wait outside. But Nancy – I want you to come away if this is too much."

She gave a vague nod and passed into the dim, medicalised abyss.

May's bed was at the far end. When she pulled back the curtain, a pale Chinese face came into view: eyes closed, chest ticker taped with monitor pads, a ventilator tube bulged at her mouth. Her head was bandaged, her hair shaved. Some of the iodine from her operation streaked her scalp. Beneath the bandage another tube led to a monitor. She looked like she was on a charger. Nancy was thankful May's comatose body looked nothing like her mom's, bloated with seawater.

Nancy's hands felt suddenly empty and she wished she'd brought something: flowers, grapes, anything to hold onto in the strange, scientific place where lives hung on threads pinned to beds. She dragged a chair forward. It felt important to be close to May in case she showed any signs: a twitch, a frown. A white tag on the edge of the linen sheet said 'Property of Hope Hospital'. She wasn't sure if that meant May or the bed linen.

May's toes formed meringue-peaks in the sheet two thirds of the way down. Clearly, it wasn't designed for a woman like her. Like most hospital equipment – wheelchairs, stretchers, bedpans, Gideon Bibles, flight socks and the red emergency pull cord for when the soul gets itchy feet – the bed was standardised, built for functionality, an average Caucasian male. The incongruity of May's petite Chinese body in that huge bed made Nancy want to scream: she could have been looking at the body of a child, and had never noticed, until that moment, the similarity between May and her daughters. Her mouth was exactly like Ricki's, even the same dimples.

"I…"

She waited between bleeps, unsure what to say, like a long lost relative who slowly gets to know the face behind the face in front of her.

"I'm…"

A nurse, who was writing notes about the elderly woman in the bed next to May's said, "It would be good for you to speak to her. She'd find that reassuring. I speak to Sybil all the time."

Nancy glanced at Sybil: the oxygen mask, the wire spewing from her wrist, her chalky, capsized face and thought: *why?* Sybil only needed drugs, maybe May did too.

When Nancy's mom chose to die – her one decisive act in an otherwise unmoved existence – Nancy had kicked and screamed and cried and dug an imaginary hole to bury her mother as she raged with a kind of blame that felt like heaps of earth, piled up and final. How could she leave her? A child of eleven! Didn't she care about her Math test on Monday? About their summer vacation? Didn't she know her dad couldn't look after her and Lizzy?

She placed her fingertips on the linen sheet, careful not to get tangled up in May's wires. Her skin was the texture of a faded petal, except that it felt cold – so unmistakably, life ebbing cold. Nancy pulled back; she hadn't meant to kiss May's forehead, only to feel cool, detached rage for the woman – this stranger, this psychopath – who'd come to take her babies.

"You lied to us," she whispered, "you made us believe you were our friend...we had no idea..."

She waited and watched May's lips to see if they might speak her side of the story, but the inert body was no more likely to confess its secrets than the wide awake May.

"How could you do that to us, May? How the hell did you do it? It's not like the embassy gave you our details, hell, they barely told us anything and we were paying them three thousand bucks."

Nancy stooped her head, exasperated. The smell of May trapped between worlds, took her right back to Sunnyside and the sewing room where her mom's body had been laid out for three days. Afterwards, the smell of her permeated the house: the carpets and the kitchen linoleum, the buttercup wallpaper of Nancy's childhood bedroom, even the banisters thrummed with the physicality of death.

"What am I supposed to tell Jen? And Ricki? All those photographs you stole...it's sick. SICK. I can't tell them. I can't put them through that, they've already lost their mother – and now I can't tell them it's you! Because it is you, isn't it? You in there." She prodded her arm, more forcefully than she ought to have done.

May's hand gave an involuntary twitch.

Shit. Nancy recoiled. She checked May's face. Of course she was still comatose; stupid, how stupid of her. Comatose like Sybil in the next bed, and the old guy in the bed next to that and the young guy over the way whose face was bandaged up. *Get a hold of yourself, woman, this isn't ER. People don't just wake up!* She might never get the answers.

There were callouses down the sweep of May's thumb and forefinger. It struck her now as being a working hand, not a teacher's. She tried to recall her daughters' hands – were they the same? Were their fingernails square, like May's, did each phalange correspond to hers in length, were their thumbs inflated at the joint? She couldn't remember...she couldn't remember. But she should be able to remember.

When the twins had arrived, Iain took so many photographs; they'd spent hours gazing at the girls, taking in their solidity, their dimensions; each micro gesture drawing them in. But now, sixteen years on, the details were vague; her memories slippery as soft-boiled eggs.

She pictured a younger version of May stroking Ricki's cheek, her hand cradling Jen's baby-soft head. Her ownership of them, her motherhood, made hot tears swell in Nancy's eyes. She and Iain had waited years for their babies.

"Why abandon them?" She pinched May's hand, where the blood had retreated from the surface of her skin, leaving it oddly mottled.

"How fucking selfish of you to come here, to our home, to ruin their lives all over again."

She wrung her knees. Nancy needed a clue, something – anything – that would join the dots to those vast empty years between what she knew and what she didn't know about May. Six years they'd been 'friends', six years to the month since she'd turned up at Iain's photography studio in tears, asking for a portrait to send home to her fiancé…Was Yifan a lie as well? Or was he the twins' father? Six years and never a word about the flesh and blood that belonged to May, the twins she'd made and left in China. What kind of a mother would abandon her kids to then hunt them down? What kind of a mother would let a stranger into her home without ever apprehending the truth? Nancy found herself pinching May's thumb as if to extract a stubborn thorn.

That's when she noticed the tattoo: a faded blue Chinese symbol beneath the sleeve of May's white hospital gown. The symbol looked like two people holding hands, it reminded Nancy of the concertina dollies the girls liked to make when they were little. What did it mean? May didn't seem like the kind of woman to have a tattoo – too straight-laced – but what did she know? May could be a former convict or a worker in a hostess bar. Nancy flopped back in the chair. A migraine tightened behind her right eye like the onset of toothache.

Someone gave a cough.

She turned round sharply in case it was Sybil. But it was only the nurse, standing at a respectable distance. Behind her stood Iain and a stranger.

"There's no rush, but Inspector Meadows would like to speak with you," said the nurse.

The inspector gave an official, conciliatory smile – the only kind possible in intensive care. His hair was dark and curly.

"I don't want to leave her yet. It's too soon, there are things I need to…"

"It's about the accident," said Iain.

"Just a few questions at this stage," said Inspector Meadows. "I've also got some effects and belongings from..." He glanced in May's direction.

Iain put his hand on her shoulder. "Come on, darling, let's go with the inspector. We can see May again tomorrow."

He turned and spoke to the nurse in a low voice. Nancy heard the words "dreadful shock," and knew they were whispering about her, the way adults whisper about grieving children.

She rubbed her eyes, the pain there intensified. The room seemed to be closing in on her, the life support machine rolling towards her.

Iain held out an encouraging hand. She didn't want to leave May. She wanted answers, real and true and sure, not more questions. Not the inspector with his conciliatory smile.

For the next hour, she found herself in a small side room with little in the way of furnishings. The seats were puce-coloured, the carpet beige, the lighting poor.

"And that was the last time you saw her?" said Inspector Meadows. "In the gardens?"

"Yes, I've already told you. After that, she was in the ambulance. The receptionist told me there'd been an accident and I left straight away."

"What time would you say that was?"

"After lunch, sometime late afternoon."

"Three...four o' clock?"

"I'm not sure. Half past three."

"And how long were you together in the gardens?"

"About ten minutes, I suppose."

He jerked his head, as if trying to shake off a wasp. It was an unfortunate tic for an inspector. Nancy fixed her eyes on the witness statement form.

"Am I free to go soon? Only my daughters are home alone, they'll be waiting for me. If I leave now I can be back in time to say goodnight. It's my birthday too, Inspector."

"Just a few more questions, Mrs Milne. You said earlier that May seemed 'a little strange' at the party. Can you tell me what you meant by that?"

"Maybe not strange; maybe nervous – oh, I don't know! Please, I really would like to see my daughters now."

"Is there another word you can think of that would better describe her behaviour?"

27

Nancy sighed. "She hardly spoke all afternoon other than to explain the food to our guests. Honestly, I don't know."

"Was she shy? Aloof?"

"No, not aloof, just helping out – unobtrusive. She was being Chinese!"

The Inspector raised an eyebrow.

Nancy wanted to get home and hold Jen and Ricki tightly for a very long time until it didn't matter whether May was in a coma or that she might be their blood mother.

"Look, she wanted to leave early because she'd arranged to phone her fiancé. She was probably just missing him."

"Fiancé?"

"In China. His name's Yifan – I don't know his surname."

"Do you have his contact details?"

"No."

The Inspector jotted on a separate sheet of paper. "And so he doesn't know about her accident?"

Nancy shook her head. "May kept herself to herself. I only know that Yifan's a doctor."

"Do you know where he works? Which city?"

"Yes…No." Nancy rubbed her eyes and propped her elbows on the desk. She felt like she was carrying a concrete slab inside her skull. "I don't know. I just don't know…"

"So you don't know May's home town?"

"She never mentioned it. Can I please leave now?"

Inspector Meadows scribbled his signature on the witness form. "I need you to read over your statement and make sure the details are correct, that we haven't omitted any information, then sign at the cross."

Her hands were sweating and left damp marks on the paper that soaked through to the carbon copies. "I hope that's everything, Inspector."

He opened his briefcase. "I'm sorry Mrs Milne, but there is one more thing that's required." He put the plastic bag on the desk. "As you're the only available next of kin, I need you to tell me what's in the bag."

Nancy gave him a quizzical look. "Well, they're shoes."

"You recognise them?"

The heels were a greyish pink, made from worn, grubby satin that must once have looked elegant, but not anymore. There were water marks along the toe and down the sides, the satin was bobbled. A fake diamond clasp was missing from the buckle of the right shoe. She'd only ever seen them worn by one person.

"Yes, I recognise them."

"What about the purse?"

"That's hers too."

"You can confirm that the effects and belongings contained in this bag belong to May Guo?"

"Yes."

She had a strong urge to rip it open and empty May's belongings onto the desk in the vain hope that part of her would come back to life. She needed to talk to May, shout at her, shake her.

"I'm afraid we'll have to keep them," the inspector said. "At least until May regains consciousness or the enquiry's over." His words floated somewhere in the background, pin pricks of sound that burst and vanished.

"What's this?" said Nancy at the discovery of a small manila envelope inside May's purse.

"It appears she kept some clumps of hair. I hoped you might be able to shed some light on that Mrs Milne."

"What kind of hair?"

The inspector looked puzzled.

Dumb question. Hair's hair, it wasn't as though it mattered what kind of hair it was; the important point was that May carried hair in her purse.

"Baby hair, at a guess," he said. "You don't know if she had any children, do you, Mrs Milne?"

"No." The lie came out before she could stop it. "She never had children."

"Hm. Well, this is my card. Call me if you remember anything. Otherwise, I'll be in touch in the next few days."

"What about May?"

"I'm afraid circumstances mean we just have to wait."

"How long?"

Inspector Meadows ushered her towards the door. "We'll get a witness appeal together as soon as we can; I'll be in touch. The nurses here are taking the best possible care of your friend, Mrs Milne."

Nancy hovered in the doorway, shivering. She wondered if she might be coming down with flu. She'd sat too long amidst the fatally sick, breathed in their chill; but she wouldn't let herself cry, not until she was safely back home, locked inside the bathroom. It wouldn't do for the twins to see her so upset, especially not on their birthday.

"Mrs Milne –"

She glanced back at Inspector Meadows, standing with his hands in his pockets, looking awkward as a school boy.

"I'm sorry this hasn't been a happy birthday."

She turned, eager to get away.

Iain stood in front of her. "Steady on, darling," he said. "I've brought the Lexus round the back to save you trekking through the hospital... Darling, are you alright?" He felt her forehead. "You're burning up."

He guided her out to the car park. A heavy December fog had drawn in and with it a fine drizzle that prickled Nancy's clammy skin. The sound of an extractor fan whirred from the back wall of the hospital.

She had done it in cold blood; told the police a lie. She knew exactly where May had lived in China, or at least where she'd studied, where she'd been photographed in front of a ferris wheel. *Tallest in the World! Welcome to Nanchang.* A young student, unmistakably May, caught in a moment years ago.

Nancy's second lie? The same one May guarded for sixteen years: the lie of her childlessness.

High school certificate

The snow in Nanchang had melted, leaving the station platform filmed with sludge. Zhi and I crowded into the square, and onto a packed bus smelling of clothes worn day and night. Zhi pushed towards the back of the bus, where the air hung thick with cigarette smoke. I took a window seat and gazed out at the thronging square.

"We made it…" I whispered.

Zhi yawned and pulled down her sunglasses.

The rusting trolley bus belched and began its struggle through a tangram of roads onto a main highway. Unused to the motion of buses, I felt nauseous. Other migrants held plastic bags to their mouths and were discreetly throwing up. I wiped my sleeve against the window and peered at the vast concrete patchwork: row upon row of corrugated-roofs that covered an area bigger than our whole village, rice fields and all. Entire mountains seemed hollowed out, leaving a lunar landscape in which cranes bent their backs instead of peasants. Blocks of cement and girders swung hypnotically through the air. Occasionally, a farm would appear to be holding out between the storm of swirling construction dust; the crop coated in an eerie layer of ash. Piles of rubble and debris littered the roadside, bare wintry trees rose up brittle and cinder-coloured.

As we approached the city centre, newer high-rise buildings, hotels, restaurants and shopping malls crowded one on top of another; the overpass that spanned the river was frantic with cars and wagons.

"It's huge…" I said.

Zhi filed her nails, disinterested. "It's a circus. They're building a bridge to the sun. Every month a new road appears – what you see here wasn't here last year. They can't make the maps fast enough."

A huge portrait smiled down from a brightly-lit restaurant. "Chairman Mao doesn't wear glasses!" I protested.

Zhi glanced up from her nails, rolled her eyes. "That's not Mao, noodle brain, that's The Colonel. We'll go when you get paid and eat chicken burger and fries. Then we'll hang out in the park." Zhi pointed to a white island glistening amidst the smoggy shades

31

of grey: pagodas and a humped bridge, a partially frozen lake laced with snow-burdened willows.

"Girls go there on Sundays, when they're tired of window shopping. But you have to watch out for the snake." Her eyes widened. "A few years ago, the park keeper went missing; he was swallowed alive by a python twenty feet long and a foot wide. They found his eyeballs in the reptile house."

"Aiya!"

"Come on, wimp, or we'll miss our stop."

We wrangled for the exit and jumped down from the bus.

Zhi threw out her arms. "Welcome to Nanchang, Cousin! Fastest growing shit-heap in the motherland."

Our national pride – a limp red flag – drooped from a flagpole at the centre of the square.

"I didn't imagine it to look so…grubby"

"You'll get over it," said Zhi, already several paces ahead.

We walked in the shadows, coiling through the crowds that shifted and churned. The frequent blast of car horns hurried cyclists along as they wheeled against the kerb and out again, netting together in an unfathomable formation. My heart leapt when I passed a man in a straw hat pulling a barrow of coal bricks and for a moment I thought it was Father. Along the kerb, I found a pair of wet, discarded biker gloves and stuffed them in my coat pocket.

We turned a corner down a back alleyway where a group of big noses in suits rolled out of a bar called The Blue Banana. Their gruff laughter rose to meet us and the smell of fish juice and liquor smarted in my nostrils. A couple of women wearing low-cut sequinned tops staggered after them. Mother always said the westerners were decadent and unruly, but this was the first time I'd seen them.

"Zhi," I panted. "Can't we stop for a rest? I'm hungry."

"Not now, we've got to make you official." She beckoned me over to a street phone, hemmed in by looming slabs of coal-stained buildings, and was already tapping in a number.

"Hi, I'm going to need a fake high school certificate, an unmarried status card and a work permit pass. How soon can you do them?" Zhi's voice didn't falter. She rummaged in her pocket for a lipstick and daubed a street name on the back of her hand. "I'll meet you there, *ciao*."

She hung up. "Now we need to fix your hair so you look like a *dagongmei* with prospects."

I'd come too far to turn back and needed a new identity, one good enough for the city and the factory gates.

That night, Zhi and I slurped hot and sour soup at the junction between Zhongshan and Shengli Road, where street vendors traded hats and felt bags, ivory boned-fans, high heeled shoes, flip flops and jewellery. I browsed the stalls, exploring the treasure trove of textures, letting threads of wool, silk, linen and gauzy chiffon glide through my fingertips, each conjuring a different image - of Empresses and Beijing Opera singers, film stars like Priscilla Chan. I flushed, remembering the tall, professional westerners at The Blue Banana – *"No shame, they have no shame,"* corrected Mother's voice in my head.

The stalls were swarming with young workers like Zhi, *dagongmei*, who buzzed with a newfound taste of freedom. They sang Cantonese pop songs, bartered loudly, bragged about their pirated Hong Kong movies. They puffed Marlboro cigarettes, whose smoke coiled upwards in the sharp night air and mingled with the smell of rendering duck fat.

Zhi saw a couple of factory girls she knew from Forwood, but she pulled away suddenly in the direction of a stall selling necklaces. We tried on beads made of pearls and fake rubies. For a few hours, I forgot about my family and was free. Zhi, I noticed, kept checking over her shoulder.

I steered the conversation onto Forwood. "It must be strange coming back to the city; everything here is so different, so exciting compared to the village."

"But at home, I get to rest."

She wouldn't tell me what was bothering her. That evening, as we huddled together beneath her coat, dovetailed inside a shop doorway, I lay worrying. I felt sure that Mrs Nie, my figurine, was urging me to keep an eye out for Cousin. Long after Zhi had fallen asleep I watched the streets empty around us. I promised my figurines that I'd keep Zhi closer than my shadow. It was the early hours of the morning when finally, I let sleep take me. A shallow sleep stippled with questions – like why, if Zhi was so successful, could we not afford to sleep somewhere warm?

Outside The Dragon Hotel, the boy arrived late with the fake documents that would help me secure work.

"So where are they?" said Zhi.

"Cash first," he replied.

"Only when she gets the documents – I want to make sure it's not a photo of some northern girl who looks nothing like her."

"*Sssh*. Keep your voice down, lady, the cops are everywhere this time of year." He marched us away from the hotel entrance, into a nearby alley.

The boy gripped Zhi's arm. She tried to brush him off.

"Let go of my cousin, you're hurting her!" I yelled.

"Ah, so the *manglieu* can speak? Your boss will soon have that knocked out of you." He took an envelope from inside his jacket and dangled it above me, just out of reach. "This what you're after, eh? Ask politely, eh?" The boy's teeth were yellow and uneven. His breath smelt of rice vinegar. He gave a thin snigger.

I punched out, flattening him to the wall.

Zhi grabbed the documents. "Run!" she screamed as we bulleted into the thronging street.

We didn't look back until we reached a square where I knelt, panting on the pavement.

"Well done," Zhi wheezed. "I didn't know you had it in you."

The factory buses were all blazoned with a green arrow. Zhi told me the arrow was Forwood's logo. She gave a sardonic laugh, "It's supposed to represent the company's *progressive and dynamic ethos*."

Voices ricocheted down the workers' bus as the girls talked.

"Will there be enough work for us all, Cousin?"

Zhi examined her red, newly painted nails. "Don't ask me! The gates open at midday. You stand as good a chance as any of this lot, because I work there."

"What? You mean there's no guaranteed work? But you said – I ran away because you promised there'd be a job for me at your factory. What will happen if they've all gone? Mother and Father will never speak to me again."

"Mai Mai."

"Don't call me that, I'm not a child any more."

"You ran away because you didn't want to marry a coffin maker's son, not because of anything I promised."

I grew angrier then, but a voice whispered in my ear. "We stand a better chance than the girls on the next bus." An ashen face, as narrow as a sunflower seed and with grey eyes, peered through the gap between our seats. "Personnel usually dole out the jobs quickly," she said. "My advice: keep your head down, show them your hands and let them see they're nimble. It doesn't matter if you're a child, so long as they can put you on the line."

"And if they don't?"

"They will. I've been around. After a few years in the city, I've seen it all." The girl's smile faded and she held out a hand. I locked fingers with her, nervous that she might not let go.

"It's her first job," Zhi interrupted, "We're Hunanese. She wants to know everything about everything."

"Ah, so she's sky eyes."

Sky Eyes. The name fit me well, like a new winter coat.

I was about to ask where she was from when the bus swung into the factory compound. A group of women were already gathered at the factory's metal gates. A uniformed guard blared into a megaphone, *"Get off the bus, get into line!"*

We surged towards the gates and I squeezed my way as far forwards as possible, thinking Zhi would follow, but when I glanced round she was gone.

Two women in suits were checking everyone's documents. They let a few pass through the gates, but more were turned away. One woman refused to go.

An official yelled at her. "You think I care? You're wrong," He pointed, "Look around you. Many women want these jobs. Why should I care about *you*?"

She held onto the gate. "My husband, my husband," wailed the woman.

"Go, before the guard removes you."

"My husband can't work. His legs are withered. I beg you, give me a job." She sobbed. A guard pulled her away, avoiding her kicks and claws. He was tall with an ox-like physique and bundled her swiftly to the edge. Even above the chatter of the crowd, I could still hear the woman crying, "My husband, my husband!"

My heart thumped as I pulled out my fake documents. The details were as requested: I was now a twenty year old graduate of Zhushan Number One School. The sixteen year old nobody from Hunan was gone.

For the next hour, I scanned the faces of those around me. One young woman's two front teeth were missing; I was close enough to see her tonsils as she laughed. Others looked as if they had been in the city longer; their appearance was more up to date: denim jackets, lipstick. Their elbows dug into my sides. The ones directly ahead spoke a dialect I didn't recognise. Their clothes were shabby. They couldn't understand a word of Cantonese when presenting their documents.

"How did you expect to find work if you cannot speak the language of your bosses? Answer me, can't you even tell me the year you were born?" asked the official. "Get away you stupid women and stop wasting my time."

I felt so thankful to Zhi, who'd taught me some stock Cantonese phrases over Spring Festival.

"Who's next? Show me your ID."

I elbowed forwards until I was standing in front of the gates, bearing my documents.

"Hunanese?" she said, rifling through them.

"Yes." I lowered my head respectfully.

"And you are twenty?"

"Yes, born year of the pig. Whatever I do, I do it with all my strength and that includes working for your great corporation."

I half expected her to inspect me the way Madam Quifang had. But there was no prodding of my abdomen this time – only sharp eyes, obedience and nimble hands counted.

"Go through," she declared.

My fake documents had worked! I slipped through the gate and walked calmly to the side entrance with the other hopefuls, my eyes fixed on the path.

Inside, I was ushered up a flight of stairs and into a vast room, where about fifty young women waited to be interviewed. The room was frigid. Its walls were white brick, peeling in places. Waist-high metal containers lined one wall of the room to create a counter. Two slogans on the walls read: "*Don't eat excessive food, don't talk excessive talk*" and "*A little dirt is good for your system.*" Through a hatch, I could see a boy scraping vegetables into a vat – perhaps the cook responsible for the awful smell?

I wondered what kind of food the workers ate and whether the dishes would be spicy like they were back home. Zhi hadn't talked much about the meals, only that workers gulped it down in fifteen minutes and hurried to their desks for a nap.

There was so much still to know about the salary, my hours, time off, the bosses. She gave me the impression factory life was hard, but that there were prospects for someone like me, a girl with ambition.

The grey-haired woman handed me a form. "Sit there and fill this in," she said, pointing to a nearby table. One girl struggled to write using her *Forwood Motor Corporation* pen and I wasn't sure whether her fingers were numb with cold or if she'd never been taught. At least Little Brother had shared his school books with me and I wasn't a complete dumb ox.

I sat down next to a young woman whose application form was almost complete. The first few questions were easy. I copied the details of my fake identity, but struggled when it came to the question about my previous experience. Should I mention *jia*? I'd only fed animals, washed clothes, planted seeds, chopped wood, made food – and run away from home. I must not forget that. I must not forget the courage it took to find my own way in the world. I leant over to see the paperwork of the woman next to me; she'd written nothing about her parents or farm work, simply: *Toy Factory, Shenzen. Two years.*

The official hovered behind me. "You have ten minutes to complete the form, there must be no errors." She gave no guidance as to what I should write in any of the boxes.

I left a blank and moved onto the questions about my health. Did I have poor eyesight? Did I lack energy? Did I have any physical deformities? Any tattoos? Was I pregnant? I stifled a giggle and filled in the form as best I could, then waited to be called up.

It was impossible to tell just by looking at a girl whether she'd be accepted or rejected. I earwigged as the young woman who'd worked at the Shenzen Toy Factory was interviewed.

"What did you do in Shenzen?" said the interviewer.

"I was on the assembly line for one year."

"Was your residence permit renewed?"

"Yes."

"What were your hours?"

"Six to six, with one hour break for meals. Overtime six to ten."

"So what was your reason for leaving?" said the male official, tapping his factory pen impatiently on her form.

"Because...because...I wanted to progress. I had set up a company magazine full of stories about the best workers. I wanted to inspire people and give workers a good feeling. But there was no opportunity for me to use my skills, nothing in the clerical department, and so I left."

The man looked up and nodded. "You have the right attitude. Go back to your seat and wait."

Her feet were restless. She looked older than most of us, in her mid-twenties, but there was a spark in her I admired.

Soon after, a young man in his late thirties entered the canteen. He strode over to the desk, flicked through the interview forms and gave a deep sigh.

"Are there no perfect candidates here today?" As he spoke the muscles rippled beneath the skin of his temples. He had a very square jaw. "You," he pointed straight at me, "let me read your form."

I stepped up to the desk. His eyes darted over my paperwork. He stroked his jaw thoughtfully. His hands looked soft and veined, reminding me of a cow's udder.

"According to this, you have no previous experience. How can I employ someone who doesn't know what they're doing? Tell me, where have you worked since graduating from high school?"

"I worked for *jia*."

"Peasants?"

"Yes, Manager. I come from Hunan."

He frowned. "The home of Chairman Mao."

"I have completed middle high school," I added boldly, sensing I must pen my own destiny.

"Really? Then you should be able to write the English word *open* as in *open door policy*." He handed me a factory pen.

I stared at it blankly.

"What's the matter?" he laughed. "Has your education deserted you?"

"No, Manager...I..."

"Then show me some other skill."

The room was silent as snowfall. I reached into my pocket for my wooden figurines. "I carved these over Spring Festival. My hands are very nimble, Manager. I will use them to work hard for you."

He raised an eyebrow and examined the delicate flower pattern I'd carved into Mrs Nie's *ch'ang-p'ao*. A long time seemed to pass before he responded.

"Show me your hands," he said.

My cheeks flushed at his request. They were farm worker's hands: rough and calloused. I hid them behind my back. It was not proper for a man to look so closely at a young woman's hands.

"Very well." He set Mrs Nie on the desk. Her face was serene; her silk shoes seemed to glow a deep lucky red. He flicked back over my application form.

Was he going to shout at me? Call for a guard? Have me thrown out? "You have no experience... But the work of your hands is..."

Tell me quickly, I wanted to say.

"Very fine."

Excitement pumped into my veins. The Manager reached for his rubber stamp. My eyes fixed on a grain of black rice on the floor.

"Take your belongings," he said, "leave via the door on your left."

There on my form, was the word EMPLOY. My peasant hands were to be put to work once more.

ID

I was photographed in the central courtyard of the Forwood factory compound. My new fringe fell unevenly across my forehead, the face beneath now flat and featureless after Zhi's haircut.

A young woman seated at a desk beneath the mei trees copied my details onto an ID badge. "Carry this at all times," she said. "You are now officially a worker at the Forwood Motor Corporation. Your worker number is 2204, you have been allocated to Electronic Circuitry under the control of Manager He. You are to be monitored by Line Leader Zhen Zhi."

"Cousin!"

The woman shook her head. "Kin relationships are discouraged at Forwood, Worker 2204. You'll do well to remember that. Now take this and read it in the waiting room." She passed me a document several inches thick, entitled *Forwood Motor Corporation: Official Rules and Regulations Manual.*

There were no windows in the waiting room and the lighting was poor. The manual began with a list of production regulations covering several sides. Arriving late, leaving the line without permission or punching someone else's timecard were all punishable offences that carried fines. A second set of rules read,

> *Daily Behaviour*
> 1. *No talking, eating or playing at work.*
> 2. *Anyone caught stealing will be dismissed on the spot.*
> 3. *Hair must be tied back and overalls cleaned weekly.*
> 4. *No spitting.*
> 5. *One day's holiday per month, to be taken on a Sunday.*

I was a few pages into reading the resignation regulations when someone called out my number.

"Yes?" I spoke into the gloom.

"Your time is up. Proceed to the door."

I looked towards the halo of light coming from the small glass panel in the outer door. Figures moved in silhouette.

"Did you not hear me?"

40

I shifted in my seat, apparently alone in the waiting room. "Yes, but I can't see you. Where are you?"

"Worker 2204, I'm not here to make idle conversation! To your right, you'll find a door. Tap in your worker number. The door will open onto a corridor. Follow it."

"To my dormitory?"

"No, it leads to the workwear room, where you will be provided with overalls."

"How will I find my dorm?"

The voice cut out.

Where were the other girls? They had already passed through. I was the last, I reasoned. I stumbled towards the machine and entered my worker number. The door clicked open and I followed a dingy passageway leading to a dead end.

"Is there anybody there?" I banged on the far wall.

No-one answered.

I banged again. "Hello. Can you hear me? Did I turn the wrong way?" This was silly. "I need you to direct me," I called out.

I slumped against the damp wall and closed my eyes. Within seconds a white light filled the room and a jet of icy water fired down on me.

A voice called out from above, "Worker 2204, do not scream in the showers. Do not scream in the showers! Can you hear me? I said do not scream."

"What's going on?" I cried, my clothes sopping.

"Calm down Worker 2204. You must get undressed and wash, before receiving your overalls. Can you hear me? Undress immediately."

I peeled off the layers of wet, smelly clothes. Minutes later, the water cut out. The shower door opened and a familiar figure emerged carrying a towel and a pile of overalls, folded neatly into a square.

"Zhi!"

"Put these on."

Her face was stripped of warmth. She dropped the pile of clothes and pushed it towards me with her foot. "My name is Line Leader Zhen. Now get dressed, you're the last one. Bring your wet clothes and follow me."

"I don't understand, Zhi. Why aren't you looking after me? Why am I being humiliated?" I said dressing hurriedly.

But Zhi's back was already turned.

I collected my belongings and stepped into an adjoining room where a group of girls had gathered in dazed silence.

Zhi began doling out papers. "Everyone, get into line and sit down. There's work to do."

Music crackled all around. The noise of it grew louder with each line. I looked down at my sheet and realised they were song lyrics.

Arise!
You workers of our nation
Fresh as morning sun
Full of vigour and vitality.

Forward!
Goes our nation,
From the factory lines
It's you who drive the world.

Toil!
For today is the day
You make the cars,
Faster, better, stronger.

I sang through tears. No-one even heard me cry. At the end of the song, Zhi instructed us to leave via a thick, green-glass door. I scrambled to my feet with the others, more uncertain than ever as to whether the door was a wall, a tunnel or a trap. Surely nothing could ever be what it seemed again. I pulled my work cap down, wanting only to disappear like the magical paintbrush in Ma Liang's tale.

Ricki closed her eyes. She liked the pattern of the water: the teeny pinpricks coming from the shower head and the *hissssss* that drowned out everything. She was a tribal leader, surrounded by women with udder-breasts in a remote lagoon. She lathered her scalp with acacia shampoo and enjoyed the soft slide of suds down her back. Her open mouth engorged with water; she gargled and squeezed it out through the irritating gap in her two front teeth.

Why didn't any part of her look right? Her hair was limp and fine. Her tits, small. Her whole body was square, short, Chinese. Pink highlights would bring it together.

"But, sweetheart! You can't ruin your beautiful hair…" Her mum was so chronic. Thankfully she didn't know about her eyebrow piercing. One teeny hole, one act of rebellion. One mark of distinction from Jen, her twin.

She stepped onto the bathmat and wiped the steam from the mirror. Her chest was pink where the blood had levitated to the surface. If I was a vampire, there'd be no reflection. No boxy Chinese kid in the mirror.

She pictured Lowrie: her long purple hair and brooding eyes, ringed in black kohl, her cobweb look. She wouldn't have taken any shit from a hit-and-run driver – she would have got up like *The Terminator*, chased after the bastard and made him suffer. She wished she had Lowrie's guts. Wished she was her.

A primitive feeling clawed inside her belly. Ricki sat down cross-legged on the bathroom carpet and explored between her legs. She pictured Lowrie on her stool in the garage workshop, wearing a black top, her shoulders exposed and edible, her tattoo flowering between the shoulder blades, the boned fabric of her corset open like a wing and beneath her skin, the frame of her back. Her breasts, she imagined how they would be larger than hers, cool like the skin of a melon. Ricki wanted to. Explode. Wham!

The door handle rattled. "Are you going to be much longer?"

Fuckistre.

"Give me a minute, will you." She lay still. Her voice breathless. Her heart thudding. The image of Lowrie zapped by annoying relative numero two.

"I need to come in," said Jen.

"You'll have to wait."

43

Jen scratched on the bathroom door. "What are you doing in there, anyway? You've been ages."

She splashed cold water on her face and rubbed away the imprint of her damp, charged body from the bathroom carpet – because Jen, as everyone liked to remind her, was no half-brain.

Ricki opened the door wide and stood to one side. "What's the great rush for the bathroom?" she said "Stuart's not coming today is he?"

"Your face looks red," said Jen.

"Does it?"

"Like a lobster."

"Let me past will you, I need to get my clothes."

"*Sshhh.*" Jen pointed to their mum's bedroom. "She's catching up on sleep."

A voice croaked, "Girls, are you there?"

"Sorry Mum," said Jen.

"It's alright, come in both of you, I want to see you."

Ricki rolled her eyes.

Nancy lay beneath the huge duvet. The heating was on at its highest setting and the bedroom smelled kind of rank.

"What is it Mum, do you need more painkillers?" said Nurse Jennifer Milne.

Ricki stayed by the door. Her sister could be such an arse-licker at times.

"I wanted to make sure you were both alright after yesterday. I'm so sorry your party was ruined."

"It was your birthday too, Mum. Besides, it wasn't your fault." Jen held her hand. "Dad says Doctor Emery's calling by after surgery."

"Thank you, darling."

Why did Jen do that? thought Ricki. It would take more than her sister's goody-goody routine to butter their mum up. It would take drugs, a large quantity poured down her throat, before Jen's boyfriend, Stuart, was ever allowed to watch the ten o'clock news in their house – let alone sleep over.

"Tell me how you're feeling, Jen? Are you worrying about May? Ricki, you must feel sad too?"

She wasn't, not about May at least, maybe she should have been – poor cow had just been run over, but it wasn't like the woman actually meant anything to her. No, Jen was the bilingual prodigy of the Milne family.

Jen poured her mum a glass of water from the jug on her bedside table. "I'm trying to stay positive. Where there's life there's hope, right Mum?"

"Yes, she's in good hands, the staff at Hope are…"

"Did you want me for something, cos I'm kind of dripping here?" said Ricki. She didn't have long if she was going to catch the tram into town.

"Sorry, Ricki, it's just…May cared a lot about you both…she really loved coming here."

"She gave me fifty quid," said Ricki.

"I know, and she had so little. I think…I think she cared more than we realised."

"That's nice, now can I go get dressed?"

"Do you have to be such a cow?" said Jen.

Her mum slumped back into the pillows and gave a small moan. "Girls, don't fight. There's something I have to tell you both."

"Mum, don't get upset. Do you want me to get Dad?"

"No."

"He said to call him."

"I don't want your father, sweetheart, I want you…I want you to know that May…that she –"

Ricki was never so pleased to hear a doorbell. She rushed downstairs to find Doctor Emery on the doorstep, wearing ear muffs like the nineties had passed her by. She showed her upstairs then slinked away to her bedroom to get ready for Lowrie.

Jen stopped Ricki in the hallway. "Don't you think you should stay here with us after what happened yesterday? We could at least go and visit May in hospital."

"Why would I waste a day off school with someone who doesn't even know I'm there? Come on, Jen, get real." She swung her new Nikon over her shoulder and checked inside her hoodie for May's birthday money.

"I can't believe you sometimes. You only ever please yourself. You never think about other people."

"There's nothing I can do. You heard what Dad said last night, Mum needs sleep. I'll only be gone a few hours."

"That's what you always say."

"Yeah, well."

"What am I going to do all afternoon?"

"Ring Stuart, swat up on your irregular Chinese verbs, administer Mum's drugs…it's not my problem." Ricki zipped her hoodie and threw on a scarf. Seeing her sister on the verge of tears,

45

she softened. "Look, I'll be back before Dad gets home. There's something I need to do that's all."

"Can't it wait? Mum needs you," called Jen. "I need you."

No you don't, thought Ricki as her boots crunched down the driveway. *Jen, the brain of Britain, is an island and an island needs no-one.*

She cut across Piccadilly Gardens, over the footbridge surrounded by geysers that sprouted cold water from the concrete when people least expected it. No kids played there in winter, only a handful of skateboarders, whipping onto the low wall, jumping freestyle off the steps and sometimes tripping uncoolly over their boards.

The woman giving away newspapers from a yellow booth next to Primark was blowing into her cupped hands; her sawn-off mittens unthreaded with age, her fingers blue-cold with December's dirty news. Ricki reached for the new Nikon her parents had bought for her birthday and took a few shots of the vendor before crossing over the tram tracks onto Tib Street. On the street corner: the whistle of tram wheels, the smell of candy floss, hot dogs, shop doors too heavy for bag-laden women with bronzed, unseasonable faces to open. The winter sun had disappeared behind the back of Debenhams where the silhouetted pigeons roosted. She felt an overwhelming urge to be some place warm.

Top Café, part of Affleck's Palace Emporium, was her spiritual home. She loved its easy, 'stay all day drinking a can of coke' feel, the comers and goers, the students, the grungy entrepreneurs and dealers in junk; its *Budweiser* bar stools, with split open seat wounds, the brown HP sauce bottles and the chalkboard menu whose contents were grouped according to *Good Stuff, Bad Stuff* and *Snax*. Top Café was on the third floor, near the bead factory and the shop unit which sold leather clubbing gear.

"Hi," said Jules, as Ricki approached the counter. "How's it going?"

"I'll take a mug of coffee, please Jules. Oh and beanz on toast, with plenty of real butter." Ricki took a plastic spoon from a wicker bowl on the counter.

"It's not often we see you here on a Monday."

Ricki shrugged, like the woman of mystery she wasn't. Jules knew as well as anyone the reason she hung out in Afflecks.

"She's been talking about you all week."

"Yeah?" said Ricki.

The coffee machine steamed in Jules' pierced face. "Yup. Seems like you've wowed her with those photos."

46

She let the possibility sink in and it felt sweet. "They were just pictures I had on my camera."

"That's not what Lowrie says. She thinks you're a visionary. I heard she's put in a good word for you with Noel."

"Really?"

Noel was like God around Afflecks, he decided which artists would make it and which got relegated to bum fluff.

Ricki took a seat by the window, overlooking the multi-storey car park and pretended to read her library copy of *Ariel*. The sun was weak, the window grubby with fingerprints. The sound of cutlery and mugs, a dishwasher being unloaded in the afternoon felt comforting; a good background vibe. Her shoulders loosened. On the wall-mounted TV a guy in a tweed jacket droned on about an old pot found in someone's attic, it was exactly the kind of rubbish her mum liked to watch when she was 'working' from home.

Lowrie struck an entry like Shock and Awe.

"Well hi there, Lady Lazarus." Lowrie flicked her hair. "I didn't know you were into Plath."

"I...she...her poetry's kind of cool." She'd only borrowed the book because she knew Lowrie was a fan.

"Well, don't stick your head in any ovens, kid, I hate to see talent ruined." She slid into the booth and swiped up a menu, her purple talons pristine against the coffee-stained paper.

Jules set down Ricki's plate of beanz. "Speak of the devil. I was just telling Ricki about Noel."

Lowrie rapped her chunky ring against the table. "I can't think without caffeine, Jules. Make it large and black will you. Me and the kid have to talk."

Jules ran a cloth over the table. "Sure."

"So, would you be up for it if Noel gave you a unit?" said Lowrie.

"Are you kidding?"

"Listen, Noel isn't the kind of guy to be easily impressed and believe me, he loved your stuff."

Lowrie wore a lacy top and long velvet gloves. Tattoos budded on her upper arms; a tiger crouched on the branch of a bonsai tree, its tail curled seductively above the glove like a beckoning finger. Two eyes wrapped around her other arm. Lowrie once told her they were the eyes of Hathor, an Egyptian Goddess. Ricki looked it up on the Net and found Hathor was lady of love, music and intoxication, as well as the patron-goddess of unmarried women, which figured. Lowrie never talked about boyfriends, except the ones from 'before' - by which she meant before prison - and it was usually dissing.

"But I'd better ask my dad first."

"Sure, your dad, you ask away. Ask your dad. You know sometimes, kid, I forget you're only fifteen."

"Sixteen," Ricki corrected.

The coffee arrived and Lowrie gulped it down. "So, business over, are you going to tell me why you're here, or what? I figured it was urgent."

"I needed to get out of the house. We've had some family stuff going on. It was my birthday at the weekend. My sister's teacher got mowed down. She's in intensive care. Looks like she might snuff it."

"Shit, kid. I'm sorry."

"I need your help." Ricki reached into the pocket of her hoodie and took out the red envelope from May. She slid it across the table as if planning a heist, same seriousness. "Open it," she said.

"Fifty quid?" whispered Lowrie. "You should be more careful, kid. This is Afflecks not John freakin' Lewis."

"I want to get a tattoo at Slither." Ricki held her gaze. "Lisa's a friend of yours. If you're there she'll do it."

"No way. I can't ask her that."

Ricki stared at the congealed heap of beanz, feeling suddenly small and stupid and desperately hungry for more than the cold carbs on her plate.

"Look kid, I see you're disappointed. All I'm saying is think about it. If you still want one in a year or two there's nothing to stop you."

"You sound like my mother."

"It's breaking the law."

"And? You were sixteen when you had yours."

Lowrie rubbed her forehead. "So what design were you thinking of?"

The studio was quiet. Lisa, the owner, sat on a stool behind the counter, reading *Total Tattoo* and eating noodles. She was one of a handful of Chinese with units at Afflecks, along with Tony and Steph who owned Kin-ki.

"Hi stranger." Lowrie leant over the counter and they kissed briefly near the mouth.

"Good to see you, tiger," Lisa said.

"I've brought a friend. This is Ricki."

48

"Another BBC thank God, I was beginning to think they'd gone all moral about inking," said Lisa.

"A what?" said Lowrie.

"A banana like me. Yellow on the outside, white inside."

"She means I'm British Born Chinese," said Ricki, "which I'm not."

"What, you don't like being half and half?" she said resuming her noodles. "How old are you anyway, kid?"

Lowrie shot Ricki a quick sideways glance. "Eighteen," she said.

She eyed Ricki with suspicion. "You don't expect me to believe that. Come on, guys, I've got my licence to think about. Imagine what Noel would say."

"He'll be sweet, Lisa. You can't ID everyone; most of them are fake anyway."

Ricki handed over her design folder. "I've been sketching out some ideas."

Lowrie flicked through, pointing to the double happiness couplet. "I like the way the little people are joined. Are they screwing or what?"

"The frig, they're not screwing, it's double happiness," said Lisa.

"Well I like it."

"Me too," said Ricki.

"Lao Lao, that's my grandma, she lived through such shit under Mao. She used to tell me about the student and the village girl when I was little. It's a cool love story, all that dreamy destiny shit."

"So that's a yes? You'll do me that tattoo?"

Lisa sighed. "Okay, but I don't do faces, necks, hands or sleeves."

Lowrie laughed. "You'll do anything with a pulse, you old slag."

Ricki emerged from the room at the back of the shop feeling elated. The skin on her upper arm felt raw, but reborn.

"It looks really distinctive," said Lowrie.

Distinctive meaning interesting, unique; distinctive in a good way, not a Chinese freak in a class of white kids. Lisa strapped it up, neat and secure. The ointment and tape, the care and cleanliness were reassuringly clinical.

"How long should I wear the bandage?"

"Twenty four hours. If it sticks to your skin, don't yank it away. Make sure you soak it in warm water and peel it off gently. Wash it and leave it to breathe, okay kid? I'll give you some Tattoo Goo."

"And it will be okay?"

"You know where I am if there's a problem – just make sure your parents don't look me up." Lisa snapped off the gloves and tossed them in the waste bin.

Ricki's hoodie rubbed against her bandage. "You've done an awesome job. I'm really pleased, how much do I owe you?" she said, unsticking the red envelope containing her birthday money."

Lisa stared at May's Chinese handwriting. "Listen, kid, I don't want any trouble, I've got my licence to think about."

Ricki took out May's tenners and fanned them across the counter. "They're not fake or anything, it's my birthday money. I promise I won't tell anyone you did it."

"Not even your mum?"

Ricki had a sudden vision of her mum crying her eyes out at the sight of it. "Especially not my mum."

"Won't she wonder what you've done with the money?"

Ricki laughed. "I know how to lie."

"Lie to the one who wrote a note like this?" said Lisa, pointing to the envelope.

"What does it say? I can't read Chinese."

"It says, '*To my precious daughter who I wish long life. I am sorry this gift is so poor and I have cost you dearly.*' I think she'll want to know how you spent her gift. The last thing I need is an irate Chinese ma in my shop, losing me my licence."

Ricki pulled back the envelope. "You've got it all wrong," she said. "The woman who gave me the money wasn't my mother. She's a friend of the family; she teaches my brainy sister Mandarin on a Saturday."

Lisa shook her head. "No, no, it's definitely from your mum. Look at the way she's signed it."

Ricki stared blankly at the characters. "Why would she call me her daughter?"

"I'm only telling you what it says."

"That she's my fucking mother?" Ricki yelled. "My mother's British, alright!"

"Hey kid, calm down," said Lowrie.

"She lives in fucking Altrincham and has just been made redundant and likes sewing and watching *The Weakest Link*. I haven't even met my real mother. I don't know her. She left me in fucking China, alright? So there's no way my real mother is ever going to know about my stupid tattoo or your stupid shop so why don't you... Just shut up." Ricki snivelled into the sleeve of her hoodie, feeling like a proper lunatic in front of Lowrie.

"Now look what you've done," said Lowrie.

Lisa scowled. "Eighteen my arse."

Lowrie pushed the cash across the counter. "Come on, kid, let's go. And I'll see you later."

They picked their way towards the stairway.

Ricki tried to stay composed. Man, did her mum have some answering to do. She would make her talk about it all: China, May, all the messy adoption shit. Nikon or no Nikon, flu or no flu, coma or no fucking coma.

The invitation

Clang-a-lang-a-lang-a-lang-a-lang-

I am running down a corridor whose walls drip with sap, the sap of poison ivy. It oozes from my skin. The poison is within.

A-clang-a-lang-a-lang-lang-a-lang-

Ivy curls around my ankles, tangles me up inside. It will smother me bone by bone if I don't escape. I can't find a door. There's no-one to help, not even Zhi. I'm alone in the dark. I trip and fall and…A noise shakes the walls, roars, sprints through my blood.

Clang-a-lang-a-lang-a-clang-clang-a-

The corridor, the shower, my Cousin…

I was awake, screaming into my pillow. Someone took it away steadily, calmly and rocked me until I quietened. Her face as narrow as a sunflower seed. Her eyes, so hauntingly hollow. Had she touched my cheek? Did that grey hand stroking my forehead belong to her or was it the roots of poison ivy retreating beneath the blanket as daylight chased away the nightmare?

"Sky Eyes," she said. "It was just a dream. Wake up now and eat. Work starts soon."

This wasn't my *k'ang*. The room was too gloomy and cold. I heard strange voices – accents different to my own.

"Who are you?"

"Don't you remember? We met on the bus. I'm Ren."

I wiped my eyes and spat. There were four bunks besides mine. The windows were shuttered. Wires hung from the ceiling, draped with washing. Sets of blue overalls – one, different to the rest, was an-off white blouse and grey skirt. A pipe jutted from the wall and out of it spewed something sludgy. Girls hurried, jostling to fill their bowls.

Ren took my bowl. "Wait there, I'll get you some congee."

Someone shouted, "Stop her! She's taking double!"

Ren was pushed aside. The pipe spat and puttered out. The small, dingy dorm reverberated with barely satisfied murmurings.

"Thanks," I said and spooned up the little congee she'd managed to collect in my bowl.

"This shit doesn't get any better does it?" protested a girl, half-dressed inside the bunk opposite. Her skin was the colour of candle wax, translucent and taut across her chest cavity. Her ribs stuck out in rows like a fire grate. She pulled her blouse down from the wire and her casket black eyes met mine.

"Only slugs can eat that shit, y'know. It's like slug shit. It's like eating your own shit." She pulled her blouse over her shoulders. "What are you looking at?"

I pulled my blanket up under my chin. "Nothing. I…"

"Take your nosy, creeping eyes off me. What are you, some kind of spy?"

The girl's arms seemed thin as kindling. "New ones are such weirdos these days. Where did they find you two – the Security Bureau? You both act like you've got hang ups."

Ren scraped the last congee from her bowl.

"Stop scraping, slug, it's getting on my nerves."

"You heard," said another, concealed behind a dirty rag of curtain. "We don't scrape our bowls, OK?"

"I never read any rule," said Ren, climbing down from our bunk. We watched her limp to the window and pull on the shutters. Light from the courtyard streaked in. The bully shielded her eyes, like a bat blinded by daylight.

"You think you're so smart," she said. "I don't know where you've crawled from, slug, but believe me, a few weeks in this shit hole and you aren't going to think you're so smart."

"We'll see," said Ren.

The bully laughed. "Stupid as well as ugly. Where are you from?"

"Hubei."

"Hubei *mei* – so you're a drudge worker. They must be desperate if they're hiring cripples."

"*Forward! Goes the cripple with her little slug…*" the bully changed the company song and mimicked Ren's limp. "*Crawling on the earth, begging to be crushed.*"

"*Damei, bee-jway,*" warned another girl, "before your mouth gets us all fired."

"*Have Joy! For tomorrow you'll be gone…*"

I wanted to stand up for Ren, but daren't.

"Look girls, the Hubei *mei* is deaf as well as crippled!"

Ren span round and lurched for Damei, clutching her by the wrists.

"Don't think you're hurting me," said Damei with false bravado.

"*Niou-se,*" spat Ren, as though Damei was a piece of cow shit. She pushed Damei onto her bunk and swung past, out of the dorm.

Clang-a-lang-a-lang-a-lang-a-lang-a-

The room shook again, in disbelief, relief. Someone had stood up to the scrawny bully – had anyone done that before?

I dressed in silence, pulled down my work cap, rubbed the sleep dragons from my eyes and pushed my feet into the cold, black slippers beneath my bunk. I was lost inside my new shapeless overalls. As I checked my appearance at the mirror, a face I recognised appeared.

"You okay? She's not always that cruel."

"It's Fatty, isn't it?"

"I was at the train station."

"Hunan *mei*, I remember. I need to speak to Zhi. Do you know where she sleeps? I want her to find me another dorm."

"You shouldn't rely on family any more," Fatty said. "The managers don't want us in our village gangs. They say it makes us lazy workers. We're supposed to leave the countryside behind."

"But where can I find her?"

Fatty shook her head. "Forget it. She has no authority round here. She won't help you now. You can only rely on yourself."

Fatty disappeared into the swarm of girls teeming from their dorms; face after unknown face indistinguishable beneath work caps and matching overalls.

Clang-a-lang-a-lang-a-lang-a-a-a-

I followed the girl in front.

"Blues go that way, idiot," said a stranger pointing to a door marked 'Sanitary Room'.

The water was cold as I splashed my face. A girl, a blue like me, said there'd be hot water at ten that evening, when the stove got lit. I went to the toilet and climbed up on the seat to look out the window. The sanitary room backed onto the courtyard. In the distance, over the roof of the factory compound and the high risers beyond, there were pastel mountains. Suddenly, a blast of music, the company song. I sang half-heartedly and filed down to circuitry with the rest of the blue overalls. Waiting at the door, was Cousin Zhi.

"Move it girls, or there'll be two yuan coming off your pay packet," she yelled.

I copied another girl and held up my ID badge, wanting Zhi to hold me to her chest like a sister. But she checked my badge without even looking at my face. No glimmer of warmth. We were strangers.

54

The girl behind pushed me forwards into the workroom. It was an eerie bottle green and smelt of bleach. Several conveyor belts were interlocked in a grid, with work stations on both sides.

I hesitated, unsure where to sit. Then a girl shepherded me onto a stool in 'Zone B' and plonked down wearily opposite me.

"Whatever I do, you copy, okay?" she said.

Her accent was southern. Perhaps a Chaozhou *mei*? Just visible beneath her overalls was a pretty heart-shaped locket glinting in the gloom like a small relic from a different world. Her name was engraved in tiny characters, *Xiaofan*. I stared at the locket, wishing it was mine.

The lights flashed above the line, Xiaofan straightened and snapped on a pair of gloves. I did the same and turned the lamp on above my work station to fathom the instructions that hung on my shelf. A klaxon echoed in the cool of the room and the belt began to flow, bringing small plastic boards in front of us. Stationed at the far end, Xiaofan and I were first to start work. I was scared to even touch the board. Xiaofan worked swiftly and handled the board's minutiae of plastic buttons and wiring with great delicacy, as if plucking fish bones from a *tou yu*.

The board was inert in my hands.

I daren't ask her what to do; factory rules forbid talking on the line. I copied Xiaofan and inserted one of the plastic cards, the size of a fingernail, which were stored in a tray on my desk. A series of English words flashed up; fat and curly as worms.

Zhi's voice breathed down my neck. "You must follow the instructions precisely, 2204," She pointed to step two on my diagram. "It's a six-step process. Soon you won't need to think, it will be familiar. For now, be sure to study the diagrams. You can follow rules, can't you?"

I nodded. Was she referring to me running from Li Quifang or what? The coldness behind her eyes told me otherwise; there was no past between us now, no New Year's Eve, no escape from the farm or bold talk of better futures.

"And remember, for every one you get wrong, we deduct two yuan."

We. She counted herself a manager, but where was the real boss?

No sooner had the thought entered my head, I noticed a staircase, leading to an upper office. Inside, a man paced back and forth before slumping onto his chair. It was the young manager who'd hired me.

Zhi stood with her hands on her hips and huffed, "Get on with it then. Time equals money!"

Several boards had piled up in front of my station. The regular, heavy beat of the company song jangled my nerves.

Produce!
Your hands are like those
who built our Great Wall

No, my hands felt gnarled and numb as root ginger. I couldn't keep up with the beat. There wasn't always enough time to check the display screen properly and a few times I skipped step six, the bit about checking for defects in the glass. Press this, press that… My hands fumbled with the pincer tool used for handling wiring and a tiny shock shot up my forearm. Was it my imagination, or was the young manager watching my struggle?

By mid-morning, I improved, and the conveyor belt started to move faster. The coldness of the room kept me alert. I decided I would write down the English words at the end of my shift and learn them in the dorm. At the start of the day, the circuit boards were coming every two minutes, but by the end of the morning I counted only ninety seconds between each klaxon. It was like counting lightning strikes in the fields back home, working out how long until a thunderstorm broke.

"This one is not functioning at optimum efficiency," said a sudden voice from behind.

I jumped and dropped my board.

"I agree," said a second man.

"Too much time wasted on inserting the COMMS card."

"Yes. Far too much time wasted."

"Five seconds, to be precise."

"Five seconds."

"Almost two and a half fewer circuit boards per hour."

"Two and a half."

"Not sufficient."

"No."

One of the men straightened me up, while the other pushed my stool closer to the work station. They angled the tray of COMMS cards so there was less distance for me to reach. I felt like Little Brother's clockwork toy.

"Time improvement?" asked the first man.

"Two seconds," said the other.

"Two seconds."

"Increase per hour?"

"One board."

"One board."

"It will need to be monitored."

"Yes."

"Yes."

The men went over to Xiaofan's station. The one with the clipboard whispered in her ear. She nodded. He gave her an encouraging pat on the shoulder, like the owner of a well-trained dog. The men passed down the line, checking each girl's speed with a stop clock.

The light above the conveyor belt flashed and the next shoal of circuit boards swam down the black belt towards us. Zhi seemed hardly to acknowledge the arrival of the two men and I could only assume their presence was a normal part of life on the line, even so, they gave me the creeps. They appeared twice more that morning and each time recorded the speed of my work. They always spoke to Xiaofan who worked more swiftly than anyone else, twice as fast as me.

Only once, that first morning, did the belt slow down. Fatty raised her hand for an *out of position permit*. She needed to go to the sanitary room.

To break the monotony, I counted five minutes and twenty six seconds. When Fatty returned, Zhi ordered her to stand on her stool.

"Oh, come on," said Fatty. "I used my permit."

"That's irrelevant; you spent too long away from the line. Now get up."

Everyone stopped and gawped as Fatty climbed unsteadily onto her stool.

"Worker 1946, you've neglected one of the main principles of factory life: your time is factory property. You are factory property."

Fatty hunched her shoulders.

"You will spend the rest of the morning standing on the stool while your workers finish the order. As repayment to Forwood, you will spend the night cleaning equipment."

A groan rippled down the line, with murmurs that we were going to miss lunch making up for Fatty. An hour later, she was swaying badly. I thought she might fall headlong onto the belt. But she never cried. Instead, she made the mistake of tutting at Cousin behind her back.

"What was that?" said Zhi, reaching for the pincer tool.

Fatty yelped as Zhi jabbed her ankles.

"Don't ever undermine me, 1946. I'm your line leader. Now get back to work, all of you!"

The conveyor belt resumed.

What kind of a monster had Zhi become? I glanced up at the manager's office. Surely he wouldn't condone Zhi's behaviour – didn't he have anything to say? To my surprise, he lay with his head on his desk looking, for all the world, sound asleep.

I resolved to find Zhi's dorm and take things into my own hands as soon as possible. Perhaps she slept in a different part of the factory, with the other line leaders?

When Damei, the bully, arrived two hours later, Fatty was still standing on the stool, limp and miserable, her legs shaking.

Damei kowtowed mockingly at Zhi. "Line Leader Zhen, what an honour it is for me to escort you to Personnel."

"What's this all about?"

"You've been caught on camera."

"What? I'm not going anywhere. I've done nothing wrong."

"My boss wants to know why you pulled a worker off the line. This order's due out tomorrow."

"It will be ready."

"Save it for the boss," said Damei, helping Fatty down from the stool. "The rest of you have fifteen minutes to eat your lunch then you're to come straight back to the line."

"You can't tell them what to do."

"Instructions are instructions Line Leader Zhen, I'm only fulfilling management's desires – you of all people should know about that." Damei smirked.

Zhi refused to budge. "You must think I'm stupid, believing Personnel have sent a low life like you here to get me."

"Watch your mouth, Hunan *mei*," said Damei and grabbed Zhi by the arm.

She let out an undignified squeal.

I dropped my circuit board. The conveyor belt ceased. A worker on my line got up from her station. The others quickly followed, including Fatty. Xiaofan, however, continued working. I thought she muttered the word 'traitors'.

"Come back, girls," said Zhi. "I have not instructed you to go. I'm the line leader, you must show me respect!"

The pull of food was too great for most and they scurried off. I hung back to stick up for Zhi.

"Oh it's you, *slug*," said Damei. "What's wrong – don't you Hunan *mei* eat?"

Zhi's eyes caught mine and she softened. "Leave her out of this."

"How sweet, your cousin's sticking up for you. What would Manager He say if he knew you were showing favouritism?" Damei laughed and nodded up towards the upper office.

So that was his name. Manager He, the one who'd interviewed me, who'd praised my wooden figurine, touched my hands. Manager He, the one asleep in his office.

Zhi glanced towards the bureau where he sat slouched over his desk.

"Come on, let's get this over with," said Damei, "I want my lunch."

Damei shepherded Zhi towards a different exit on the far side of the room.

"Wait! Zhi!" I called, "What will happen to you?"

"Go and eat," Damei said.

"Zhi!"

She didn't look back. The door closed with a deadening bang. I rattled it in the silence, but it was locked and I was left behind with Xiaofan.

I hurried away down a white tiled corridor that led not to the canteen, but a door marked *Bonding*. The smell was nauseating. I pressed my ear to the door but there was no sound. It seemed an unlikely place to find Zhi. I pulled gently on the handle, slipped inside and the door closed behind me, extinguishing the wedge of light from the corridor. My steps were tentative, but I was determined to find my cousin.

Through the darkness, I edged forwards, feeling for a surface, a wall, a handle. I sensed a presence, but had taken too many steps into the room to get out quickly.

"Who's there?" I called.

The sound of breathing deepened. I stumbled into a blunt edge of machinery. Instinctively, I raised a hand to stop myself falling, but instead caught hold of a lever. The machinery creaked into life. A klaxon sounded and I could hear the whirr of a fan, the drop sound of cog teeth moving. A warm gust of air blew over my face and a voice screamed. It was mine.

Torchlight loped over the ceiling. It afforded me a brief picture of bodies bent double at their desks. Suddenly, a hand covered my eyes. I was hauled into a bright adjoining room and directed onto a chair.

"And to think, we were about to send out a search party, 2204!"

The woman peering down at me wore a nurse's gown. Her mouth was covered with a cloth mask. She reached out a gloved hand and shone her torch into my face.

"Where's Zhi? What have you done with her?"

"Don't worry. This won't take long."

I squirmed, trying to free myself as the woman held my mouth open.

"No obvious dental problems," she said to the assistant who unclipped my ID badge.

"Please take off your overalls, 2204. We need to check you over."

"What for?"

"Just do as I say."

"Let me go. I want my cousin."

"Be still."

"But you're hurting me."

"Be still."

"I'm not taking my clothes off."

Something stung my skin and I yelped. The light was so bright. Somewhere in the background I heard a voice calling, "Sky Eyes, Sky Eyes," and then, when blackness swallowed up the words, there was a name, "It's Ren, Ren…you'll be okay."

The room I found myself in had no furniture. The walls were white, the windows long and open, the ceiling high. A breeze clacked at the blind. A bird hopped onto the window sill, cocked its head as if to ask what I was doing there. Other birds flowered in the courtyard's bare mei trees, singing.

The door opened and a stranger entered. She didn't speak but handed me a small square of folded paper, then left.

It smelt of Father's tobacco. *Please, let it be a note from him, begging me to come home.* I brought it to my face and breathed deeply. The smell was his hands, the insides of his pockets and the winter melon candy he stashed there. It was also his face, his mouth puffing on the bamboo pipe. I ached for him to come and take me home. My tears spidered an ink-stain on the paper. It wasn't his writing.

Due to the ~~inevitable~~ unfortunate incident with Line Leader Zhen this morning, and her departure, I now require your assistance. Come to my bureau tomorrow night, 3am prompt. Do not tell anyone. Destroy this note immediately. Mgr. He

Candy

I wasn't so stupid as to go to his bureau wearing blue overalls. I waited until Damei's mouth slackened into a lazy 'o' and her body bunched worm-like beneath the blanket. Damei – the only girl in our dorm to have a clerical job – would be the one caught on camera slinking through Forwood in the middle of the night.

The doors of the dorms were all closed along the corridor. I picked my way through space which seemed to shrink into darkness. I felt for the banister. Fifty-one steps to the sanitary room. Another fifty and I was in *Circuitry*. After that, Manager He's bureau.

A desk lamp glowed in the distance. Something dark hovered up there, but when I looked again there was nothing.

Be brave, he's a man not a tiger, I told myself as I tiptoed down the line.

"*Tsst*," came a voice. Manager He hovered on the bottom step of the staircase that led to his bureau. "You're late." He hurried up the steps and disappeared inside the office, leaving the door ajar. "Don't just stand there, come in."

The room was warm and dark. He gestured to the corner and I grappled in the half-light until I found a stool. He shuffled through the papers on his desk. The vacuous gloom of the circuitry room stretched out below.

He wasn't the manager I remembered from my interview: no tie, no suit jacket or shiny black shoes. In fact, he wore soft slippers and a velvet coat. Balls of scrunched up paper were strewn across the floor. The bureau smelled stale.

"Time…frittered away again," he muttered and slumped back in his chair. "Talk amongst yourselves, I need to clear my mind."

I searched the shadows and an old man leaned forwards into the skirt of lamplight, his eyes wrinkling into a smile. "*Wǎnshàng hǎo*, young lady," he said and tapped the leg of my stool with his cane.

I startled, forgetting to bow my head.

He looked at my chest, the nipples pert as goji berries beneath Damei's thin blouse, and removed his deerstalker. "Want to try it on? I see you're cold."

I folded my arms. "A man's hat does not sit well on the head of a girl."

"Ha-ha! Wise and stubborn, you'll make a wonderful wife," his thin lips smacked together to make a *tac-tac* noise.

He set a pipe to rest between his gums and produced a small metal tin filled with dark shreds of tobacco. He pressed the shreds lingeringly into the bowl of his pipe as if savouring it with his fingertips. His eyes closed and he inhaled deeply, manipulating the tobacco with a needle. A few short puffs then he sucked contentedly on the stem. The bureau filled with a sickeningly sweet smell as the smoke uncoiled like calligraphy ink in water. The old man's eyes rolled and the pipe fell from his lips.

Manager He blew out the spirit lamp. "It is time to talk about the greatest of all honours. Can you imagine what that might be?"

"Erm…"

Manager He stood up and gazed at the portrait of Deng Xiaoping on his wall. "I'm talking about the honour of leadership." I glanced around for Chairman Mao's picture but it wasn't there.

"Worker 2204," he said, beckoning me to his side, "I've brought you to my office because I am going to make an example of you."

His hands were very warm on my shoulders. His breath smelt of peppermint. I swallowed purposefully, trying to suppress the urge to hiccup brought on by the sudden tension.

"What, no reply?" he said.

"I…I don't know what to say. If there's a problem with my work, then I promise to correct it. I can't afford to lose this job."

"Eh?"

"You said you were going to make an example of me."

"I have no intention of firing you – quite the opposite."

Manager He took a flask from his drawer and poured himself a cup of peppermint tea. He also produced a tin of candies, removed the lid and offered me one.

I salivated.

"Let me speak more directly," he said.

The candy dissolved slowly – ever so slowly – on my tongue.

"As you know, Line Leader Zhen is no longer able to assist with my project and so I have been on the lookout for another helper – someone brand new to factory life."

My ears pricked up at the mention of Zhi. She had never mentioned any project.

"I have great plans for our factory, Worker 2204. A strategy that will bring glory to the city and make us a shining star in our nation's future." His eyes widened with a new, effervescent energy. "By this time next year, I expect our 4x4 model to be sold all over the West. Imagine it, thousands upon thousands of Europeans – Americans even! All driving Forwood 4x4s."

He scraped back his hair. Standing beneath the light, I could see his velvet coat was, in fact, a dressing gown and that Manager He wore pyjamas. I tried not to gawp.

"May I ask how Line Leader Zhen helped you?"

He recoiled. "She's no longer of any importance. The girl was too untrustworthy, too scheming and greedy –"

The old man jumped in his seat as if he'd fallen from a mountain ledge in his dreams.

"Worker 2204, let me speak candidly. Our best chance of success in Europe currently hangs in the balance. In a few months, an important businessman will arrive at the factory, one we must impress. His name is Herr Schnelleck. When he comes, Schnelleck must see first-hand that all workers are at the peak of their productivity."

I nodded, aware that the old man held a pen in mid-air and seemed to be measuring my physical proportions like a master draftsman – or a mother-in-law.

"Your task is to motivate the workers, 2204. You're to be a beacon of light, shining the way to a brighter future. Do I make myself clear?"

"Erm..."

"Just do what I say and everything will be fine."

"I'm not sure I understand, are you saying Zhi's been fired? That you want me to replace her?"

Manager He huffed.

"Promise me I'll see her again," I said.

"Only if you do what's asked."

The thoughts of not seeing Zhi, or finding out why she'd lied to me, were too much and I nodded.

"Good. Now take this." Manager He held out the tin of candies. "What's the matter, don't you like them?"

I swallowed back the saliva that had pooled in my mouth, my hunger immediate. "Yes, I do."

"Then take the whole tin, they're yours to keep. Think of this as a sign of what's to come, 2204. A little treat. One day, I'll make you wealthier than all the others. Then they'll see that hard work, efficiency and diligence are rewarded."

"But I've only just started. I need to master the processes, the English words…"

"Oh, don't worry about that. I see your newness as an advantage. I'll work out the details: the checks, the time analysts et cetera. Soon you'll get a day off. I want you to go with the other girls into the city and buy new clothes, make-up, shoes, music – anything that will make them jealous. Until then, you should work your hardest. They have to believe you've been rewarded."

"What about Xiaofan? She's too fast. I can't work harder than her."

"Listen to me, 2204, she's an old school pace setter. You belong to the future. Remember, I've seen your figurines. These hands are capable of creating great beauty." Manager He reached out and closed his hands around mine as though they were the winning tiles in a multi-million yuan game of mahjong.

I quivered.

"This is strictly between us," he said.

The old man, who'd been occupied with his artwork, gave a manic laugh. "Ha-ha! Truly, this pear is ripe for eating, He-Chuan."

Manager He smiled awkwardly and led me onto the staircase. I fumbled with the tin of candies. The atmosphere had altered and I had a fleeting suspicion that he was going to kiss me on the cheek, but he didn't. He drew the rope of his dressing gown more tightly around his waist and shuffled backwards into his bureau.

"Make sure you're early for work tomorrow, 2204," he added.

Inside the bureau, I could hear the *tac-tac* of the old man's lips followed by the whistling of his pipe.

I ran my tongue behind my teeth, where the sugar hadn't quite dissolved. The candies were sweet and pink and soft. I couldn't help but wonder if Manager He's lips might taste the same.

"She won't come in. Lie back down," Stuart said.

Jen pulled on a vest top and perched on the edge of the bed. "I can't, not when they're all downstairs."

"The hawk's always downstairs. Can't we go somewhere?"

"Like where? The golf club bushes?"

"But I need you," he clutched his crotch. "If we don't do it soon, I'm gonna be ill."

She slipped on her trackies. Stuart was right about her mum being a hawk; she'd know, the minute they had sex.

"Do it yourself."

He hesitated briefly, "If you're sure?"

She shrugged, unsure about everything to do with their relationship, and hurried to the bathroom to fetch Stuart a loo roll. Afterwards, he lay very still, satisfied enough. But what about the next time? She couldn't keep fobbing him off if she wanted to stay his girlfriend. Did she want that? She wanted chocolate, she wanted to pass her GCSEs, she wanted to go to China; she wanted to die of embarrassment every time her mum called her "clever girl" in front of Ricki.

Jen switched on the desk lamp and sifted through her mock exam papers. "I can't believe May got mowed down at a golf club! In Altrincham, of all places. What kind of bastard would leave her lying in the street?"

Stuart opened one eye; the candlelight caught the blush of acne across his forehead. "Maybe she was looking the wrong way? They drive on the right, don't they, in China?"

She blew out the tealights and flung open the window, sickened by his smell. Stuart's ignorance was beyond.

"Now what's got into you? First you give me a hard-on the size of Beetham Tower, then you go cold. I don't know where I am half the time. Like at your party, why did you leave me in the bushes like a perv? I just want to have sex with my girlfriend."

Jen busied herself at the desk. Her exams were six months away. She felt pressured to get a GCSE results card dotted with stars. May was always telling her she could do more, more, more! *Jen, Jen, Jen. How you going to be top international businesswoman if you not practising Chinese?* Work harder, be better, excel... Her mum must have thought she'd struck gold when she found May; the only woman who could nag more.

66

"I'm going downstairs. You'd better come, she'll be getting suspicious."

In truth, she liked Stuart best when they were hanging out with his petrol head friends; she felt safe, it was okay for him to feel her up and make claims about their non-existent sex life – it never led to anything. Turning him on amused her, made her feel confident, proved she wasn't frigid, if only to herself. It also gave her an edge. Swots and bad boys weren't supposed to mix. Stuart fitted the criteria of badness perfectly, having dropped out of school and been cautioned by the police more times than Jen liked to dwell on. But doing it with him? Stuart Crisp being the first man to put his thing inside her!

One of the last things May said to her at the party was, "I know you not loving him in here." She had pointed to Jen's heart.

Jen left Stuart to clean himself up and went downstairs. In the living room, Ricki was arguing with her mum – again. She'd become totally emo since hanging out with the dropouts from Afflecks.

"I don't believe you. You're lying," Ricki cried.

"Sweetheart!"

"I'm not your sweetheart…you're not my mother…you're…"

Jen entered and saw Ricki's face misshapen with tears. "Now what's the matter?" she asked.

"Ask her." Ricki towered over her mum who'd shrunk back in the recliner. Jen felt like the teacher breaking up a playground fight with the school bully.

"Jen, thank goodness you're here…you'll understand."

"Have you even heard yourself? You're pathetic. Jen don't listen to her, she's lying. She's a liar."

"Ricki, what's got into you?" Not upsetting their mum was one of the unspoken house rules. Why was she breaking it so spectacularly?

"Where's your envelope, Jen?" said Ricki.

"I dunno. Probably with the other presents."

"I have it, darling." Her mum rubbed her temples. Her body looked fragile, like that of an injured bird. "It's upstairs, in my handbag."

Ricki charged upstairs and stomped across their parents' bedroom.

"Mum, what's got into Ricki? Why's she calling you a liar?"

Her mother stayed oddly silent.

Ricki thundered downstairs and thrust the red envelope into Jen's hands. "Read it," she said. "I'm guessing May never gave you a practice paper like this before."

Jen took the envelope. It was May's handwriting. Her characters were wavery like an erratic cardiograph. "It's her birthday present to me."

"I'm not stupid. I'm asking you to tell me what it says."

"It says *to my precious daughter…*"

Ricki wheezed.

"Listen, it's not May's fault we're Chinese. You shouldn't hold it against her – or me. We're both China's daughters, it's May's way of making us feel connected."

"You must be joking."

"You don't need to be jealous," she said. "When May gets better, you can have lessons too. It's not a competition. I'm sorry if she gave me birthday money and you didn't get any. Here, take it." Jen held out the envelope, "Take the money. I'm really not that bothered." In fact, she had been saving up for the Olympics in the hope they might all go to Beijing.

"Darling, Ricki already has an envelope."

"Then why are you so mad, Ricki?"

She glowered. "Mad…I'm mad because…"

"Ricki, stop. Jen deserves to hear this from me."

"I'm mad because that fucking May woman abandoned us at birth and you didn't see it and I didn't see it and all the time our own fucking mother kept it a secret!"

Her mum lunged and slapped Ricki fast and loud, on the side of her cheek. "I told you not to," she shouted.

Jen managed to grab her sister's wrist before Ricki struck back. "No. Stop it."

"Tell her that's the truth," Ricki screamed.

"Mum?"

"The day of your party, the day May…went into a coma…I went to her bedsit. All her belongings were there. I only realised when I found her things."

"She's lying, Jen."

"I'm not. I promise. I knew nothing until Sunday. May was the one who lied. Oh God, I'm sorry I hurt you. Ricki, let me see your face, is it bleeding? What have I done?"

The blow had left a red imprint in the shape of a hand.

"When were you going to tell us?" Ricki wheezed, her asthma worsening.

"What are you saying?" Jen interrupted. "That May's our mother?" She wanted to laugh out loud it sounded so crazy. May was her teacher. Their birth mother was thousands of miles away in China, anonymous, faceless, unknowable.

"When were you going to tell us? Next week, next year? Or were you going to keep up the lies. How convenient that May's in a coma. I bet it would suit you just fine if she died right now?"

Her mum shook her head. "I didn't know, I didn't know." She covered her face. "I tried to tell you this morning."

"What do you mean, you didn't fucking know? We have a right to know about May."

"You're not to swear at me like that Ricki. I've brought you up better than this."

Ricki gave a sardonic laugh. "I'm getting out of this nightmare." She wiped her face with her sleeve where the thickly clotted mascara had streaked her cheeks and hurried out the door. It slammed behind her on its gilt hinges.

"Ricki," called her mum. "You've forgotten your inhaler."

When the front door clicked moments later, Jen knew it would be Stuart, escaping from the house as fast as he could. If she wasn't part of the mess she would do the same.

Jen trudged through to the kitchen and switched on the kettle. She covered the casserole she had made earlier with tin foil and wiped the surfaces mechanically with a J-cloth, picking up bits of leftover food. She sat at the breakfast bar, where she'd shared so many meals with May, and waited for the kettle's whistle. It didn't sound so homely now.

A few hours ago, she'd cooked a family meal in the deluded hope Ricki would return and her parents might let Stuart eat with them. Before all this happened, her biggest worry in life – apart from exams – had been how to give her boyfriend a blow job without her mum hearing. Now winter cold crept beneath her skin.

That fucking May woman abandoned us at birth.

Jen looked around her...*The Pelican Chinese* take-away menu, the lucky dragon fan on the fridge, the cheap lunar calendar. Was China really a warehouse of red tat, made for pence? What about the terracotta army, the Great Wall, the mighty emperors, Confucius... The things May had been so proud of. May was the most genuine part, the most real, living, breathing piece of memorabilia Jen knew. All this, was the fake.

Jen had longed to learn Mandarin: not to please her mother, not to piss off her sister, but to create a space, a language in which to find herself. Could May really be anything other than her teacher, the little, bumbling lady who came every Saturday? May's English was flawed. How could either of them invent themselves into languages they didn't fully understand?

It wasn't until later, when her dad came home, that Jen realised what she'd done. The lunar calendar was scattered in shreds across the floor, there was a burnt smell emanating from the Aga. Her dad opened it to find the cindery remains of the lucky dragon fan.

He didn't shout, only held her. "It's all right, love, it doesn't matter now. The inspector's here with news."

The kitchen felt foreign, invaded by the inspector in his fluorescent jacket and stab vest.

"We've found what we believe to be the car. It was a 4x4," he said. "We're taking it in for forensics. We've also got CCTV from the golf club. We're working on a witness appeal for the media."

"What can we do, Inspector?" Iain said.

"I need you to confirm May's details. Tell me, if you would, everything you know about her: date of birth, residence, any friends in Manchester, work colleagues, anyone who might hold a grudge."

Her mum leant against the doorframe, her face pale and vacant. "May Guo," she said. "That's all we know."

The inspector's pen hovered over his notebook. "Excuse me, Mrs Milne, but I understood your friendship extended over several years? That's what you said, in your statement at the hospital."

"Yes. She visited us every week for six years."

"And you only know her name? I find that hard to believe, Mrs Milne."

Jen wished the floor would open up and the inspector would disappear. His shirt was pristine, she wondered who ironed it, what he looked like when he undressed at night, whether his wife made him happy? She wondered if he had kids and whether they were clever...whether they were his own flesh and blood and not someone else's cast-offs?

"We'll be searching May's residence on Burton Road for more information. We've been unable to trace any family members, seems she was something of a mystery."

"You mean Yifan doesn't know?" Jen said. "You haven't called him?"

"Impossible I'm afraid, there's no number – we're not even sure of his surname. I understand you have the keys to her bedsit, Mrs Milne?"

Nancy didn't respond.

70

"Nancy." Her dad placed a hand on her knee. "Inspector Meadows needs to see May's place."

"I'm sorry. It's such a terrible mess."

"Where are May's keys?" Iain said, more firmly.

Jen felt like shaking her mum, telling her to snap out of it.

"I never expected her home to look so grubby. I imagined her to live in a nice semi on a leafy street. I even pictured her kitchen to be like ours, because she cooked such extravagant food for us. Her cooker was like your mother's old Belling. Why did she lie to me, Iain?"

The inspector raised an eyebrow.

"A small misunderstanding, Inspector," said Iain.

"No, it wasn't," Jen interrupted. "She told us the biggest lie of all time. My teacher conned us into believing we were her friends, when all along she despised us."

The inspector stopped writing and combed a hand through his curly hair. "Mr Milne?"

"Inspector, our daughters were adopted from China. It appears this woman – May Guo – was their mother. We just didn't know it until after her accident. My wife found several photographs of our daughters in her wardrobe. Today Ricki discovered a birthday gift from May – addressed to *my dear daughter*."

The inspector stroked his neck, unable to suppress a tic. "I see."

Nancy handed him the keys to May's bedsit.

"So no telephone numbers, no names, no addresses, no family in China. We'll put a call into the Home Office."

"Are you saying…?"

"I'm not saying anything Mr Milne until we have more facts. We may have to consider repatriation, but first things first. We'll get this witness appeal out. Don't be surprised if you see posters up around the place. The photo you gave us was very clear Mr Milne, it should help a great deal."

Her dad seemed poised to say something. Maybe it was the anxiety of the moment which could easily have led to a half-hearted quip, a dad joke, about his camera never lying. He opened the door wide onto the freezing night air and thanked the inspector for coming.

Jen could feel the bitter cold all the way through to the stuffy living room. She knew her dad would rather stand there all night than turn indoors, to face his home, his wife – the kids that could now never fully be his.

Pink satin shoes

Nanchang crackled with activity. Bayi Square, where I'd first stepped off the bus with Zhi, was awash with Falun Gong practitioners. A teacher on a dais sat cross-legged, arms outstretched. The calm, meditative bodies of the Falun Gong students were so unlike my aching body. My fingers throbbed where I had pushed, prodded and poked the circuit boards. Two weeks! Already I heard the klaxon in my sleep. I woke to the sound of the alarm clanging. Sleep was never long or deep enough for me to recuperate. Dreams were shallow. My head ached constantly. The whites of my eyes were turning pink and my hair had lost its sheen.

I hurried, anxious to find the bus that would take me to the train station and back home to my parents. I couldn't bear another day checking a thousand circuit boards.

I skirted a path around the square, feeling in my pocket for Manager He's spending money. He'd slipped an extra wad of notes into my pay packet and I was rich. 300 yuan!

The Falun Gong teacher brought his hands together, and the practitioners dispersed. For a moment I followed the general flow before being swept into the bright lights of a restaurant doorway. I glanced up and saw Chairman Mao, actually *The Colonel*, his benevolent face smiling down on me. Surely this was a sign, a confirmation that I should go home, to Hunan. Mao's country, my country. The place where Li Quifang waited at the coffin maker's door.

The smell of fried food wafting down the line was so different to the pig's blood soup Forwood doled out and it lifted my spirits. Chicken burger, fries, Coca-Cola, chicken nuggets, thousand year old eggs, breakfast *youtiao*, rice... With Manager He's money, I had enough to buy the entire menu.

"What can I get you?" asked a worker who looked more like an American movie star in her baseball cap.

Even the waitress mopping the floor was nice to me, warning me not to slip with my tray, urging me to walk where it was dry. What a fuss pot. I perched on a stool by the window and gorged myself like a proper peasant, letting the chilli paste drip down my chin, chewing and sucking on the tender wing meat. It was more expensive than I expected: ten yuan for Hot Wings, six for fries and three for a green tea. I gobbled it down, making my toes curl with a strange mixture of pleasure and guilt.

The bizarre slogan said, *Eat your fingers off.* Was this supposed to make customers feel hungry? Maybe westerners weren't so cultured after all?

In the far corner, a bride and groom were celebrating their wedding banquet with a dozen or so guests. They drank Coca-Cola, flush-faced and high spirited. All around, the Colonel's smiley face bobbed approvingly, emblazoned on bunches of red balloons. Her wedding dress was western in style and billowed out around her ankles. Honestly, I thought it swamped her. Still, it seemed like a fun way to celebrate and, fleetingly, I dared to imagine my own wedding party. Then mother's sour face came suddenly to mind as she muttered the word 'vulgar'.

I thought of Li Quifang, the reality of being his wife: the wedding, the wedding night, followed by a long life serving Madam Quifang. I sat a whole hour in KFC, becoming less and less sure of my decision to leave Nanchang. I took Mr and Mrs Nie from my pocket and asked what they thought, but they remained silent.

Several times, I had the sense of being watched. I had grown used to the electronic eye in circuitry. I turned round, but there was no-one there, no camera. The feeling was hard to shake off.

I wandered listlessly in the direction of the bus stop. If I stayed a little longer at the factory things might improve. It might not be so easy to find another job with my fake high school certificate and documents. Manager He had promised I'd be rewarded for my loyalty, promised I'd see Zhi again.

My head spun as the traffic blurred past. I drifted in search of a water fountain. Someone moved in a doorway and I went to see who it was, but there was no-one. The factory had driven me senseless. The restrictions, the rules – so many stupid, pointless rules! I slumped in the doorway.

The events of the past fortnight flickered one after the other. All those circuit boards...where did they all go? What did they do? And what was Damei's problem? I replayed the moment she shoved Zhi out of circuitry, the way she continued to taunt Ren. I remembered my humiliation in the showers, Zhi's blank face as she dropped my overalls on the wet floor. Everyone hated me for being Zhi's cousin; even Ren cooled off when she heard about the incident with Fatty on the stool.

73

Night after night, Damei re-enacted Zhi's departure. *"Let me go, I'll make sure you're rewarded. Whatever it is you want: promotion! Wages! A hukou! I can get them all! I am Line Leader Zhen! I deserve respect!"* She would say, refusing to let up until she got bored or until Fatty cajoled her into playing cards.

I heaved my aching body up off the step and dragged a path down the busy street towards the bus stop.

"Sorry, no notes." The bus driver screwed his nose up at Manager He's money.

Passengers pushed past me, tutting.

"You can keep the change, it doesn't matter." I heard myself begin to rant.

Someone tugged on my coat. "2204."

The girl was younger than me, her face open to the world and all its possibilities. Her hair was tied back, wisps of it curled around her childish features.

"That's you isn't it? You're the new one?"

She offered a hand, I pulled away.

"Don't leave now," she said, "Give the factory another chance. The first month's always the hardest. It gets better when you have money to spend."

"Who are you?" I asked.

"I'm a cleaner at Forwood. I saw you just now and thought I'd say hi. Where were you going?"

"Nowhere."

She shrugged. "I'm Sichuan *mei*. My name's Fei Fei, I noticed you could do with a friend."

"Why aren't you with the others?" I asked. "They've all gone shopping."

"Personnel ordered me to buy melons for Cook. The bosses give me all kinds of errands on top of my cleaning work." She played with the cuff of her cardigan the way Little Brother did when he had something to hide.

"I've not tasted fruit for so long…"

"Then come with me to the market, there's bound to be a little they won't miss," she offered.

The bus was about to leave, there was no way of getting on without loose change. My best option was to go with Fei Fei to the market and get the fruit. After that I'd be able to shake her off, pretend I had to wire money home at the Post Office, then return to the bus depot. There was still time to escape Nanchang, if I kept my head about me.

But Fei Fei dawdled by the shops. On Ladies Street, she paused in front of a shop called *Phoenix* whose window mannequin posed naked apart from a short jacket made of paper and a leather mini skirt emblazoned with the national flag; its yellow star barely covering her privates. The outfit was labelled *Neo-Punk*, but I knew what Mother would have called it.

"Have you worked at Forwood long?" I asked.

"About a year. They say my salary will go up this month because I've been a good worker and not caused the company any bother. I hope so, I have dreams."

"What kind?"

"The kind your cousin had before..." Fei Fei tugged nervously on her sleeve again. "I'm sorry," she said.

It wasn't the first time I'd heard innuendos about Zhi. At lunch, the girls from circuitry whispered about her, but when I sat down their gossip trailed off, they changed the subject and left me to eat alone. Once, in the dinner queue, I overheard someone say, "Line Leader Zhen could no more keep her mouth shut than she could her legs."

Did Fei Fei think my cousin was a slut too?

We sauntered from one shop window to the next. Fei Fei irritated me. The clothes would look awful on her scrawny body. How naïve to think she could ever afford them. Who did she think she was? I was the one walking around with 300 yuan in my trouser pocket. I was the one Manager He called 'worker of the future' – not Fei Fei with her silly pigtail and goofy eyes.

I pulled her sleeve. "I thought you had to buy melons?"

Fei Fei's giggle faded quickly.

"Listen," I said, "There's something I want to ask you. I've heard rumours about my cousin and I don't know what to think. Do you know if she had a boyfriend at the factory? I heard there are some cute guys in engineering. Is that why personnel fired her? *Rule 46: Any worker caught engaged with a male on factory premises, either employed by the corporation or otherwise, faces immediate dismissal.*

No-one's willing to talk in that place. They're all watching their backs the entire time."

Fei Fei's face still bore the softness of youth. For a brief moment I thought she might blurt something out, then suddenly she changed her mind.

She pulled away. "Say you'll come with me. Let's enjoy ourselves. You should spend your first pay packet on yourself.

Don't send it all home. All that work without any fun, we might as well be dead."

The moment for revelations was gone.

At The Pacific Department Store, I felt out of place in my sloppy, unwashed cardigan and trousers encrusted with red mud from the farm. Even the air inside the store smelt expensive, a heady mixture of perfume and fresh coffee. Around me women browsed, unhurried, through the shoe section, taking time to feel the quality of leather or hold a handbag to their side, checking in the mirror to see if it matched their coat. The women bore the same grave seriousness as Madam Quifang, deciding whether I was a good enough prospect for her spoilt brat.

Fei Fei headed to a nearby shoe display. "It's not only urban people who can afford these," she said, squeezing her foot into a black shiny slip-on. "I earned a hundred yuan because of my extra errands this month, that's on top of my cleaning salary. If I keep putting some aside and don't tell my family, I could own a pair like this." She held up the hem of her frayed jeans. The shoes were far too stylish for a girl playing fancy dress. Realising the shoe was too small, Fei Fei placed it back on the stand.

"Here, this one's lovely. Try it on," she held out a different shoe for me.

The pink satin opened at the toe and strapped around the ankle, with a jewel on the buckle that demanded my attention. The sole was like a tongue, uncurling itself into a question: *can you resist me?*

I kicked off my trainers and slipped it on. I would need a smart dress with a matching pink handbag to be like the ladies milling around the store. Madam Quifang's words came back to me: *Your feet are too broad...I cannot allow a peasant's foot to rest under my table.*

"Wow, Hunan *mei*, you look like a fairy tale Yeh-Shen!" said Fei Fei. "Now all we need is Prince Charming."

I laughed and brushed her off, but glanced over my shoulder in case Manager He was there.

*Make the other girls sit up and take note...*he'd said. I imagined wearing the shoes around the dorm. That would give those gossiping idiots something to talk about. They'd be so jealous, especially Damei.

"Can I help you?" asked a shop assistant in a voice that really meant '*What are you two greasy hats doing here?*' Her nose

76

wrinkled as if we smelled putrid. "What exactly are you looking for?"

"We're admiring these pink satin shoes."

She held up the price tag. "They are very exclusive. Only to be worn by educated women of class."

The shoes were 250 yuan. I had enough, but not for the train fare to Hunan as well. I decided not to bother.

"Sorry, ladies, but if you do not intend to purchase those shoes, then remove them at once. Proper urban ladies do not appreciate the smell you migrants leave behind."

I smarted. "And what if I were to buy them?"

"I doubt very much a worker like you could afford..."

I reeled Manager He's money onto her palm. "This is enough isn't it?"

She held each note up to the light, saw they were real, and then was forced to kneel and tie the buckles for me.

I gloated.

The assistant wrapped my new shoes in a pristine box lined with pink tissue paper, and I thanked her with extravagant sarcasm.

When we left the store, Fei Fei flung her arms around me. "That was brilliant. What a show, what a posh woman you make!"

"Just because I'm a peasant, doesn't mean I have to be treated like shit."

She stared at me. Her face seemed to suddenly lose some of its spontaneous happiness. I guessed we both wanted to be fairytale Yeh-Shens at heart.

We spent another hour or so inside the store. Fei Fei talked me into having a free makeover. The make-up was imported from America. A beautician asked what look I wanted?

"New," I told her. I wanted to look brand new. She performed a miracle: applying creams, powders, even whitener to make me look more western. She plucked my eyebrows and outlined my lips in pencil, saying I had a pretty face if it weren't for the bags under my eyes. It was the nicest thing anyone had ever said to me.

"You've got to buy some," Fei Fei said. "You look amazing."

We joined the dwindling crowds on Ladies Street. Fei Fei had a spring in her step. I asked if there was still time to go to the market.

"Oh, yes. I almost forgot."

We walked in contented silence. I felt much more optimistic now that I had bought my own make-up and shoes – more rational about the whole situation. In fact, away from Forwood, I wondered why I had ever thought of leaving the place. Besides, did I really

77

think that I could walk back into the farm and expect forgiveness? Where else could I go all alone? I needed to stick at it. If I was clever, Forwood still offered a world of opportunity. I should stay smart – smart and beautiful! Before long, even Damei would be eating out of my hand. I'd be the friend of every worker – it would be in their best interest.

I hurried Fei Fei along, eager to get back to the dorm and try on my new shoes. The hairs on my neck quivered as I imagined slipping my feet into their pink satin, snug as a love letter inside its envelope. I gripped the bag's taffeta handle as we left the market and didn't let go, especially not to help the little Sichuan *mei* carry her melons.

No-one noticed me in the dingy half-light of the dorm that evening. The lights had gone off at nine. The bosses had probably decided to save on electricity. I expected the girls to improvise and light candles or open the shutters, but they were all too exhausted from shopping in town. Fatty's slender body hunched in purposeful sleep and the bunk wires rasped. Damei snored. Ren brushed her hair in the darkness, chafing her comb against a cotter. She had washed earlier, but the smell of Forwood was still on her: flinty, metallic, cold.

"You still awake?" I whispered and tugged gently on the edge of her blanket.

There was no reply.

I turned onto my side to face the cold wall. At home, I slept with Little Brother and would lie awake listening to his tiny snore, his snuffle. He'd fling an arm across me and it would stay there, heavy and warm all night.

"Can we talk?"

"Go to sleep," said Ren, drowsy.

"But there's something I want to show you."

Soon after, her breathing deepened and a snore caught in the back of her throat. She slept mostly on her left side, her bad leg stretched out like a stork.

I reached beneath my bunk and felt for the bag with the pink taffeta handles. It didn't matter that I couldn't see what I was doing, I could feel. The satin was cool and perfectly smooth. I lay down and ran the satin up my bare leg, soft as a cat's tail. Soft like the hands of Manager He. I closed my eyes and imagined him in his dressing gown.

"*Du*," Ren mumbled in her sleep, "*Du*…"

I couldn't help feeling annoyed; she was spoiling the pleasure of my new shoes. Perhaps I should wake her as I did Little Brother, when he dreamt about grass snakes.

"Du, come back!"

She jolted and I heard her racing breath, then a sigh as she lumbered over to face the wall.

I replaced my shoes in their box and curled my pillow into a tube, imagining it as Little Brother beside me in the narrow bunk. My nose and toes were cold. I packed my hands into my armpits where there was a measly residual heat. The skin on my face felt strange beneath the make-up. Tomorrow morning, the girls would wake and see how beautiful I looked.

But I couldn't sleep. My mind flowed like the traffic in Nanchang. In the end, I decided to go and show Manager He my new belongings. I pinched the skirt and blouse from the foot of Damei's bunk, where she kept it folded, and hurried out of the dorm.

The way was becoming familiar. Even in the dark, I could navigate the thirteen steps to the sanitary room, though it took a little more effort in high heels.

The place was eerily quiet without any workers. I walked over to the sink and set about refreshing my make-up. The mascara had smudged, my white skin was blotchy. I washed it away then re-applied the whitener, concentrating on my dimples. White, said the beautician, was the desirable colour for women who wanted to look beautiful: Western white, the shade of a garlic skin. I re-curled my lashes, freshened the eye shadow and softened my lips with gloss. It glided on easy as a silk *ch'ang-p'ao*.

Already three o'clock. My feet hurried down the corridor into circuitry. A green light flashed above the pipework. I could have sworn it tracked me down the line, but I was distracted by a sudden movement in the bureau. It was him! I recognised his outline and the ruffled look of his hair. I teetered up the staircase, my knees wavering like willow. He sat hunched over his desk.

I expected him to tell me I was late, to point at his watch, to sigh, to set about shuffling his papers, but there was a silence between us that made my throat feel suddenly dry. I took up my stool in the corner, poured two cups of green tea and waited for him to speak.

He tasted the tea quickly, a few mouthfuls and it was gone. He poured another, his hand shaking.

"Let me," I offered.

79

He startled as I moved closer.

"Productivity dropped again on Friday by half a percent." He pulled back his swivel chair, crunching over some papers. "That's almost a quarter of a car we're losing every day."

I hadn't noticed before, but Manager He had a habit of resting the tip of his tongue on his bottom lip.

"A quarter of a car per day, a whole car every week, two cars per fortnight..." he gasped. "Something must be done before Schnelleck arrives. If he sees us in this state, our chances are up in smoke, along with our exhausts."

I waited patiently for him to notice my shoes. "Every four days," I corrected.

"Eh?"

"We are losing a car every four days, not every week; that is if we are losing a quarter of a car per day," I said.

Manager He gulped. "Yes, exactly."

Maybe my transformation was not so successful after all? Perhaps it was my turquoise eye shadow or the shape of my lips or the way my dimples looked beneath the white powder?

"What's the news on the floor, 2204? How are they responding to the new food?"

"New food?"

"I had the menus changed yesterday after you said the pig's blood soup wasn't filling enough."

"You listened to me?"

Manager He let out a laugh. "Don't sound so surprised, that's why you're here. I can trust you. I knew that the moment I laid eyes on you."

He glanced down at my shoes. I tried not to bunch my toes. "I see you made a purchase," he loosened his tie. "Have the others seen them?"

"Not yet," I said, "I'm waiting for the right moment. Tonight the lights went out early and..."

"Alright, alright, just don't leave it too long, we're in a sticky situation and I have to do everything in my power to speed up the department."

Over his shoulder, I could see the towering papers on his desk. The sight of all that mess made my hands itch.

"Manager."

"What is it, 2204?"

"I see you're always so busy. It must be hard for you to keep order in your bureau on top of leading our department. Perhaps I could encourage productivity a little by helping you in here, with your papers?" I said, sensing the perfect excuse to see him more often.

He wiped his brow. "I'm impressed by your attitude. The others never... Oh, I'm living in the past, what do they matter now?"

The heat in his bureau seemed to be intensifying.

"So, that's a yes?"

"Let me take a closer look," he said suddenly.

At first I thought he was talking about his paperwork, but instead he gestured to my pink satin shoes. I felt myself redden, but lifted my left foot and he grasped it. A shiver ran all the way up to my belly. His hands were warm as newly laid eggs, his fingers solid around my ankle. Was it my imagination or did he stroke the skin there? I kept very still and let him touch me, pushing aside the memory of Madam Quifang's inspection.

"You've done well," he whispered. "Your shoes, your face, I can see the way you've transformed yourself."

I grinned stupidly and may even have laughed with nerves.

"Aren't you hot?" he said.

I felt myself swell like a red-lipped eugenia under the noonday sun, but I was frightened to say yes in case it led to something beyond my control.

He lifted the hem of Damei's stolen skirt and put his hand on my knee. I sensed he was about to move closer and that I would let him. I wanted to know: would the silk of my lips fall away easily? The taste of sugar tickled on my tongue as I remembered his candies.

"Ha-ha! The cherry's surely ripening by the day," came a voice from the doorway. "You'd better watch out or she'll become a weed, growing where you don't want her."

Manager He smarted.

Old Artist's cane clinked the edge of my stool. "What's this, a new face for old?"

"I was instructed to buy make-up."

"Ha-ha! Light me the spirit lamp, He-Chuan, before I set to work carving out this beauty."

"You mean he's staying?" I said, forgetting my place.

"There'll be no opium tonight, Old Artist. I need your full attention. The portrait has to look perfect."

The man removed his deerstalker, his yellow-white hair wafted into soft peaks. "Whatever you say, Manager, whatever you say." He eased himself into the chair, creaked open his sketch book and began drawing.

Manager He returned to his paperwork. Occasionally, he paused to look at my portrait. "Good!" or "Yes, that's it!" he'd say.

"Stop gawping at the Manager," said Old Artist. "Or your likeness will be cross-eyed."

After that, Manager He did not look until Old Artist declared it finished.

"You've not lost your talent," he said. "Be sure to include the 4x4, as we discussed. Make it shine – shine like a new dawn at the beginning of a new era."

Of course, I didn't know what the portrait was for or why anyone would want a picture of me.

"Have you got everything you need? The shoes, the face?"

Old Artist rubbed his chin thoughtfully. I could feel his eyes roving towards my chest. "I suppose, there is more I could do to highlight the girl's natural assets…"

"No, definitely not. Not this time. She must remain covered. I don't want a riot on my hands. You know what those squabbling women workers are like these days. Even if the randy monkeys in engineering were to approve, what good are they without the women following suit?"

Old Artist shut his sketchbook and gathered up his battered attaché case. There was an awkward silence and I realised it was time for me to leave the men alone. My job was done, although an aching part of me wished it wasn't.

Manager He walked with me a little way into the circuitry room. His tongue rested thoughtfully on his lip, as though fishing for the right words.

"You've done well, 2204, you've made yourself look very different, very… distinctive."

Distinctive…I breathed in the word. That meant interesting, unique; distinctive in a good way, not a woman hidden in a factory of identical overalls and lives.

I felt his hand squeeze mine and I reciprocated by rubbing my thumb against his. Just this once, what harm would it do? His breath became shallow.

"Am I good enough for you?" I whispered.

"Good as new."

The green light above the pipework flashed, and Manager He promptly let go of my hand. "Come back tomorrow night and do some paperwork," he said.

I nodded, feeling suddenly adrift. He gestured towards the exit and I hurried away, clumsily knocking into a chair. Once in the corridor, I ran dream-like in my beautiful fairy-tale slippers. I ran through a factory of bodies, breathing walls and fading lights, until finally my bunk found me and I became a feather settling down to sleep, falling where the wind had blown me; swept up and weightless in a gust of his breath. Unsure what separated my day from my night. I fell to sleep wearing my Yeh-Shen shoes, my pink satin dreams – content for the first time since arriving at Forwood.

The bitches...traitors. Ricki turned the corner with fire in her heels, her breath whipped by a cross-wind of winter air. *Lying, two-faced cows, the pair of them.*

The house numbers were too small to see.

Idiot...Moron... Ricki Milne, thick as pig shit. Can't tell a lie if it bites her on the arse. Can't tell her real mum a mile off.

The house was somewhere mid-terrace. Princess Street, too run-down even for Cinderella. Ricki rapped on the door of number 28. *Please be in. Just answer this one time.* The house sat in darkness. Lowrie was probably at a party, her eyes crinkling around a joint in some smoke-filled boomer of a club.

A light came on upstairs then the door opened and Lowrie peered out. She wore a kimono from Kin-ki. It was black, with gold flowers and white cranes flying across the chest. Ricki followed the winding tracery of her veins to where they disappeared beneath the silk.

"Ricki, what are you doing here at this time of night?"

"I needed some place to go."

"What's happened? Your tattoo's not gone mangy has it? Don't tell me your parents found out?"

"It's not that."

Lowrie pulled her dressing gown tighter. "It's late, kid. I've got work tomorrow."

"I'm sorry, I'll make it up to you, I promise. It's only for a night. I'll be out of your hair by morning." Ricki packed her hands into the armpits of her parka. "It's cold," she wheezed, "getting colder."

"You're not in a good way, kid."

"Families fuck you up, isn't that right?"

"You should try reading less miserable poetry."

Ricki's teeth chattered. "Are you going to let me in or what?"

A voice called from upstairs. "Who is it, Lou?" A blonde appeared wrapped in a towel, she was in her early thirties, maybe younger, with a pierced bottom lip.

"Ricki, this is Esme."

"Your bath's getting cold, Lou. Don't be long."

Ricki had a sudden urge to punch the blonde goddess. "I'll go."

"Sorry, kid," said Lowrie. "Why don't you talk things through with your twin?"

Ricki gave a bitter laugh. "Yeah," she said, turning away.

My fucking double.

She didn't know where to go. Behind the counter of the chippy, the kebab spike was bare, a lace tablecloth hung over the fryers. Pinned above the till was a postcard: *Madonna and Child.* Mary's flat, sad eyes met hers. She must have known from the beginning how it would end, losing her baby.

What about May? Had she known? Ricki raged inside her parka. How could May do it? What was she thinking, coming to England? Ricki glimpsed her reflection. Who was this Chinese kid staring back at her? She blew into her hands to keep them warm and hummed.

What about May's voice? Had she sung to them in the womb? Had she talked to the bump of babies, the stump of flesh heaping up in front of her? What kind of a mother was she all those months and why didn't she listen when people told her to scrap the babies while she could? Or did May smoke pot and sniff glue? Was she off her head half the time and couldn't think straight? Maybe that's why Ricki inherited asthma and Jen's teeth turned out soft as rotting bark. Did May really – in her heart and in her empty belly – believe they would open their arms, wide as the Yellow River and let her steam on down? Pick up where she'd left off in China?

Fuck you, May.

Ricki sat for a while in the freezing bus shelter. She couldn't feel her toes. A bus pulled up and she shook her head at the driver. The couple kissing on the backseat faded out of view. She wandered towards the park.

A bench *In loving memory of Herbert, 1919-2007* was freckled with frost. Ricki curled up on it, knees tucked beneath her chin, her parka like a fly sheet, her teeth protesting at the cold. She was woken by car headlights.

A guy whistled piercingly. "Hey, lady!"

Ricki's heart pumped faster. The car bumped over the frozen grass and a guy rolled out with a bottle of beer, burbling about the stars, saying he could see his anus, with its mother of a ring.

"That's Saturn and you're talkin' bollocks."

A guy staggered towards Herbert's bench. "Bit young to be here alone," he said.

"Who's asking?"

"Come over here will you," called the driver. He had a thick Manchester accent. A woman in an itsy-bit of vest top sat sideways on his knee and began pouring *Woodpecker* down his throat. They fell out of the open door, and he groaned.

Ricki stared through the car headlights at the figure on all fours: the leather jacket, the biker boots, the ponytail.

"Stuart?"

Spittle hung from the corner of his mouth.

"Stuart what are you doing? I thought you were with Jen?"

His eyes were unfocused. "I'm letting off steam."

"Letting off steam? You piece of shit. Who's that slapper with you?"

He wiped his mouth. "I don't see you holding Jen's hand."

Ricki hugged herself, overcome by the cold inside her. She was miles from home. She couldn't even remember the way back.

"You want to sleep in the car? There's room in the back if you can put up with Dave trying to have a feel."

"Do I look that desperate?"

When she woke, the slapper had gone. Stuart wound down the window and spat a gigantic gob that twinkled on the frosty grass. Ricki caught his eye in the rear-view mirror and looked away.

"Alright?" he said.

"What do you think?"

He got out and scraped the frost off the windscreen with his fingers. She could see tyre tracks in the desolate park. Stuart reversed, wheels crunching, towards a track and an exit leading to a terraced street.

He drove to ASDA and disappeared off in search of breakfast. Dave trailed after him. Ricki stayed in the car and checked her mobile. There were ten missed calls and a text from Jen, *Plz, call NOW*. The first voicemail was from her dad, telling her to *Get yourself home, your mother's beside herself*. The next was from her mum, sobbing into the phone, saying she was sorry, she didn't mean to hurt her, she didn't know what to do... Ricki deleted them. The final voicemail was from Jen.

Ricki, I know how you're feeling. I'm shocked too. I need you. We need to talk right now. I promise I won't pretend everything's okay. No-one else understands me. You're my twin sister.

Ricki's fingers hovered over the green button to call her back, when something caught her eye. It was a policeman, passing in front of the car on his way into the supermarket. She shrank back in the seat. No doubt her parents had reported her missing. Her mum had probably declared a national state of emergency because she'd stayed out for one poxy night. Abandoned babies aren't supposed to run off, they're supposed to be eternally grateful, loyal as rescued puppies.

Ricki watched the policeman hand over what looked like *Wanted* posters to a member of staff. She waited until the policeman left then went to see what was was going on. A woman from customer services had pinned a poster to a community notice board.

"At least it's not another shooting," she said.

Ricki stared at May's face in the witness appeal poster. It was like a creepy Scooby Doo painting, the kind with moving eyes. So this was her Chinese mother. They even had the same dimples... No wonder May always seemed so lost and out of place in Manchester. She was never meant to be here, never meant to find her and Jen. That's what the authorities would have said: the adoption agency, the Home Office, the Chinese government. Was a clean break too much to ask? She'd left them once, in China, wasn't that enough?

"Can I take one?"

The woman gazed at Ricki. "Why don't you go and have a nice cuppa, you look like you've seen a ghost."

Stuart appeared at her side. "She's coming with me,"

At the car, he prised away the poster.

"That's her innit? Jen's teacher. Don't tell me she's snuffed it? Should have been watching where she was going."

Ricki looked into his pasty face and wanted to smash it into orbit.

"What did I say wrong?"

"What do you ever say right, wank-stain?"

She snatched the poster and stormed off, to who knew where or how long it would take her...she just wanted...

To be.

Anywhere.

But there.

"And stay away from my sister or I'll tell my parents you've been trying to get her laid."

"Oooh, big fucking deal," she heard him laugh.

87

Portrait of a young woman

Oh, Mrs Nie, his hands are soft, his thumb graceful as a swan's neck. Last night, when he touched me, I thought I'd float away. His name is Manager He. I don't know what I've done to deserve his attention. He says I am the future. He held my hands, those I thought were ugly, and told me I could inspire others. "You are the light," he said, "shining the way to a brighter future..." Oh, Mrs Nie, how can I work when my hands won't stop trembling at the thought of him?

Clang-a-lang-a-lang-a-lang-a-lang-a-

I bundled Mrs Nie into my pillow case. Ren was first to the pipe and brought me a share, as she often did. We hurried to the sanitary room to fight for a place at the sink. There wasn't a chance to show off my pink satin shoes, but that time would come. Soon they'd all want to be rewarded like me, even cynical old Ren.

I was getting the knack of the circuit boards; although not quite up to Xiaofan's speed. I completed most of them before the klaxon. The time analysts no longer checked my efficiency or whispered to Xiaofan. My study of basic English was also paying off. I recognised words like *quit* and *defect warning* without having to refer back to the instructions. I'd prove to the shoe assistant in the department store, as I did to Madam Quifang: not all peasants are dumb pigs.

I glanced towards Manager He's bureau. For the last half hour, the chief executive, had been laying into him. I was scared it might be something to do with me and Rule 46, the one forbidding *improper relations*. The bureau door slammed and the chief executive strode down the line, tripping over some plastic packaging. His armful of papers fanned across the factory floor.

"Which imbecile left these here? Can't you see it's a safety hazard?" He dusted himself down. "Star of Forwood? Pah! Just remember, it's me who pays your wages and feeds your families back home. Now get back to work and you, pick these up." He pointed to me.

Manager He stepped out of his bureau, his hair ruffled and his shirt marbled with sweat. "You heard! Get back to work."

I hurried to pick up the chief executive's papers, which were identical portraits of a young woman in a sequinned dress and pink shoes. The word *STAR* was printed in red characters at the top of each sheet. Old Artist's portrait! I tried to catch Manager He's eye, but he disappeared into his bureau, red-faced, like a boy who'd received a good whipping. I handed the chief executive his papers and returned to my desk.

A self-satisfied smile curled at the corner of Xiaofan's mouth. She was onto us.

At lunchtime, Ren showed up late and slumped down next to me, her face increasingly sallow since her recent overtime in bonding. Her eyes were strained as if she'd been staring at the sun, but there was no daylight in the work rooms.

She rubbed her bad leg under the table. "Three hours' sleep. It's not enough, Sky Eyes."

Ren pushed the food around her bowl. There was not much improvement to Manager He's new menus. The pig's blood soup contained a few more rubbery strands of noodle and a tiny portion of chicken's feet was given to every third worker in the queue. A far cry from KFC.

"What is it that you do in bonding?" I asked. We were all trained in one process, which we performed endlessly. It was rare for anyone to venture further than their own line, let alone section.

"I stand in a cold room, gawping down a microscope and bonding minuscule dies onto a frame. My hands get so numb I can't hold the tweezers to separate out the electronic dies. My line leader badgers me constantly because the dies are expensive and we're told not to waste a single one." She pushed away her tray. "I can't eat this shit." The blackened rice was stuck together in a clod and the knife beans had been steamed until translucent and were now falling apart.

"Maybe things will improve?" I said. "It's pay day again soon. Fei Fei's hoping for a rise."

Ren snorted. "Fei Fei, the cleaner? Don't be daft; she only started a month before us. The girl's soft as butter, and she loiters around gossiping too much. There's no way they'll increase her pay."

"She told me she'd worked here a year."

"People say anything to gain respect. But here's the truth: one day you'll wake up and wish you were dead in a place like this. They call it Forwood, but this factory isn't moving forwards or getting better. We're going nowhere. What have we got to show for our lives spent on the line? We stay because we can't lose face and go home empty handed."

At that moment, Fei Fei rushed over and slapped one of Old Artist's posters down in front of us.

"Look Mai Ling, look – you're like a movie star! And to think, I was there when you bought the make-up. Your portrait's everywhere. You're famous."

The poster showed me wearing a sequinned dress and pink shoes, standing in front of a shiny 4x4. The slogan read: *The Star of Forwood. Workers, you too can light the way to a better future.*

"Propagandist shit," said Ren, "What will they come up with next? If they think that's going to make me work any harder..."

Fei Fei pulled on my sleeve. "Come on, I'll show you the rest. I've been helping to put them up."

"Come too, Ren," I urged.

We were supposed to tidy our tray away. Ren left hers on the table and followed us out of the canteen.

Fei Fei turned left, knocking into a group of workers swooning over a postcard of Andy Lau, the movie star. We followed her down an unfamiliar corridor to a large, unexpectedly sunny part of the factory. I blinked at the sudden wash of natural light. She said it was Forwood's official visitor entrance – she knew a lot for someone who started the month before me. The reception desk was empty, music echoed dreamily from a radio in the glass atrium. All around, on the walls, shone a hundred pairs of pink satin shoes, a hundred gleaming 4x4s and my smile on a hundred posters.

"Now everyone can see how gorgeous we are beneath our boring old overalls. You've made us more than just *dagongmei*, 2204. We're working women with prospects."

Old Artist had made me taller than in real life and more Western-looking; I didn't remember posing: hands on my hips, my chest puffed out in pride.

"You've done a good job," said Fei Fei.

"How did you get their attention?" Ren asked.

"I did exactly what you told me to do, Ren. I used my hands. The harder you work, the more rewards you get."

I wished Ren would hobble back to work and leave me and Fei Fei to talk about my new shoes and make-up.

"Ha! Don't you think I work hard? *Core of the factory* they call us. So why do the girls in bonding only get 50 yuan more than the rest? I feel my eyesight getting weaker staring down that microscope. Last night, in the dorm, I walked straight into our bunk. And you talk about rewards? The only reward I've got from any factory is this," she pointed to her damaged right leg and then reached up and tore my picture from the wall. "This is what I think to your stupid poster." She ripped it to pieces.

"Hubei *mei*, what's got into you?" Fei Fei scolded. "You know the city's better than home: bowing to a mother-in-law, scraping to a husband."

Ren shook her head. She was sweating and pale. "I'm not sure I can take much more…I'm so tired…every day the same…"

Fei Fei helped her onto a chair. "Maybe I should get the nurse?" she said.

"No," shouted Ren. "I don't want any more of her bloody pills."

"I'll go," I said.

She flung off my hand. "I don't want any help."

"Ren, you've not been sleeping well, you're exhausted. All those nightmares, sometimes I don't know whether to wake you up."

"You've got the wrong impression, Sky Eyes," she whispered.

"But I hear you, calling Du's name in the night."

"I want you to forget that name. Don't say it around here again."

I nodded like the old obedient Mai Mai.

"Promise me, you won't change, Sky Eyes. Factory life, it can turn you into something you're not. Bosses get under your skin after a while… It happens so slowly. You won't even notice. First the posters, then one day you'll wake up and you won't know who's in the mirror."

She was right. I was already changing so fast. But the person I was becoming at Forwood, the one trying to make a living for herself, was a better person than I could ever be under Li Quifang's heel.

"Just promise me, you won't forget the girl you were, your family, your blood."

Fei Fei picked up the scraps of my poster and went to put them in the bin.

"Is that what happened to Du?" I whispered.

Ren wiped her eyes with her sleeve, pulling down an invisible shield to her past. I realised then, for the first time, that to survive in the factory, that was how it was for all of us. The past could not exist anywhere but in our own private thoughts, to share it would be to admit weakness. And a weak body, a vulnerable one, was not a working body. Not a *dagongmei*.

I handed her one of Manager He's candies, hidden in my overalls, and she sucked on it without argument.

"I'm sorry I ripped your poster," she said, eventually.

"It's only a stupid portrait," I lied.

Overtime finished early, around eight, and I seized my chance to show off my new purchases. Fatty was washing in the sanitary room when I breezed in with my new make-up bag. She dried her face and watched transfixed as I lined up my beauty products on the sink next to hers.

I had re-played the beautician's instructions a hundred times on the line that day and it was a thrill to act it out for Fatty. "First, use a primer to prepare the skin," I said, dabbing it over my cheeks. "Next rub on the moisturiser, being careful not to drag the delicate skin around the eyes. Then smooth out any blemishes using concealer – a speck on both cheeks is all that's needed, don't make it too thick or you'll look like a peasant who's trying too hard. Next add whitener, for a refined look, and finally a highlighter to get rid of the dark circles."

I stepped back and smiled at Fatty. "Well? What do you think? Not bad for a girl from Hunan."

"You look stunning, Hunan *mei*. All grown up!"

"Thanks. I need to practise more with the highlighter though, I can still see the bags under my eyes."

"But I don't understand, how can you afford all this stuff after one month? Did you not send any money to your family?"

"Of course," I lied. "All this, I bought with my reward money, Fatty. I got a bonus for working hard during my probation." I added another blob of highlighter below each eye.

"I never got anything for my probation."

I shrugged, "Maybe the rules are changing? Maybe Manager He is trying to inspire his workers and make them feel happy."

Fatty picked up a lipstick and flipped it over between her thumb and forefinger. "This colour is striking. Try it on," she held it out to me.

I pressed my lips together and carefully followed their contours until a crimson pout appeared.

"Can I try it?" Fatty asked.

"Oh, erm."

"I won't spoil it, I'll be careful."

"Probably best if you don't, Hunan *mei* – otherwise they'll all want to borrow it," I shoved the lipstick quickly inside my make-up bag ready for my next visit to Manager He. "I'm sure if you pick up speed on the line, Fatty, you'll be rewarded too. I've set myself a target of one board every forty five seconds. Why don't we have a competition? You'll probably beat me hands down."

Fatty's face fell, she seemed not to care about the boards. "I only wanted to try the lipstick, there was no need to be mean. I stole an extra piece of melon from the canteen and was going to share it with you tonight."

Just then a couple of workers from the dorm next to ours entered, giggling and pointing in my direction.

"You're the Star of Forwood aren't you?" said one, whose bun was scraped so tightly above her head she resembled a gourd. "We saw your posters outside the canteen and we think you look unbelievable."

"Oh...thank you."

"We wanted to see you in real life," said her friend, hurrying to my side, her eyes fixed on my newly made-up face. She leaned in close and I smelt the cooking oil in her hair. A canteen worker. "Is that whitener you've used?" she asked.

I tried not to recoil as she ran her plastered fingertip along my jawline. "Yes, I bought it in town on Sunday."

"It makes your skin looks so fresh."

"No spots at all," remarked the worker with greasy hair and skin to match.

"I earned the make-up through hard work. You can do the same."

"What colour is that lipstick?" said the girl with the bun.

"Cherry."

"I want some! I think it would suit me."

I smiled, unsure.

"What would Kwo say if he saw us looking like this, Hakka *mei*?"

"He would forget to boil the rice, Hakka *mei*!" laughed her friend.

"You too can light the way to a better future!" Fatty said sarcastically.

"That's right," I interjected. "Your work in the canteen is very important. It is not simply rice and dumplings you make every day, it is a satisfied workforce. With a full belly we can work many hours and still have energy for overtime."

"Mai Ling," said Fatty, tugging on my sleeve, "I'm going to play cards. Come on, don't waste time talking to these Hakka *mei*, come with me."

"No, please stay," said the greasy kitchen worker, poking around inside my make-up bag. "We want to see what else you have in here."

"Show us how to put eyeshadow on properly. I'm sick of my eyes looking so dreary."

"And tell me how I can get rid of these spots."

"She wants to impress the engineers."

"No I don't!" she elbowed her friend. "I already have a boyfriend, waiting for me at home."

Fatty skulked off. I stayed to demonstrate my eyeshadows and talk more about what it took to become a 'star'. They promised to try harder at cooking the food properly so that it didn't taste like pig swill.

With my fame spreading, Damei's personnel uniform was no longer a convincing disguise for my night visits to Manager He, but I continued to wear it out of spite.

That night, I found him hunched over his desk asleep. I entered without invitation and began sifting through his papers, as we'd agreed. The ones on his desk were all letters, addressed to Herr Schnelleck. There were about thirty, of varying length, written in English. My poster was stapled to one of them. I spent an idle moment tracing my outline, before slipping the poster into a new file at the front of the cabinet.

"Shipment!" he cried and sat up abruptly.

I coughed gently. "Excuse me, Manager, I've come to get ahead with the filing."

He looked particularly handsome, a certain spongy softness to his features after sleep. "Yes, yes…the filing… I must have dozed off. I don't know what came over me. There are invoices that need processing and an important schedule to work out for tomorrow."

For the next hour we worked solidly. My presence seemed to be a comfort. I listened to him read aloud phrases translated from his latest letter to Schnelleck. I admired his intellect and education and held his pens like a proper assistant. Sometimes, I made green tea and cleared papers from the floor, quietly arranging the files in the cabinet to regain order. The work wasn't at all taxing compared to being on the line. It gave me the opportunity to study him in more detail; to let my eyes linger on the back of his neck. I imagined the shape and texture of his back beneath his dressing gown; solid as wet clay against my cheek.

"You've not said what you think of the portrait," he said eventually. "Don't you approve? I'm keen to know its effect? Are they jealous? The time analysts have reported a minor increase."

The bureau felt suddenly hotter.

"They're all talking about me – that's for sure. I'd say the posters have been a success."

"But what are they saying?" he asked. "It's not enough that they should be gossiping. I need action, or my work here is finished. I'm finished."

"They asked what I did to deserve rewards, so I told them I worked hard."

"And did they buy it?"

Ren flashed into my mind, but I pushed her out again. "Of course; they'll believe anything if they think it's going to make them richer or more beautiful."

He gave a knowing laugh. "How true," he said and took a bottle of liquor from his drawer, swigging from the neck without offering me a sip.

"2204, something has been bothering me and until now I haven't had chance to raise it with you. The fact is… I've been trying to remember your name."

"My name?" A name was contraband in a place like Forwood. To Damei, I was 'slug', to Ren 'Sky Eyes'. To most, I was simply another Hunan *mei*. "My real name is Mai Ling."

His knee jittered. Perhaps the liquor had made him forget the normal order of things. He reached out suddenly and laced his fingers around mine. He brought me to my feet. I smelt the liquor on his breath.

"Mai Ling, I need you to promise never to tell anyone."

I nodded.

He leaned forwards, the features of his face blurred and I closed my eyes, believing he was about to kiss me. A heavy weight pressed against my face. The weight of his forehead.

"Good," he pressed tighter, "because no-one must ever know. Do you understand?"

I felt like a firecracker in a tin box. He would have gone further if I hadn't resisted. His tongue slipped inside my mouth. I squeezed myself from underneath him and scrambled through the darkness of the circuitry room. I kept my head bowed, fearful of the electronic eye hidden in the pipework. I lunged for the sanitary room door and went straight to the mirror. My cheeks and neck were flushed; my cherry lipstick was smeared and clownish. The creature standing in front of me was unfamiliar. I closed my eyes

95

for a moment to see if the girl Mai Mai was there, behind the painted face. When I opened them, there stood a different young woman. There was also blood. Damei's uniform was freckled with my blood.

I stuffed my knickers thick with toilet paper and tried to wash the stain from Damei's skirt. Niether water, soap or scrubbing helped. I returned to the dorm, draped the uniform over the foot of Damei's bed and tiptoed to my bunk.

Tin box

I woke feeling someone's breath in my ear. Believing it to be Manager He, I turned to welcome him with a smile, but a hand whacked me across the head.

"That's for making all that noise when I was trying to sleep. Don't you know I'm on early starts this week?" said Damei.

I whimpered.

"Next time you feel like a night wander, make sure it's a long walk over that balcony, alright Slug?"

Damei pulled back my blanket and grabbed me by the nightshirt, ready to strike me again. Quickly, I told her Kwo's new menu had given me the shits and pleaded with her to stop. Then the breakfast alarm rang out, Damei dressed hurriedly and swept out of the dorm without food. She didn't notice the crimpled bloodstain on her uniform.

I wasn't interested in congee either. Instead, I found the pink satin shoes from beneath my bunk and put them on, determined not to hide beneath a date tree.

Fatty paused by my bunk with her congee. "They're pretty shoes, Hunan *mei*," she said.

"I couldn't resist."

The girl who slept by the window looked up from her bowl. "How can you afford that stuff, and I can't? We do the same job, don't we? We have the same boss?"

The girl worked with me in Zone B and was known for her competitive streak. I had seen her check a board in forty seconds and felt she could do more given the right persuasion.

"I worked like a dog during my probation. I even memorised the English on the boards."

"You did what?" she said, pulling on the shutters in a vain attempt to keep out the drafts.

"It's not that hard if you put your mind to it – it gives me the edge."

"Easier to get ahead winning mahjong," she said, approaching my bunk.

After the episode with Fatty in the sanitary room I knew I needed to be more generous and so I told the girl she could try my shoes on if she wanted. "They're not like other shoes, they're finished with real satin," I added and passed them to her.

She put them on and teetered towards her bunk. "Look at me. A proper Miss Canton!" she laughed.

"A tall *mei*," said another girl, flicking her toenail clippings on the floor.

"Worker, you have thirty seconds to clear that mess or I'll fire you on the spot!" she stamped on the toenail clippings with my beautiful shoe.

We all laughed.

"Have you been mixing with the managers, Waisheng *mei*?" jibed Fatty. "You sure sound like a boss."

"She plays mahjong in high places, don't you Waisheng *mei*?" said the girl cutting her toenails.

Ren, who was combing her hair in the mirror, spun round and shot me a warning glance. "Take the shoes off her, Sky Eyes," she hissed, "it's you they mock."

The afternoon passed slowly. In Zhi's absence, we got away with listening to the radio. Some of the girls brought in sweets they'd bought on their day off and passed them down the line. Manager He didn't seem bothered, so long as we were getting through the work. The noise of the conveyor belt droned on, punctuated by the sudden blare of the klaxon which kept my head from dropping onto my chest.

My period pains were dreadful. I disappeared to the sanitary room and climbed onto the toilet to look at the beautiful square of daylight. I spent as long as I could by the window, staring at the mountains above the city skyline. I hoped Little Brother had forgiven me for leaving.

When I returned to work, one of the workers from Zone B gave me a mock salute. Another kowtowed all the way to the floor. Her accomplice shrieked with laughter and before long everyone in circuitry had joined in, calling me 'Hong Kong cat' and 'Miss bossy top'. The girl who had tried on my shoes laughed along. Xiaofan put down her circuit board and the others followed suit, abandoning their stations to gossip. The conveyor belt ground to a halt.

Suddenly, a loud whistle pierced the chaos. Two young men entered and stood imposingly at the managers' entrance.

Manager He stepped out of his bureau. "Workers, meet Mr. Chen and Mr. Ting." He paused. "Men, I trust you'll deal with this situation?"

Mr Chen bowed and Manager He scuttled back inside his office.

Chen wore horn-rimmed glasses and stood straight-backed, feet together. Ting was younger and shorter, with a perfectly proportioned frame, his clothes immaculate. A dopey young worker on my line grinned like a buffoon, silly *mei*, as if they'd be interested in her.

"Back to your stations, girls," said Ting. "What we have to say won't take long."

Chen read from a sheet. "This week, a worker was caught wearing another worker's ID badge in her absence. This violation is unacceptable and will incur a fine of 50 yuan. There is no excuse for anybody who covers up for best friends, relatives or fellow villagers. Remember the factory is not like the field. You are each responsible for yourselves."

Ting continued, "Also this week, production tools were found in a worker's dorm. Remember, workers are not permitted to take anything outside the circuitry room, not even waste material. Everything in this room belongs to Forwood. Let me repeat, you must put an end to the bad habits from the field. Theft is a serious violation of factory rules and incurs dismissal."

There was a pause as Chen and Ting scanned the room. The two girls from Zone B who had mocked me were singled out. I clapped inwardly as Ting muscled them towards the door.

One cried like a baby, "I never stole a thing!"

The other hung her head in resignation.

"We will return next Wednesday and every week thereafter, until you are all fully compliant with factory regulations," said Chen.

The door slammed behind them, and we were left stunned by the girls' sudden eviction.

Manager He spoke over the tannoy, "Let that be a lesson to all of you. I will not let unruly workers jeopardise the productivity of my department."

The company song resumed along with the conveyor belt. My hands trembled as I picked off a board and I vowed never, ever to be caught.

The next day, during evening meal, I posed next to Fei Fei as she plastered more of my posters to the canteen walls. Workers from every department gawped in our direction.

"Do you think they're jealous of me like they were of Zhi?" I asked.

99

Fei Fei hesitated. "They say your cousin was not a nice line leader and that she forgot her place in the factory hierarchy. I believe you are much wiser."

"But a line leader needs to be firm. They are almost impossible to control. Yesterday, they mocked me on the line – and for what? Being a worker with ambition?"

"Workers don't like being bossed around by an uppity *dagongmei*. The trick is to inspire them from within, not rule over them like a proud tyrant – I believe. But then, I'm young and not all that clever, what do I know?"

Her words sounded uncannily like Manager He's, I thought, as I passed her another of my posters.

Suddenly, there was a commotion in the dinner queue. Fei Fei and I left the posters and hurried over to where Damei was squaring up to another worker from personnel.

"You bitch, you think you can play with me? You think I'll take it?" Damei held the girl by her wrists. She was of an equally scrawny build, but with fire in her belly. She retaliated with a stream of insults.

"Fight! Fight! Fight!" Called out the factory girls.

Kwo appeared, pushing his way to the centre of the crowd that had formed in a circle around them, and shouted for the girls to stop.

Damei pulled her adversary by the hair. The girl's fingernails clawed back at Damei's face, making her eyes bulge.

"No-one messes with my stuff!" yelled Damei.

"You crazy bitch, I never touched your dirty uniform. If you washed, it wouldn't get so filthy!"

Damei stamped on her toes and the girl hopped like a startled chicken.

"Slum-bitch."

Damei's eyes flashed. "What did you just call me?"

"Look around. There's no-one to stick up for you. You have no family."

Damei punched the girl square on the jaw, sending her sideways to Kwo's feet. I hurried from the crowd, knowing that the bloodied heap of flesh on the canteen floor should have been me.

Later that night, after overtime, I flung myself onto the bunk and grappled for Mr and Mrs Nie. I started to ask them what I should do, but whispering to a wooden doll suddenly seemed childish.

It was all going wrong. No-one was taking me seriously. There was only Fei Fei and what did she matter? I needed to pull

100

myself together. *If you can't impress Manager He, you'll be out on your ear. Help me, Mrs Nie, help me! I need all of them to like me.* I need...

The door creaked open. Ren was returning from her shift.

I shoved my figurines beneath the pillow and lay still, pretending to be asleep.

She sat on the edge of my bunk, lit an illicit cigarette and asked, "What's all this about Damei punching someone's lights out in the canteen?"

I inched back the blanket. "I'm too tired for gossip, Ren. I need sleep."

"Is it anything to do with the uniform you've been stealing? You'd better take care, Sky Eyes. Damei would eat you for breakfast if she found out it was you. Whatever you're doing, stop now, before it's too late."

She leant into my bunk, her cigarette almost suffocating, her face ghostly in the smudge-grey light of the dorm.

"I'm so scared, Ren," I whispered.

She touched my arm, then seemed to remember something.

Over by the door, Ren knelt and inched up the loose floorboard using the stolen screwdriver from her overalls. There was something hidden in the cavity.

She handed it to me. "I want you to have this."

It was a battered tin box. "Where did it come from?" I asked, shivering.

"I didn't pinch it if that's what you mean," said Ren, climbing in beside me.

The box was decorated with a picture of a factory. Inside a brooch glinted in the half-light. It was a pricey-looking pearlescent dragonfly.

"I can't let her go..." Ren stared past me at the wall. "In my nightmares, she's always standing by a river; it's the canal that runs through the Kingmaker Factory."

"Du?"

"They found her in the canal... A manager dragged her out and took her away. No-one knew what happened after that, not even her family came for her body. I don't think the factory told them."

"Oh, Ren."

"No-one cared, Sky Eyes, so long as it went unnoticed – do you understand? I need you to understand." Her tired eyes searched mine. "We shared a dorm, there were ten of us. The rest were from Guangdong, but we were both Hubei *mei* so we stuck together,

101

always side by side. But the day they made her a line leader she changed, almost overnight. They made her work harder than her body could bear. They told her not to associate with her kin or her villagers... They separated us into different dorms and transferred me to another department where I had to learn the bonding process from scratch. For a while we lost touch completely."

"Did the brooch belong to Du?" I asked, sensing it was the last trace of something precious.

Ren's teeth chattered. "She gave it to me in secret the day before..."

I pulled my blanket over her shoulders. Her feet were icy and she slipped them between mine.

"We weren't allowed any personal effects and belongings. She made the dragonfly using scraps of leftover silver from the factory floor. I don't know where she got the jewels, or how she got them past the factory gates. It was her last gift to me. She said dragonflies represented summer, times when we'd been happy, before she got so tired. I should have known, I should have realised she was saying goodbye..." Ren covered her face with her hands and sobbed.

"I didn't know how much I loved her until she was gone. Du was the only one who made the factory bearable. After she died, my days became endless...I stopped eating and tried to starve myself. It was hard to get up for work, harder than you can imagine. I was punished for not working fast enough. When I saw your posters the other day it set this rage off in me, because you wouldn't listen... But you have to listen, Sky Eyes, you have to know that sooner or later whoever's controlling you will try and take away every scrap of what's precious. You don't know it yet, but one day what happened to Du will happen to you too. There'll be no past, no family waiting to welcome you home, no Hunan. They've already got rid of your cousin like she's some cheap part." Ren's grief rioted from her like a ball of flames.

I wished she hadn't said I was being controlled. I wanted to remind her of all the rewards I received. Manager He wasn't like the other factory managers. He aspired to be a different kind of leader, a better one that would take us to victory in the workplace. He was young and wanted change. Ren was wrong, things were improving all the time. Soon I would ask him for more days off for workers. As for Zhi, perhaps she'd brought it on herself – that's what the gossips were implying and maybe they had a point.

"What made you want to work here if you hated factory life so much?" I said.

She laughed bitterly. "Isn't that obvious?" she said and pulled at her damaged leg beneath the blanket, like it was a piece of rotten meat attached to one of Kwo's chicken feet. "You really don't see what's in front of you, do you? But you can trust me, Sky Eyes," she softened and drew me into her ashen embrace.

But I didn't want her. I only wanted Manager He – to be his star, to light up the night sky, to lie with him, to be his woman in a sequinned dress. My eyelids closed, I could bear their weight no longer.

When I opened them, a minute or a day may have passed, I wasn't sure – all I knew was that Ren had vanished from my bed and the wires overhead rasped as she turned in her bunk. The dorm was completely black.

An envelope inside an envelope. Jen's hands trembled as she opened the red *hongbao* to read May's letter for the second time. It had been such a shock to find the smaller of the two envelopes, its cool manila coated in a fine layer of dust. The seal had lost its tackiness, shrunken by time. It was addressed simply, *To my babies*, and written in Chinese on faded paper ripped from a notebook.

My dear child,

Who grows inside me as secret as a flower in the soil; who turns and moves and is stirring me up at night. A small grain of goodness in this bitter agony of life. I love you before you are even born.

I think of you all the time, from the start to the end of the day, and all during the night... I cannot sleep in my bed tonight... Thoughts of you burn like a fire over wild plains. When will I see your face? I see it already... I know your eyes and nose. I feel your tears inside the secret place. How much longer until these arms hold you?

You are my shadow... flesh not for cutting...essential as the beating of a heart...

Jen pressed it to her face. The note paper smelled of unknown places. She tried to imagine May pregnant, but saw only her teacher, standing in the living room, talking interminably about time and tense, nagging her to practise her tones. This May couldn't be her mum. Hers was poor, illiterate, unloving, without any notion of how to be a good mother. That was an easier version, everything neat. But adoption was not neatly boxed with a taffeta bow.

Jen's only knowledge of her past was that she had been abandoned on the steps of The Nanchang Welfare Institute. A member of staff had found her and Ricki wrapped up in a blanket. May had wanted them to be found, but had left no other clues – until now.

She was not reserved like some Chinese women. May was loud and full of things to say about education, food, China, Britain. About the strangeness of being a stranger. It made Jen laugh when May talked about *shavs* on the bus, who gossiped all their business into mobile phones. "Have they no shame?" May asked. During lessons, she would lean in so close that Jen could smell her shampoo; joss sticks from Shared Earth. There was a spicy tang to her skin. Her teeth were small, child-like. Could May be the origin of Jen's bad teeth?

What about Jen's square jawline, her high cheek bones and inquisitive eyes? Knowing May was her 'tummy mummy' was only half an answer.

If X=Mum, Y=??? Yifan, she guessed?

The puzzle ended in frustration. It was always the same. Brainy as she was, she could not fathom her origins.

May talked about him. Yifan was her big yellow sun. She smiled at the mention of his name. *He prefers eating: steamed pork with rice flour dumplings. He likes: walking, usually in the People's Park. He is a chess champion at the hospital where he works. His eyes are so twinkly. He has a talent for sitting cross-legged in meditation for hours - no stretching! Special talent: putting his feet behind his head. He knows all the names of every bone in a human body. Sometimes he sings when no-one's listening. His voice is very bad. Very outside of what is "musically safe,"* she'd say, as though singing was a drawer of sharp knives. Saw the tune in half, cut the family in two. One half May, the other unknown. Who needed a dad straight out of the Chinese state circus, anyway? thought Jen. She sounded like Ricki. *China is crap, China stinks, China is nothing to me.*

Strange how Yifan's number had not been found at May's bedsit.

Jen lined May's letter up with her coursework from the week before. May wrote like she danced at the birthday party, crazy and off-kilter. She had hung around awkwardly by the buffet table, trying to be helpful, offering people wantons. Offering a plate of lies.

Jen slid a fresh sheet of A4 from the printer on her desk. Carefully, she translated the first few lines. She would give May's letter to Ricki.

To write like May – all peaks and troughs – she held her pen tight, near the nib and wrote so as to taste the words, breathe them.

Don't forget in China, we write in the present tense. 'X' in Chinese is halfway between English 's' and 'sh' and 'R' buzzes like a bee, it never rolls. Not Ddddddrrrrrrrrrrrr.

You understand, Jennifer?

Are you listening? Or are you thinking about that boy?

The nouns came easily: child, flower, night, grain, secret. She whispered the verbs… to grow, to turn, to move, to be born. May's

105

voice corrected her pronunciation. Jen's Chinese was improving; the two-hour lessons every Saturday were not wasted. Or maybe, Jen's tongue had never forgotten its motherland?

She checked her mobile – still no messages from Ricki. There was a tap on her door. Jen shoved everything into her desk, beneath a makeup bag.

"Can I come in?" her mum said. "I was wondering if you'd heard any news?"

"No."

"We'll give it another hour, then I'm calling the police. I've tried phoning all her friends. No-one's seen her. She's not been admitted to hospital."

"Ricki will come back, Mum. She always does."

"I'm not so sure this time."

Nancy shuffled into the cavity of the bedroom and sat down on the bed.

"Mum, can we talk?"

"Of course, what is it?"

"I've been thinking about the orphanage…Were they all girls? I mean, is that why we were abandoned, because nobody wants girls in China?"

Her mum dabbed her eyes. "We were never allowed inside, Jennifer."

"You never met her, did you?"

"No, never."

"Were there many other babies?"

"About a dozen. The orphanage staff brought you to the hotel. You were everything to us. You always will be."

"But it is true? I mean, did May abandon us because we were girls?"

Her mum shook her head. "I don't know her reasons, darling. I could never leave you. Not ever."

"I need to know," said Jen.

"I can't magic her out of a coma."

"We could go to China."

Her mum got up and went to the window. She glanced back and forth at the street.

"We could go and find out about May," repeated Jen.

"Where is she? It said on the News there might be snow. What if she's had one of her asthma attacks?"

"Mum?"

Nancy dropped the edge of curtain.

"May never talked much about her past, but we know some things…Yifan was a doctor, right? And you said May was in Nanchang, so maybe we could start there? We could go back to the welfare institute or the embassy…There must be somebody who can tell us more."

"I can't think straight right now, Jen. All I want is to see Ricki's face again."

"She can't avoid us forever."

"I hit my daughter. What if something's happened to her? It's all my fault."

"What if, what if! What if I need answers, Mum?"

"Jen, I'm so sorry."

"I have to go back. I'll go myself if you won't."

Her mum stood motionless, staring into the dwindling light. "My mom always used to say that if you faced your fears they became smaller. You're a very bright young woman, Jen. Very bright and very precious to me. I'd do anything for you, to protect you and Ricki."

Jen squeezed her mum's trembling hand. "Let me go back."

"I know, darling. I know. And I will, I promise. I promise we'll go. Just as soon as… Oh God, what if she never comes home?"

The fox and the chicken

"*Herr Schnelleck, I write to inform you of the details of your visit to Forwood Motor Corporation. The enclosed itinerary includes maps, contact names, accommodation details and, most importantly, our productivity figures which, I'm sure you'll agree, are exceptional and that –*"

Manager He broke off and gazed into space. "Wait," he said, "Delete that last bit. It needs more... more –"

"More grease?" I suggested, wondering how much longer it was going to take and whether I'd ever get any sleep.

"No, not grease – more about me."

Manager He began to pace back and forth across the small bureau. This was his fifth version of the letter to Schnelleck.

"I disagree."

He spun round. "What did you just say, 2204?"

"We want him to feel important, don't we? To understand he is like a god to us. Schnelleck is our gateway to the West, you said. Why not ask what he wants to see and do in Nanchang? Play to his European temperament – his ego."

"Hm."

The wall clock in his bureau ran half an hour ahead of time; it was now five thirty. I was tired and still hadn't asked him about Zhi's whereabouts or floated the subject of weekly days off for workers. For the last three hours it had been all Schnelleck, Schnelleck, Schnelleck and I was sick of hearing about him. Who was he anyway, that he should be so important? China was a big country. Did we really need to impress the big noses in Europe?

"Do you mean we're to flatter him? You honestly believe a man of Schnelleck's judgement won't immediately see through it? Ha! 2204, you have a lot to learn. You forget Schnelleck is a European."

I stared at the characters on my typewriter, shot down by his remark.

"Although, I suppose a little Chinese courtesy never hurt anyone. It is what we're known for. Let me see... This shouldn't tax me. I just need to think clearly."

I stifled a yawn. What was taking him so long? Why couldn't he see the obvious? Important visitors need buttering up or bribery. He should have seen the way Mother and Father fussed after Madam Quifang: the slaughtered pig, the new bottle of baijiu, the expense of the matchmaker. None of which mattered, now that I had pink satin shoes, lipstick and whitener. Perhaps it had not been drummed into Manager He as a child? To impress requires total humility of body, soul and wallet. He was a boy, a 'little emperor', of course he had not learnt it.

Manager He suggested we take a short tea break. He took out his stash of candies and pulled up a chair beside me, sucking as he gazed into space. I took one without him noticing.

"Manager, there's something important I've been meaning to ask you. It's that, well, many of the workers are so tired. Exhaustion is starting to affect productivity. The other day, I caught one dozing at her station holding a pincer tool!"

He stirred. "Where were the time analysts? Useless cretins. Chen and Ting will do a better job, I'll get them onto her. Nothing a pay cut can't put right." He loosened his tie and undid his top button. "Tell me, honestly, do workers not read factory regulations any more? They must know sleeping on the job is a punishable offence?"

"Yes, yes, we're told it every week, we sing about it in the company song. The rules are pinned up everywhere in this place."

"And still they don't comply? Unbelievable. You see the scale of the task I'm up against, 2204?"

"Yes Manager," I said wearily. "The problem is, we're all too tired to work anyharder. Physically, we're exhausted to the point of passing out. It doesn't matter how many extra hours you ask of us, we need more rest – time to recharge our batteries."

"Like robots," he laughed, clearly taken by the idea. "Tell me, what would you be doing at home in the village? Working the fields all day? Gathering firewood, mucking out animals. I remember it well, even from childhood. You can't seriously be saying the factory is more taxing than work for *jia*? Of course not! I know it and you know it. Any worker caught slacking on the job is a lazy mutton."

I wanted to laugh in his face. Had he sat for twelve hours on a stool staring at tiny wires and plastic buttons? If so, he would know factory work was twice as hard as farm work, where you could get away with being lazy for an hour here and there. Sometimes I wandered off into the woods and lay down on the pine needles with Little Brother; together we breathed in the smell of the earth.

I stood up, deciding to take a different tack. "Manager He, may I ask you a question?"

He rolled up his shirt sleeves and reached for his velvet dressing gown which hung on the back of his chair. Over the course of our night-time meetings, it became clear Manager He rarely left Forwood.

"What is more important: productivity or accuracy?" I said, pacing behind him.

"Without accuracy there are no sales. Without productivity there is no profit. They are of equal importance."

"But without enough time to rest, your workers are becoming both unproductive and inaccurate. The women in your department are like machines – from what I observe on the line, and in the dorm, we are desperately in need of repair."

"I don't like what you are suggesting. I can't send workers to be fixed. Ha! It's easier to get new parts. They're cheap and disposable, especially at this time of year. An inexpensive machine doesn't need servicing, it needs scrapping."

"Can you afford to scrap your entire workforce?"

He spluttered on his tea. "2204, that's enough. You are talking above your position. I'm worn out by your inane prattle about tired workers. Next you'll be recommending I give women a lie-in every weekend! I know I asked you to inspire them from within, but this is taking things too far. Stop this foolish talk or I'll have a mutiny on my hands. Workers are here for one reason only – money. The same reason I am here. Money makes this factory churn out cars and money will make the world sit up and take note of our country. Money can take a boy like me out of poverty and make him the most successful businessman this city has ever seen. What it can't do is fix a bad machine. Now remember that."

"But our health…"

"Ha! That's it!" Manager He threw his hands in the air.

"What is?" I asked.

He clenched his forehead. "Money – ha! – genius. Why didn't I think of it earlier?"

"Think of what?"

"Get back to the typewriter. I need you to get this down before it goes out of my head."

Our discussion was over. I resumed typing with a heavy heart. For a clever man, he could be incredibly short-sighted.

Schnelleck was to receive the best money could buy. Five star accommodation, expensive restaurants, personal tours of the city, privileged entry into Nanchang's historic sites and the opportunity to see Forwood at the peak of its productivity. As an extra sweetener, he would be given all the spending money he could possibly need. Oodles of it! I was staggered when the figure of ten thousand yuan was mentioned and Manager He raised it to twenty. It struck me that a factory that fed its workers pig's blood soup, could ill afford a visitor like Schnelleck. But I kept my gob shut. The sooner he finished dictation, the sooner I could get back to bed.

"Truly, I've excelled myself. Schnelleck will be overjoyed by such lavish expressions of Chinese hospitality. He'll see we're ready to open ourselves up to Europe and the world." He gazed at the poster of Deng Xiaoping, as if he were a father. "He'll realise any dream is possible in China."

Manger He's dressing gown flapped open. The skin beneath his shirt was smooth, hairless.

"This calls for a little celebration. Look in my filing cabinet at the back. Get the bottle will you?"

"Yes, Manager."

I stood by the cabinet and poured two cupfuls of baijiu.

We drank quickly.

"Why the long face, don't you like it?" he asked as he settled in the corner.

"I was forbidden at home."

"Well you're not at home now, 2204. I thought we'd established that." He held up his cup for me to pour him another. His chest brushed my arm.

"To productivity, accuracy, profit and great wealth!" Manager He downed it in one gulp. He wiped his mouth with his sleeve. "Aiya! Drink of the gods – I swear it gives me a clear head – started drinking it at university and never looked back."

The baijiu tasted of warm honey, sweet and rich on my tongue. A sudden memory pulled on my heart, of father drinking liquor at the kitchen table, his cheeks pink after a day in the fields. Would they be coping without my hands? Had Madam Quifang made their lives unbearable since I ran away?

"Funny," said Manager He, "I always dreamt of this moment: standing on the cusp of success. There's a real possibility Forwood will become the province's most profitable factory."

I watched his lips and imagined them breezing across my face, planting kisses down my neck.

He kicked off his shoes and settled deeper into the corner where the light didn't quite reach. He poured himself another cupful of baijiu and then another. "Strange how life works out…"

His voice was disarmingly woeful. "How a small amount of good might come from those bastards of destruction."

His head drooped and pressed against my thigh.

"Do you know what it's like to lose someone you love, Mai Ling? How old are you...twenty? The Cultural Revolution would have ended soon after you were born.You were lucky. It would have been better to have grown up in your time – in the new era."

I realised he was talking about our society and the way things were changing. I'd seen it for myself in Nanchang, what Manager He called the new era. Changes in the way people dressed and spoke, the brightly lit shops and restaurants like KFC which smelt of fresh paint. Even back home in the fields things were going a different way, only worse. Father could no longer rely on the State to buy our grain for a good price. He struggled to know how to be enterprising. The new era was not necessarily better for everyone, but I held my tongue.

Manager He buried his head deeper onto my thighs. "My eyes saw things a young boy should never see. My father, my brother... they refused to give up the little food we had. The men, they didn't even take them out into the yard. They did it right there in front of mother, I thought they were going to turn the gun on me too. Mother was wailing. She fell to her knees and, in her weakness, she surrendered our grain. One of the militia had a cut across his cheek, where his scarf did not reach. I thought about his scar for a long time afterwards, trying to work out where I'd seen it before. I realised he was the father of a boy I knew from the next village. That's what happened back then, men betraying men in their commune, fighting to survive. I had barely the strength to pedal my bike, and was terrified of what might happen. I wanted to stay and protect her like a proper son, but Mother ordered me to get out. That's how I ended up here in Nanchang. I fled to an aunt with every secret *fen* my family ever owned. The last I heard, everyone in the village had starved to death. I never heard my mother's voice again."

I stroked his hair. The famine and the Cultural Revolution that followed were times my parents never talked about openly.

"I refuse to worship Mao. I survived and I owe it to my family to seek change. Deng Xiaoping is the one I salute – he's a realist. He does not make excuses for what happened, but there's no doubting his change in direction."

"Yes. President Xiaoping talks about the future, like you."

"There is nothing in the past worth holding onto, Mai Ling. We must always move forwards. That's why we must secure

Schnelleck, with him on board Forwood can expand. We are ready, I know it."

If only Ren could hear Manager He speak about change and progress, she would feel less cynical.

"Have you heard about the President's plans to create Special Economic Zones?"

I shook my head.

"I think we can do it, Mai Ling. If Forwood secures enough business overseas, we can put forward a case to make Nanchang a city for redevelopment. Consider the benefits: we'd be free to trade and make money without all the petty bureaucracy that has stifled business for so long."

He was talking fast, losing me in a flurry of words. His lips glistened with baijiu. I was still trying to imagine the horror of seeing my father and brother shot in front of me. No wonder Manager He got Chen and Ting to do his dirty work, it was obvious to me now. My instinct was to pull him to my breast.

The bureau fell silent, as if the walls had read my thoughts. His warm hand pressed against my leg. This time, we were alone, no interruptions from Old Artist. The loudest sound was our hushed disjointed breath.

He knelt and put his face to my feet.

"My grandmother's feet were like hooves, small and deformed. Yours are so long. They curl at the toes when I kiss them here."

"It tickles."

I stroked his face as he kissed my breasts. His talk was filthy. A vast impure ocean of desire opened suddenly before me and I felt myself falling and afraid.

His body had a fervency I had only seen in animals. It felt as though he was digging something out of me as we made love. Afterwards, he slumped over his desk. I withdrew, weak and sore, my blood in droplets on the floor.

He re-read Schnelleck's letter as if nothing had happened. Silently, I willed him to put it down and talk to me. I wanted the comfort of hearing my name. *Mai Ling.* Comfort like a piece of home, like red soil, or the smell of peasant tobacco.

I longed to be innocent again. I wiped my tears, dressed and cleared away the baijiu cups. Replacing the bottle inside his filing cabinet I felt my hands shake. The strange, hot twisting of our bodies had turned to formalities, empty words. He was Manager, I was 2204. I hovered in the doorway. He had been so quick at the end – a fox stealing a chicken.

"Before you go…" he said. "I want you to take this, in addition to your next pay packet." He held out a thick wedge of yuan. "Go into town on your day off and treat yourself. Buy more clothes, find yourself a suit. Observe what the women wear in the city and emulate them. Buy underwear made in England and French perfume."

"I'm not sure that's a good idea, Manager. I'm really not like the urban women."

"You must."

"I…"

"I want you to look like a lady who belongs to the new era. Come back and show me. Do you understand?"

I nodded and took the money, curling it tight into my trembling hand. It felt as cold as the bureau floor.

"I won't forget what happened tonight," he said. "You were very lovely. The best…"

I silenced him with a kiss and pretended that he'd called me his special lady. The alarm was already ringing through the walls.

The restaurant was half full of the usual lunchtime crowd. Businessmen who ate dim sum, a few local Chinese and their kids. On table six, a young couple cosied up in one of the white leather booths, playing footsie under the table. Stuart never took Jen out for a meal. He didn't earn enough at the vinyl shop.

A guy from the group on table eight signalled her over.

"We're wondering what the special is today?" He was in his fifties, but acting like a twenty-something. "We can't see anything we fancy on the menu. It's not exciting enough."

"We're very particular about what we eat," said his friend.

Five pairs of eyes x-rayed her uniform; Jen felt like a Peking duck hanging in the cabinet.

"We only do dim sum at lunchtime, sir."

"What a shame. I was just fancying something tasty and exotic."

"Are you ready to order?"

He reached over and toyed with her apron. "I'd have thought that was obvious, wouldn't you?"

She flinched, knocking into Michael, a waiter. Jen hurried to the kitchen where the smell of chilli soothed her.

Later that afternoon, her shift over, she gulped a glass of lemonade on the back doorstep.

"Are you alright?" asked Michael. "I'm sorry those idiots tried it on with you."

"I'm fine, honestly."

Michael was in his second year at Manchester Uni. His grandparents were from Hong Kong.

"So you're okay then?"

"I said so, didn't I?"

She hadn't meant to snap. He wasn't to blame for May, or Ricki, or the idiots on table eight. "I'm sorry. There's a lot going on at home, that's all."

"Another time maybe?" he said and put on his coat to leave.

Jen pulled her jacket tighter. If only time could go in circles rather than straight lines. If only May hadn't come to her birthday party, or they had danced a minute longer. If only she'd wake up and explain why she had tracked them down in Manchester. Life felt so tangled, Jen couldn't find the ends.

She checked her mobile, still nothing from Ricki. Her only text message was from Stuart.

Meet me outside mcdonalds after yr shift. Please?

Maybe she'd got him wrong? He wasn't all bad.

She texted back, *Cu half hour*.

Jen finished her shift and slipped away without phoning her parents as she'd promised.

Stuart tucked into a Big Mac outside McDonalds. He offered to go back in and get her something.

She refused, "I can't eat when my sister's missing."

A woman with a bucket of roses asked Stuart if he wanted one for the lady. To her surprise, he fished out some loose change.

"You didn't have to do that," she said.

"I've been an idiot, I owe you an apology."

They drifted across St Ann's Square and perched on an oversized pebble near the Royal Exchange Theatre. Stuart wrapped Jen in his leather jacket to shield her from the wind. A quartet in evening dresses and dinner jackets shivered as they played *The Four Seasons*. The air smelt of fried onion from the hot dog stand on the corner of Cross Street. It reminded Jen of good times, trips on the tram into town with her sister. Now Ricki hung out with a different crowd.

Stuart's biker boots padded the pavement. He lit a roll-up. "About your birthday, Jen…I'm sorry I didn't stay when your parents were at the hospital. And sorry things have been getting a bit heated about, y'know, sex and everything. I don't mind waiting if that's what you prefer."

"You don't? But I thought…"

"It's your choice, I shouldn't have been so pushy."

He kissed her forehead.

"Where were you that night? I called your mobile like a million times."

Stuart dragged on the roll-up. "With the lads. I'm sorry. Like I said, I've been an idiot. What can I do to make it up to you?" He held her face in his hands and brushed back the hair that had blown into her mouth.

She had longed for tenderness. The next thing she knew, she was tugging on his arm, beckoning him away from the square.

Lots of people passed by, all too busy thinking about parcels, passports, pensions to look down the Post Office alleyway. She silenced the voice in her head which said STOP. NO. DON'T. Instead, she put her hand up the back of his shirt and clawed her nails into his cold skin. He pressed her to the wall, his kisses little wounds. She fumbled for the zip on his jeans and felt him already hard.

"Wait," said Stuart, taking a condom from his jacket pocket.

Jen pulled down her tights, then her knickers, enough to guide him inside her. He was eager and cumbersome; she clutched a nearby window ledge to stop herself falling. Just as Stuart was getting close to coming, a voice bellowed down the alley.

"Oi, you!"

He shouted something about calling the police.

She pushed Stuart off and hitched up her tights. He discarded the condom in the alley and made a run for it, fastening his trousers as they ran. They spilled out onto Spring Gardens, breathless and exhilarated.

"Shit," said Jen outside HMV. "I left my rose."

They laughed and hugged each other. Jen nestled against his beaten leather jacket.

"You're fearless. I love you," said Stuart.

The skin on her back felt raw where it had scraped against the wall. There'd be other times, other men. The right one. At least now she knew how it felt.

"I need to ask you something, Stuart. I want you to tell me the truth," she said, suddenly serious.

"Sshh, let's hold each other like this. Don't talk. "

"We have to. I want you to tell me."

"Babe, it's cold. You're acting strange. What is it?"

"I know about her."

"Who?" His laugh sounded fragile. "You're starting to freak me out a little here, Jen. I don't see you for days, you tell me you're not interested in sex, then we go at it like rabbits in an alleyway. Who are you talking about?"

She kissed his wind-chapped lips and pushed her tongue into his mouth – their last kiss.

Jen broke off. "I know about the petrol head friend you've been screwing behind my back. Don't pretend. I've worked it out. I just need you to admit it."

He shook his head. "Jen, you're losing it. I haven't done anything. I mean...what gave you that idea?"

"Tell me the truth."

"I can't... Jen, you don't need to ask me that... Let's just get in a taxi and you can come back to mine. My flatmate's out. We can put the heating on. I'll make you some pasta."

"Admit it."

She forced herself not to be swayed by the mournful look in his eyes. It wasn't his mother in a coma, his sister who'd run away from home.

"Admit it, Stuart."

He shook his head. "She means nothing to me."

"How long have you been seeing her?"

"A couple of months." He wiped the snot on his sleeve. "This is the end isn't it? I've been so fucking stupid, Jen. She's a mistake."

"Mistakes are one-offs. What you've made is a complete balls-up of everything."

"I can make it up to you. I'll never see her again, ever."

"You know what?" said Jen.

His bloodshot eyes were suddenly hopeful.

"Everyone's lied to me: my mum, May, even Ricki covers her tracks, but I don't need to take it from you, Stuart."

"Then why did we just do it if you hate my guts?"

Because she could, because there was a pain inside that needed to come out, because she was sick of being clever Jen, top of the class, Little Miss Perfect – so studious, so Chinese.

She left him in the doorway of HMV and hurried towards Piccadilly Gardens. The mobile in her pocket was vibrating. From now on, Jen would be in charge of who came and went in her life.

When they were little, Ricki would come running through to Jen's bedroom in the middle of the night, caught in a reoccurring nightmare about the house burning to the ground. The house was big, Ricki said, like a warehouse, with more rooms than she could count. Jen's job was to check all the rooms to make sure there was no fire; sometimes they even stood barefoot in the garden which backed onto the railway line. Eventually Ricki accepted it was just a dream and would fall asleep, warm in the nook of her twin's arm.

So when Jen saw Ricki standing in her bedroom doorway the night she came home it was only natural that she should say, "It's okay, Sis. Just a bad dream. Everything's all right now."

She pulled back the duvet and Ricki climbed in, her knee a small cold slab sliding between hers.

"Everyone's okay."

"Yeah," said Ricki, dragging the duvet around their ears. She snuggled deeper. Inside it they were safe together. Jen held Ricki until the air grew moist beneath the duvet. She had never felt so glad to hold her twin. There had been no asthma attacks, no disasters.

"I heard you burnt Mum's lucky fan," said Ricki after a while.

A smile curled at the corner of Jen's mouth. "What about you? Are you okay?"

"Cold."

"But alive."

"Jen... Did you ever think May was...you know...the one?"

"Never."

"What about Mum. D'you think she knew?"

"She did a pretty good job of hiding the truth, if she did, Rick."

"Mum said she was going to tell us, remember? It was the morning after our party, before Dr Emery arrived," said Ricki.

"Oh, I'd forgotten."

"I can't stand her."

"Mum?"

"Both of them, I suppose."

Jen rolled the duvet back. "I've told her I want to go to China," she said suddenly. "I need to find stuff out."

"What's to know? May's our birth mum. The secret's out – what more do you expect to find? It's not like she's going to wake up and spill the beans, is it?"

"I don't know."

"Face it, May will probably die anyway."

"There's a chance that if we go to China, we'd feel better."

"And what if we don't, Jen? What if we go there and feel worse? I don't think I can take much more." Ricki rolled onto her back. "Besides, there's other stuff to think about."

"Like what?"

"Like living! You've got exams, I've got my photography. There's a unit coming up at Afflecks that could be mine. It's the best chance I've got if I want to make a name for myself."

"Yeah."

"You could sound more pleased."

"I don't think this is going to just blow over. Not for me at least..." said Jen. She reached out for Ricki's hand. "But I won't go without you."

Her sister was pale in the early morning light; her face washed in fear. Jen wanted to say it was just a bad dream, everything would be okay, their mum and dad were safe. But how could she?

Into the gloom rattled an Intercity on its way to...? Glasgow, Edinburgh, Birmingham, London... And from there a plane could fly them both away. To China. Maybe even home? Maybe.

Book of traditional tales

Sunday. Finally a day off after weeks of mind-numbing work on the line and our pay overdue by a fortnight. Workers grumbled that their families relied on money to buy fertilisers or support siblings through school. I felt smug with Manager He's money tucked safely into my trousers and left Fatty, Fei Fei and the others window shopping.

A pineapple-coloured haze hung over the newly-built dual carriageway, where early morning traffic zipped over the river. Nanchang was an unfinished city, its maps continually rewritten. The weather was getting warmer, and I decided to take a stroll through the People's Park to breathe in some fresh air. The park's magnolia trees had blossomed early. I wandered in the direction of the panda enclosure, where the zoo keeper shovelled bamboo from his wheelbarrow.

A young couple caught my eye. The boy was taking a photograph of his girlfriend. I followed them to the bridge, feeling unbearably envious, and dropped back a few paces, concealed by an overhanging willow. They kissed for a long time on the bridge and eventually drifted off, unhurried – the boy's arm flung loosely around her shoulders. I guessed they were part of the city's floating population; workers, like me, enjoying a rare day off.

Since my intimate encounter with Manager He, I had received no special attention: no glances down the line or requests for help with Schnelleck's letters. I missed him and slept hugging my pillow lengthways down the bunk, pretending it was him.

Feeling even more lonely, I abandoned the park and its peeling pergolas, and headed back to Women's Street where I lingered around the teahouses, observing the clothes of urban women: suits with shoulder pads and shiny patent ankle boots. I tried on a few outfits in the Pacific Department Store; they made me look like an auntie. What would the others call me, *Hong Kong cat* or *bossy mei*? A beauty assistant asked me if I had considered hair extensions, fake hair glued to my own messy tufts. Manager He was wrong, women were easier to fix than machines.

By midday I felt tired and deflated. I couldn't find French perfume or English underwear and had spent barely half of

Manager He's money on a new suit. I left Women's Street and took to the back streets in search of The Blue Banana, the bar I had seen on my first visit, telling myself the visit was 'research' ahead of meeting Schnelleck.

Away from the main drag, the city was a confusing grid of alleyways, the names of which sounded modern and reminded me of Manager He: Merchant's Way, Street of the Free Thinker, We Seek to Prosper Place and New Era Street. I turned right and an unpromising narrow alley gave way to a mixture of high-rise office buildings, restaurants and bars. Mixed into this were several shops with blackened windows. *For the Discerning Businessman of Tomorrow*, said one sign.

Unable to locate The Blue Banana, I stopped instead at The Agile Rabbit. Inside, TVs lined the bar. A few worn-out westerners were reading newspapers. The barman was ultra-moody and reminded me of Kwo, the canteen cook. Unlike Kwo, he was also ultra-cool in his black shirt and thin white tie.

"Can I get a baijiu?" I asked him.

"We don't serve that during happy hour. It's cocktails only. Look outside, on the board."

At the far end of the bar, a big nose westerner sipped a glass of bright pink liquid through a straw.

"I'll have whatever he's drinking."

The moody barman set my glass on a beer mat that said *Club Tropicana*. He decorated the drink with a parasol and some fancy ribbons; lit a sparkler. It tasted cold and fruity. I stayed on to drink more. When I got up to go to the toilet, my legs felt unsteady and I had to hold onto the columns of mirrored glass.

When I returned, a crowd of young Chinese had congregated at my end of the bar.

They chanted. "Who's the man? He's the man! Who's the man? He's the man!"

I loped to the other end of the bar and resumed drinking courtesy of Manager He's money. The big nose lit a Marlboro. It hung off his wide, fishy lips.

"Let me try one of your American cigarettes?" I said, bold with drink.

"Sure, take the packet." His Chinese was near-perfect, with a Hong Kong accent. "And while you smoke, you can tell me all about yourself." He took a long, slow drag on his cigarette.

What did he want to know? I could tell him about my job, the 4x4s we made for people like him. Yes, he liked that, the big nose.

His fat white fingers inched across to my knee.

The moody barman turned up the moody music to drown out the rowdy drinkers. The atmosphere was anything but happy.

"Who's the man? He's the man! Who's the man? He's the man!"

"Stop, put me down!" protested the skinny fellow as they flipped him easily into the air.

"I feel sick. You're going to break my glasses."

He landed on the floor. They clamoured to pour cocktails over him, and then the barman screamed at them to get out. They scattered, laughing, and staggered into the street. The big nose was distracted by the young men. I swiped his Marlboros and made for the door, figuring they might earn me a few favours back in the dorm.

I was halfway down New Era Street, when someone grabbed my arm. I spun round ready for confrontation. But it was the skinny Chinese fellow from the bar.

"Mai Ling. That's right, isn't it?" He smiled as if I should know his name. "Don't you recognise me?"

I shook my head.

"We met on the train from Hunan. It's Yifan. How are you? You still look a little pale."

The young medical student! His hair had grown longer and flopped over his glasses, but his gentle eyes were unchanged. I recalled how he'd revived me with green tea.

"I'm fine now, how are you? I thought you were going to land on the bar."

He rubbed his back. "Silly games... It's my birthday. They always do that, I don't know why. You'd think us medics would know better."

"Um...Happy birthday!"

"So, how's it going?"

"Good."

"I bet those 4x4s are rolling off the line?"

"Sort of."

"New designs take time, I suppose. Not much margin for error."

"No."

"It's good that you get time off – everyone here seems to work twenty-four seven."

"Yes."

"Stress does terrible things to a person's health. Neck pain, back pain, tension headaches, high blood pressure, blurred vision..."

He should see the way *dagongmei* work like mutts.

"So…"

"So…"

"So…there is a nice teahouse not far from here. Would you like to come with me? I think I need to sober up a little. If you have time, that is, I don't want to keep you from your business."

I glanced over his shoulder to make sure the big nose wasn't following me.

"I'd like that," I said, pleased to leave New Era Street.

The Suseng Teahouse was very traditional, its décor shabby. We sat on a bench by the window. I waffled about the factory's vision, our eagerness to enter global-markets. The plans could have been my own.

Yifan nodded in silence.

"Is everything alright?" I asked after a while. "Has your tea gone cold? The hostess will bring you some more water. I'll ask."

He covered the tea pot, "No, my tea's fine, it's delicious, thank you. I was listening intently to everything you were saying. I'm sorry if I seemed a little distant."

It was easier lying to Yifan than I remembered. In fact, the more we talked, the more I revelled in the possibility of leading my own department. I began to believe it. Alcohol helped the lies flow readily. I told Yifan that in the near future I had an important business meeting with a German investor named Herr Schnelleck, whom I planned to impress with extravagant gifts and shows of Chinese wealth and hospitality.

Yifan spluttered into his tea. "Your plans are very grandiose indeed!"

"You have to think big, Yifan."

"That's quite a liberalist bourgeois mentality you've developed since we met on the train. It shocks me coming from a girl who lived in Hunan, Mao's own land."

What was he talking about? Yifan was too smart for me. But I did know Chairman Mao was from Hunan. No-one in China, not even the stupidest peasant, could fail to know Mao was born in Hunan.

"Perhaps you've left behind more than your village in coming to the city," he said, raising an eyebrow.

I wasn't in the mood for a lecture. "If you mean I'm not the girl I used to be, then you're right and perhaps that's not such a bad thing."

"I'm not talking about the status of women in our society, Mai Ling, or about education. Clearly, you are very educated indeed. I am talking about your loyalty to the past and the true Chinese way of life – not this fake modernity occurring all around us."

My head hurt. I was beginning to wish I hadn't bothered coming to the teahouse. It was nearly four o'clock and I still had to buy French perfume.

Yifan reached into his satchel and handed me a battered book, not the *Little Red Book*. It was called *Traditional Tales and Other Stories from our Great Past*. I hoped he wasn't going to ask me to read, my comprehension was still only average.

"I want you to have this," he said, "I think it will help."

He was right, if my literacy improved, Manager He and Schnelleck might think better of me. I took the book and opened it at the first page. The inscription read: *To our pride and joy, our dear son, on the occasion of your graduation with distinction and successful completion of your high school education. May you live a long and happy life, working your hardest for the good people of China.* It was signed by his parents and grandparents.

"I can't take this."

"I want you to hang onto it for a while"

"But I hardly know you and this must be very precious."

"It is."

"Well then, you keep it. Really, Yifan, I've done nothing to deserve this gift."

Yifan shook his head, insistent, and I slipped it inside my shopping bag.

Manager He would never read such a book. For him, there was nothing great about China's past. There was only the death of his family, the starvation of his fellow villagers. I would have to hide the book under the loose floorboard in the dorm.

As I thanked Yifan, the feeling of being watched returned. I glanced over my shoulder to see if anyone had entered the teahouse – a quick movement, a swish of hair! It was so sudden I couldn't tell exactly. When I looked again, there was no-one. I hurried my tea, unnerved, and made my excuses to Yifan.

"So soon? But there's more tea in the pot."

I didn't want to hear about how wonderful Hunan was and how I should treasure the place above all else. Where I'd come from was becoming less and less to me. I said my polite goodbyes and was almost to the door when he caught up with me and put a hand out to bar the exit.

"Mai Ling, wait. I don't want you to go like this. I'm sorry if I said too much. I didn't mean to upset you. I can see how seriously you take your work. It's not my place to tell you what to think... At least say you'll meet me again. A new ferris wheel is coming to town. A group of us from the university are going. Please, come with us."

"Maybe. I need to get back to work."

"Very well, I must let you. But here's my dorm number, take it and call me if you're able to."

He passed me a page ripped from his notebook. I buried it inside my trouser pocket.

"Take care of yourself, Mai Ling. It's easy to get carried away. Even with the best intentions, you might find yourself in a situation you can't –"

"Let me go."

Yifan stepped aside and whispered, "Just don't forget: there are people, forces, in this city who wouldn't be so tolerant if they were to hear you speak. Nanchang's heartbeat remains strongly traditional." He glanced over his shoulder at the cast of ageing men, some playing cards, others puffing Red Double Happiness cigarettes.

I forced a smile and flung open the door, desperate to get away from the small, old-fashioned teahouse that stank of smoke and incense. As I hurried away, eager to find a shop that would sell perfume, the alcohol still sloshed in my stomach and I felt queasy. I couldn't wait to get back to the factory and the safety of Manager He. The yellowing sky had turned dark amber. Unexpected hailstones began to beat against my Western-white face.

In her dreams, Nancy returns to the sea.

She takes up the latch of the picket gate and wades through the lumpy dunes, desperate to get to the pier in time to save her mom. The seaweed feels soft as it wraps around her toes, holding her back.

She is too late.

Her mom's housecoat flaps against the granite, slapped in and out by the tide. The same one she wore every day, sometimes to the corner store. Her hair floats on the surface, bobbing in and out of view as the sea coughs up foam. Nancy screams into the wind. No sound comes out.

She dives in, kicking like a frog, but her mom's swollen body is too heavy. Seagulls rebound in the wind above, cawing as though laughing at their own game. Sunlight floods the waves. Then the shape of a man, a fisherman, drags them out.

Her mom whispers. *Please put your things away. It's time for supper.* Her voice turns to thin air.

Nancy wakes in tears, always.

Iain squeezed her hand. "Should I call Dr Emery, maybe you do need antibiotics?"

Nancy could still taste the saltiness of the Atlantic Ocean and her legs felt tired from running through the dunes, though she had not left her recliner all day.

"It will pass," she told him. The dream will fade, she reassured herself.

"You nodded off again."

She vaguely remembered Countdown. *Bada-bada-badabadum...pooum!* Iain must have turned the TV off. Falling asleep in her chair! How much longer before she started playing outdoor bowls on a Sunday afternoon? Or occupying her time with hobbies she'd never imagined satisfying in youth. Suddenly, the room felt stifling: the carpets and cushions and coal-effect fire were closing in on her.

"I think we need to get away," she said, panicked, "someplace sunny."

"Away? I don't think now is a good time."

"Geez Iain, nobody's actually died."

126

He let go of her hand.

"Let's do it," Nancy urged.

"How can we, with the business of May hanging over us?"

"Let's go to China."

"Nancy, that's ridiculous."

"Not it's not. It could be weeks, months, until something happens with May – God knows, she might never wake up... Can't you see we're stagnating here? This is not my vision for us."

Iain searched her face.

"These four walls..." she looked around her; the heating was unbearably stuffy. "You've got your own business, I don't expect you to understand. My work – well, I've already been made redundant. The girls are growing up. I need to get out before it's too late. I need to..."

"I know, Nancy, but you're not like your mother. You don't need to run away. And the girls aren't going anywhere yet. We are not going to lose them."

"I need to lie down," she said, exhausted.

"Let me bring you up a camomile tea."

"No," she held up her hands, "I want to be alone."

Iain gathered up her leftover toast.

"Don't think I'm not feeling it too, Nancy. I'm just trying to hold things together."

At times, and in certain lights, Iain looked like her dad. A man worn back to sand.

Upstairs, their bedroom was cooler. The day had turned out bright; clouds scudded across the sky. She sat on the edge of the bed and watched them change shape. She thought of pebbles skimmed into the sea as a child, her attempts to shatter its surface and destroy memory, undo death.

Nancy reached into her bedside cabinet for her favourite photo of the twins, taken on the beach at Formby one exceptionally hot day in July, when the girls were about three. In the picture, Ricki's sun hat flopped over her eyes and Jen lifted its edges, poking a triangle of peanut butter sandwich into her mouth. Afterwards, they followed the red squirrel trail up through the forest. The smell of cool, soft pine needles, the springy path beneath her flip-flops. It was a relief to be out of the bright sun. The twins slept all the way home, and Iain carried them to bed.

May's effects and belongings were under police charge; her life reduced to the dank and poky bedsit on Burton Road, so different from Nancy's own, with its high walls and picture rail, her

Regency dressing table bought from an antique shop in Chester. What would someone make of Nancy from these things? Could they boil her down like jam?

There was the jewellery box, the one with the ballerina in a pink tutu. Her sister Lizzie had given it to her at JFK the day she emigrated. Nancy had clutched it as she crossed the sea: a piece of home. Also a locket, the last shred of her mom. It had been her eleventh birthday present and inside was a happy photo of her parents. No warning of the tragedy that would blast them apart.

She wished her mom was alive now to tuck her up; wished she could pick up the phone and call home. "Hi Mom, it's Nancy…No, things aren't so great, can we talk?"

She returned the belongings to her bedside cabinet, climbed into bed and pulled the duvet to her chin. Energy drained from her, like falling from a granite rock, pulling down the fluffy clouds, the broad blue sky, the furniture and her belongings, and she fell into a deep sleep.

She awoke, sweating, to see Iain holding a cup of tea.

"Sweetheart, we need you downstairs."

"Iain, what is it? What's the matter?"

"Everything's fine, Nancy."

"The girls…"

"The girls are fine. But the inspector's here."

He put the tea on the bedside cabinet. So much bloody tea in England.

In the kitchen, Inspector Meadows stood awkwardly by the breakfast bar.

Ricki leant against the back door, as if she might run away.

"The news is we've found the car, a 4x4, and from that, we've traced the driver."

"The killer, don't you mean?" said Ricki, picking at a hole in her tights.

"It's early days, but it's looking like he'll give a full statement. We've been very fortunate. It's rare in cases like this. Usually the vehicle doesn't belong to the offender."

"That's fantastic news," said Iain.

"I can't go into too much detail, but the driver was found in possession of drugs, traces of which have been found in the vehicle."

"An addict?" said Nancy. But who was she to pass judgement? A few days ago she'd struck her own daughter. She

128

was officially an abusive parent – at least that's how social workers would have seen it during the adoption process.

"So what happens next?" said Ricki. "The driver gets nicked while we hold candlelit vigils?"

"Questioning. The offender will be kept at the station until he's given a full statement. If we're satisfied there's enough evidence, we'll get it to court as soon as possible. The DNA samples are crucial."

"And how long will that take?" said Iain.

"Hard to say but, at a guess, we're looking at several months."

"Months!" Jen burst out. "Can't you do anything sooner?"

"I know this is a difficult time for you all, but trust me, we're doing all we can to move the case forwards."

"So she's a 'case' now?" said Ricki.

Iain showed Inspector Meadows to the door. Jen helped Nancy wash up in silence. Ricki plugged in her headphones.

"Girls, I've made a decision…" said Nancy with urgency in her voice.

Jen dried her hands.

"I've decided we should leave sooner rather than later."

Ricki, realising something was serious, removed her headphones. "What are you talking about?"

"About China, I've made my decision. We're are all going, including you, Ricki."

"What? You can't make me do that."

"No, I can't. But I'm hoping you'll come to the same realisation, that we owe it to ourselves."

"But…"

"Do you mean that?" said Jen, "Can we really go?"

"We should probably have gone before now. I'm sorry I never bought you tickets for your birthday," said Nancy.

Jen hugged her. "Mum, that's fantastic news."

"Ricki?"

Ricki huffed like the five year old Nancy adored.

Uniform

I could hear shouting as I climbed the stairs to the dorm, my arms ladened with shopping bags. Girls queued the length of the corridor as far as the sanitary room. A dirty-faced worker from another floor told me Damei was in the shit.

"Silly cow shouldn't have punched someone's lights out – in the canteen of all places."

"Where is she now?"

"In there," she pointed to the sanitary room. "She's jammed the door. They're saying she's stuck her head in the sink."

Girls brayed on the door, calling for her to come out. Sunday, the day off, was also laundry day and we needed the sinks. I squirted on some Chanel.

"Pew! What's that?" A girl nearby gawped at my shopping bags. "Oh, I know who you are. You're the slut of Forwood."

I smarted. "What did you just say?"

Suddenly, the sanitary room door opened and Damei staggered out, dazed. Her hair was wet, but neatly combed, her face strangely vulnerable. She was wrapped in a Forwood towel which, despite its meagre size, enveloped her completely. The girls parted to let her walk through.

"Hey, Damei, if you like sticking your head in water, there'll be plenty of that where you're going. The managers in personnel can be proper nasty," someone shouted.

"That's if they don't fire you."

"Don't be daft," said another, "they never get rid of their own. It's only us on the line that cop it."

"She's used all the hot water," called out someone from downstairs. "There's not enough to douse a tic up here!"

I followed Damei into the dorm. "I hope you think of Zhi when they boot you out onto the street."

Damei dried her hair slowly, deliberately, as if drying it strand by strand.

I slid the shopping bags beneath my bunk and climbed onto my bed. To hell with her – she could spit in her own oil for all I cared.

There was an eerie silence in the dorm that night. We dreaded work after a day's freedom. I drifted in and out of sleep. In my dreams Manager He came home to the farm. Mother was stir frying vegetables. There was someone at the door, I screamed not to let them in. It was a cadre ready to shoot us. I woke up panting, tossed over in my bed and told myself that it was just another nightmare, like all the others I'd had since coming to the factory.

In the bunk opposite, Damei curled against the wall. I sensed she was also awake. The door creaked opened. The loose floorboard squeaked by the door and I heard the sound of slippers shuffling across the floor. Someone whispered, "Damei."

I peered into the blue-black shadows. A couple of workers from personnel towered over her bunk. "Quickly now, you're coming with us."

"Where? What will happen to me?" Damei's voice sounded vague, weak, the fighter resigned.

They led her towards the door. I flung back my blanket. Ren must have felt the bunk give and she whispered like a bossy mother. I ignored her and slipped out of the dorm, hanging back in the shadows. They led Damei in the opposite direction to the sanitary room. I wavered, eager to see her suffer but, scared of being punished myself, I ran to the only safe place I knew.

The lamp glowed in his bureau, warm and reassuring and, through the window, I could see his papers strewn across the desk. I rattled the locked door.

"Manager...tsst Manager...it's me, are you there? I need to see you. They've taken Damei."

Was he alright? Was he asleep? Had he gone home? What if personnel had come for him too? Manager He said if we were ever to be found out, they'd make sure we never worked in another factory again.

I called his name again.

A movement from his bureau.

"Manager!"

He was frowning and shaking his head. His lips – his lovely, soft candy lips – mouthed something like, "Go away." Was he saying it wasn't safe or that I was late?

"I can't hear you."

He pointed to the green light in the pipework.

"Open up," I cried. "Don't let me get caught. Open it now."

Manager He shouted louder. "Get away!"

I banged on his door until it opened a crack, and I forced it until the door flung open.

"Hold me." I threw myself into his arms.

"No. You have to go, it's too risky."

"But I need you – they've taken Damei."

"You can't come here anymore. I don't want to see you here."

He pushed me out onto the staircase. "Get out," he screamed. The door to his bureau slammed in my face.

A few hours later, the alarm pierced the silence and the breakfast congee spurted from the pipe. I looked at it, sickened. Fatty straightened the bottom bunk, where Damei's blanket had been thrown back in the night, and plumped her pillow. I think we all knew there was no hope of her return.

At work, the seconds dragged like hours. Manager He wasn't in his bureau. I persuaded myself that he was on business in another part of the factory and would soon return.

In his absence, the workers chatted more freely over the din of the company song. I could hear them gossiping about my new perfume, which I was happy to wear on the line. Perfume was a luxury no other worker could afford. One of the bolder girls on my line left her station to ask if she could borrow the bottle that night, she wanted to spray some on a love letter to her boyfriend. I explained she needed to earn her own privileges and not rely on handouts. I told her to speed up her work, which she did.

At 11.30am, Chen and Ting arrived unexpectedly. Tuesdays weren't their usual day.

"This week, there have been cases of spitting, sleeping on the line and using the telephone during work hours."

"The offenders are: 2256, 2292 and 2378. All stand."

Their salary was to be cut in line with the regulation manual, they would spend the rest of the week on cleaning duties with Fei Fei. No lunch for any of them, plus a freeze on their wages. They'd got off lightly.

"Where's the boss?" shouted a loud mouth from Zone A.

"If you are referring to Manager He, then I am afraid we are not at liberty to divulge any information as to his whereabouts."

"Has he been bollocked as well? I bet Damei's landed him in it?"

"I know a girl in personnel; she says they were caught doing it up there, in his office, that it was all on camera."

Ting gasped. "Mr Chen, get these two gossips and take down their number. They can be fined today along with the other rebels."

One protested. "We were only asking!"

"In that case, 2320, you won't be concerned if we make you surplus to requirements."

"What Mr Ting means is…"

"What I mean is you're fired."

"Now come with us," said Chen, taking her by the arm and leading her towards the manager's exit.

"And back to work the rest of you," called Ting.

The door closed behind them, and Xiaofan leaned into the light above her station, "What's the matter 2204?" She whispered, "Worried you might be next?"

I stiffened.

"It's only a matter of time. They'll get rid of you the way they do all troublemakers. I'll make sure of it. No-one gets ahead of me in this place."

"You're just trying to scare me."

"Don't think I don't know what you've been up to with Manager He. How you've been stealing Damei's uniform. I was there, in the toilet. I saw you scrubbing your blood from her skirt. You're the same as your cousin. You Hunan *mei* can't help yourselves."

The klaxon sounded and another batch of circuit boards flowed towards us. A self-satisfied smile wormed its way across Xiaofan's mouth.

Our lunch break was delayed 26 minutes while we made up for lost time. I had no appetite and hurried to the dorm in search of Damei's uniform, eager to destroy the evidence that might incriminate me. I was relieved to find it folded beneath her blanket and bundled the skirt up tightly beneath my overalls.

As I descended the basement to the bins, the stink of rubbish hit me. I side-stepped the stray bin bags heaving with trash: the empty packets of noodles we weren't supposed to eat, newspapers with the job adverts torn free by those hoping for a better life. The air was thicker in the basement. The stench overpowering. My footsteps sounded loud against the concrete. I found the bin marked *Overalls*, flung open the lid and pushed Damei's uniform towards the bottom. As I turned to leave, someone pulled me into an alcove.

"Shhhh," he covered my mouth. "Don't make a noise or they'll find us."

Manager He kissed me, hard, like a starved comrade tucking into meaty ribs. He tugged urgently at my overalls. We didn't have long and did it right there, amidst the trash, pinned to the wall.

Afterwards, he spoke with urgency. "You mustn't come to my bureau again, do you understand, Mai Ling? Someone has told them I'm fooling around with Damei. They're on my case. They're watching me all the time."

"But that's not true. You've only been with me – haven't you?"

"I denied everything. They have no evidence; the cameras don't really work, Mai Ling, they're only empty boxes, there to make you work harder. The boss warned me to keep in line, but I can take care of him. I'm his best manager. He won't fire me in a hurry."

"I'm frightened."

"Keep doing what you're doing with the workers, 2204. Show off your new clothes, show them your rewards. Tell them you're going to be promoted – anything! I need them to be ready for Schnelleck. He's responded to our last letter already. He's coming! Much earlier than planned. Another week and he'll be here. I need you to step it up a gear."

"But what about the boss?"

"He doesn't need to be involved until the deal in Europe's secured. By then I'll have him eating out of my hand. He might be a traditionalist, but no-one at the top can resist tripling a profit."

"I love you," I said. "I'm so glad you're safe."

I went to kiss his cheek, but he pulled away and I ended up kissing thin air – the smell as rotten as mouldy congee.

Ricki's tattoo tingled. The bluish-black outline of the 'double happiness' symbol had turned strawberry-coloured, the skin on her upper arm peeled away like sunburn. She should have waited longer before pulling off the gauze patch.

But there was no way she was going back to Afflecks after what happened with Lisa and the red envelope. How could she begin to explain? Well actually, Lisa, you were right, the woman who gave me the envelope was my real mum – my Chinese one – and yeah, somehow, God knows how, she tracked us down... She taught my brainy sister Chinese on Saturday mornings for more than five years and we never realised what took you five minutes to see plain as day.

#Totalfreakinmuppet

She twisted the lid of Tattoo Goo and applied a thin layer. It smelt like weed. Then she climbed into the hobbit hole of her duvet and flicked on her laptop. A *Wiki* link came top of her search, followed by *Lonely Planet, BBC, China's Tourist Office, China Today*... She scrolled down.

Blah-blah-blah.

Who cared about China's etymology, history, pre-history, geography or politics? She was looking for a face like hers. A link to *Chinese inventions* caught her eye at the bottom of the page: chopsticks, exploding cannonball, kite, rice, toilet paper... Surely rice wasn't an invention? Unless they meant genetically modified rice. Hell, maybe the Chinese invented a super-grain that could multiply enough times to feed the whole population? She put nothing past the ingenious folks who spawned a new baby every two seconds. Two seconds! No wonder they needed rid of her and Jen.

In infant school, her teacher Mrs Wimperis, 'Wimpy' as she was known, had asked them to choose a country for a special project. Wimpy told Ricki to enlighten the class about China. Ricki looked up 'enlighten' in her dad's big dictionary, it said *to shed light on*. So she borrowed his globe and took it to school. Ricki spun it round in front of the class until the small magnifying glass shone directly over the yellow blob of land that was China.

"...And?" said Mrs Wimpy. "What are you going to tell us about China, Ricki?"

"Tell you?" she panicked. She hadn't planned on saying anything, only to enlighten.

She couldn't ask Jen for help. Jen had been moved up to Mr Matthews' class.

"You must know something about where you're from?" said Wimpy.

Some of the kids started to giggle.

"I know my tummy mummy lives there," she said.

"Your what?" said Wimpy.

Tummy mummy, it sounded like a cross between a Tamagotchi and a Teletubby, a person who would die if she wasn't fed enough custard.

"She means her proper mum," said Keith Gait. "The one with narrow eyes." He pulled his eyelids up at the corner, and Amber Jenkins rolled backwards clutching her sides with laughter.

After that, Wimpy never asked Ricki to talk about China again. She suspected her mum had given the teacher a gob full at parents' evening after Jen blurted the story of the globe over dinner. Ricki sulked for a week and wouldn't let Jen borrow her binoculars to spy on James Best, the boy from year seven who lived in the house opposite – and who Jen fancied the pants off.

Ricki never fancied anyone, not even at secondary school. She tried to like a boy called Philip, who was very serious. He was also shit hot at art and drew political cartoons of Tony Blair in the art room during his lunch break. His nickname was Pullup. He was so scrawny, always pulling up his trousers. Ricki tried to fancy him because she liked his drawings. But after a whole term, she realised she didn't want any boy, irrespective of how slack they wore their trousers.

She clicked on a few more sites about China then wandered onto one selling cheap airfares to Beijing. For £384 she could be leaving Manchester that evening and arrive in Beijing fifteen hours later.

Three hundred and eighty four quid!

It probably cost May twice that amount six years ago. She must have given up a good job in China to come and find them in Manchester.

Ricki closed the session. She switched back to her photographs and watched the thumbnails of her recent pictures load, anxious to find ones good enough to impress Noel. They were mainly shots of the city centre: shoppers and office workers taken low angle and long-range. She'd gone for people on mobile phones with urgent looks on their faces; the end of the world was coming and they knew it. Last phone calls home to loved ones.

A couple of shots were pretty good. Especially one of a little kid crying and holding her hands out to be picked up. Ricki managed to get it just right so the kid looked abandoned in a stampede of legs. She double clicked it to full size and stared at her blubbering face. Her red bobble hat was vivid against the greyish street. She was holding a bag of Buttons, her mouth smeared in chocolate like any ordinary kid on any ordinary day, except the picture said otherwise. Sometimes photos fell into place. It was luck, she guessed. Her dad called it "waiting for the sun to dip." She would run it through Photoshop, change the skimming clouds to blood red and hey presto, *Apocalypto*. That was her theme.

She flicked on through the series, but stopped, suddenly, at an unexpected photograph of May at the party, the day she was mowed down. She'd forgotten it was on there. Ricki's finger hovered over the delete button. It didn't belong with the rest of her pictures, any more than May belonged with their family. But if it didn't belong there, then where? Every picture has a home. Could she find the balls to take it back to its rightful place?

Hot tears rolled down Ricki's face. She knew the answer.

Maybe Nanchang would have a Metrolink like Manchester? Maybe the Chinkies all rode bicycles? Cycling proficiency was the only thing she'd ever been better at than Jen. Yeah, she could ride her bike and fit right in with the other millions of faces that looked like hers. All the other billions of babies.

Slowly, her finger moved away from the delete key.

Snapshot

The idea came to me on waking, the way good ideas often do. It wasn't new clothes or fancy shoes that workers wanted most, they could save up for those themselves. What they couldn't buy was freedom. We heard on the radio that the new ferris wheel had arrived in town and everyone wanted a ride. If I could get permission for a few of us to go, the others would be jealous. They would soon pick up speed if the reward was excitement and adventure away from the line. I had little more than a week.

I searched under my bunk for the tin box. It had been a while since I'd spoken to my wooden figurines, what with working so hard all day and visiting Manager He. I stroked the smooth pinewood of Madam Nie's head. She smelt of the forest back home. "I'm sorry," I whispered, hoping Mother might hear my apology.

Mrs Nie agreed the ferris wheel was a good ploy. I lay her back inside the tin box and set off in search of Fei Fei.

In the empty courtyard I wavered, disorientated and weary. My memory was increasingly hazy and I couldn't remember the exact location of Fei Fei's dorm. The cold, petrol-filled air assaulted my senses and I jolted as someone tapped me on the shoulder. I turned to see Fei Fei.

"I was just looking for you," she said.

What a funny habit she had, popping up out of the blue. "Shouldn't you be tidying the canteen before breakfast?" I asked.

"The boss sent me on an errand. What are you doing?" Her question was strangely pressing.

"I have some good news."

"Oh?"

"Manager He's agreed to let me out for a night. I worked my backside off last week for a big order. As a reward, I'm allowed to take two friends into Nanchang to see the new ferris wheel. I'm going tonight."

She shook her head. "I don't believe you. Managers don't let us out at night."

"It's true and he suggested I choose you because of the great work you did cleaning our equipment in time for that order. Say you'll come, Fei Fei? We'll have fun. It will be like the last time."

"That can't be right."

The alarm reverberated in the courtyard.

I squeezed her hand. "Listen, meet me after work. I'll wait by the gate. Wear something nice."

Like a dupe, she nodded in agreement.

Ren was harder to convince. I sought her out over lunch and took a different tack.

"No-one wants to know me, Ren. They say I suck up to management. You were right, 'Star of Forwood' was a scam to con us into submission."

She pushed the rice around her bowl. "Like I said, there are no stars around here."

"You know so much about factory life. I've been naïve. Not like you, you're experienced."

"Look where experience got me," she gestured to her leg.

"You need more time off – away from this place." I let the words hang in the air.

Ren chewed slowly on her food; I could tell she was thinking about Du.

"Why don't we do something rebellious?" I said. "You and me, let's escape for a night."

"Not many stars go in for acts of rebellion."

"I'll bribe the guards."

"You're still not listening, Sky Eyes. I said trust no-one in this place."

"But I trust you."

Ren caught my eye. "Maybe not even me."

"You can't go on like this, Ren. You need a break."

"They'll be all over us. We could lose our jobs."

"Not if we're careful."

"But if I go, I might never come back," she said and pushed away her tray, unable to face any more of the old green egg at the centre of Kwo's 'two dish surprise'.

Luckily, the guard on duty that night was a greedy southerner whose eyes darted all over the bribe as I pressed it into his glove. He didn't seem to notice the tremor in my hands or the way my voice wavered as I told him we'd be back around midnight.

"If anyone asks, say we're on a private errand for the Chief Executive."

He nodded, disinterested, as he counted his fistful of yuan.

Feeling bold, I said, "And don't breathe a word about the money I gave you, or he'll fire you."

Beneath the glare of the perimeter floodlights, my heart thudded. One small glitch and it would be us that got the push.

The gates clicked open and Fei Fei slid the heavy-looking bolt. I slipped an arm into Ren's and bundled her out, as fast as she could manage, her leg sweeping its invisible weight.

We walked the road leading to the express route and flagged a taxi over the river. The driver smoked roll-ups and played American music. Disco lights rigged along the back window of the taxi pulsed and flickered. I lost myself in a swirl of colour and sound.

The world and his girlfriend were out in Nanchang.

A gang of students cycled straight in front of the taxi as we entered the Donghu district. Our driver sprang his head out of the window and shouted,

"You got a death warrant Confucius?" His voice faded in the melee of traffic noise.

I paid the extortionate taxi fare to impress the girls, then we ditched the taxi and followed the throngs heading towards the river Gan, stopping often for Ren to catch up and Fei Fei to window shop.

"Hey, Mai Ling, have you ever seen such racy knickers?" She pressed her nose to the glass of a lingerie shop.

"What idiot would pay six hundred yuan for those?" said Ren.

"Imagine how sexy you'd feel beneath your overalls." Fei Fei giggled.

"What do you think, Sky Eyes? You've got the cash to buy it now you've flavour of the month with management?" said Ren.

"I'd never wear knickers like that. They're vulgar and expensive and made half way across the world."

But the skin on my chest flushed with excitement at the thought of Manager He peeling back the red lace.

At the market, I gave Fei Fei twenty yuan to buy a new denim jacket. Ren hung back, saying her wages were all accounted for. She was cagey when I asked about her family situation.

I knew she hid money inside her mattress, ready for moving on. Sometimes I heard her practise reading and writing before the breakfast alarm. She kept a notepad under the loose floorboard by the door. I stole it once. One of the pages said *GET OUT GET OUT GET OUT*. Glued to the page was an advert, cut from a newspaper, for a secretarial job. Judging by the faded newsprint, she'd been guarding it for some time, maybe years.

The restaurants were heaving. People of all ages spilled in and out. Lanterns lined the streets. Along the river, street vendors cooked spit-roasted skewers of fish over oil drums. We rested on a derelict wall overlooking the Gan, and wolfed down the fish. I felt intoxicated by the Canton pop songs thudding out from the funfair and the excited banter of people out to have a good time.

"It's so good to get away," said Fei Fei dreamily. "I'm not sure I can go back after tonight. Look at my hands, they're so dry from bleach and machinery oil."

"It's the same in any factory. Whether its handbags or 4x4s, we'll always be slaves to the klaxon. A *dagongmei*'s body is never her own. Isn't that right, Sky Eyes?"

"Let's not talk about it tonight, Ren. I just want to have fun."

A sudden explosion of fireworks burst across the night sky, their reflection jumped like frogs along the river. A couple of fishermen in a sampan looked up terrified, as if the penny moon had landed in their boat. I jumped off the wall and idled along the sandy riverbank where a skinny young guy approached me.

"Mai Ling?"

It was Yifan. I had not bothered to call him since our last meeting in the Suseng Teahouse and now he was alone, separated from his friends in the great maw of the city.

Fei Fei hurried over and introduced herself, "I work in the same factory as Mai Ling."

"Another engineer?"

Fei Fei giggled, perceiving irony where none was intended.

"Will you come with us to the ferris wheel?" she asked.

Yifan glanced towards me, "If that's alright?"

"Sure," I said.

Yifan dropped in step beside me and we chatted about his studies, but Fei Fei kept interrupting. It was so embarrassingly obvious she fancied him.

He told us stories about his work, "Once," he said, "there was a patient who kicked up a real fuss. He needed urgent treatment for chest pain, but had no cash or insurance paperwork, although he insisted he was a millionaire and promised to make a donation to the hospital if we agreed to treat him. The senior doctors relented because of the plans to build a new wing."

"Did he cough up?" said Fei Fei.

"Yes. Unfortunately, the man's donation was a body organ and not money. He died of a heart attack during his operation and we were left with a clogged aorta!"

Ren laughed; a beautiful, unfamiliar sound that lifted my spirits.

Yifan was nothing like the serious student I remembered from the Suseng Teahouse. We joked about the people around us, made up stories about where they'd come from and what they were doing in Nanchang.

"Look at those love birds," said Fei Fei, "kissing in the street."

"And the couple glued with their hands inside each others' back pockets," I laughed.

"What about her on the bench?" Ren pointed to a solitary young woman cradling a baby inside her coat.

"Looks like she's waiting for someone."

"My guess is that in a few hours that baby will never see its mother again. She'll leave it on the steps over there." Ren inclined her head towards a white-washed, monolithic building on the opposite side of the road.

"Welfare institute," she added.

"Is that what happens when a mother doesn't want her child?" I asked.

"Sometimes," said Yifan, suddenly serious, "If the child's lucky."

I was about to ask him what he meant when Ren pulled me aside, her voice urgent in my ear.

"Don't get in any deeper with the manager, Sky Eyes, or that could be you."

I laughed.

Fei Fei called for us to hurry. We rejoined the excitable crowds, but I couldn't help glance over my shoulder, unnerved by the sight of the young woman, all alone and rocking her child.

As we neared the ferris wheel, narrow alleyways gave way to broad avenues of neon light. I could hear screams as people reached the highest point of the wheel. It was spectacularly grand and the sight of it stopped us in our tracks.

Yifan paid for our tickets. He spent an embarrassingly long time counting out loose change from his grubby cloth wallet. I felt that not losing face cost him his last yuan.

On the ferris wheel, I bagged a seat by the window and watched the people below begin to shrink, their mouths gaped in wonder. I gripped the handrail, feeling dizzy.

"Don't look down, look up," Yifan said.

I stared up at the wheel's creaking iron structure and hoped the workers who made it were better fed and rested than us.

"The city's beautiful from up here," said Yifan. "Look! You can see the university and there's the Tengwɛng Pavilion. The river looks so wide!"

I felt a hand brush mine. At first I thought it belonged to the young boy at my knee, who stood on tiptoes, his nose pressed to the glass. Then Yifan squeezed my little finger gently, discreetly. Ren and Fei Fei were too busy admiring the view to even notice. I sat, frozen, Yifan's hand laced around mine as the wheel completed its revolution.

When we reached the bottom, I expected Ren to say it was a waste of money or complain about something.

Instead, she beamed. "We were so high! I could have flown away."

"Like a bird," I said, stepping down.

"Free," added Fei Fei, bustling to my side. "Free at last."

"We shouldn't lose this moment," I said.

I spent twelve yuan on a disposable camera from one of the funfair stalls and Yifan snapped photos of us in front of the wheel, where a large sign said, *Welcome to Nanchang!*

We took the camera to a processing booth on the corner and huddled around the machine as they popped out one by one.

"I can't believe how scrawny I am," said Fei Fei, crestfallen. "I look like I've been fighting the Japanese. Am I really that pale?"

"It's the flashlight," said Yifan generously.

Ren buried a few of the photographs in her jacket. "Come on, Mai Ling, it's getting late. Let's go back before the guard changes shift," she tugged on my sleeve. "We're never free."

We left the store and headed in the direction of Bayi Square for a taxi.

"Are you sure I can't buy you a drink?" said Yifan.

"Perhaps another time," I said, suddenly weary.

"Mai Ling – there's something I've been meaning to ask you all evening."

"I must get back. Work starts very early. I'm under a lot of pressure. I can't begin to explain."

He grappled for my hand. "Then say you'll meet me again."

I shook it away.

"I'm sorry, I didn't mean to offend you."

"You haven't, I'm tired."

"Take my number again. Call me this time." He fished in his satchel for a pen and some paper. "My exams will soon be over. I need to see you again."

I nodded and shoved his number in my pocket just as Fei Fei and Ren rounded the corner.

Back at the factory, Fei Fei said she needed to sit a while before she could sleep. The excitement had made her head spin. Ren and I left her in the courtyard.

We paused on the landing to our dorm and caught our breath. I looked out over the courtyard expecting to see Fei Fei, but in the few moments it had taken us to climb the stairs, she had disappeared.

"Strange, she's never in the places you think she's going to be," I muttered.

"You need to watch her," said Ren, "She's not who she says she is."

I laughed. This was such a typical Ren-statement. "What makes you say that? Fei Fei is hopeless at keeping secrets."

We stared at the empty courtyard.

"Ren, not everyone in this factory is out to get us the way they got Du. Some people would actually be your friend if you let them."

Her face flashed. "You don't know what you're talking about."

"The managers here aren't all…"

"You think you can silence me with a 'reward' trip?"

"I thought you might enjoy coming."

"Can't you see what's in front of you, Sky Eyes?"

"What's that supposed to mean?"

"I'm faithful to you without bribery. I'll never tell anyone about you and him, but you should end it. Stop seeing the manager before it's too late, I mean it." She let go of my arm and hurried away, leaving me adrift on the landing.

So that was all the thanks I got for treating her to a night out. Perhaps I should have had Manager He cut her precious wages.

I waited until my resentment subsided. Waited and watched for signs of Fei Fei, whose gossiping mouth and solidarity I was going to need more than ever.

Something moved behind the mei trees - a bird, perhaps? But when I looked again there were two pairs of legs. It was definitely Fei Fei, I recognised her trousers. Something swished again. Someone else paced back and forth behind the tree. A voice inside told me to keep watching, even though I didn't want to. Just then a figure stepped out of the gloom and marched purposefully across the courtyard in his dressing gown. The figure, I realised, my legs suddenly leaden, was Manager He.

Mr Nie

Ren gave me the silent treatment for two whole days after our exchange. She was touchy and her moods drained my *qi*. Energy that could be "better spent leading others in the way of productivity," as Manager He would say.

Unable to meet in his bureau, we had agreed to see each other in the basement at lunchtime whilst workers ate or napped at their work stations. We were kissing by the bins, when I broke off to ask him about his encounter with Fei Fei in the courtyard. What had he been doing in the early hours of the morning, talking to a nobody like her?

His eyes closed at the mention of her name.

"I was taking a stroll to clear my head. Why do you ask? And why were you snooping on me? You should be sleeping when not on the line, otherwise how can you expect to do a decent day's work?"

"But I saw you talking to her."

"Yes, yes, I did bump into Fei Fei. Nothing wrong with that." He pulled away. "If you must know, I issued her a warning."

"For what?"

"Stealing is rife. Workers like Fei Fei think they can take a few bits of metal here, a few tools there, not to mention all the titbits stolen from the canteen."

"Fei Fei? Are you sure?"

She wasn't a bad worker, immature perhaps, but not a thief. She desired beauty and glamour, and for that she needed cash. She needed to stay in line.

"It's unacceptable, 2204, and must stop before Schnelleck arrives. Imagine if he caught her at it."

The mention of his name was sobering. I was barely meeting my own targets, let alone inspiring others to amazing feats of productivity.

"Did Schnelleck say which department he wanted to see first?" I asked, hoping it wouldn't be ours.

"I got a fax this morning from his secretary; he wants to see it all, starting in bodywork – but I think I can engineer it for him to come to circuitry and bypass those idiots altogether. Ha ha!

Engineer it…Ha! Sometimes I don't know my own wit. Schnelleck will be eating out of my hand this time next week."

He kissed my forehead as though it was a lotto ticket.

"When the Chief Executive hears I've secured foreign business, he's sure to put me in charge of overseas accounts. And you know what the West represents?"

I wasn't sure if he expected me to answer when he was in full flow. To me the West was Wrigley's, Americans with money to burn in bars and fat white fingers that strayed too far up my leg; then there was white beauty, sexy knickers and French perfume, a language I'd never master beyond the odd word on the circuit boards and, of course, The Colonel – although I didn't think any of this was the answer Manager He wanted.

"A potential goldmine, that's what! I'm going to be so rich, I'll have enough yuan to fill my bureau, floor to ceiling."

I buried my head into his chest. His heart went *tic-a-tac-tic-a-tac* like a wind-up toy.

He guided me to the front of his trousers. I touched him until his mouth slackened and his eyelids screwed up with a pleasure that looked almost painful. He slumped back and the bin took his weight, cushioned by a heap of overflowing trash – thinking of his productivity figures, no doubt. There was nothing for me in return. I was left wanting, burning – the fire dragon who stirred whenever he was around.

Manager He straightened and pushed some of the rubbish back into the bin.

"It's such a mess, Mai Ling," he muttered.

I stared at the bags that surrounded us.

"I need Fei Fei to shift this crap – can you tell her? There's far too much rubbish everywhere. Bags and boxes and bubble wrap and buckets of scrap metal, old worn out hand tools, I can't have Schnelleck thinking we're slap dash."

"Of course, Manager." I kissed his cheek.

"Be sure you ask her today. I want to see it looking tidier when we meet here tomorrow."

I found Fei Fei in the canteen, fluttering her eyelids at Kwo and showing off the new denim jacket I bought her in town. Kwo, the dumb egg, succumbed and gave her an extra spoonful of bean sprouts.

A girl behind us in the lunch queue noticed and demanded the same.

"They're only for certain workers," said Kwo.

147

"What's she done to deserve extra? She's only a cleaner."

"Excuse me!" Fei Fei spun round. "Who do you think tidies your work stations and keeps your conveyor belt running? Without me, this place would grind to a halt."

"I doubt that," said the girl, wearing green quality control overalls; her friends huddled around to gawp at Fei Fei's pristine jacket.

"Don't be so quick to look down on her," I butted in. "She works hard to get ahead. Everyone has the same chance of being rewarded." I nudged Fei Fei. "Isn't that right?"

"Oh, yes...rewards," she faltered.

"Was your jacket a reward too, Sichuan *mei*?" A girl stepped forwards from the huddle and touched Fei Fei's sleeve. "I've been wanting one like this."

"She got it last night," I said.

"Last night?"

Fei Fei nodded. "I went to see the new ferris wheel."

Her friends gasped in collective disbelief.

"They let you out?"

"How?"

"What was it like?"

"Did you ride the wheel?"

"Was it scary?"

"How high does it go?"

"What did you see?"

"Move it, girls," shouted Kwo. "You're slowing everybody down."

Fei Fei pulled away, but the group followed, encircling us.

"The view from the top was breathtaking. I saw the whole city," Fei Fei said.

"Even Forwood?"

She laughed.

"What did it look like?"

"Did you meet any guys?"

"Did you go to the funfair?"

"Oh, tell us, tell us everything," said a worker who looked barely sixteen with heavy, bloodshot eyes.

Fei Fei beamed, pleased to be the centre of attention for once. "We saw it all: the twinkling lights spread out below, fireworks exploding along the river, young couples kissing as they waited their turn. The wheel looked five times bigger than the factory tower and wider than this canteen." She gestured to the walls.

"Who did you go with?"

148

I slipped my arm through Fei Fei's. "She went with me."

"Oh, I get it. You're the one on the posters."

"We work hard, we get rewards. It's simple." I tugged Fei Fei's arm, wanting her to back me up, but she stared at the floor.

"Well your jacket is pretty and I think a trip out to the ferris wheel is worth the hard work," said a sturdy, square faced woman, probably a Guangdong *mei*.

"I agree, we're already knackered, we might as well get the benefits," added a wiry girl. "Do you think the bosses in quality control would let us go?"

"Of course!" I said. "But you've got to work faster and speed up on the checks. No radio in the afternoon, no sweets on the line when the boss isn't looking, no disappearing off to the sanitary room pretending you need the loo when really you want to try on your friend's lipstick."

They laughed.

"I'm serious. If you girls want to live happily and richly you'd better start by making a difference to your lives today. No more wasted time. You only have yourselves to blame if you can't shine like stars."

"She's right."

"I don't want to be stuck here forever."

"We should carve out our own worlds."

"Yes," I nodded. "Our time here is brief, it's best to work our hardest while we are young and reap the rewards. Isn't that right Fei Fei?"

She glanced up at the expectant faces. "I...I want to eat my lunch now."

"But there's so much more we want to know," said the youngest girl with bloodshot eyes.

Fei Fei swayed slightly, a few beads of sweat had gathered at her temples.

"You heard her, girls, leave us alone now and go and sit with the others from your department."

The girls wandered off, gossiping enthusiastically about the ferris wheel and how they would work hard for rewards. Apart from one dumb ox, who tutted and complained that her rice was stone cold.

I waited until they were out of earshot, then grabbed the sleeve of Fei Fei's denim jacket. "We need to talk now," I said, manoeuvring her sparrow-like frame towards a table in the corner, away from the rest.

"I'm sorry, Mai Ling, I don't know why I didn't praise you in front of them. I was only sharing in your reward."

"Never mind that, what's this about you stealing?"

"Stealing?"

"It's against the rules. Don't you know they'll fire you?"

Her eyes widened, as if she might cry.

"But I've not taken a thing."

"Don't lie, you'll only make things worse. Listen, I'm the star of Forwood, do you understand? A star can't be friends with a thief. If you know what's best, you'll put back whatever it is you've stolen. If it happens again, we're finished – no more trips into town, no treats. You're on your own."

She snivelled into the sleeve of her new jacket. "I understand."

"Good. Because from now on I need you and this factory to be squeaky clean."

That night, Ren wasn't in the dorm. I threw back the covers and ventured into the familiar gloom of Forwood's corridors, figuring she must be on overtime.

I could hear voices in the canteen. The women from personnel were eating late.

There was even more rubbish lying around outside their living quarters: food wrappers and plastic bags, cigarette butts, drinks cartons, even pairs of worn-out shoes. It was as if the lazy sheep had tipped up their rubbish bins.

Directly outside Bonding there were more obstacles: cardboard boxes stacked waist-high, some labelled *hazardous*. I tried pushing them aside, but they were too heavy. I climbed over, trying to fathom out why the entrance was blocked and by whom?

As I reached for the handle, I heard arguing coming from inside.

"…And another thing, she can't save you if that's what you're thinking. She won't last much longer and he'll get rid of her, just like her rotten cousin."

It was Xiaofan. What was she doing away from her dorm, arguing with Ren so late at night?

"What's it to you?" said Ren, "You're only jealous because he isn't interested in you anymore. As for her saving me, you don't know what you're talking about. I don't need saving, I can look after myself."

There was a sharp slap, a gasp from Ren, followed by silence. I stepped back from the door and crouched between the nearby boxes.

Ren was silent on the other side of the door. I imagined her face, slapped and humiliated. She had been faithful to me, after all. I waited until Xiaofan left, then crawled out and hurried back to the dorm, leaving Ren to finish her work.

For another hour or more, I lay awake listening to the sounds of the dorm. Fatty muttered to herself then tossed over. The girl by the window screamed intermittently in her sleep.

I grappled for the loose floorboard to find Ren's notebook. A lot of it was boring: mainly slogans from around the factory, things like *Don't eat excessive food, don't talk excessive talk*, and *A little dirt is good for your system*. She had doodled squares that looked like prison bars. There was nothing in the notebook about me. I closed it, feeling disappointed.

Then I heard Mr Nie whispering from inside Ren's tin box.

What is it? I asked, lifting him out.

Bad leg, he said, *bad leg…*

The patina of his little wooden face caught the half-light.

What about her bad leg?

Bad leg, bad leg, he repeated.

But I was so tired I could hardly keep my eyelids open anymore, and Mr Nie's warning faded into oblivion.

Mrs Nie

The next morning, Ren wasn't in her bunk and I hurried to the line to find Xiaofan.

"What have you done to her? Was it you who blocked the corridors near the bonding room?"

"I don't know what you're talking about. Get your hands off me," said Xiaofan, pulling on her work gloves.

"I'm talking about Ren. I heard you arguing in bonding. Why did you slap her? She's not in her bed. What have you done to my friend?"

"Friend!" laughed Xiaofan and leaned over the conveyor belt. "Nobody here believes you're a star, 2204. They all know you and him are having some kind of pathetic fling. It won't last and then you'll be out on your ear just like your slutty cousin."

I grabbed the pincer tool, forgetting the rules, and was about to jab her when suddenly there was a crashing noise at the far end of circuitry. Manager He had tripped on the stairs and fallen flat on his face.

"See how pitiful he is? You really think he'll come running to help you when the Chief Executive finds out? You're not a star; you can't even do 60 boards an hour."

"At least he still wants me. I'm not an old has-been. He said you were like a car that groans and moans and eventually packs in. Face it, Xiaofan, you're history. You've lost your chance."

The smirk fell from her superior face, and I rushed over to Manager He.

"Get off." He pushed me away and scrambled to his feet as a bell rang out. It wasn't the usual bell, it was louder, more persistent.

"Everybody, stop what you're doing," he cried.

"Manager – what is it? What's the matter?"

The ringing made me push my fists over my ears.

"We've got to get out," Manager He shouted.

I hurried back to my station to tidy away my tray. "Leave it, Mai Ling."

"I don't understand. What's that bell?"

Fatty grabbed me by the hand. "It's the fire alarm!"

152

I glanced over to see Xiaofan's chair kicked over. She had run for the door.

"Don't just stand there, Mai Ling," shouted Manager He from the door. "Quickly! We must all get to the courtyard. Leave your equipment. Come at once. Come on, girls."

Manager He flung open the door and immediately the acrid smell of burning plastic hit us. The corridor was full of smoke.

"Back," cried Manager He, coughing, "you all have to go back."

"We can't stay here," somebody wailed above the noise of the alarm. "It's not safe."

"Try the manager's exit," said another.

We retreated to the far exit, Fatty still clutching my overalls. She grabbed a couple of soft cloths, used for dusting the LCDs, and held one to her mouth. The other, she pushed into my hand. "Take it," she said, her eyes wide.

Manager He fumbled for his keys to open the door.

I lurched towards him.

"Let him do it," said Fatty. "Or we won't get out."

"Hurry up!" cried a worker.

A hand pushed me to the floor and I crawled after Fatty towards a rectangle of light, out into the cold bright daylight. Some workers were already huddled in the courtyard, outnumbered by the white blouses and grey skirts of personnel. Everyone stared up at the main building in gripped disbelief. Above us the sound of breaking glass attacked the air like gun fire. A loud explosion sent smoke spewing from an upstairs window. The upper part of the bonding room where Ren worked was completely ablaze. Flames gobbled up the air.

Another almighty crack and girls scrambled to their feet, screaming shrilly, "It's going down!"

I looked up to see a blackened part of the upper wall tilting in the wind. It seemed to sway forever until it eventually succumbed to gravity and the whole wall collapsed in a gush of choking smoke that enveloped everyone, including me.

I rolled into a tight ball and closed my eyes, fearing it was my time to die. For a while all was black. But death never came and eventually I heard someone calling out for me.

"2204? 2204? 2204?" My number was getting louder.

"That's me," I croaked, my throat clogged with the taste of ash.

A personnel worker knelt over me with a clipboard. I turned my head to the side looking for Fatty. Instead, there were bloodied

153

faces, some charred, others with gashes. The woman closest to me wailed indescribably. Two of her fingers were missing from the knuckle, lacerated to the bone by a large shard of glass still wedged in her hand.

A personnel worker clenched the woman's blood-soaked hand. "The ambulances have arrived, the doctors are coming."

"Where's Fatty?" I asked, meekly.

"Can you confirm your department?"

I shook my head, which felt leaden. Then I felt myself being lifted up. At the head of the stretcher was a familiar face. My head fizzed, and there was Yifan and then there was nothing.

The fire was still out of control when I came to. I was surrounded by row upon row of women, their charred faces still and unmoving. The stench of the dyes used in bonding filled the air completely. Maybe I was close to Ren, after all. I rolled over onto my knees and tried to haul myself up, desperate to find her. But someone pushed me back to the ground.

A sketchy outline of a young woman towered over me.

"You're supposed to be dead," she said.

Xiaofan.

"Where's Manager He... and Ren?" I mumbled.

"Forget them, 2204, half the factory's burnt to the ground. Your sweetheart left you to perish. You're all alone now – like the rest of us."

Xiaofan's shoe dug into my shoulder and I began to blubber. "It was you... You started it? You left Ren to burn!"

Xiaofan started to kick me and I fell back, with the overwhelming urge to sleep.

Later Fatty woke me saying she was sorry over and over, which was strange, because she'd done nothing wrong. It was all Xiaofan's fault. She nudged something wooden and familiar into my hands, Mr and Mrs Nie.

"We can't find her," said Fatty, whispering a name. "We can't find Ren anywhere."

She cradled me, sobbing.

It took three days for the last embers to be put out on account of an exceptionally blustery north wind which had destroyed large sections of the factory. Electronic circuitry was one of the few areas relatively unscathed. Manager He's bureau was covered in fine black ash, but still standing.

Our dorms were also in tact and we were told to return to sleep amidst the soot as if nothing ever happened. Other workers joined us from different departments and took the beds of girls who were missing. A younger, less experienced Bei *mei* slept above me in Ren's bed. I could barely understand her northern accent.

When the girl was out, I climbed onto her bed and butted my leg against the wall as Ren used to. I still expected to see her hobbling towards the breakfast pipe or perching on our bunk. Some nights I heard her calling out for Du. Once, I saw her standing by the shutters, holding her notebook and learning to read.

My sadness for Ren was only surpassed by my longing for Manager He. He was rumoured to be alive, recuperating in hospital, but I couldn't be sure. I stopped eating. Food seemed irrelevant. The conveyor belts no longer operated. With so much machinery and equipment wasted, we worked at making the place clean and safe. I found comfort in this and used every last scrap of energy in the clear-up operation. Without Manager He, it was my duty to keep things going.

Fei Fei never showed for work in the weeks that followed and we heard she was amongst the hundreds convalescing in the recovery quarters. Fatty did her best to comfort me. We played cards; she taught me Rummy and Quick Fix, a game from her village, which involved slight of hand. I wasn't very good, I couldn't concentrate for long. Sometimes we talked about Hunan, about our families – who felt like ghosts. Fatty told me she had worked hard and stuck to the rules because she had planned to bring her sister-in-law to Nanchang. We agreed it was better than housework. We laughed and cried, sorry for all that we'd lost.

We never really talked about the fire, or our injuries, except once I thanked her for bringing me my figurines. She could not have known our dorm was untouched by the fire and had hurried to salvage what she could. She said it was nothing. She said the real saving work was done by the ambulance men and doctors. The events were already so vague and muddled, but I knew it was his face, his gentle eyes – Yifan had saved my life.

Once, when the wick of the candle was burnt almost to nothing, I confessed to Fatty that Manager He was my first love.

"I don't know how long I can keep going without him. I have to believe he's coming back."

"I'm sure he'll be alright," she said, "try and stay strong. He will come back, you'll see."

Secretly, I worried what he might look like and whether the fire had disfigured his beautiful features and soft hands. I shivered inside at the thought of him touching me with hands like stumps. Immediately, I felt guilty.

Fatty sighed, unsure how to comfort me. I didn't know either and hoped sleep might blot out the pain.

Personnel were less harsh with us for a while. They didn't fine us for talking as we worked and we were allowed to keep the radio on all the time. Chen and Ting never showed up again, which distressed me. I was desperate to have Manager He get rid of Xiaofan. I couldn't even bear to look her in the eye.

Manager He would be incurably frustrated, away from his work, away from his great plans and from Schnelleck. Would he still make a deal? If there was even the remotest chance, Manager He would find a way.

It was half past two on Thursday afternoon when personnel sent a message that Manager He was alive. My fighter had survived again! All thoughts of what he might look like, his injuries, flew out of my mind. Dizzying joy soaked through my body. I wanted to say, "Ha! You failed!" to Xiaofan. He would be returning to the factory.

That evening, in the dorm, I unfolded my crumpled suit with a renewed sense of purpose. I had a second chance at happiness. Fatty said I looked as powerful as one of the top dogs in personnel, wearing shoulder pads like that.

"Good enough to be his wife?" I asked.

There was no answer in the darkness.

Our reunion in his bureau was just like old times. He poured me a glass of baijiu and offered me candy. His face was unblemished, apart from a small cut on his forehead which I discovered whilst stroking his hair. He was a little stiff, having fallen in his hurry to escape the factory, but I was very gentle with him. The subject of his leaving me, of not making sure I was safely out, was never mentioned. What point was there in upsetting each other?

I told him over and over how much I missed him as I planted little kisses over his face and neck. I waited patiently for him to undress, and slid off my overalls to make it easier. For the first time ever, Manager He was concerned to give me what I wanted. He nuzzled at my ear and stroked me with tenderness.

"Tell me how," he murmured. "Here?"

He spent a long time holding my feet, rubbing his face against them, he put my toes inside his mouth and his tongue darted like a fish. It reminded me of wading barefoot in a warm river. The bureau was nicely lit; the spirit lamp gave off a steady glow.

He kissed between my legs. It was a feeling of becoming taller, the dragon waking. I tugged Manager's hair for him to stop, before it was too late, but he kept going. I put my hand in my mouth and bit hard. He watched me.

We made love on his bureau floor. I bathed in his weight, so solid, so real – so alive! My hand fell across his shoulder blade.

Afterwards, in a doze, Manager He murmured "performance quotas."

"What did you just say?" I asked, aggrieved that he should mention work so soon.

"It will please him, my star… my amazing star."

"What will?"

But he rolled over to sleep and I put it down to him talking gibberish – something which often happened after his climax.

By the time he woke up, I was already seated at the desk, flicking through some recent paperwork relating to productivity, though not really concentrating on the numbers. I was still swooning over the idea of marrying Manager He. I pictured us living in one of those brand new apartments on the outskirts of the city, driving to work in our 4x4.

"Mai Ling," he said dreamily. "Come here, I want to talk."

I knelt beside him.

"It's about Schnelleck."

"I guess he isn't coming any more?"

"Yes, of course he is. He doesn't know anything about the fire, only that I've been in hospital. He believes that's why I postponed his visit. I have no intention of letting him know the truth."

"Surely he can't visit a burnt out factory?"

Manager He frowned and his top lip curled in a way I had never seen before. "You mean you don't believe we can do it? You've lost faith in me?"

"No, no, that's not true. I just don't know how. I thought you would have made a contingency plan, that's all."

"I didn't waste a minute in hospital. I have it all worked out. You and I will meet him in town."

"Won't he want to visit the factory?" I asked. "No foreigner comes all the way to China to meet up and sip tea, even Chinese tea."

"There isn't time to explain it all now."

He was right; it was already five o'clock in the morning. I had stayed longer than on any other occasion.

"I need you to promise you'll go along with the plan and not question my judgement. Do you understand?"

Manager He's pupils were deep, endless. I wondered if he was capable of sound judgement after the fire. How could he possibly win Schnelleck over? And how could our factory – blackened and destroyed – be impressive?

"I'm not sure," I whispered.

He lit a cigarette and stared at the portrait of Deng Xiaoping that now curled away from the wall. The smell of tobacco sickened me so soon after the fire.

"How can I achieve the four modernisations without labourers?" I heard him say, as though he was making a direct plea to the president.

I hadn't noticed before, but Manager He's shoulders sloped terribly. He also had a little hump beneath his neck on account of the long hours he spent stooped over his desk. I felt suddenly repulsed. I had given myself away too easily.

"I will leave you in peace, Manager. You must be very weary, after such a long day at work and so soon after being in hospital."

"So now you're deserting me?" he snapped.

I didn't like his bullish tone.

"What's got into you, 2204, are you too proud to even answer a straightforward question? Has being a star gone to your head?"

"No," my voice was sulky, childish. "We should talk more tomorrow."

"There isn't time tomorrow, don't you understand?" he spun around, extinguishing his cigarette on the tin of candies and clutched my face between his hands. I need you more than ever, Mai Ling. Things have gone badly wrong for us... But I'm not going to give up. I'm still holding onto my dream for this factory – which is more than can be said for the other managers. They're already talking about shutting this place down and moving onto a different city. It's as if no-one believes in anything anymore. That's why I need you." He smothered my face with kisses.

I felt a sudden rush of pity.

"What must I do?"

"Trust in me."

The sensible part of my brain said it was stupid to trust a flawed plan. Mother always said, "Dishes without salt are tasteless, words without reason are powerless." But since when did I ever listen to reason? Running away was not playing by the rules. If I had been a good, obedient daughter I would be living in the coffin shop with Li Quifang and his mother, knitting jumpers for our baby and funeral gowns for the dead. Didn't Father also say, "A craftsman is thirty percent free and seventy percent beholden to his employer"?

"Alright, I'll do as you say," I acquiesced.

"And will you trust me completely?"

"With my life."

Manager He breathed a visible sigh of relief. I thought he was going to wrap his arms around me and hug me tenderly, like a lover should. Instead, he reached over and pushed his desk drawer shut.

I reached for him. "Hold me, I've missed you."

He held me so tight, I could barely move. If I hadn't loved him I would have found it unbearable, I would have wanted to push him away and run. But I did love him and so I stayed there until he let go and when he did, when his arms dropped to his side, I felt weightless, like a kite caught in a pocket of air. I remembered Ren, so high above the world and free, riding on that ferris wheel, the way I would always remember her.

Nancy expected to see a yellow haze of pollution as the plane nudged its way through the cumulus. But that had been sixteen years ago. The Beijing air now was crystalline, and the tops of buildings sparkled against a stratospheric-blue dawn.

They took a high-speed train from the airport into the city. Iain and Ricki were in their own world, taking pictures. Jen was quiet. Already her daughters looked more at home in China than they did in white, suburban Altrincham. Nancy worried that a stranger would not guess they belonged to her. That old familiar dread of losing them clutched at her stomach. She fanned herself with a copy of *The Times*.

She'd read about China's olympian attempts to clean up the air: banning half of the city's three million cars from the roads on any given day, closing down factories, relocating entire industries. There were to be 50,000 bikes available to rent. Their efforts had not been in vain, thought Nancy, as she breathed in humid, unpolluted air.

Their room was on the twenty-first floor; worth every penny of the measly pay-off money Nancy had been given for her redundancy. They took a stroll before dark. Billboards were awash with the Olympic slogan; *One world, one dream*, translated into English, French, Spanish and even Greek. Chinese flags hung proudly from almost every store on the torch relay-route. A small sign of the unrest over Tibet were a few students wearing *Anti-Riot & Explore the Truth* T-shirts. Otherwise, the atmosphere was one of exuberant, well-controlled patriotism. Still, Nancy held tightly to her handbag which contained almost £500 contingency funds in RMB.

They bought burgers from McDonald's and ate in a square near the Olympic Village. Barely a minute had passed, when a volunteer asked if Iain needed assistance. Her English was so slick it verged on robotic.

"No thank you, we've just stopped for a bite to eat."

She pointed to an undefined distance. "A bite to eat, very well, sir, enjoy your meal over there, please."

It wasn't worth arguing the case for liberty. "Come on girls, let's find somewhere else," Nancy said.

They joined the crowds taking photos around the perimeter of the Bird's Nest. The stadium was a jaw-dropping feat of engineering, an iconic building, created with the same indomitable optimism as those who built The Great Wall. Nancy imagined the thousands of construction workers who'd toiled for five years to assemble its vast steel structure. Imagined, too, the local women, older than her, made homeless in order that China might appear ready to welcome the world.

Nancy scanned the passing faces. May was the street vendor selling Olympic headbands, the young Chinese woman pushing a stroller, the suited woman rushing home as she talked business on her mobile phone. There was no turning back from her country, her street, her sky, her face. They had come to find out about May and she was everywhere. But had May ever been to Beijing? Or walked its streets? What did she know of China's Olympic fervour, their campaign to win the most gold medals and the single-minded way they went about bringing honour to their nation? May said she was part of a new generation of Chinese that could afford foreign travel and wanted to see beyond her national borders. That's what brought her to England. She also said she was from a small village in Hunan and had won a scholarship to study engineering in Nanchang – truth or lie? Maybe Beijing was her birthplace? Maybe her family had lived in this very district before it was bulldozed to make way for the 10 million tourists and athletes and global media?

There was only one person who would know. She smoothed the piece of paper on which she'd written the name of his hospital.

The next day, Nancy scrutinised her daughters for signs of 'emotional trauma', as the social worker called it. She guessed Ricki might retreat into herself or wander off alone, but in fact her daughter appeared relaxed, happy even, to be away from Manchester.

At Tiananmen Square, Jen and Iain went to buy a souvenir and some postcards, leaving Nancy and Ricki alone to share a pot of green tea.

Ricki stared into the distance, where Mao's portrait hung above the gate.

"How did he get to be so powerful?" she asked. "I mean why do people still come here and take photographs?"

Nancy didn't have an answer.

"Well, I'm not going to take any."

This part of her daughter's history was unreachable, unfathomable, even after Nancy read a stack of books on Chinese culture and history.

"Are you pleased we came?" asked Nancy.

Ricki shrugged. "The people are okay. I dunno... I guess I expected to feel more of a connection, a shock or something."

"Perhaps when we get to Nanchang you'll feel differently?"

"Perhaps. What about you?"

"I was so excited about meeting you for the first time I didn't sleep for three nights. I was supercharged."

"No, I meant in England. How did you feel being a foreigner there?" said Ricki.

"Oh, now you're really making me feel old!"

"Seriously, did it take long to feel at home in a different country?"

"I suppose, darling, I was pleased to leave and so I embraced my new life with your dad."

"Didn't you miss America?"

"I was born there – it's where I have all my childhood memories. There are certain people I miss."

She didn't want to burden her daughter with talk of her past.

"Did you leave America because of what happened to Grandma?"

Nancy fussed with the corner of the tablecloth.

"Sorry to bring it up. You don't have to answer if you don't want to."

Nancy gazed across the square. "It wasn't only Grandma's death that made it hard for me to stay in America... There was a boy, Peter." Nancy set down her cup. "I've never talked about him to anyone."

"Was he your boyfriend?"

"When I was fourteen, we took a school trip to Syosset, a camping trip. Your Aunty Lizzie had a nasty virus and stayed at home. Peter was a young man who I met while we were away. He was helping his father in the fields over summer... He was the first person I thought I loved, which you'll probably laugh at. But the heart can persuade you of anything, I suppose. It's not always about age, is it darling?"

"What happened? Did you see him again?"

"He did come and visit me after the camping trip was over. We hung out on the beach, he met my friends. You can imagine how, in the fifties, sex wasn't something I felt able to talk to Grandpa about and well... Grandma wasn't there."

"Was he cute?"

"I thought so. I kept a few photographs of him, right up until the time I met your dad."

She paused, remembering the picture of Peter in his Speedos. Nancy had kissed his photo every night. All that was a lifetime away and yet talking to Ricki its rawness made her smart.

"So what happened to him?"

Nancy's eyes flitted back and forth across Tiananmen Square, expecting Iain to arrive back at any minute.

"Peter and I took things a little too far."

"You slept together?"

"Please, don't think badly of me. Everything was different back then, I didn't know anything about contraception. I only wish things had been explained more clearly, but your Grandpa never told me a thing and the rest was just school girl gossip."

"What are you saying, Mum? That I have an older brother or sister out there somewhere?"

"No, there was no baby – we decided it was for the best," said Nancy. "Although sometimes I wish…"

"What is it, Mum?"

Nancy blinked back the tears.

"After we decided to terminate – well, that was the end of everything. I needed to get away. Too many ghosts, Ricki. I needed a fresh start and a few years later my chance came along when I met your dad in New York. I don't mean to upset you by telling you all this, I don't even know where it came from…"

Nancy shifted in her seat and smoothed the tablecloth as she saw Iain and Jen approach.

Iain shrugged. "We decided not to bother."

"It didn't feel right, buying a postcard of this place. It gives me the creeps," Jen added. "What have you two been talking about?"

"Just some history," Ricki said. "That's right, isn't it Mum?"

"Yes, sweetheart. It really isn't important anymore."

Iain skimmed through the guide book, reading out Fodor's top ten sights. "How about we go to the markets after tea, Rick? Take a few night shots for *Apocalypto*."

"Oh, that," she said, "I've scrapped it."

"Don't Afflecks have a unit coming up? I thought that was your theme?"

"Yeah well, I'm not sure I want to work there. Maybe it's history, like a lot of stuff." Ricki scraped back her chair. "Are we going now or what? I'm sick of staring at Mao's porkie-pie face."

"I see what you mean; he does look kind of like the pig on our Chinese calendar," said Jen.

"The one you trashed," Ricki smiled.

Was Nancy imagining it or was there warmth in her daughter's smile? Had her confession broken some invisible barrier?

"Do you need to go back to the hotel for a rest?" Iain asked.

Nancy counted silently to five; truly she loved him, if only he could be more as he was when they first met.

"No," said Nancy, "I want to do whatever you're all doing. It's not as though I'm decrepit."

"Sorry, I never meant…"

"Those boutiques you were telling me about, Jen, are they far from here?"

As soon as they were distracted, Nancy would slip away, buy a phone card and make a call to Yifan.

The telephone kiosks in the Bird's Nest were located in the foyers. The phone accepted her card, and she held her breath as she dialled. She had rehearsed this so many times, but when his voice came on the line, she momentarily forgot what to say.

"*Wǎnshànghǎo,*" said Yifan.

She took a deep breath and asked if he could speak English. "My name is Nancy Milne, I am from England. I have something important to talk to you about. Please, don't hang up."

There was a silence.

"What name?" he said. "You tell me again, more slow this time."

Nancy repeated her name. "Thank you, thank you for not hanging up. I'm phoning about May – I believe you knew her as Mai Ling? She perhaps mentioned my name to you before? I want to talk to you about..." She took a deep breath. "I believe you and her were together. Girlfriend and boyfriend? Her name was Mai Ling. Please, tell me if I'm wrong."

Was he still there?

"Yes."

"Sir, can you hear me?"

"I don't know you."

"But, but this is Dr Yifan Meng at God's Help Hospital?" She checked the address torn from her notebook.

"My time is low. Please, I ask you not to waste it."

Nancy sensed him about to put the phone down. "Wait," she said, "I have news that you need to hear, sad news. Whatever has passed between you and May, please, at least let me tell you the news. She talked fondly of you."

She heard a door click on the other end of the line. "What is this? Why are you calling me? It's been years…"

The time had come to tell him his fiancee hung by a thread, if indeed they were engaged.

"I have been to sit with her every day at the hospital, Dr Meng," said Nancy. "Before she slipped into her coma, she asked me to tell you…to tell you that she loved you and wanted me to meet you." Her lie hung in the silence that followed.

Two days later, Nancy was on the phone to Yifan again.

"I must apologise," he said, "Your phone call took me by surprise. I hope you can forgive my rudeness. You must understand, it came as a bad dream."

Nancy was alone in the hotel bedroom; Iain believed she was taking a nap on account of her migraine.

"I understand this must be difficult," she said.

"It is not a straightforward situation I find myself in, Mrs Milne."

"Pardon?"

"I cannot say, but since Mai Ling's departure, my life has taken a different path to the one I once hoped."

"Dr Meng, excuse my bluntness, but am I right in thinking you are engaged to be married to May?"

Yifan cleared his throat. "Your assumption is correct, but only in my heart, a long time ago. The current reality is somewhat different."

"But the way she talked about you…"

"Mai Ling said many things that were not true."

"But…"

"Mrs Milne, it is now time for you to answer some of my questions. I want to know more about you and how you come to know Mai Ling?"

Nancy propped herself up on the bed. The AC unit whirred noisily above the bedroom door. "I'm sorry," she said, "this is very confusing for me too. I know May because…"

He waited.

"May is the mother of my children. I adopted her girls from China sixteen years ago. We are here now, in Beijing, we've come to try and find out more. Since she fell into a coma so suddenly it has left us with many questions – you understand? The twins want to find out…"

"You're telling me she came to England?"

"Yes. Six years ago."

"Six years."

"Dr Meng we are flying to Nanchang soon. I want my girls to meet you and know where they come from. You're the only one who can help us. Please, if you have any affection left for May in your heart then say you'll meet with us."

"It's not possible."

"But she loved you and the twins."

"You don't know how hard it would be for me. What a compromising position you would be putting me in."

"An hour of your time, that's all I ask."

"It is impossible. I can't."

She sensed he wanted to meet the girls; that he wouldn't deny her.

"Very well, Mrs Milne," he said, suddenly decisive. "Meet me at the university; have you got a pen? It's the Mo Building on University Way. I have only one hour to give you and your family."

"*Xièxiè*, thank you so much."

"I wait at the university on Friday at three o' clock in the afternoon. If it rains I am in the foyer."

Yifan put the phone down before she had chance to thank him again. She'd done it. Her detective work had paid off. Nancy glanced again at the name of the building where Yifan said to meet.

What would he look like? Would the twins have his eyes, his nose, perhaps even some of his gestures – they say that's possible, don't they? Didn't her own sister, Lizzie, have that funny way of crossing and uncrossing her legs that she'd inherited from Aunt Valerie in Montreal who they saw maybe twice the whole time they were growing up?

Then it hit her, hard.

If Yifan was not her fiancé, as May claimed, there was a distinct possibility he might not be the twins' biological father. In trying to uncover the stones of the past, had she only succeeded in finding another lurking worm?

So she'd lived too. Ricki never saw that one coming. You never think your mum, especially a mumsy devoted mum like hers, would have an abortion. Maybe she thought she deserved not to have kids after getting rid of that baby? But finding out about Peter wasn't even in the same ball park as discovering May was her birth mother. That lie had cut right into the squidgy tissue of her heart.

Ricki propped her laptop up against her knees in bed. It was late, but she couldn't sleep and watched YouTube. She hit play for the third time; Liu Xiang limped hopelessly away from the track – he had been China's gold favourite. Ricki felt cold – this wasn't her country, her hero, her disappointment. She couldn't connect 'China' with 'home' or 'May' with 'mother'. Her imperfect mum, she realised, was the one she loved.

It was dusk when they arrived in Nanchang. The sky trembled in the still-strong heat of the day. They took a taxi from the airport, and the Bluewater Hotel was as her mum had described it – down to the plastic palm trees around the lobby. Ricki realised she was stepping into the story of her life: this, the hotel where the welfare institute staff had delivered her and Jen, these the rotating doors, the actual ones she'd passed through into her new life.

As a kid, Jen had asked the questions Ricki found impossible to ask: "Where did you find us, Mummy? What were we wearing? Did I have a teddy bear with me? Did Ricki have one too?" It was as though Ricki had a snowball in her throat that wouldn't melt, the ball only got harder and eventually she swallowed it – along with the pain of knowing she'd been abandoned.

Her mum's story: "You were sleeping in the fresh air, peacefully, in a very safe place and a kind lady picked you up and cuddled you and offered you some milk to make you grow strong. She found you a new mummy and daddy who would be able to cuddle you and look after you. The lady chose us very carefully because you were such special, important girls."

"And when you came for us," Jen would say, "what happened next?"

"We held you and you smiled and all the people in Nanchang said what beautiful girls you were; wherever we went people admired you. Then, after a few days, we flew high up into the clouds in a big aeroplane and when we came down you were in England which was your new home. Mummy had painted you a new bedroom and Daddy filled it with teddy bears."

Ricki wanted to ask why 'Tummy Mummy' left them if they were so special? She wanted to know why her skin didn't match the other kids? Why couldn't anyone tell her about the very beginning of her beginning?

She felt a tug on her sleeve and realised it was Jen, moving her towards the reception desk. Her touch was reassuring. They were in this together, the way it had always been.

The hotel receptionist was an efficient, slender kid. They took the glass elevator to the third floor, Room 111 – the room Nancy and Iain had stayed in during their adoption. Nancy said the room had fresh paint and new furnishings. Ricki bunked down with Jen next door. They ate dinner at nine (more rice) and Jen turned in for an early night, leaving Ricki restless.

The roof terrace consisted of a few potted maple trees, shrubs and trellises built into an arbour. Ricki's eyes were drawn to the red glow of a cigarette, its smell rich and woody in the humid night. She stepped towards the arbour, expecting to find another sleepless guest. Instead, the girl from reception sat alone, curled inside the seat.

"Sorry," said Ricki. "I didn't mean to disturb you."

The girl anxiously flicked down her cigarette to stub it out. "I leave you in peace," she said.

"Please," Ricki sat down next to her. "Don't go."

"The boss doesn't want us here. It's supposed to be for guests, but they never come here at night." She tucked her cigarette butt into her pocket and settled back into the arbour. "You stay a week?"

"Yeah, family holiday – kind of."

"Not somewhere families normally come unless they adopting – not much happens in Nanchang."

The girl had dimples, but on her they looked right.

"So…how long have you worked here?" Ricki said, avoiding the subject of her adoption.

"Long time," she said.

"You like it?"

The girl shrugged. "I'm getting some cash together. Couple of years, maybe I have enough for university. I really want to go to England and study Shakespeare."

"I wouldn't bother."

"Yes!"

"National heroes can be overrated," said Ricki.

"So, what are you doing here? One week – you are bored?"

"Family stuff."

The girl stared up at the amber, night sky then sighed. "I should go. I worked a long shift. I'm sleepy." She rubbed her eyes.

"Hey, listen," Ricki said. "Do you know where I can get a drink? Something stronger than green tea?"

The receptionist brought Snow beers from the hotel's cellar. She loosened up after her third bottle and revealed she worked at the hotel because her parents wouldn't pay for her education.

"They're filthy rich, made it big in property development," she laughed, "but I never get a yuan. Losing face is not good in China... they have their reputations. Having a daughter 'confused' like me spoils their image. They ignore the truth because they want me to settle down and get married. We don't see each other that much now. I make my own way. I've been promoted twice already. I find happiness on my terms."

The arbour felt snug, womb-like. Ricki nestled safely inside, mesmerised by the gorgeous creature sitting next to her and wished she could stay there all night.

When morning came, Ricki was sick from the Snow beers. Her mum insisted she saw a doctor and said she'd booked an appointment. They all had to go.

The doctor waited on the steps of a large domed building, watching for them. He ushered them inside quickly and without bowing. They followed him to his office.

"Mrs Milne, you wanted to see me and here I am. What it is you really want from me?"

Ricki looked up, puzzled. "I'm not feeling very good."

Dr. Meng looked at Nancy. "There really is little else I can tell you."

Iain reached into his trousers and opened his wallet. "It's alright, Doctor, we can pay you for medicine."

Nancy gestured for him to put it away.

"I fear I have already told you everything I know about Mai Ling."

"Mai Ling?" Iain frowned and glanced down at Yifan's name badge on his lapel. "Nancy, tell me this isn't... That he doesn't mean May? "

"Iain, I didn't want to tell you because I wasn't sure if he'd even be here."

"Mai as in *May*?" Jen asked.

"And you're Yifan?" blurted Iain.

Ricki looked to the doctor who looked at the floor, which gave nothing away and yet said everything. This guy, this white-coat, her mum seemed to be saying he knew May.

"I was doing it for the twins' sake and for mine. There are still things we need to know."

"This is too much, Nancy."

Yifan stood up, his voice calm. "Mr Milne, please don't raise your voice in my office. My colleagues are working next door. Your wife, I believe, had good intentions. It is my fault for agreeing to meet; it was against my better judgement. You are quite right, Mr Milne, this meeting is a mistake."

"What were you thinking, Mum?" Ricki said.

"Are you really Yifan?" Jen said.

"Yes."

"You do know she's...dying? Shit, Mum, you have told him, haven't you?" Ricki said.

"Yes, I know about the accident. Her chances are..."

"I can't believe you brought us here without telling us," interrupted Jen.

Yifan removed his glasses. Without them, he looked myopic, vulnerable. He walked steadily to the door and held it open.

"Wait, don't throw us out, you promised me you'd talk to us," said Nancy, "Please, Doctor, you must tell us what you know about May, anything at all. I can't bear any more lies or half-truths. My girls need to know about their biological mother."

Yifan replaced his glasses and gave a deep sigh. "We met on the train," he began, closing the door. "She was on her way to the city to work as an engineer; I was a student at the university. I was training to be a doctor. She happened to faint and I helped her, we chatted and things went from there."

"Where was she travelling from?" asked Nancy.

"She was Hunanese like me. A small village, in the countryside, I'm sorry I forget the name..."

"The village was called Xiashu Wang," Jen said. "She had a Little Brother who she missed all the time they were apart. Mum, I already know this stuff."

"That's right. She missed him in Nanchang but, forgive me, to my knowledge she never returned home."

"Why not?" asked Ricki.

Yifan bowed his head; Chinese for 'no more questions'.

"What about her job in Nanchang?" said Jen, desperate for facts.

He let slip a smile. "She was always busy, always rushing from one place to another. Your mother worked very hard," he turned to them, "she cared a lot about her work, she put in long hours at the factory. She wanted to be the best."

"The factory?" asked Ricki.

"Yes, she worked at Forwood, a car manufacturing plant, her job was to engineer their new 4x4, now sadly no more. The factory closed down some years ago. Of course, it was the fire which ruined everything. They couldn't possibly continue production after that. Mai Ling was lucky to survive. I was part of a team of doctors on the day of the fire. I helped drag her away from the blaze, others were sadly not so fortunate."

"She never mentioned any of this! She told me she was a civil engineer who worked on the new highway to Beijing," said Jen. "She told me teaching was something she did in her spare time to earn extra cash so that you and her could make a new life for yourselves in England."

He shook his head.

"How do we know you're telling us the truth? You could just be saying that to make yourself sound heroic," Ricki said.

"It's quite possible her memory was affected by smoke inhalation, I've seen that in a number of cases. But please, believe me when I say I have no reason to make these things up. If it wasn't for Mrs Milne's persistence I would not be here talking to you now."

There was a knock on the door of Yifan's office. A student poked his head around. Yifan dismissed him, and he bowed in a flurry of apologies.

"The School of Medicine does not look approvingly on unexpected foreign visitors," he said.

"It's very good of you to meet with us, Yifan, we're very grateful. I know we don't have long. Can you tell us where May lived in Nanchang?"

"No, I'm afraid she never told me. When we met, it was always in public places, the People's Park mainly, or some of the teahouses in the old quarter. I think she liked it when I took her there, she had a good appetite. I don't believe she ate properly most of the time, she was always so busy."

"So she never came to your place?" asked Ricki, confused.

"What you have to understand about May is that she was first and foremost dedicated to her work. It meant everything to her. Whenever we met, she was always watching the clock, eager to get back. She was very committed to the *principles* which governed the factory." His tone became more scathing. "Of course, that all came to an abrupt end."

"So what happened after the fire? Did she come to live with you or what?" said Ricki. "When did you do it? Us, I mean."

"I brought May to God's Help Hospital. She was in terrible pain; I found her wandering the streets, haemorrhaging. She was carrying you both and had just given birth. After several weeks of recuperation, she was dismissed from the hospital in accordance with our policy. We last saw each other the night before she was discharged."

"You mean she never called you or tried to meet up?" said Jen.

"Called me?" He seemed genuinely surprised. "If only that were the case, then perhaps I could have cared for her. She was a dear friend, I had the greatest of affection for her. But no, she never called me and I had no means of contacting her. She left the hospital without a word of goodbye. I never knew she had come to England. The call from your mother was a complete shock. It has been sixteen years..."

"Oh God," said Iain. "What a bloody shambles."

"So are you our dad or not?" said Ricki.

"No, no, on my life I am not your father," said Yifan. "May and I were only ever friends, nothing more, even though I once hoped that might be different... It came as a shock to find her with babies. I was unaware of her pregnancy."

"Do you have any idea who our dad might be?" Jen asked.

Yifan shook his head as if shaking away the memory. "I'm afraid I can't tell you what I don't know. I must go now, Mrs Milne, I'm already late for my rounds."

"But there's so much we still have to ask you."

"Nancy, that's enough. Let him go for goodness' sake. The poor man has said everything there is to say."

Ricki felt powerless as she watched Yifan gather up the papers into his satchel. She knew this was the best opportunity she'd ever have to ask about May, but instead she found herself walking out of Yifan's office, clutching onto her dad. Jen hung back, persistent and still digging for answers. Her brain, as big as it was, didn't seem to get the simplest of messages: Yifan = not Daddy.

Back at the hotel Ricki declared she was going out. Her parents stopped sulking with each other momentarily.

"I'm not sure that's wise," said her mum.

"You weren't feeling good this morning."

"Darling, listen to your father."

Jen offered to keep her company.

But Ricki said, "I'm fine, I just need to be alone."

"At least promise me you'll take your mobile and your inhaler? Here's some money in case you want to call a cab. Please be back in time for dinner or we'll start to worry."

She took the money, along with her Nikon and left the hotel without looking back.

It was a hot, airless evening. She kept to the main roads and walked until she could see the Tengwang Pavilion rise up like giant Lego. She forked right, heading for the People's Park where Yifan and May used to hang out. The panda enclosure was closed for the night so she found a bench and chewed the straw of her soda water. Her tattoo itched. Ricki clawed away her hoodie and stretched out on the bench, gazing at the cloudless sky. The park was peaceful – she could see why May liked meeting her geeky doctor buddy here. She didn't feel so stupid knowing May had duped everyone, even a clever guy like him.

So who was her real dad?

She closed her eyes. The sunshine made the insides of her eyelids white and blank – exactly what she wanted her mind to be. The noise of the birds and the skateboarders in a distant corner of the park started to slip away.

When she stirred, it was with a start. What was she doing? There was somewhere she needed to go, a picture she needed to take and, more importantly, a picture to leave behind. She raced across the park and didn't stop running until she reached Starbucks.

If she turned the corner, the building would be right there in front of her. But it was one thing looking on Google Maps, another to actually stand on the steps where she was abandoned. What was wrong with her? Why couldn't she go through with it? It was only a building. Maybe if she looked at the welfare institute through her camera lens it might be easier?

She pulled out the photograph of May at her sixteenth birthday party. It was taken a few minutes after May gave her the fifty quid, neatly wrapped inside the red envelope. Ricki stared hard at May's dimples.

She couldn't do it after all. Not on her own. She needed Jen there, side by side, the way twins should be. She tucked May in her pocket and headed back, taking the short route through the park and not stopping, not even to check out the skateboarders' moves.

White scar

The day of Schnelleck's visit and a bruise-yellow sky dragged over Forwood. Birds clung to the burnt-out mei trees in the courtyard. A heavy downpour seemed inevitable.

I skipped breakfast under the pretence of a sickness bug and waited for workers to trudge from our frigid dorm before changing into my suit. I sneaked out to hide behind a skip in the courtyard until my taxi's appointed time. While waiting, I watched the workers.

We'd all been cleaning up rubble and glass, sawing down the jagged remnants of phantom staircases and heaving mauled ironwork and concrete slabs over to the perimeter fence – always in the vain hope of finding a living hand or limb. Ren's body, among others, was never discovered. We were all listless and exhausted. Soot had turned the water in the sanitary room taps to sludge. We collected rainwater in the refuse bins and doused off the worst of the grime from our limp bodies at dusk. The state-allocated water that had arrived in a tractor taxi after the fire was in short supply.

Since Manager He's return, we had met many times to discuss Schnelleck's visit. His bureau, although standing, was cold, dark and blackened with soot. I think we made love twice, but it was of no comfort; sadness coiled like smoke through my veins.

I slipped from behind the skip while my co-workers stood idle at the canteen door. The guards received the bribe with relish, pawing over the money as if they couldn't believe their luck at finally being paid at all. If anyone had caught me, I didn't have a cover story, no fake errands were believable in a factory laid in ruins. I relied on the fact that workers were too disordered to notice my absence.

Manager He and I had agreed it was best to travel separately to avoid punishment, or rather, a worse punishment.

The hotel was in the old town, The Sweet Mandarin, overlooking the Tengwang Pavilion, one of Nanchang's most sacred and historic monuments, a place where ancient Buddhists came to worship and meditate on the beauty of their natural surroundings which, in those days, were mainly pine groves and the meandering river Gan. This is what Manager He told me by way of a brief history lesson, in case Schnelleck asked.

I wound down the taxi window and peered dolefully at the other pristine factories standing robust along the highway. A string of optimistic construction sites gave way to towering apartments and advertisements for a new health drink promising eternal love. In between, the cheap corner stores sold packets of noodles for workers to rehydrate after fourteen-hours of toiling on the line.

The driver took me half way up the sharp, narrow road to The Sweet Mandarin. I climbed the last stretch in my pink shoes. I made it to the courtyard as the rain clouds opened, and I hurried for shelter beneath a stone pilaster. A cool relieving breeze tickled my face. The rain bounced off the elegant flagstones and wrought-iron fencing. At the centre of the gardens stood a tree, ancient and stately – the so-called 'sweet mandarin'.

"For the tree, six hundred years it is growing," said a stilted Chinese accent.

I turned to see a westerner; a weedy man with sooty hair, thinning around his temples.

"Herr Schnelleck?" I had been expecting a blonde giant.

"*Ni Hao.*" He kowtowed unnecessarily to the ground, as though standing at the grave of an ancestor. His smile was strained. I wondered how he recognised me, so thin and dreary compared to Old Artist's portrait?

"Sir, there is no need," I said, embarrassed. "Are you alright?"

Schnelleck straightened, red-faced. "Xièxiè, a little stiff. I am delighted to meet you at last – The Star of Forwood. Tell me, how is your Manager? I trust he has recovered from his unfortunate spell in hospital."

"He has made an excellent recovery and will be joining us shortly."

A young waiter wearing a traditional *ch'ang-p'ao* shuffled forwards with a tea tray. We followed him inside the restaurant. My stomach gargled at the sight of soft dates on his tray.

"Do you mind?" I asked as we took a seat overlooking the courtyard.

"Be my guest," said Schnelleck.

I crammed a handful of dates into my mouth and sucked until their skin turned gluey.

He poured the tea carefully and dabbed his mouth with his serviette. What a strange smiled chiselled his face! Was he real? If I prodded him, would he fall and break like a terracotta warrior?

We sipped our tea in silence. Schnelleck smiled at the rain clouds, he smiled at the table, he smiled at the old couple eating dumplings next to us. Then to break his monotony of smiling, he pointed at the sky with a strange, violent hand gesture that seemed to mimic the rain. The old couple wearing traditional Zhongshan suits scowled. Did Schnelleck think we'd never seen rain in China?

The clumsy waiter didn't help matters; several times, he spilled hot water when replenishing our tea. Schnelleck wrung his serviette beneath the table.

"Are you having need to be eating?" he asked.

I stopped sucking on the dates and flicked the stones from the roof of my mouth into my hand. A gob of spittle landed on the tablecloth.

"It would be an honour to eat with you, Herr Schnelleck, but Manager He will be joining us any minute now. He's usually starving by midday, that's why he keeps candies in the desk – made in Europe, of course."

"Oh."

"Yes, but he's very professional. He wouldn't eat them in front of you. Should I request more tea?"

"Exactly. So far, I am an idiot," he chortled.

After many long and silent moments there was still no sign of Manager He. Schnelleck's smile was wearing me out. *The man sitting opposite you holds the key to your future, remember that Mai Ling from Hunan.* I steered the conversation onto work matters.

"At Forwood, we work very fast you know? The girls on my line can check a board in under a minute, sometimes faster if the screws – I mean, the managers – permit the radio."

Schnelleck set his tea cup down and leant forwards, neat as origami.

"The company song is very inspiring but it gets on our nerves after a few hours. The girls prefer love songs."

Once I started talking it was difficult to stop. "Mainly the time analysts don't inspire us to work harder; it's not like clipboards and stop clocks are the answer. It's the fear of losing our jobs – "

I had meant to say it took leadership, true vision of the kind Manager He possessed, for workers to exceed targets.

"And what happens when workers don't meet their targets?"

"That's what Chen and Ting are for; they hold admonition meetings every week."

"Admonition?"

I explained it was another word for punishment. Poor westerner, he could barely string together a sentence of Chinese. "Girls are fired for not sticking to the rules. Sometimes we're fined or food's withheld or our pay's delayed. But it's all for our own good – the good of the factory."

I poured him another cup of tea. "But Herr Schnelleck, there's so much more I can tell you about how productive we've been." I launched into a speech about the reward system.

"Excuse me, I want to know more about the punishments."

"Some of those lazy sheep deserve everything they get... If workers break the rules what do they expect? Manager He says that without rules Forwood would fall into chaos and we'd never impress any foreign –"

Schnelleck's smile weakened. I realised it wasn't a serviette he fiddled with beneath the table; he was writing in a notebook.

To distract him, I demonstrated how to use chopsticks.

"What an expert you are! So adept with your hands," he said as the chopsticks slipped noodle-like between his fingers. "No wonder they call you The Star of Forwood."

I felt my face redden. The only person ever to have drawn attention to my hands was Manager He.

"No need for shyness." He cleared his throat and straightened his tie.

I smiled meekly and offered him the dish of dates. "Ha, ha! Manager He will be here any minute, I can't imagine what's keeping him. We've been planning this for months. We even rehearsed."

Schnelleck placed his small, hairy hand on mine. I swiftly withdrew as though from a trap.

"Calm down, you look terrified. Besides, we have been talking all this time, and I still only know you as the Star of Forwood. May I ask, what is your real name?"

Outside, the rain crackled hard against the glass. I had a sudden vision of Mother making soup on the stove. What would she think if she could see me in a posh hotel having lunch with a foreigner? But then, I knew exactly what she'd say.

"Will you tell me or must I guess?" Schnelleck's voice brought me back.

"They call me Worker 2204."

"Please, you misunderstand my question."

I understood perfectly. My real name hid behind the wall; the past untouchable. "What name was given to you by your parents?"

Only here, outside the factory, could I begin to remember myself again. "Mai Ling," I murmured.

"Mai Ling... Mai Ling... Does it have any special meaning?"

"It means beautiful forest. There is a pine wood above our farm where the pine needles there are soft enough to sleep on... I remember them."

He nodded silently. "Do you ever see your family, Mai Ling?"

"Not since I started work. The girls at Forwood are my family now."

"That must be very hard, to have no relative you can call on for help?"

I don't know whether it was the rain, or maybe the mention of my family or, most likely, the absence of Manager He, but I started to feel intensely lonely sitting opposite Schnelleck. Tears welled in my eyes at the sudden memory of playing figurines with Little Brother.

"Mai Ling, dear girl." Schnelleck passed me his serviette.

"I'm very sorry, sir, I don't know what came over me."

What was it about this man, this 'big nose' that had got me so on edge? We should have been knocking his socks off with our productivity figures, instead I was snivelling like a baby. I needed to save the situation.

"I have an idea," he said, rising from the table. "Will you follow me?"

The air outside was fresh from the rain; we dashed across the courtyard and Schnelleck produced a set of keys from his suit pocket which he used to unlock a glass door. I wiped the rain from my face and stepped inside what turned out to be a giant greenhouse filled with large elephant-eared bushes.

"Wait a moment, then come and find me," said Schnelleck, disappearing down a path hemmed in by huge waxy plants.

The greenhouse smelt pleasant, very sweet and intense and I recognised it as orange blossom or, more precisely, sweet mandarin. It wafted over me, bringing to life a lost image of my grandmother picking cotton with an orange-scented flower in her hair. I must have been about seven at the time, back in the days when Grandmother was still six inches taller than me.

Gradually, I heard music. I followed the sound to a clearing in the centre where Schnelleck was already seated at a grand piano. His music was very good, the piece fluid – I had never heard anything quite like it. I rested on a rock beneath a hairy-leaf plant and thought again of Grandmother; of her blue jasmine bowls buried in the ground and the precious memories of her I hid, far down where the other girls wouldn't find them. Also memories of the way Little Brother tugged my hair as he fell to sleep sprawled across my *k'ang*; Father's happiness following a bumper rice crop and the rabbits he bought back from market. I remembered, too, the way the sky settled into a familiar painting every night over the top of our valley – as though it could only ever look one way. The soil in Hunan was red and when it dried up in summer, I spat it into a paste and dabbed it on my cheeks to look like Auntie, whose rouge-red complexion had seemed so sophisticated.

Schnelleck paused. "The piece is by Beethoven – a German composer. Do you know where Germany is?

"No."

"No matter... Beethoven is our finest composer; everyone who lives must hear his music at least once. He dedicated that piece to his pupil, a girl your age, with whom he was in love. It's known as *Mondscheinsonate*...how do you say...um, *Moonlight Sonata?*"

I wanted him to play on; this Beethoven was giving me permission to remember things I had not thought of in months. But Schnelleck said he preferred the doleful first movement to the livelier second.

I said, "Sadness is not what Manager He wanted; his desire was to make you happy, delighted even, by our hospitality."

Schnelleck reached into his suit and held out a black and white photograph of a woman, smiling as though caught off-guard. Her clothes were nothing special, a plain white T-shirt, the kind a migrant might wear. Her long hair was pinned back in a sloppy ponytail, her fringe brushed the top of her eyebrows, reminding me of Fei Fei's hair. The woman's large Western eyes creased around the corners in contentment. She was seated at a piano.

"Her name's Isla, she's my wife. I left her at home with our daughter, Gerda, who wanted to come. It wasn't possible. Gerda is... she is not well."

"Gerda's your only daughter?"

"Yes, our only child."

So maybe China wasn't the only country to say, *Popularize the first, control the second and exterminate the third...?*

Schnelleck seemed jaded now in the drab light. He clearly missed his wife as painfully as I missed my family and Ren. I should have tried harder to find her that night... She should never have died alone.

"Find who?" asked Schnelleck.

"A friend, Ren."

"You say she is missing?"

179

"It was her legs, they were no good. She didn't stand a chance. She couldn't run and even if she could, she had grown weak."

"She was in need of medical attention?"

"Partly because of the work but also because of Du. She missed her every day and every day part of her died..."

Schnelleck stared at the piano keys. "Please, go on."

"It's all so unfair. I found out she was learning to read and write. She wanted to leave Forwood and find a new job. At first, I was angry with her. I couldn't understand why anyone would want to leave – well, there were times, early on, when I longed to go home, but those feelings didn't last long and Manager He soon made me see sense. Ren was never happy. She carried her sadness like a dead baby, clinging onto it. She would say things like, 'Can't you see it's all a game, Mai Ling, that we're being used?' But Manager He cares a great deal about his workers, he wants to make things better. That's why he chose me. He knows together we'll make a better future."

"That's what he told you?" Schnelleck's voice cut through the air.

"Winning your business, Herr Schnelleck, will take Forwood into a new era."

"I see." He closed the piano lid.

We didn't intend to reveal this card so early, but things had taken a strange course – Beethoven had changed everything. I peered over the piano for signs of Manager He.

"And what exactly does your Manager think Europe can offer Forwood? Does he really believe that expansion will cure all the factory's problems? Money can't buy everything, Mai Ling. Things like equality and a fair society."

"He never said..."

"I'm sorry, I don't mean to upset you. Please, accept my apology. I brought you here to hear my music, to relax. From everything you say, Mai Ling, you have a great need for peace."

"I should go."

He looked at his watch. "Please, stay a little longer. There remains several hours until my next appointment. I am already so lonely in this city. I miss my family, Mai Ling – you understand how that feels?"

"As you wish."

We walked the gravel path around the greenhouse. Schnelleck asked me to read aloud the Chinese names of the plants on display.

He paused next to a dense cluster of crimson Ixora. "You have treated me like an emperor and I'm very grateful for your welcome, but there has to be more to my visit than extravagant hotels and personal tours of your city. I want to know about your life at Forwood, Mai Ling, not the things you are supposed to say, but how it really is to be a worker."

I bowed my head.

"What is there to hide, if everything Manager He writes in his letters is true?"

"How can I begin?"

"Tell me more about the people you work with."

"I've already told you about Ren."

"There must be others."

"I share a dorm with seven others. You soon find out who to avoid."

"The atmosphere is good or bad?"

"That depends."

"On what?"

I pursed my lips and pulled nervously on the sleeve of my blouse.

"On the hours?" he asked. "The food?"

I nodded.

"So the girls in your dorm don't like working at Forwood?"

"It's not really a question of liking it, Herr Schnelleck, we're there to work because we have to and because we want to live for ourselves; most of us came from the country. There aren't many jobs back home apart from looking after your husband and his family."

His wife no doubt filled her time with much more exciting pursuits than washing Schnelleck's socks. She could play the piano in her T-shirt whenever she wanted; her cares all light as rose petals. "For you, in Europe, there's no such thing as an arranged marriage?"

He paused, gave a laugh, and pointed to his shirt sleeves. "No, in my country a man must learn how to press his shirts using a travel iron!"

I was confused; did he mean the women were lazy?

"So you're from the country?" he said.

"Hunan province."

"Ah, Chairman Mao."

Hunan. Mao. They weren't words I felt as proud of as I was supposed to.

181

"Mai Ling, it strikes me you're neither happy at home in the country nor in the city."

"Happy?"

"Yes, *gāo xìng*. Is that the right word? I'm sorry my Chinese is below average, I'm learning it for business purposes."

"I'm very happy at Forwood, as are the other workers," I said, pulling myself together. "If I've given you any other impression, Herr Schnelleck, then I'm afraid it's not true. Forwood Motor Corporation is the best opportunity a young woman like me could have in life. I have a great future there. I believe my job is well-paid and the prospects are the best of any factory and…"

A porter stepped before us. "Herr Schnelleck?" He offered a note on a tray.

Schnelleck read quickly. "I should never have come. Isla told me my daughter's condition is worsening. Mai Ling, forgive me for dashing off like this." He clasped his bristly head. "Please, give my regards to your Manager. Thank him for his hospitality, but tell him that there will be no business deal."

"Pardon?"

"I can't grant Forwood our account."

"But…"

"It's been a pleasure to spend time with you. But I fear I may have been too easily impressed with the cost-savings your Manager highlighted in his many letters." He headed for the door.

"Wait! Don't go! You must not have analysed the figures correctly."

He hesitated. "Figures are not enough, your Manager will see that in time – maybe twenty years from now it will become clear. For now, he is a child learning to walk."

Manager He was no child. He was the most enterprising man I'd ever met.

"With respect, you don't know all our plans for Forwood. He's a good man and you're making a big mistake by leaving me here like this."

"Please, Mai Ling, don't be upset. My daughter needs me now."

I grabbed him by the arm. "How can you say that? Don't you know the effort we've gone to? At least talk to him, phone him now before you leave. I'm begging you to hear what he has to say about the future…"

"Let me make this clear to you, Mai Ling. From everything you've told me, I now realise that your Manager has no concept of how to run an effective business. You cannot cut corners with your staff and their safety – as was proved. Yes, I heard about the fire, it was in the local paper provided by the hotel. If I was considering investing in Forwood prior to this visit, then I am very sorry but that is no longer a correct option for me." Schnelleck's smile had vanished. "I wish you every good thing life has to offer, Mai Ling, but I must say goodbye."

I watched as he darted through the rain towards reception and knew that my future, my luck, went with him. And in that moment I hated Beethoven, almost as much as I hated Isla with her ponytail and Gerda, poorly in some distant land.

Hours later the rain still beat against the shutters of our dorm. It was time for our evening meal, everyone was in the canteen, but I lay alone in my bunk, staring at the wires on what used to be Ren's bed, wishing I was dead.

A scratching at the door interrupted my thoughts. At first I believed it was a rat, I had seen a few since the fire.

I opened the door to see Manager He. "Well, well," he said, "you're back early."

"Manager, what are you doing here? We're not meant to see each other in the dorm. We can't…"

"I've come especially to find you, my little star." His words were slurred. I could smell baijiu.

"You look unwell Manager; can I get you a drink of water?"

He shook his head, kicked a pair of work slippers out of his way and batted the overalls from around his head where they hung on the drying wires. "Not much space in here, is there?" he laughed, "Still, enough room for the *dagongmei*, eh, my little star."

I didn't like his tone of voice.

"So, how did you find him?"

"Herr Schnelleck?"

"The very same – was he good? Better than me? Was it large? That's what they say about foreign men: big nose, big –" he broke off to belch. "Aiya! Pardon the hog. Don't keep me in suspense, 2204, how long did it take before you and him got down to business?"

"We waited hours for you. What happened? Where were you? I've been so worried, I thought maybe the boss... Has there been an accident, you don't look yourself?"

He fell down on Damei's bunk and bounced, "How d'you sleep on this thing? And is that the breakfast pipe? I keep telling them to turn it off."

"Manager, I think you should go, the others will be back soon. We could get into trouble if they find you here."

He laughed cruelly, as though I'd told him the funniest story of his life.

"I might get into trouble? Since when were managers ruled by workers?" He scratched his belly. "Not learnt much since you arrived have you? Still thinking like you did back in the fields, up to your arse in mud? Anyway, you still haven't told me how it went with Schnelleck? I tried calling him but they said he checked out hours ago."

Why was he being so nasty all of a sudden when only yesterday he'd held me in his arms and we'd made love? I perched on my bed.

"Speak up, 2204, I can't hear you. Tell you what, I'll come and join you."

He lumbered out of Damei's bunk and pinned me down on the bed, his stinky breath all over my face.

"Now tell me, why would a man like Schnelleck decide to leave all of a sudden without even saying a proper goodbye, without calling to thank me?"

"There was an urgent family matter – his daughter was very sick."

"You expect me to believe that, 2204?"

"It's the truth," I squirmed, frightened. "He told me all about her."

"You weren't there to talk, 2204. Your job was to be the bait. Tell me, did you screw him like I taught you?"

"Manager, you don't know what you're saying. Please, get off me, the others will find you."

"Did you talk dirty like you did for me?"

I started to cry, but a sweaty hand clamped my mouth shut.

"A man doesn't travel halfway across the world to be disappointed, 2204. You said yourself he should be treated like an emperor. I hope you did a good job?"

"I never did any of those things – you're hurting me."

"What happened? Didn't he like the Chinese way? Wasn't he interested in your little breasts? It's not as though we didn't practise enough, was it? How many times did I screw you?" He shook me by the shoulders. "How many?"

I was crying too much to answer.

"Stupid, dirty peasant." He slapped me hard across the cheek, his ring slicing my skin. He wiped the blood on my pillow as

184

though it were poison. "And now what's happened to my chances, eh? You've ruined it all, you dumb bitch."

He held me down so I couldn't move, undid his zip and took down his trousers.

I counted the seconds until it was over. In my mind I counted the lighting strikes in the fields back home, the seconds between the klaxon on the conveyor belt, the wires on Ren's old bunk. I counted anything but the number of thrusts it took to hollow out my stomach.

Afterwards, I bunched my knees up and stared at the wall, terrified. He demanded a cigarette and dug one of the hidden Marlboros from beneath my mattress. I heard the click of his lighter and smoke filled the space inside my bunk; eventually there was a sudden give in the bed. The stub of his cigarette lay discarded on my sheet.

Even if I scrubbed myself raw with soap, his stain would never come out. A deeper wound throbbed urgently, multiplying, growing out of my control: one new cell dividing every second, too many for me to imagine, let alone count. Too fast to be monitored or recorded or checked by any time analyst.

I started at a movement coming from the doorway. I looked up to see the face of Fei Fei, pale and horrified, before she disappeared to shadow.

Letter to my baby

I worked the bare minimum, stole sugar from the canteen, avoided overtime and, returning to the dorm numb with exhaustion, fell into oblivion until the alarm woke me and I began again; an endless repetition of seconds which dragged into days. When Fatty asked me why I'd swapped my bunk for Damei's, I told her the new Bei *mei* farted in her sleep.

I think it was a Thursday when he returned, unshaven and wearing the same clothes he'd worn the night of the attack. He brushed past me down the line; the unmistakable odour of baijiu lingering in his wake. Bile rose in my mouth, but I swallowed it – as I had swallowed the secret of what he'd done to me.

Xiaofan grinned to see the end of my relationship with him; it was all a game to her. She had won. I was the star of nothing. Not one of my posters remained after the fire; if it did, I would have torn it to shreds, as Ren did that first morning.

He stayed in his bureau all weekend, until it developed a powerful, fermented stench that made several girls cover their noses with scarves as they worked. They nicknamed him the 'wilder beast'.

My time of the month came and went, with only a few brown freckles on my underwear. Mother never really explained to me the ins and outs of sex, but she did give me this warning: "never do anything stupid with a boy." If I did, "no life would be spared."

April began slowly and with yet more rain. The mei trees in the courtyard remained black and spindly.

I was skiving around there one day when I heard the familiar sound of a girl crying. There, crouching on her haunches behind the black stub of a mei tree, was Fei Fei, her face buried into her knees.

"Fei Fei, what's the matter?"

"Leave me alone," she said, "I want to be on my own."

"You can't stay there, it's going to rain."

"I don't care."

"What is it? What's happened?"

"I don't want your help."

"Alright, stay there, but you'll be drenched." I said angrily, wondering what she had to cry about?

"Everyone should leave me alone!" she screamed suddenly and bolted in the direction of her dorm, her lank hair slapping like a dead bird against her back.

I stared vacantly at the stub of the mei tree where she had squatted. There in the ash something had been crossed out. It was a heart and the word "Manager." It was so obvious! How could I have missed the signs? Even a dog's body like Fei Fei could have a crush on someone in charge.

A sharp twinge in my side made me double up. Another and I was limping to the dorm.

"Let me guess, Kwo's rice has given you shits again?" Fatty joked.

I collapsed onto Damei's bunk, clutching my belly. "Must have been that second helping…"

Fatty's face dropped as she watched me curl up in agony. "You'd better get to the nurse."

"No!"

"At least let me help you."

Fatty guided me to the sanitary room and I threw up. She splashed cold water on my face. The colour returned to my cheeks, but I was still shaking. A memory of his urgent breath thumped inside my ear, the pain as he had forced deeper into me. *Stupid, dirty peasant…dumb bitch…* What love speaks like that? What love leaves a scar? I nursed my cheek and the cherry-coloured scab shaped like a sickle, inflicted by Manager He's ring.

"Don't worry, Mai Ling, whatever it is I'll take care of you. Hunan *mei* stick together."

I leant over the sink as the nausea washed over me again. "Thanks, Fatty. I'll be better in a few days."

Missing a period was nothing unusual, I told myself; other girls at the factory went months without theirs and everything turned out alright. It was just hard work, bad food and worry that had caused my bleeding to stop.

But the date of my next period came and went, again without a trace of blood. The sickness intensified. At all times of day I ran to the sanitary room, heaving to rid myself of the thing implanted within. I told the others it was the shit we ate, or made up a story about my *qi* being weakened by the fire. Fatty offered to come with me to see the nurse. I could feel my belly start to thicken for the first time since working at Forwood. The baby would soon protrude beneath my overalls. Unwilling to face it alone, and frightened because I had no means to care for a baby, I set out for Manager He's bureau.

Empty bottles of baijiu and reams of papers lay strewn across the floor. The filing cabinets once so neatly ordered, were a jumble of loose sheets. In the middle of it all, he lay slumped over his desk, snoring. The place stank.

"Who's there? Mother, is that you?" he called without lifting his head.

I refused to pity him this time.

"What's going on?" His voice sounded hoarse, his head seemed rooted to the desk.

"It's me."

He groaned. "Turn off the light, 2204, my head's killing me."

I ignored him and opened the window overlooking circuitry.

Eventually he roused, his sweating face was the colour of congee. "I thought you'd come," he said.

We sat in silence, neither mentioning what he'd done to me.

"I suppose it's only right you should know," he muttered.

"Know what?"

"You're going to be transferred, 2204."

"Who says?"

He bowed his head. "It's come from above."

"Where are they sending me?"

"I don't know. They hardly tell me anything these days. I'm amazed they've not chucked me out. Look at me 2204. Not exactly a picture of success, am I?" He gave a sour laugh and reached for the bottle of baijiu. "There's no point arguing with them; they'll come for you one day next week. You'll be told what to do and instructed how to use the new machinery."

"So that's it? All over, just like that!"

He slugged at the bottle and wiped his chin against his sleeve.

"I can't go until I've told you…" There was a sharp twinge in my side, as though the baby wanted me to stay quiet. "I'm feeling sick all the time."

"Normal in a place like this."

"I've also missed two periods."

He rose and swayed over to the door, as though he was going to throw me out immediately. "What are you saying?"

I put a protective hand over my stomach. "I promise I'm telling the truth. I'm sure of it…a baby, I mean."

"And you expect me to believe that? After everything that's happened, I wouldn't even trust you to bring me liquor. First you

188

con me out of hundreds of yuan to buy yourself new clothes, then you get me to have sex with you – more than once – not to mention treat you like an empress. Now you say you're pregnant? I don't think so, 2204."

"I'm telling you first because I can't keep this a secret for much longer," I pointed to my belly. "I can hardly fasten my trousers. Listen to me, I'm pregnant with your child."

He shook his head. "If that's the case, how many weeks are you? Tell me. I want the exact date. Give me some proof it was me and not one of those adolescent grease monkeys in engineering."

I burned with shame and anger. "It's been two months exactly; it was the time you forced me to have sex in my dorm. Thursday 21st March."

His face fell and immediately he began searching the mounds of paper on his desk, rummaging through the drawers with increasing frustration.

"Manager?"

"I know I left it here somewhere, I can't find anything in this dump. I can't think straight!" he screeched. "No wonder I'm not performing, not achieving. Arse-licking Maoists every one of them… Ah, here it is."

He counted out a series of twenty yuan notes from his wallet. "This should cover it."

I looked at the grubby notes. "What are you saying?"

"Well, you didn't expect me to say 'keep it,' did you?"

"But I can't…"

"Oh yes you can, 2204, and you will. If you think I'm going to risk my reputation, you're mistaken. There's no way this can ever get out. Understood?"

He scribbled something on a scrap of paper and shoved it into my hand – he said it was the name of a place he knew that could do the 'work'.

I hurried down the steps into the gloom.

"Do it straight away," he called after me, "then come back and tell me it's finished."

The street was set back from the main shopping district. Never-white washing hung between buildings while the smell of onion and fried ginger wafted from an open window. "A chilli for every dish, a teardrop for good flavour," mother used to say, as she taught me to cook. Now my tears were all in vain.

Fortune Alley was longer than it first appeared and I walked for a good ten minutes to reach Building No. 136. The red paint on the front door was peeling, the lower windows were barred. The upper balconies, though dilapidated, harboured a couple of rusty bicycles, some chairs, several bags stuffed to the brim with clothing, a vacuum cleaner and a broken TV.

I rang the bell. The door buzzed and clicked open.

Inside, the apartment smelt like the waste disposal unit at Forwood. A ragged-looking cat hunched protectively over a chicken bone on the stairwell. A door was ajar and opera music drifted out.

The abortionist's room was piled high with bric-a-brac: books, chairs, a desk, vases, paintings, papers, an easel, radios, tins of bean sprouts, several rails of clothing, most of which looked too moth-eaten to wear. At the centre of it all, a woman sat still as a cobweb on her meditation mat, the radio playing by her side.

"If you're wondering what all the stuff is," she said, reaching out to turn down the music, "not all girls have the cash to pay me. Sometimes they nick things on the way here."

She unwrapped her legs and stood up in one fluid motion. Her eyes rested on my stomach. "But I have the feeling you're not one of those kind of girls. Thirteen weeks, and large. Of course, the placenta could be at the front? Or maybe…" Her arms fanned over my ripening belly like a book opening at an old favourite page. "Probably best not to dwell on it."

"How do you know how far gone I am?"

"Practise," she said and picked her way over the junk.

A slight breeze from the open balcony lifted my hair, but not my spirits. She told me to take a seat wherever I could find one.

"But don't make yourself comfortable, it's better if we get started straight away. What's he given you?"

I thought that was obvious, why else would I be standing in her junk-filled apartment? It took a moment for me to realise she was asking for payment. The yuan totalled exactly one hundred. I gave her seventy five and she folded it inside a tea caddy.

"A businessman, eh? What happened, did he have a wife?"

I shook my head.

"Do you need rice wine?"

I nodded.

She turned up the volume on the radio. "Just a precaution."

From a drawer, she took out several lengths of rubber tubing, an unlabelled bottle of liquid, a long sewing needle, some matches and soap. "It will hurt and you will bleed. You can have a bed here and an hour to recover, that should be long enough for the demons to leave the soul in peace. Once I start there's no going back, do you understand?"

My stomach twitched when I looked at the dirty mattress.

"No."

"You want me to say it again?"

"No. I don't want the demons to come after my soul. I don't think I can do this. In fact, I'm certain. Keep the money. I've got to go." I scrambled for the door.

"But –"

The air was hot and the sun shone directly onto the porch where I paused, blinded momentarily by its brilliance.

When I opened my eyes, some guys wearing white doctor coats were heading up the alley in my direction – one of them looked like Yifan. I reached for the buzzer and pretended to ring it. They stopped close by the porch and I could hear them talking.

"This street is typical of where we find a lot of the women in our gynaecological unit," said one.

"What percentage of patients are found here, compared to those who self-admit?"

"Around seventy. Quite often they're in too bad a condition to make it to the hospital alone. They have little or no funds for any proper medical attention. They might have suffered haemorrhaging, secondary infection, perhaps show early signs of pneumonia and occasionally pulmonary…"

I held my breath.

"What kind of conditions do they work under? Any anaesthetic?"

"Primitive, very primitive."

I glanced around. It was Yifan! And he was only a few feet away. *Please don't let him see me. Please don't let him see me…* I stared at the buzzer, as if waiting for an answer.

"Mai Ling? Is that you?"

I turned into the light. "Hello Yifan."

"I can't believe it! What are you doing here?"

"Research," I said, off the top of my head. "Work asked me to see what cars people are driving these days."

"Ah, testing the water, as we'd say?" He gave a nervous laugh.

"I'm only supposed to be gone an hour."

My heart ached. I wanted to tell him about Ren, about Xiaofan starting the fire, about losing Schnelleck's business deal and then the horrible thing Manager He had done to me. Most of all

I wanted to tell him about the life growing inside of me. I blinked back the tears and shielded my eyes.

"Are you alright? Pardon me for saying, but perhaps it's a little early for you to be back at work so soon after the fire... That cut on your cheek looks inflamed. You should be resting.Your managers promised they'd take good care of you all. I'd rather hoped you might be convalescing at home on the farm."

"I'm fine. I need to get back."

"Well be sure to drink plenty of water in this heat." Yifan hung back. "We're always in such a hurry, you and I. It would be wonderful to spend more time with you. I had so much fun that night on the ferris wheel. I've thought about you often. After the fire I feared maybe…"

I gave him a brief hug. "Thank you," I said. "For saving my life."

He reached into his attaché case for a pen and scribbled down his phone number for me a third time. "Please, please call me. My exams finish next Tuesday. Say you'll be there for lunch – meet me outside the medical library?"

"Dr Meng!" called another doctor. "Are you with us or not?"

"You'd better go."

Yifan kissed my cheek, near the cut. "Goodbye Mai Ling. I hope we'll speak again."

I trembled at his touch, so kind, so gentle. Even in my bunk that night I quivered at the lightness of it.

There was little hope of sleep. I tossed and turned in Damei's bunk, the springs dug into my sides where the baby flitted about like a netted butterfly. The girl in Ren's old bed had a habit of grinding her teeth as she slept and, for several hours, I listened to nothing but the eerie hum of the factory pipes and the irritating sound of her teeth. That was until I lost my temper, stood up and batted her with my pillow. She grumbled sleepily and turned over, but within minutes the grinding started up again.

I cracked open the shutters and peered through the slats at the bright lights that bleached the Nanchang sky. A row of illuminated factory windows meant workers were toiling into the night. It wasn't like in the countryside, where the stars made the blackness seem bigger and deeper. I'd left home for this.

Ren's notepad was still hidden under the loose floorboard by the door. I sat by the window where a little light seeped through the shutters, and felt the coolness of its pages. It smelled of the dies used in bonding, but there was also an earthy smell to the paper, like mud. Ren had grown up on the banks of the Yangtze. However far we travelled from home, some things always remained part of us. Her pen was heavy in my hand, burdensome. The page was striped with shadows where I began to write.

At first, I jotted whatever came into my head, random phrases or memories that became a torrent, flowing into paragraphs. Soon a letter formed on the page. A letter to my baby, to my dear child.

Who grows inside me as secret as a flower in the soil; who turns and moves and is stirring me up at night. A small grain of goodness in this bitter agony of life. I love you before you are even born.

I think of you all the time, from the start to the end of the day, and all during the night... I cannot sleep in my bed tonight... Thoughts of you burn like a fire over wild plains. When will I see your face? I see it already... I know your eyes and nose. I feel your tears inside the secret place. How much longer until these arms hold you?

The page was damp. I wiped the tears form my chin and tore it out, anxious it should be kept perfect. More perfect than the person writing it.

I shut my eyes and pictured my baby's face. It would look like me and not the evil bastard who had forced himself upon me. It would look like Mother, Father, Little Brother. I resolved not to let Manager He persuade me into going back to the abortionist. I kept his name out of the letter, as he would be kept out of the baby's life, at whatever cost.

You are my shadow... flesh not for cutting...essential as the beating of a heart...

They cannot take you from me. I will guard you with my life. No harm will ever reach you. Whatever they say, we'll never be parted – not even for a second. Ha! Listen to the way your mother talks before you are born.

I signed it 'Mama' and replaced Ren's pen and notepad beneath the floorboard, exhausted. I clenched and unclenched my fists, my hands numb. "Trust no-one," Ren once said and she was right. I tucked the page inside my overalls' pocket. I'd carry the letter to my baby with me wherever I went – safe, as I carried the child.

The next morning there was no breakfast alarm. Circuitry was deserted. The blinds were drawn and the door to his bureau locked. I banged several times and called out his name. No response, not even the sound of his snoring. I was about to call a final time when a hand clutched at my shoulder.

The clean-shaven man raised his sunglasses. Manager He gestured towards my stomach, his impeccable face unmoved. "Did you get rid of it?"

"Why haven't the food pipes come on? What's going on?"

A look of smug satisfaction crept over his face.

"Was it you who turned them off?"

"Maybe."

I pushed him on the shoulder and he faltered, gripping the handrail. He straightened his tie, composed his sunglasses. The old determined Manager was back.

"I suppose you'll only find out sooner or later... I'm the new Head of Production, 2204. The Chief Executive was a puppy dog in the end, he just rolled over."

I stepped back in disbelief.

"Most of you will probably walk out once you realise you aren't being fed. That gives Forwood a clean start. Remember how we talked of change, 2204, the bright future? News of Schnelleck's visit – even though no business was done – has been in my favour. The factory's practically mine now to do as I want." He rattled the bureau door to check it was locked, "Anyway, that's irrelevant now, especially for you."

"Sorry?"

"I said you were being transferred, but omitted the details."

"What details?"

"You're officially being transferred to the street. Understand? It's over. You're out."

"But – you can't do that."

"I'm firing you on the grounds of material damage. It's all there in the rulebook."

"Material damage?"

"Damage to the physicality and functionality of this factory."

"I didn't do a thing!"

"Trespassing, theft of factory property, deception, contaminating the water, spitting, absenteeism, intimate relations with a worker of the opposite sex...need I go on?"

"You can't sack me for being loyal to you, for doing everything you asked of me, for helping you achieve your dreams. Your bureau was a mess, the workers didn't respect you. They laughed behind your back! If it wasn't for me..."

He passed me a brown envelope. "Here, think of this as a leaving present, a bonus for all that rubbish sex. The thing is, 2004,

I had someone follow you. That's how I know you didn't go through with the abortion. In the end, you were just like your cousin. No doubt she's learnt how to fend for herself on the streets and so will you."

He inhaled. "But that's the past and I refuse to let this whole episode sour me. In fact, I want to thank you. You've taught me something very valuable. I am only young – a young manager has many things to learn on the road to success. You've taught me never to trust anyone ever again. This time, thanks to you, I'm going it alone."

He bowed mockingly as I clutched the brown envelope. My first reaction was to throw it after him, shout an insult. Then my baby jumped suddenly and I steadied myself.

On the envelope, he'd written two addresses. The first said *Madam Feng, Straight Street, Market District*. The second address provided the clinic of 'Doctor Quo', a place off Shongshan Road in the heart of the city – an area I knew well from my shopping trips.

The addresses burned my hand like a firecracker. Damn him, the envelope was too thick to throw away, but too thin to bring me security.

I kicked at his door, never wanting to see him again in my life. It was time to leave Forwood. Every important effect and belonging accumulated at the factory was already safe; buried in a secret place, like Grandmother's jasmine bowls.

So there it was: The Truth. Yifan wasn't the twins' father. He wasn't even May's fiancé.

"What were you thinking, putting the girls through that? What if he had been their father – were you just going to drop it on them?" shouted Iain. "Haven't we been through enough?"

Nancy snapped. "Don't preach about what's best for our girls. I know what it's like: growing up with a mother who rubbed herself out of the picture. Every day another part of you disappears. Okay, so you don't want to be here, but don't make me feel like I'm the mad woman who can't let go."

"That's ridiculous. Of course I want to be here – they're my children, I'm trying to help them. But you're being so…"

"So what?"

"You don't have the monopoly on pain, Nancy."

She spat out the last remaining wick of her fingernail. Her mom's gold locket felt tight around her neck. "I'm going out."

"Can I come?" he softened, knowing she would say no.

Nancy hurried into the settling dusk. At first, she drifted through the streets unsure of herself, a Western woman alone. She reached a large crossroads and turned right, hoping it would lead down to the river. Her pace quickened. By the time she reached the river banks she was out of breath and perspiring in the humid night air. The bridge stretched out in front of her, as she remembered, its footpath dotted with fishermen. Beneath it, others trawled their nets. She raced up the steps onto the bridge and walked some distance to a solitary place. They had walked the twins out here those first evenings, when they wouldn't settle.

Nancy gripped the wooden railings. The water was dark and intoxicatingly deep. In a few seconds, she could leave it all behind. Dare she? What would her mom say if she saw her daughter standing above this river black with silt?

A sudden memory surfaced, of her mom buying Neapolitan ice-cream from the drug store. But six months later she was dead, drowned; how bloody awful the turns a life can take, the pull of water inside a person, tugging in all directions. The old familiar feeling in Nancy's stomach returned, of waves breaking, rolling, breaking and consuming.

She removed her mom's necklace, stepped onto the railings and leaned over. Nancy felt light-headed, her sandals unsteady on the damp railings. It was time. Her grip slackened on the wet metal. She closed her eyes, unable to watch in case she bobbed back up to the surface and like a fool it didn't work. She could do this. She could let go.

Mom...

When she opened them again, the locket was nowhere in that wide, dark river. It was only Nancy, alone, leaning over the railings. A chill lifted from her. The lanterns bobbed and flickered in the water's gloom. The locket containing her mom's photo had vanished and in its place: water – water, fluid and weak. Water, overcoming fire. Water, the most transforming of all five elements: turning solitude, privacy, nervousness, insecurity, introspection, mystery to truth, honesty and maybe, just maybe, a dashing peace.

She waited until the fishermen had gathered in the last of their nets; then turned and walked purposefully back to The Bluewater Hotel, wanting only to hold her girls.

Queen

The shadows shortened and the glazy Nanchang sun drew out ever longer. For the last time, I glanced across the square where I'd once queued for a job. I had been so excited, rushing off to the factory bus with my fake high school certificate and big aspirations. Now there was nothing worth staying for.

I trudged the highway to the university. Fast-food restaurants and market stalls sold books, fruit and posters of Western singers with crazy ice-cream hair whipped into headbands. The students in white coats were my age, but lacked the stooped shoulders of a *dagongmei*. They sauntered along in twos and threes, talking a foreign language, *sphenopalatine ganglioneuralgia blah-di-blah...* There was no mention of the herbal remedies I'd grown up with: ginseng, dragon bone, bitter cardamom.

I sought out a bench opposite the medical library and watched as students filed by, laden with books. Eventually Yifan surfaced from the grey building.

"Mai Ling, I'm so glad to see you." He reached over to hug me, but I shrank back, mistrustful after Manager He.

"How did your exam go?" I asked as brightly as I could.

"The physiology questions were the ones I had practised; I guessed some answers on the endocrine system, types of intracellular vacuoles... No doubt engineering exams are equally hard to predict?"

"You're much cleverer than me."

Yifan blushed. "I still have a lot to learn."

I suggested we go for a burger. The baby was always hungry and I was forever daydreaming about my next meal. I ordered the biggest cheeseburger on the menu and ate so fast the ketchup smeared around my lips. I gulped my Coke and slurped on the crushed ice at the bottom of the cup. Several students had congregated inside the burger bar while debating facts from a textbook. They were the real stars of the future. They had the potential to be whoever they wanted to be, go wherever they wanted to go. They were in high spirits and eager to learn compared to the weary, resigned women of the factory. I feared the shoe assistant had been right all along; maybe I was just an uneducated peasant.

Yifan passed me his napkin. "You can have my fries, if you're still hungry. I'm not sure I can eat them all, so soon after the exam."

I stared at him, saddened by fate. Our paths had crossed, but could never be joined.

"Mai Ling? Are you alright?"

I wiped the ketchup from my lips. "I'm trying to imagine the future. I have a picture of you in my mind: a doctor, sitting by the bed of an old *wài pó*, caring for her the way you do."

Yifan found this amusing. "My family say I must use my education wisely; by that they mean a respectable, well-paid job in a state hospital. I'm not so sure."

I bit my tongue. A good wage wasn't to be sniffed at.

Yifan said he had an idea to work for a missionary hospital, "Where I can work independently to help those in need. But there are so few remaining."

"Anyone who's sick needs a doctor."

"Not everyone has the chance. The other day, when I bumped into you on Fortune Alley, you probably didn't realise, why should you? But that area is where young women, loose women, go."

I thumped my Coke cup onto the table and huffed, "Oh, really!"

"It's shocking," Yifan continued, "That's why I want to live a life helping others, not just myself. I don't like the way people our age have become so selfish. Many people in the city have no-one to turn to – people are nicknaming them the 'triple withouts'. You know the sort, Mai Ling, the villagers our age who come here looking for work and end up destitute because they have no home, no job and no income. I don't know how the future will fit together or how I'll find the right job. It's not easy going against your parents' wishes, is it? I can't imagine there are many girls like you who win an engineering scholarship and leave their family."

I bowed me head, ashamed.

"I didn't mean to offend you. Please, I've been too direct."

"Don't keep apologising, Yifan. You are a good man."

"You have every right to a successful job. I believe more kinswomen should be granted opportunities in life. It's not fair us men have been so long in charge. Forgive me. I would love for you to talk more about your work – the 4x4 sounds a superb vehicle, so practical! Do you know how many road traffic accidents there are in Nanchang? How many legs are amputated, how many head injuries? A safe vehicle is a worthy..." Yifan talked on but I couldn't bear to listen.

I had eaten too fast and was feeling queasy. I made up a story about a work meeting, saying I was already late. My hand went automatically to Manager He's brown envelope stuffed in my trouser pocket. It was still there.

"At least say we'll meet again. I really like you, Mai Ling. In fact, I don't think I could bear it if this was my last chance to..."

"We will, but I have to go now."

He beamed. "May I call by after work?"

"No! I mean, the Managers don't like unapproved visitors, you know how it is?"

He gave a resigned nod. "Meet me in the People's Park. I have a day off a month from today. I'll be waiting in the shade, beneath the willow trees."

I hoped a month was long enough for me to find my courage and tell him the truth.

"Yes, the shade is best, too much UV is bad for the skin, all manner of melanoma can..."

"Goodbye, Yifan," I kissed him on the check and stepped out into the midday heat, unsure of the direction to Straight Street.

Madam Feng opened the door cautiously, took one look at me and said, "Who the hell are you? And who sent you?"

She did not look like any Madam I had ever come across before. She wore men's trousers, her shirt sleeves rolled to the elbow. Her hair was slicked back from her square jaw and when she yawned, a side tooth glimmered like stolen treasure.

"I was with Manager He. He gave me your address."

"Speak up, kid. The hell, you're going to have to speak louder than that if you want to come in."

"I was with Manager He. He gave me your address."

"He-Chuan? I thought I'd heard the last of him, hell."

She extinguished her cigarette against the doorframe and disappeared inside. I followed her trail of smoke.

The apartment was dark and humid, becoming lighter towards the end of a narrow hallway. I could hear Madam Feng's laughter and followed the sound to where she sat at a dressing table strewn with make-up. Some machinery was hooked up to a pincer tool and she focused on jabbing the back of her left hand, the telephone receiver balanced under her square jaw.

"Hell, Solino, you think I can get away with that? Don't you remember the last time, at my place? I'm not joking, the guy's a maniac," she said.

I wandered over to the open balcony and perched on a blow-up chair.

"Don't sit there!" she yelled. "She's on my inflatable, Solino. Hell kid, get off that piece of art."

The neon sign of a bar flashed across the empty street, and I wished I was on the doorstep of our farm.

Madam Feng's voice was raspy from smoking. Her pincer tool buzzed continually as she talked. I craned to see what she was doing, there were no wires or circuit boards. The tool was being used to mark her skin. She winced as it jabbed the tiny bones in her hand. After each new incision, she wiped it with a cloth and dragged on her cigarette. Slowly the words 'Take a Chance' appeared in her raw pink flesh. A chance on her? On life? On love? I wondered how Manager He came to know a woman like this – there was so much I hadn't understood when I staked all my hopes on him.

She held up her hand for me to see. "What do you think, kid? You like my tattoo?"

"I've never seen one before."

She bandaged it with a pad then undressed, still holding the telephone. Her body was firm and contoured, with a blue serpent tattoo writhing down her back.

"Sorry, what did you say Sol? I'm getting ready for work here."

I came to understand they were work friends in the same night club. Their boss, Mr. J, owed Madam Feng money and she was hatching a plan to make sure he coughed up.

"Hang on, Solino... Listen, kid, go find the spare room, get some sleep you look like garbage... I know, I know, but she's new and I'm a sucker – you want to see the way she's staring at my ink. It's okay, kid, the needle won't bite, unless you want it to. Go dump your bag. Go on! I've got work tonight." She shooed me out of the lounge.

The spare room consisted of a mat on the floor, a bare light bulb, a rope hanging from the ceiling and a sink in the corner whose taps were furry with mould. The place could have been a cell in the public security bureau. Would Madam Feng make me write self-criticisms? Deny I was pregnant? Force me to have an abortion? Without a city resident permit to make me legal, it was

Madam Feng's place or the street. I hunkered down on the mat, cradling my stomach, and began to count out the money.

It must have been five or six o' clock the next morning when I was startled by the sound of someone breaking in. I awoke panting, asleep on the money I'd been counting.

Madam Feng was staring down at me. The bandage on her hand was gone and I could see the angry writing ringed in puffy, red flesh.

"You decided to stay? A good decision for someone in your situation."

My fists unclenched.

"You gotta be careful around this part of town," she said. "Don't carry so much cash. Be smart. Maybe we'll get you a tattoo to help you to fit in."

"I don't think so."

"Ah come on, kid, lighten up. Your face is too pretty to look so miserable. Whatever brought you here, forget it now. Trust me, you'll survive. But I have to sleep, I'm wrecked after last night. The clients thought 'Take a Chance' was an open invitation. Anyway, got to sleep."

My bedroom door clicked shut.

As Madam Feng slept, I rummaged in her cupboards and found dried egg noodles, some powdered spices and a jar of coffee. Her fridge contained a tin of half-eaten lychees that tasted off. I sat at her desk and held the tattoo needle, as if I was back on the line. It was actually made up of a group of small needles. The sudden memory of Zhi jabbing Fatty made me drop the equipment. Where was Cousin? I wondered, staring at my washed-out reflection in the mirror. Violet circles had appeared beneath my eyes, I dabbed them with Madam Feng's whitener and told myself to forget Zhi.

Over the days that followed, Madam Feng and I fell into our own separate routines. Her days were largely spent sleeping; occasionally I'd hear her singing in the bedroom. The albums kicking around on her bedroom floor were Western stuff – a black female singer with tightly-cropped curls, a man playing a trumpet as shiny as his soulful face. I wondered how she'd got hold of them, but I didn't ask questions and she didn't either, nor did she refer to Manager He. There seemed to be only one rule at Madam Feng's place: no drugs. If she caught me with opium I'd be out on my ear, she said.

Every day, she spent exactly one hour in the bathroom before leaving for work. She wore sequin-studded gowns and covered herself up in a long grey trench coat on her way out. The gowns hugged her muscular body in a way Mother would call scandalous. She was a very powerful woman dressed like that. She stayed out all night, almost every night, and her key turned in the lock at six every morning, as predictable as the breakfast alarm. She never answered personal questions, though, and would leave the room if I asked about her work, "Hell, kid, since when did you become one of them?" I knew she meant The Party.

During the day, I emptied bins, mopped floors and cleaned windows so she had no reason to get rid of me. The work was child's play, I couldn't believe my luck. It ceased to matter how she knew Manager He, she gave me free digs and didn't care I was living illegally in Nanchang.

Occasionally, I left the apartment to buy cheap melons from a stall on the corner. My baby had started to crave anything juicy and refreshing. Going out was well worth the swollen ankles and terrible fatigue. It gave me space to think, sometimes to plan – but never to dream – dreaming was for naïve little girls who didn't know any better.

I had agreed to meet Yifan on a Saturday and got up early to wash my hair. The water was cold, but that didn't matter. At least, I didn't have to share the sink with a dozen others. Away from the factory, my hair started to regain its sheen and my nails grew longer and strong.

I found Yifan pacing the shaded footpath near the panda enclosure in the People's Park. He wore a pair of smart, khaki trousers and a brilliantly white, crisp shirt which dazzled in the sun. His head was bowed and he seemed to be talking to himself. I approached via the side gate and crept up on him through the willow trees, nervous in case Manager He's spy was still tracking me.

Yifan was singing off-key. It jarred compared to Madam Feng's perfect voice. He turned round embarrassed.

"Awful isn't it?" he said, "I only sing when no-one's listening. Stretching the bronchial tract is a great form of relaxation. You should try it."

I smiled. "I don't think the Beijing Opera will be calling you any time soon."

He asked if I'd eaten. There was a stall selling his favourite steamed pork with rice flour dumplings on his way into the park. We bought some and ate on a nearby bench; two tame ducks waddled around our feet.

"How does it feel to be free?" I asked. "I mean, without revision."

He tossed his last scraps of pork to the ducks. "Actually, I've been playing a lot of chess. The guy I share an apartment with likes to think he's better than me. So far I've beaten him ten games to one – though he put me at an unfair disadvantage by playing rock music throughout our game."

"You got any other hidden talents?" I asked jovially.

Yifan slid off the bench and sat crossed-legged on the grass. He pulled his feet up behind his neck and grinned. "I can do this!"

"Ay! That looks painful!"

"Not if you're flexible in the gluteus maximus."

He jumped across the grass on his backside, his legs wrapped around his neck like an acrobat from the state circus.

"I'm the only one in our meditation group who can sit cross-legged for four hours without even stretching. Did you know, Mai Ling, the femur is the longest bone in the human body, but your intestines are ten times longer than you?"

"That's a lot of guts."

He gave a shy belch and unhooked his legs from around his neck.

I suggested we take a walk now that the sun was less intense. It pleased me to stroll along the winding footpaths, and we crossed a bridge leading to a highly scented area of the park. The pineapple trees were ladened with ripe fruit and the borders crammed with exotic-looking plants. Yifan told me some of their names and we chatted about our families, the villages we'd left behind in Hunan and the characters we'd grown up with – we had a lot in common, although being an only boy, he'd known privileges I could only dream of, such as his education. He described his school and Teacher Herzu who sparked his interest in biology.

"She encouraged me in every way possible and would let me spend time in her laboratory during lunch hour and also after class – that's when I started to learn how amazing the human body is."

I glanced sideways, feeling a mixture of curiosity and something else.

"My parents say I'm more inquisitive than a honey bee."

I broke a palm spear from an overhanging pineapple tree and threw it over the bridge into the little stream. Yifan did the same and we rushed to the other side to see whose spear came through first. I wished Little Brother was with us at that moment.

"Mai Ling," said Yifan, gazing into the stream. "I'm sorry if I bore you. I feel so free to talk that sometimes I lose track of time."

"You don't have to say sorry," I said. In fact, I wished he would stop apologising all the time. "I'm the one who should apologise to you."

His gentle eyes looked steadily into mine. For a split second I thought I'd tell him everything, the whole story from start to finish. "There's a lot I haven't told you," I began, but trailed off.

His hand fell lightly on my shoulder. "Tell me then, I promise to listen."

He was so kind and earnest; he may even have agreed to see me again. But Yifan deserved better than a reject. I leant over and kissed him on the cheek. "Maybe I will, one day," I said. "But for now let's walk."

Our meetings continued along this vein for several more weeks over the summer. The baby grew heavy in my abdomen and I disguised the bump with loose-fitting shirts stolen from a neighbour's washing line.

Yifan decided to stay in the city rather than return home to Hunan. He wanted to improve his chess game. By mid-August, he'd been spotted by a local scout from the State Federation of Master Chess Players who asked him to represent the province at a national competition. The tournament took him away from Nanchang for a week while he travelled the long train journey up to Beijing. He returned dejected, having reached the finals and lost out to another student his age from Guangzhou.

We met up shortly after he returned and took our usual stroll around the park, followed by tea in one of the rooms overlooking the panda enclosure, popular with tourists, especially Americans – who were around every corner in those days. I always did a double take whenever I saw a couple of big noses with a Chinese baby girl in the park.

Yifan filled me in on the chess competition. The winner, Ban Ji, hadn't spoken to anyone throughout the whole tournament, not even a polite hello.

"He never ate or drank. Some say he didn't even go to the bathroom. When he wasn't playing, he watched the other contestants – he was very intimidating."

As the sun crept over our table, Yifan put a hand out and covered mine.

"Close your eyes," he said. "I've bought you something."

The gift was small and wooden inside my palm.

"She's my winning queen," he said proudly. "I played with her all the way through to the finals. She brought me luck."

I turned the chess piece over and found a double happiness couplet carved into the base.

"You do know the story of double happiness, don't you?"

I nodded, blushing at the mention of my favourite love story.

"When I was a young boy, I dreamt of being the student in that story. I think to find someone who you can love from the heart, someone to share life's journey, is the greatest gift of all."

I thanked him with a kiss on the cheek. "It's lovely."

He reddened. "It's not much. I am glad you like it. I was desperate to find something personal, something you could keep. There are so many shops selling so many things in Beijing. I searched a whole day and found nothing; it was only when I returned to my room I realised the most obvious gift was there all along, sitting on her square on my chessboard."

"You looked all day, for me?"

"You say I'm clever, but I am actually very slow. I didn't appreciate what mattered most was right in front of me – as you are now."

The chess piece felt smooth in my hand. I wished holding Yifan could be so easy. "We should walk some more; it's cooler now."

We stepped outside and walked a little way along the garden path, but soon he stopped and turned to face me.

"Mai Ling, you make me so happy. I love being in your company. When we're together, everything's right and when we're apart I can hardly think of anything except when we'll next see each other."

The baby rolled in my secret place.

"Speak to me, Mai Ling, put me out of my misery." He reached for my hand. "Tell me you feel the same way? Tell me this is more than just friendship and pleasant walks through the park?"

He stepped closer, until I could smell his aftershave. Or was it the roses in the tearoom garden? He pressed against the baby. How much longer could I lie to kind, gentle Yifan? He would make someone a good husband, but it would never be me.

I bowed my head and let my hand fall away from his.

"I've made an error of judgement, a very grave one…" he said.

"Yifan –"

He stepped back, his eyes brimming with tears. "I must go."

I watched the back of his crisp white shirt disappear up the garden path and out into the park. "I'm sorry," I whispered, but it was too late.

I was so miserable that I didn't go back to Madam Feng's place for two whole days and nights. Instead I slept rough in the People's Park in the hope Yifan might come back and find me there, waiting for him. I agonised over my decision not to embroil him in my messy life, and my heart ached for him. I desperately wanted somebody to take care of me and love me kindly. I cried so bitterly my baby must have felt my grief.

Madam Feng didn't ask where I'd been or why, but she was surprised when I demanded a favour from her.

"Why the change of heart?" she said.

I sat at her desk and held out her tattoo machinery. "No questions, right? You just do it. I need this."

She pulled up a chair beside me and took a pen out of the drawer.

"I want you to tattoo double happiness on me. Right here, inside my wrist. Here, here, you see. This place. Here. Where I can feel the blood. Pumping. Here. It's beating. My heart. You know? It does. Here. It doesn't. Stop. But…"

"Sshh, kid. Sshh, you'll upset the baby. Don't lose your breath."

The needles punctured me. The double happiness symbol stood proud. My skin was rubbed and raw. The tattoo she gave me was no pain at all.

The bigger I grew, the harder it was to sleep on my mat and so I moved to the settee. There, I made up for lost time: all the nights in the factory spent doing overtime, working until dawn for Manager He. Sleep like a coma. I never heard Madam Feng come in from work and could sleep through any amount of noise in the street below. Until one morning, the loud bang of a gun jolted me awake.

A man's hand was grappling to unlock the chain on our front door. His fingers poked around the jamb, feeling for the bolt. "You've gone too far this time, bitch. Open up," he shouted.

Instinctively, I rushed to hold back the intruder, but the door broke and swung open. The guy was in his thirties and wore a bomber jacket. "Who the fuck are you?" he barked and grabbed me by the hair.

"Please don't hurt me."

"Where is she?"

"I don't know, I swear."

He let go and barged around the apartment, into all the bedrooms. I could hear doors being flung open, first Madam Feng's and then mine. It sounded like he was trashing the place. I was so scared I didn't dare grab her tattooing needles.

"I want you to tell her I'll be back. She's not going to get away with her tricks, you understand?"

I nodded, shaking.

The door slammed. I waited to hear the sound of his boots on the staircase, before creeping over to the balcony. He skulked off in the direction of the melon stall, his outward appearance no different to any other guy in that part of town.

The next morning, Madam Feng arrived home later than usual. I jumped when the door creaked open.

"Shit, kid, the guy's a psychopath."

She rushed to the balcony and drew the curtains, then called her workmate Solino. "Get out now, Sol. You've got to leave Nanchang before he comes for you too."

Despite the hour, she poured us both liquor. I cradled it to my cheek.

After a while, she checked each of the rooms for damage, but I had already cleared the worst of the mess, apart from her sequinned dresses, I couldn't salvage them at all.

I disappeared to my room and hunched on the mat, looking up at the loose rope hanging from the ceiling. For a moment, I wondered if a noose might be the easy way out. Then the baby kicked me unexpectedly between my ribs and I came to my senses. *Never let you go.*

For weeks, I fretted over Mr J's return. I was nearly eight months and knew I couldn't live there forever. Madam Feng wouldn't tolerate a crying baby during the day. I had to be wise.

It was a wet, late-autumn afternoon when things came to a head. Madam Feng had woken up badly and rushed into my bedroom. She stared through me, her skin marbled with sweat.

She shook me by the shoulders. "Where is he? I heard him in the kitchen, where's he gone?"

From her breath, I could tell she had been drinking more of the hard stuff. "Is the door locked?" She ran into the lounge and called out to me. "I don't understand, I heard him, he was here. I was sure I heard him…"

"Take it steady," I said, directing her onto the settee.

Her eyes were unusually wide – had she taken too many of the pink tablets? I wondered.

"I know it's none of my business, but I want you to know that I understand – how a man can force himself."

"You don't know anything," she said.

"It happened to me too…with Manager He."

"Don't you get it?" she screamed. "I don't want you prying into my business. So keep the hell out of my life and stop asking so many questions. And if you can't cope with that, then just go back to wherever it is you came from."

"I don't want to leave you."

"This isn't a place for a kid like you, or your baby, you hear?"

I don't think she meant to say it so directly, but once the words left her mouth there was nothing I could do but to gather up my belongings. I stuffed Manager He's money inside my bra as quickly as I could.

Madam Feng stood in the doorway, blocking my exit. Her voice was flat. "Where will you go?"

I shrugged. *Just me and baby from now on.*

"Wait." She disappeared into the kitchen, coming back with a handful of yuan. "At least take this."

It was money she kept hidden in a pot at the back of the cupboard. I took it but didn't hug her.

In Straight Street, thick smog mingled with rain. Live music rose from one of the bars, *Lady Plays the Blues*. The usual crowd spilled out onto the pavement.

Half way down the street, I glanced back to see if Madam Feng was looking out for me. Sure enough, she was leaning over her balcony, waving in my direction. But there was something strange about the way she flung her arms that made me pause and do a double take. As I stared, unsure of whether to go back and say goodbye properly, someone barged past, knocking me sideways. I put a hand out and managed to steady myself.

"Watch it, mister," I called.

The black fabric of his bomber jacket was heading straight for Madam Feng's.

"Look!" shouted one of the young guys at the bar. "The woman up there's going to jump!"

The crowd blurred and a sudden pain in my haunches stapled me to the street. There were shouts from the bar; a shrill cry from the balcony.

"She's jumped!"

"The woman's jumped."

"She's killed herself."

"Mind the body!"

Whose body? What body?

A sudden flow of water issued from me. The melon seller dropped his crate. Rain grizzled down. Melons, fat and round and ready to burst, rolled into the gutter. People scrambled to see what was happening. The melon seller started to run.

"Call the police."

"It's too late for a doctor!"

Water everywhere.

This is it, baby, hold on tight.

There in the road, where the crowd now gathered, was a twisted body and a head smashed against a crimson pool of blood. One leg straight as a stork's, another tucked beneath her chest, exactly as she slept. Her arm not where an arm should naturally be, angled behind her neck.

I couldn't run. The baby wouldn't wait. There in the street, baby tells me it can't hold on.

"We should call the ambulance!"

"Look at her!"

I dug Manager He's envelope from my bra and looked again at the name and address of the doctor he had given me.

Doctor Quo, you'd better be ready.

All was unexpected. All premature, like a downpour blighting summer.

Yifan was their only footnote to the past. There had to be another meeting, thought Jen as she texted him three, four even five times. Eventually he acquiesced and agreed to meet them at the Suseng Teahouse off Middle Road in the old town. It was a dark, traditional building smelling of jasmine and half full of ageing men playing mahjong. Yifan arrived late, delayed by his rounds at the hospital.

"I'm so sorry about last time, rushing you out of my bureau. It was such a shock for me." His eyes were earnest behind his thick-rimmed glasses.

"You're not kidding," said Ricki.

"I never imagined I'd see you again after all these years. I can hardly take it all in."

"We appreciate you meeting with us," said Jen. "It's a great comfort to know a piece of the puzzle exists."

"A puzzle indeed," said Yifan.

Ricki fiddled with the strap on her Nikon.

"I see you like photography, Ricki. My son has – what's the word? An *exhibit* with the School of Art. Perhaps while you are in Nanchang you would like to see his work?"

Jen glanced at Yifan's wedding ring – sign of his life after May.

"He's working on it today; he would be pleased to explain his material to you."

"Sure," Ricki said.

A waiter, wearing a gown and traditional cap, bowed and poured the tea. Yifan tapped his finger against the cup to thank him.

"Your mother and I met here once. You see that table?" He signalled towards the window where two men sat in companionable silence, smoking.

"I know this story," said Jen, reaching into her rucksack for the book of traditional tales. "You were sitting by the window. You gave May this."

Yifan blanched.

"She held onto your book all these years, Yifan. Look, here's the inscription from your grandparents."

His hand brushed the cover, as though brushing away the dust that settles on memory, and he leafed silently through its pages.

"Why did you give her a book?" asked Ricki. "Maybe if you'd given her something more romantic you could have been our dad."

"Ricki!"

"Perhaps you're sister's right, perhaps not. I suspect, however, that Mai Ling's heart already belonged to someone else and I was a poor suitor in comparison. In my country, we have a saying: 'a broken heart has never been cured by medicine'. You know, our nation is very wise if we would listen to our ancestors."

"May taught me some of these stories during our lessons," said Jen. "She said I would never understand China unless I looked to the past. That all seems so ironic now."

Yifan closed the book. "I'm afraid Mai was never so interested in the past when I knew her. Perhaps when she left China, she could finally value our country, even with its flaws. Although, forgive me, England is also to be admired: Shakespeare, the Queen…"

May had once compared England and its language to a postage stamp – small but necessary to communicate with the rest of the world, Jen remembered.

Ricki cradled her tea cup. "So what was she like when you knew her?"

"Very beautiful, to me at least. A real sense of adventure; she was a survivor – *plucky* I think you say in English? She lived to work and was so stubborn, dogged at times," he smiled fleetingly, forgiving now of her faults.

Ricki stiffened in self-recognition. "Did you love her?" she said.

Yifan glanced towards the door. "In truth, I would have loved her all my life if she had agreed to be my wife. She was all I could think about for years after we parted. Sometimes, even now, I wake up next to my wife and believe, for the briefest of moments, that it is Mai Ling beside me. I can't tell you what it means to see you both sitting here – you look so like her, especially you Ricki. It is as though, when I came into the teahouse, it was her back turned to me, her shoulders stooped over the table, and then when I saw your face in the light..." He removed his glasses and wiped his eyes. "My wife makes me happy; she would be devastated to hear me talk this way. She doesn't even know I am here. I hate to deceive her."

"Perhaps if May had married you, we might never have been abandoned – perhaps you would have taken care of her?" said Jen. "And us?"

"Of course I would have loved you as I do my son." He shook his head. "But that was never meant to be, Jen. Life cannot be relived. It is a bitter truth I am telling you because I don't want you to live as I have done, regretting everything that has gone before. We must accept May's choices. As for what happened, I've told you everything I know. After leaving God's Help, I never saw her again."

Ricki set her cup down. "I think May didn't make choices, so much as mistakes."

"No, Yifan's right," Jen said, "May chose her own destiny. She knew exactly what she was doing when she left us behind and when she came to find us. We can't pity her for that."

"But you're a doctor," said Ricki, "you must see all sorts of women – women like May who can't cope. How can you say abandoning your child is a choice?"

"What do you want from me?" He pleaded in a whisper.

The men in the window sat motionless, pinned in time like subjects inside a painting. The muted patter of rain sounded above the noise of the radio. Yifan checked his watch and slid the book inside his attaché case. Jen sensed he had not told them everything.

"Are you going so soon?" she asked.

"I'm afraid so, my first lecture is at ten."

"What about your son's exhibition?"

"I can walk that way with you a little. He will explain it far better than me, I'm afraid my brain is scientific in nature and I admit to not knowing a great deal about the way artists think. My son and I are very different; he is the new generation." Yifan put on his rain coat and plumped the cushion where he had been sitting. He paid and left a customary half cup of tea.

The exhibition was housed in an unassuming building in a run-down part of Nanchang, not far from the old town. Yifan called up a narrow, badly lit staircase. A tall, handsome figure appeared, his hair shaved. Yifan introduced him to Jen and Ricki.

"Son, these two young ladies have come all the way from England. They wish to see your exhibition. I told them you would be happy to show them around. They are special visitors, Guan, I want you to take good care of them."

He gave a small bow. "Hi there," he said in impeccable English.

213

"Son, you look very pale, have you been working through the night again? I've warned you not to, stress plays havoc with the immune system."

"*Dad.*"

Yifan brushed the rain from his overcoat. In the half-light, his forehead looked more furrowed; Jen noticed his black hair was flecked through with white. He cradled his attaché case close to his chest as though reticent to leave. She went over and hugged him tightly, breaking the unwritten rules of formality.

"I'll remember you," Jen whispered, "the way May remembered you."

She could feel Yifan trembling beneath his raincoat. He broke away and held a hand out to Ricki. "I'm very glad you came, Ricki."

"Thanks," she said. "It has helped seeing you again."

"I'm sorry to rush, but I must go if I don't want to lose my job."

"Go!" shouted Guan. "Before the dean sends out his search party."

They followed Guan upstairs to the exhibition and sat down on a battered velvet settee next to a coffee machine, the weight of unresolved questions bearing down on them.

"So you're English… What brings you to Nanchang?" he asked. "You look young to be travelling alone."

"We're here with our parents. They're back at the hotel," said Jen.

"The hotel where we were born," Ricki added.

Guan gave a puzzled expression.

"We're adopted," said Ricki. "It's a long story."

"We've come here to find out more about our birth mum."

"Ah, so that's how you know Dad?"

Ricki shot Guan a questioning glance. "What do you mean?"

"He can be so modest at times; people don't know what an amazing job he does, with young women especially. Do you guys drink coffee? I imagine you're pretty fed up of all the tea we drink here."

"Caffeine would be good. It's been a nightmare so far," said Ricki, her eyes darting all over the random collection of junk around her.

"Interesting, isn't it?" said Guan. "I've called it *Go.*"

"This is your exhibition? All this?" said Jen.

"I wanted it to feel like you're entering someone's house. This place used to belong to a prostitute who committed suicide.

Straight off the balcony in broad daylight. A real tragedy. No-one came forwards to claim her stuff and over the last sixteen years or so her apartment sat empty until I was able to rent it. The State doesn't know I'm using it for an exhibition – not yet, anyway. Although word will spread pretty fast once it gets online."

Guan rummaged through a cardboard box and pulled out a photograph. "Here she is – Madam Feng."

"A drag queen?" Ricki asked.

"I don't think so. She worked in a karaoke bar not far from here; her regulars were mainly local businessmen. She kept their business cards – I tried phoning one; he was a senior guy, Head of Production in the car industry, but the number didn't exist after all these years. I gave up trying to trace him or the others."

Guan put the photograph in the bottom of a chest of drawers to make it look as if it had been carelessly shoved away.

"So why do you call it *Go*?" asked Ricki.

"We all have our comings and goings – the shift of life and death; it washes up personal stuff. It would have eventually been thrown in a dumpster if I hadn't salvaged it, gone forever. No family you see, the woman never had any children, no-one to inherit her belongings. I'm interested in the way objects outlive people. Freaks me out, to be honest."

"Why?" said Ricki. "That's what happens. People die all the time."

"We all like to think we're immortal, especially artists."

"Art makes you immortal," said Ricki.

"Yeah, but what if you're not an artist? What if you're just a normal, everyday person? Or a woman like Madam Feng who everyone wanted, lusted over, but no-one loved or properly knew? Your stuff is what's left of you. It can't sum you up, or tell the truth. It doesn't reveal your inner life, the parts we keep hidden, even from ourselves. But objects tell stories and can become art – even if the State forbids it." He gave a dry laugh.

Listening to Guan, Jen was reminded of the chess piece in her pocket. May's Queen. She had intended to give it to Yifan.

"Guan, do you think you could give this to your dad for me?"

He looked at it carefully, turning it over in his hand. "That's funny, Dad has a set just like it. The double happiness symbol is carved into the base, right? It's his lucky set."

She nodded. "I figured it might belong to him. Tell him it was tucked inside her pillow will you, he'll know who I'm talking about."

215

"A pillow? I love a good mystery. I won't ask who it belonged to – we've learnt not to quiz each other too much."

Guan poured espressos, black and intense. The smell revived Jen and she asked about his family.

"I'm an only child. After my first dad died, Mum and Yifan decided to play by the rules. He sacrificed a lot. Yifan's a good man. Listen, will you come with me for a walk? I should really get some fresh air; I've been sifting through this stuff all day. I can give you a quick tour of the streets around here and tell you more about my shy father."

They finished their coffee. Guan put on a baseball cap and a scarf. He stopped to buy sliced melon from a man on the corner and passed them a carton each. It tasted deliciously sweet after coffee.

They walked past the Suseng Teahouse, in the direction of the banks and office blocks. Old and new buildings jumbled together like photos in a drawer, flashes of the city's different eras. Guan took an unexpected turning and they entered a grubby residential area.

He lit a cigarette. "This is where Dad spends most of his spare time. I've taken photographs around here, but I don't store them on my laptop – the authorities wouldn't be too happy if they thought I was making any kind of political point. One must always be patriotic."

"What do you mean?" asked Ricki.

"The Party doesn't believe in creative freedom. But if you stay safe there are still ways to bend the rules. My dad's a lecturer by day and by night he comes here, looking for women to help."

"Prostitutes, you mean?"

"Sometimes, not always. They're in a bad shape for all sorts of reasons – homelessness, unwanted pregnancy, sometimes addicts... Mum doesn't approve, she worries all the time about his safety, but he's stubborn and comes anyway. I think she's accepted it now. She's stopped nagging him to quit."

"So he's like a street doctor?" Jen cut in.

"Exactly. He gives women on the spot treatment, whatever he can, and makes sure they know where to find a bed for the night. He tries to get them into God's Help, but they don't always want to go there. They don't want anyone finding out they exist – the State, I mean. It would create hassle. They've not always lived by the rules. There's plenty of people lining up to punish them."

"What sort of punishment?" said Jen.

"Prison, forced sterilisation, fines, sometimes the women just vanish. They're pretty dispensable, in some people's eyes."

"That's sick," Ricki added.

"That's what dad thinks, but it's not every man who has his guts. Especially not a man like him with a good job, a loving wife and apartment sorted. He's far braver than me; I'm just a dreamer, I want art to change the world."

"And can it?" said Ricki.

"Maybe." He shrugged. "I hope so."

"It looks pretty deprived around here," said Jen. "It's a side you don't see in the guidebooks. Who lives here?"

"Poor families as you'd expect, then there are the widows, the dealers, the abortionists. The State know they're here but they let them get on with it – so long as they stay in their bubble. I guess the abortionists are doing them a service; less mouths to feed. Believe me, your mother could have chosen differently when she abandoned you."

Jen shivered and rubbed her arms, but the chill remained.

"Come on, guys, we'd better hurry. I've probably already shown you too much. It's a shame we don't have more time, I could have taken you to see a film. There's a new indie feature out by Gao Wendong, I'm surprised it got past the censors."

"Wait," said Ricki. "Before you go marching off, there's somewhere I need to go. Please? Come with me, it won't take long."

They followed Ricki through the People's Park. Guan lit another cigarette from the packet in his top pocket. The smell reminded Jen of Stuart's kisses; Stuart who belonged to a different life.

"Are you going to tell us where we're going?" said Jen.

Ricki stopped dead.

"Don't tell me you're lost?"

It's over there. If I don't go now I never will. You'll come with me, won't you?"

Jen had never seen her sister look so scared. She realised, suddenly, where they were heading.

"You don't have to do this…"

But Ricki was already walking.

A flight of eighteen steps led to a first-floor entrance. The steps. The ones. Shit, they looked steep, thought Jen, as she approached the welfare institute.

There was also a ground floor entrance. A large porch supported by six columns, three on either side, painted red. Four-storeys, fifteen windows to every floor. Four bands of colour painted on the central windows marked out each floor; the colours had faded: white, pink, pale blue and red in ascending order. There were also six circular windows at the front of the building. It reminded Jen of something Blue Peter might make. She stared long and hard until she could remember every detail with her eyes closed. It was the least she could do – the only thing – to remember it properly and precisely.

"Be careful," Guan smiled. "If they catch you, they'll take you back in."

They crossed over to a bench shaded by overhanging trees and sat unseen. The scene played on in Jen's imagination, of May hurrying away from the steps. She pictured it to be a cold morning, frosty, her sister turning blue. Ricki's early medical records reported 'mild hypothermia', Jen's dental records said 'malnutrition' and 'bleeding gums'. They must have been half starved when May left them.

The sound of the playground bell was sharp. Jen looked up to see the small yard fill with toddlers: some running, others playing on the swings in the scrub beyond. They were monitored by a girl wearing a white coat who looked little more than a teenager herself.

The railings were damp where Jen pressed her face to peer into the compound. The kids were so tightly wrapped up, like bundles of post ready to go all over the world. The girl caught sight of them and quickly gathered up the children, who threw tantrums at being led back through the darkened glass doors.

"Are you crazy? Come back to the bench," Guan urged.

"But we're not doing anything wrong. I've not taken any photographs. What, so now they think I'm some kind of paedophile?"

"Worse," said Guan. "You're a young woman who's abandoned her baby and come back for it. Or, you're a foreign reporter out to cause trouble – especially if they hear us speaking English."

"I want to go inside. I want to see it. I have a right," said Ricki.

Through a first floor window, Jen noticed the teenage girl pointing in their direction.

"Shit, Ricki, we'd better go."

Ricki pulled away in the direction of the steps. "I'm staying."

"Let her go if she needs to," Guan said.

"I can't let her go. She's my twin."

Jen chased after Ricki and knelt beside her on the institute steps.

"I wanted to leave the past where it should be, Jen. That means leaving this here."

In her hand was the photograph of May taken at their sixteenth birthday party. Ricki tucked it inside May's red birthday envelope and placed it on the steps, as the supervisor appeared. Guan pulled them away. They ran and didn't look back.

As Ricki thanked Guan, a look of exhilaration and relief danced over her face.

"Listen, I hope you two are going to be okay? No more stunts like that. You need to take care. It's not so free here. Don't play it so risky."

"We have to," said Jen with urgency. "Or we'll never find out the truth."

"Help us," said Ricki.

"How?"

"Your grandparents are from Hunan. Take us with you. It's our best chance of finding May's relatives. Our biological grandparents. Our uncle."

Guan rubbed at his shaved head. "Remember what I said about Madam Feng's businessman, how his mobile didn't ring any more? Sometimes, the past just wants to stay hidden behind a wall."

There was a sudden shift in the clouds and the sun made everything luminous.

Guan shielded his eyes. "I suppose Dad is always complaining I don't go back home enough…"

Jen's heart quickened. "We would need our parents' permission."

"You've no idea how far we've come," said Ricki.

Guan nodded. "I'm too like my dad to say no."

Jen and Ricki walked the backstreets to the Bluewater Hotel, avoiding the midday traffic which swelled and roared. They stopped at McDonald's for a Coke, neither mentioning May. However, Ricki removed her hoodie to reveal the double happiness tattoo on her upper arm.

"Shit, when did you get that done?" said Jen.

"After our birthday."

"You know they'll kill you."

Ricki swirled ice with her straw. "I doubt that."

Jen wished she had her twin's nerve. "So how do you know about double happiness?"

"I looked it up."

"In Yifan's book?"

"On the Net, stupid. Promise not to tell them, Jen, or they'll never let us go to May's village." Ricki would tell them about the tattoo in her own time, the way she did everything. The way she accepted her past – little by little.

Jen thumbed the outline of the double happiness symbol; tried for a moment, half a moment, to work out where one character ended and the other began and realised she couldn't.

Wisps of hair

The sound of crying babies woke me. The bed felt unfamiliar with its stiff white sheets smelling of jasmine and something else – bleach. The clock said half past two. Was it day or night? I wished the babies would shut up; where was their mother?

A face came into view. He was young and wore glasses.

"Am I dead?"

He smiled. "No, you're not dead, Mai Ling, and neither are they."

I followed his gaze to the reed crib, where two screaming babies lay cocooned in white woollen blankets.

He held up a bottle of formula. "Time for a feed."

I stared, uncertain.

"Yifan?"

"Yes," he picked up the baby and snuggled it into the folds of his doctor's coat.

Two babies...? I edged up the bed; a shooting pain gripped my lower abdomen. A tube inserted into the back of my hand connected me to a bag of clear liquid by the side of my bed.

"Don't be scared, that will make you strong again."

Yifan reached into the crib and passed the second baby from his arms to mine. "Here, be gentle with her, she's still very weak."

I directed the bottle to her lips and she sucked greedily. Her eyes rolled in contentment. White spots freckled her nose and cheeks.

"I can't remember...what happened..."

"These are your children, Mai Ling. Your baby girls. You're all going to be fine now; you've been getting stronger every day."

I stared at him. He had loved me – hadn't he? And loved me now in spite of my babies? Or maybe I never told him? There were vague shards of memory – a *yīshēng*, the bucket, running barefoot in the rain to survive.

"Mai Ling, I'm so sorry, but we had to operate." Yifan paused; his shoes tapped against the side of the bed. "The operation was to remove *zi gong*." He explained this was my *infant's palace*. He said I nearly bled to death in the doorway of a block of flats.

The baby in my arms stared at me, her eyes mesmerising, pulling me into her. Just looking at her made my breasts ache.

"But I'm afraid there is something else, a more pressing problem," he said, "that is, the matter of where you will live. This is a missionary hospital, Mai Ling. We've subsidised your operation, but we can't keep you here once you've recuperated sufficiently to return home."

"Home? But I don't have a home."

Yifan peered at his shoes.

"How soon?" I asked.

"Tomorrow morning."

I gazed at the drowsy infant, swathed in blankets. *What next Mama?* She seemed to ask before her eyes pursed in sleep.

I don't know baby.

Under sleep's anaesthetic, I returned to the dingy clinic where Doctor Quo slavered to chop my flesh into pieces with a meat cleaver and boil it into soup. When he turned round, I realised it was Kwo, the factory cook. He ladled the blood out of a deep vat. Peering inside, I saw two babies bob to the surface, their webbed hands splayed. *Don't let us become broth*, they begged.

The dream felt so real, I hurried to check the twins were safely asleep. My pillow was damp with sweat; the bed seemed to be shrinking. My stomach ached from the bottom of my pelvis up to my ribs and for hours I lay awake listening to the sound of other babies crying, mothers' snoring, footsteps squeaking down the corridor. In the half-light I watched the slow *drip-drip* of liquid as it plinked through the tube into the back of my hand.

I lumbered back onto the bed. There had to be someone in this big city who could help us? I thought of Cousin Zhi, Fatty, Ren, Fei Fei, Madam Feng... And my family? I could never shame them with these children. Yifan was my only remaining friend; I would swallow my pride and plead with him for help.

An hour or so later, an insistent hand tapped me on the shoulder.

"Wake up, your babies are hungry. Time to get up."

I rolled over to see a different doctor peering down his nose at me.

"Where's Yifan?" I asked.

"Doctor Meng has been called out on an emergency; it's unlikely that he'll be in for the rest of today."

"But I need to see him."

"I'm afraid that's not possible."

"It's an emergency."

"I'm sorry lady, there's nothing I can do," he left me with two bottles of formula. "Perhaps one of the nurses on reception can see to whatever it is you want; but don't take long with that feed – we have an amputee in the corridor waiting for your bed."

The patient in the bed next to mine pulled back the edge of her blanket, enough to see out.

"*Tsst.* You got somewhere to go?"

I shook my head.

She had a weather-beaten face that looked distrustful of the world. I wondered why she was in hospital, there was nothing obviously the matter with her. No broken arm, no bleeding, no babies.

"Think you'll keep 'em?" She gestured to my arms, where one child guzzled formula and the other grasped impatiently at the air.

Instinctively, I said yes. "We've survived this far together."

She lowered her voice. "There's always the welfare institute…"

I frowned, recalling the white-washed monolithic building on Hong Cheng Road and the warning Ren had issued the night of the ferris wheel, "Don't get in deeper with the manager, Sky Eyes." I was already much too in love with Manager He to heed her warning. My 'sky eyes,' as she called them, were watching clouds, daydreaming of a different life to this shabby one.

"Rumour is, welfare sell babies to rich foreigners," I said. "The managers own fancy apartments downtown."

"Ha! You shouldn't believe everything you hear, girl. Besides, the westerners can offer them a better life." She shook her head and reached into the bedside cabinet, producing a dog-eared sheet of photographs. They were black and white passport photos of her and a baby. On two of the pictures, the woman's eyes were closed and she looked gormless. They stirred me nonetheless.

She wiped her nose on her sleeve. "Here, take it. Take a good look."

"It's a baby girl."

"Taken the day we said goodbye. You see, girl, sometimes it's for the best."

"Perhaps."

"No perhaps about it, we don't have choices."

"There's always a choice," I said, too quickly. I didn't like the way she said "we," putting us in the same category.

The woman grabbed the photograph, offended, and slipped it into the cabinet. "Well, *hao yun*, girl," she sighed. "I hope a gold pin falls in your well. You're going to need it to look after them two littlies."

The sun shone shiftily between the blocks of high-rise flats opposite *God's Help Hospital*. Between the breaths of traffic that log-jammed Jenmen Road, a police siren screamed, distant. The rain stopped. The water level receded below the kerb. Lines of buses sloughed past, spraying me as I stared into the petrol rainbows, wishing hard for Yifan to pull up, beep his horn and say, "Hurry up! Get in, we're going home!" For fifteen stupid minutes I waited, counting the seconds, believing he might come.

For hours, I wandered the nearby streets, scuffing through the crowds, going nowhere in particular. *God's Help* had sent me on my way with a pair of navy court shoes, two sizes too small, donated by their latest amputee. I felt a century old, with my feet bound into the tight leather. It didn't take long for me to develop the strange shuffle of my ancestors – women who knew the suffering road.

By midday my babies were blue from screaming to be fed. I sat on a bench beneath a date palm tree whose fronds hung spindly in the November gloom. I put my little finger in one mouth then the other. They cried harder when they realised nothing was coming out. I would have given them my breasts, but they were empty. My wells had run dry of milk.

Stealing the formula was a risk. The owner's eyes were onto me the moment I entered her low-beam corner shop. Perhaps it was the ghostly pallor of my skin or the dark circles around my eyes, or maybe she could smell it on me: the intention to rob her blind. I mooched up and down the aisles, sniffed a garland of red chillies, delved my hand into a crate of ripe pears at the back of the shop – squeezing, testing, admiring. I knelt by a sack of green tea and rubbed the leaves between my fingers.

My opportunity came when the owner fetched her husband some tea while he mended shoes on the street. I hurried over to the aisle with powdered formula and stuffed a jar into my coat, tucking it inside the blankets where the twins' heads nestled, bawling. I hoped it was enough to last a couple of days.

The owner wrestled me on the doorstep, demanding to see inside my coat.

"You migrant mothers, stealing our stuff! Wait until I get my husband onto you." She called for him.

I unzipped my coat a slither, enough to show them the bulge inside was human.

"Let her go. I don't want any trouble, Xingyan, not this time," he ranted.

I hurried away, the babies bobbing in the swag of my jacket.

There were worse crimes. That night I crouched in an alleyway and raked together a makeshift shelter out of cardboard boxes. Two adolescents carrying knives held a woman against a nearby skip and assaulted her. I sobbed the whole way through as they whooped and grunted. They both took a turn and eventually the woman's cries died down, she stopped fighting, her body limp. I dared not move from my shelter for fear they might do the same to me. Let the police catch the rapists, let the mother live, I whispered, curling myself into a tight ball amidst the junk. When I was sure they'd gone, I covered her sobbing body with my coat.

I fell to sleep on my haunches, rocked by the muted patter of rain. The babies woke every couple of hours in need of formula, which I mixed in a bottle salvaged from the skip. I had to step over the woman to get to it.

The next morning a refuse collector came peddling his cart. He picked over the rubbish, scratched at the pavement with his bamboo broom.

"What the…"

I poked my head out of the shelter.

"Move it, woman, you can't sleep here. I thought you were a stiff. Watch yourself."

I crawled from beneath the cardboard, the babies cowled in my jumper, and ran. Above was leaden sky. Cold air. A slack rain in the wind. I coughed up phlegm like a woman who'd smoked opium all her life. My clothes lingered with the smell of the street and of food waste. I was scavenging some rice from my coat when a couple of westerners bumped into me.

"Watch it," I said.

"Oh…*bàoqiàn*." The man fumbled for an apology. No doubt he was an American.

Immediately, his wife honed in on my babies. Her clothes were pristine: grey fur coat, black patent leather shoes. The hems of her tweed trousers brushed at her heels. She had blonde hair curled in waves, crowned with a beret. This one had money alright. She smelt of money. She oozed money. Money, money, money. Good enough to eat.

She reached out to touch my babies. Sensing the opportunity to earn a few yuan, I let her stroke my baby's cheek. For a moment my youngest stopped crying and I felt a pang inside like someone had plucked a zither whose strings were attached to my heart. How could she calm them like that?

The husband reached into his back pocket and pulled out a wallet fat with yuan. Mao's blue washed-out face gawped up at me. Ha! They were giving me cash and all I'd done was flash them a glimpse of my babies. My stomach leapt at the promise of food.

"Xièxiè," I said.

He thanked me back in hesitant Chinese and turned to leave. His wife stood transfixed. He had to link his arm through hers and pull gently before she would move. I watched them disappear inside the restaurant's plush interior then shoved the money quickly inside my vest. It felt crisp against my laddered ribs.

Six days and six nights passed. The rain drained away, leaving a damp film over the streets. My shoes began to stretch. When I took them off at night I noticed the leather had taken the shape of my feet, bulging at the front where my potato toes were rooted in an uneven row.

I used some of the Americans' money to buy clean *kaidangku*. The ones from *God's Help* were too soiled for my babies to wear and the stench was unbearable where their shit had seeped out. I worried constantly about disease. I'd seen first-hand the girls at Forwood falling too ill to work after eating stale food.

The best places to wash were in public toilets and department stores, although I was usually eyed with too much suspicion to get past the doors. More than once, security guards threw me out of the Pacific Department Store, calling me "dirty *mingong*" or "lazy daughter." It was easy for them to rough me up a bit, even as I cradled my babies. I had no rights on the street, the police would have laughed in my face and locked me up if I turned to them for help.

It was on the seventh morning, as the sun shone feebly though the bare trees on Bayi Avenue, that the hopelessness of my situation hit me. I was feeding my babies cold formula on a bench. I had spent my last fen on a bottle of purified water.

How can we go on like this?

The answer was glaring – we couldn't. I had no *hukou* for a home, no food, no clean clothes, nothing to keep us warm, no protection and no money. I didn't even have the will to lift my head and beg for help any more.

226

I thought about the peasant in God's Help hospital who abandoned her daughter. I kissed my babies, put my nose to their faces and let them gnaw my finger, wanting to feel pain and be reminded that we were still alive, because at that point I felt dead; at least, dead inside. Whatever it was that had kept me going - hope, fear, love, stubbornness – had finally petered out.

I got up and started walking. One foot, then the other, then another. I counted the steps and avoided the cracks in the pavement. I became annoyed with strangers who got in my way, or made me lose count. Didn't they know where I was going?

When I turned the corner onto Hong Cheng Road, the first thing I noticed was the colour of the welfare institute walls – grey, not white as I remembered them to be. More drab and hollow because of what I was about to...

A flight of eighteen steps led to a first-floor entrance. There was also a ground floor entrance. A large porch was supported by six columns, three on either side. The triangular roof of the porch and its columns were painted red. It was a four-storey building, fifteen windows to every floor. Four bands of colour were painted on the central windows marking out each floor; the colours were: white, pink, pale blue and red in ascending order. Unusually, there were also six circular windows on the front of the building. I guessed they were pure decoration, some architectural ornament intended to demonstrate to foreigners that the Chinese had taste and style, as well as babies. I stared long and hard until I could remember every detail with my eyes closed. I knew that I would never forget that building. The least I could do – the only thing – was to remember it properly and precisely.

I couldn't do the same for my babies. A child is not a building. A voice is not a brick. A baby that moves, cries, shivers, gargles, wrinkles, breathes, frowns isn't anything that will be remembered in detail. My babies were too fluid. Their skin, yes, maybe their skin would be remembered. Their skin was a naked grain of rice slipping through my fingers. Their skin was my empty hand, grasping for their memory before I had even let go.

Never let you go.

I pressed my face to theirs and kissed. Then I took the rusty pen knife the rapists had discarded in the alley, held my wrist steady and cut away some wisps of their hair. In a short while, it would be all I had left. Afterwards, I squatted in the restless dark, folded my hands into a fist against my forehead, closed my eyes and waited.

I waited for the staff to cease their bedtime duties. Waited until the lights had been turned off in all fifteen windows. Only the circular windows remained illuminated, these must have been the stairwells. The children would like having a light at the end of the corridor, it would be a comfort, a reassurance they weren't abandoned.

Never let you go.

When everything was still and all the babies in the building were surely asleep, I waited some more. Hours. I waited for the right moment: the lull in traffic, the calming of the breeze and for their crying to subside. I waited for my babies' eyes to close so that they wouldn't see me leave. Soon the morning staff would arrive and discover my girls. They would be brought in from the cold, I hoped.

My daughters were ten days old. Would they one day wake up in a cold sweat, unable to shake the memory of being abandoned on the steps of Nanchang's Welfare Institute? Would my eldest be making love for the first time and burst into tears, haunted by the sound of footsteps fading?

The right moment never came. There can never be a right moment for a mother to say goodbye, to let go, to walk away from the things she loves the most in the entire world. My precious babies, my sweet loves, my flesh… my flesh was not for cutting, was not for giving, was not for leaving behind on those frost-laced steps. Sweet babies, I wrapped you in a blanket and covered you with my hair and wiped your tears one last time, even though I knew those tears would keep on falling, would sting your cheeks in the bitter cold. I did not go quickly, or bravely, feeling that my leaving was for the best. I burned. I burned like a flame engorged with air. I burned in my breasts because to leave you was the scorch of death.

Two, maybe three days later, I passed a stall selling plastic cartons of fresh watermelon at the entrance to the People's Park. My mouth filled with the taste of their sweet, pink flesh, reminiscent of my childhood. I stole a carton and headed over to a bench. It was the first thing I'd eaten since that night.

An early-morning haze hung over the park and the elderly residents who were practising Tai Chi looked other-worldly. Their limbs branched outwards and upwards. Their movements were smooth, gentle, like the reeling in of silk. I sucked hard on a slice of melon; the knot in my abdomen pulled tighter.

At first, I didn't see her – only her pink trainers, which sparkled in the haze as she skipped towards me. She chased a ball that had rolled beneath the bench where I was sitting. I looked up from her trainers to see a pair of bright, quizzical eyes. The girl was primary school age and wore her school uniform.

"You're crying," she said.

I reached beneath the bench for her ball. "Perhaps I need a friend to play with?" I said, wiping my eyes. "How about catch?"

"Don't you have any children of your own to play with?" she asked, her face full of gravity. "Most people who come to the park have children."

I felt for the wisps of hair in my coat pocket. "Yes. I do."

I wanted to tell the girl everything, about their features, their skin, their tears, their sleep-heavy flesh... She smiled when I mentioned they were twins.

"In fact, you remind me of my first-born. I think she'll look like you one day."

"Is she pretty?" She wound the ball through the air towards me. The girl was not great at throwing, her aim was wonky. She was probably the last to get picked for games in the school playground.

"No, not pretty," I said. "Much more than pretty."

"What? Tell me." She hopped excitedly.

"They're beautiful. Like you."

"Where are they?" she asked.

I threw the ball gently underarm. There was no answer to this. For months they'd formed inside my *infant's palace* like twin pearls. Now I couldn't say exactly where they were – which of the fifteen windows in the welfare institute was theirs. I only knew that someday soon, someone else would take my babies.

"My daughters are travelling," I said. "They've gone to America, or maybe Europe. It's their first big adventure."

The girl's eyes widened. She caught the ball. "They're so lucky! Teacher Xiao says young people should see the world."

"Your teacher's very wise. It's not good for a person to stay their whole life in one place. The world is open to you." My chest strained with the memory of a home I longed to go back to, a little brother waiting by the gate, the smell of a father's tobacco and maybe even the chance of a mother's forgiveness.

The girl was about to throw the ball, when an old man strode towards us. He put a hand on the girl's shoulder.

"*Jiao Jiao*, what have I said about being late for school? Now hurry up or there'll be big trouble."

The girl sighed. "Grandpa, I was only playing!"

He took one look at my grubby clothes and grabbed his granddaughter firmly by the hand. "We can play later, after school."

They hurried down the gravel path which led past the zoo. The girl skipped at his side, springing along in her sparkly pink trainers. When they reached the panda enclosure, she looked over her shoulder and waved. I waved back until she disappeared from view.

Even after she'd gone, I continued to wave. I stood on the gravel path parting the air with my hands, knowing the air would move in and fill the spaces around me. Fearing I had been erased, fearing my daughters had slipped through my hands, forever.

It took seven hours to reach Hunan by train. Guan slept, unmoved by the changing landscapes of city, suburb, sprawling highway, river, mountain becoming rice field; the layers of change and time peeling back to Hunan and to May's village, the kernel of our origins.

"You promise me you'll take good care of them?" Nancy had pleaded.

"I give you my word, Mrs Milne."

Iain had looked Guan straight in the eye, "You better take care of my girls...and bring them back safely."

On the train, Jen scanned the faces around her: the same, yet foreign. Despite her restlessness, she couldn't sleep. Soon, she would give May's letter to Ricki.

From Yongzhou station they boarded a bus that took them deep into the countryside, where the occasional worker appeared to be stitched into the seams of rice fields. The bus was old and cramped with no air-conditioning and poor suspension. At one point it was held up by of an old lady, sitting on an upturned beer crate in the middle of a dusty track brandishing a sweeping brush as a barrier. The driver handed over a few coins and the brush was raised at the makeshift toll. Ricki took a few shots of the woman swaddled in her padded cotton jacket; she looked well into her eighties, her face riddled with wrinkles.

The bus passengers, which included a dog that didn't belong to anyone, appeared unfazed by the heat and humidity, some even wore cardigans and black woollen shawls. Jen tried to catch snippets of conversation, but it was so far removed from her knowledge of Chinese that they might as well have been speaking Russian.

On arrival, Guan led them to his *nǎinai* who lived in the centre of the village in a sturdy, modern house clad in white tiles. "Dad likes to help out wherever he can. He promised Grandad he'd look after *nǎinai* and renovate the place. I think he feels like he let them down somewhere along the line."

Guan knocked and they entered, leaving their shoes and bags on the reed mat in the dark vestibule.

"*Nǎinai*," he called out.

A small, springy woman with an all-enveloping smile appeared in the hallway. They didn't hug, that wasn't the tradition, but she stroked his arm affectionately.

"Look how big you've grown and so skinny! What are they feeding you in that big city? All coffee and french fries, your father tells me."

She let go, noticing Jen and Ricki in the vestibule.

There was a rapid exchange, then his grandma stepped aside and gave a neat bow. "Friends of my grandson are friends of mine," she said. "Now Guan, you must be thirsty, I will get you all tea – not too watery and with plenty of leaves in the strainer. Show your guests the spare room, Grandson."

They were to sleep in a room at the far end of the bungalow. The faded blue walls had little in the way of decorations. It was warm from the evening sun and Jen asked if she could open a window?

"Sure," said Guan, "It's the double glazing Dad put in, this side of the bungalow soaks up the heat. It used to be his room. *Năinai* uses it to write her calligraphy now because of the light."

Some of her work was left out on a desk by the window.

"It's *Nüshu*, a kind of women's writing from Jiangyong county. She's been copying it from great grandmother's missives – *Năinai* says it's hard to get the strokes so fine now that her eyes are failing, but she's determined to keep something of the past alive." Guan smiled, "I guess we're similar."

He was to sleep in a large room in the annexe. *Năinai* fussed after him; replenishing his cup as soon as he finished and offering him sugary pastilles, mixed in with spicy peanuts. *Năinai's* body was rumpled with age, but surprisingly lithe as she climbed the rickety wooden ladder to pick oranges from a tree in her garden. Her eyes twinkled like Yifan's. Guan translated for Ricki. He seemed relaxed, apart from when *Năinai* probed about his *jian kang* – health.

As the sun dipped below the rim of the valley, *Năinai* suggested they eat indoors. She prepared a feast, humbly passing it off as a few meagre dishes, not edible for guests.

Jen knew to compliment her. The smell of chilli wafted into her face from the steaming platter of fried tofu.

"*Năinai* is asking me who it is you are looking for?"

"The family of Mai Ling Guo. I know they were farmers, from a village somewhere in this area," Jen said.

"Xiashu Wang."

"You know it?"

"*Năinai* says only one member remains – the youngest son. His name is Jinsong. He lives with his wife and son on his parents' farm."

"It must be him."

Ricki, who'd been struggling with the spicy tofu, pushed it away. "Sure sounds like our long-lost uncle to me," she said, before bolting from the table.

Jen apologised and went after her. She found Ricki crouched beside *Năinai's* calligraphy desk, hugging her knees.

Jen knelt down. "We've come so far, Ricki."

"What if we find out who he is? What if Jinsong tells us about our dad?"

"I don't know. We'll be together." She squeezed Ricki's hand. For once, her twin didn't pull away.

Jinsong's smallholding was on the outskirts of Xiashu Wang, overlooking rice fields. In the yard, chickens pecked the dry earth. Jen ran her fingers through the red soil. She worried as she tried to picture Jinsong's face, shocked and confused in the sun's harrowing light, as he realised they were his nieces.

"Wait here," said Guan, "it's better if I go in first and explain the situation."

Jen watched him disappear around the back of the ramshackle farmhouse, his white jeans incongruous in the countryside. They leaned against the wall of an outbuilding, Ricki's camera swung idly by her side.

Suddenly there was a commotion in the yard. A buzz shot through the trembling heat. It was a young boy, arms outstretched like aeroplane wings.

Rat-a-tat-tat-rat-a-tat-tat-tat-tat!

He fell to the dust and rolled over, a wooden stick strung to his belt.

"Come out! I know you're hiding from me. Come out and fight me like a man!" He scrambled behind a water trough.

Ricki bobbed her head around the corner of the outbuilding. The boy crawled a few paces then made a run for her, charging with his stick rifle.

Rat-a-tat-tat-rat-a-tat-tat-tat-tat....DIE!

Ricki fought valiantly but, unarmed, was no match for the young boy; she fell hopelessly on her back making an exaggerated wail as she writhed on the ground dying.

The boy grinned. He poked her with the toe of his trainer to make sure she was properly dead.

"Feng-Shu! Feng-Shu!" a voice cried from the porch.

He tied the stick to his trouser belt and dragged his feet through the red soil, becoming a plane whirring through the heat again. A thin, suspicious woman met him at the back door and gathered him to her side.

Jen and Ricki sheltered beneath a prickly bush to finish the last of the mineral water. At that moment, Guan appeared. With him, a man smoking one of Guan's cigarettes, the remaining packet tucked into his T-shirt. Jen wiped the red soil from her hands and stood quickly to bow.

"I've explained everything; he knows who you are and is willing to meet," said Guan.

Jinsong's chest rose and fell quickly beneath his T-shirt, imprinted with *Rage against the Machine*. His hands remained stiff by his sides as he spoke.

Guan gave an encouraging nod.

They followed him into the house, where the walls were black from cooking fires. Chickens wandered underfoot. They were asked to sit at the wooden table, beside the ancestral shrine. Jen's eyes went immediately to a black and white photograph of a couple, presumably May's grandparents. Jinsong gave them liquor and they drank. He was a solid man, large handed.

The young boy – their cousin, Feng-Shu – lay down and read on a wooden bed in the corner. Jen wondered if he was pretending. She looked back and forth from her cup to the bed, trying to picture May as a child, tucked up with Jinsong. She had adored him, missed him.

Jinsong searched their faces. "Hen-Shu, pour some more baijiu."

His wife re-filled their cups and returned to her washing up bowl, setting the plates to dry in a beer crate by the door.

"I believe you are my sister's children?"

Jen nodded, she could just about make out his accent, but it helped that Guan was there to translate.

"What is it you want from Uncle? You can see with your own eyes, I have nothing to give you."

"Only to meet you," said Jen.

"Jinsong finds it hard to believe you have come from England. I told him the circumstances, but adoption is not so common here."

"So what do they do with unwanted girls?" said Ricki. The question hung in the air, unanswered.

"I understand *Mai Mai* is dying? Who is looking after her in England?"

Jen told him the nurses were doing everything they could. It didn't sound good enough.

Guan puffed a fresh cloud of cigarette smoke into the fug. "The doctors in England are first class, Jinsong; trust me, she will be in good hands."

"My parents said she would come to no good, but I never believed them. She is my older sister, was my best friend…"

"I'm sorry to break this news to you," said Jen.

Jinsong rose suddenly. Guan translated, "Come with him, please. There's something he wants you to see."

The pine trees provided a welcome shade. They were sweating by the time they reached the gateway that led to the centre of the forest. Guan lit a cigarette, his shaved head pinked by the fierce sun. Jinsong seemed hardly to notice the steepness of the path, and was surprised to find them growing breathless.

"You girls don't work for *jia*, no?"

"He means outdoors, for your family."

Jen shook her head. She struggled to translate how vastly different their lives were, how stuffed up into rooms, how centrally heated, polished, dusted; how they were wrapped up, bundled, all their lives spent surrounded by things. No, not outdoors, on the land, no they did not work for family, for *jia*.

Jinsong laughed. "Not so like your mother then."

They continued to a point where Jen didn't think the path could get any steeper, clawing a route that slanted diagonally through the trees, the way only obvious to Jinsong, until they reached a clearing and a level plateau where he stopped and looked up.

He got down and stretched out on a bed of pine needles, closed his eyes. "She loved the smell of these trees; every year she gathered wood from up here and used it to make wooden figurines for Spring Festival… I played with them too. What a girl I was! Nothing like Feng-Shu. Always too soft. Father had lost hope of a daughter-in-law before I met Hen-Shu."

Jen stood silent, taking in the lofty cathedral-stillness of the place. She tried to picture Mai Ling feeling the bark, searching for a piece of wood the right size and colour for her figurines.

"How old was she when she left the farm?" Jen asked.

"She was your age, sixteen. I was ten."

"That's young for a scholarship?" Guan said.

"You are joking – what good is education?"

"She never went to university?" said Jen.

He laughed.

"She told us she'd done a degree in engineering, that she'd won a scholarship!" Jen protested.

"No. She ran away to avoid marrying a boy."

"Who?" Jen asked.

"The coffin-maker's son. Mother and Father set it up, but she wouldn't go through with it."

"Jen, what's he saying? I can't understand."

"You didn't know any of this? Your parents in England didn't tell you?" Guan said.

"Will someone please tell me what the fuck's going on? Is he telling us who our dad is?"

Guan offered Ricki a hand up, "Come on, your breathing's not good… I promised your parents I'd take care of you. We shouldn't have come up here in this heat."

"I'm fine."

Jinsong rolled onto his side where he lay on the pine needles; the word *Rage* folded into *Machine*.

What else could he tell them? A whole world of growing-up, but where to start with such a vast map? Childhood so difficult to unpick.

"Did Mai escape on her own?" Jen asked.

"Funny girl."

"I'm not trying to be."

"It was Cousin Zhi that put her up to it. I think Mai Mai might have gone through with the marriage if it wasn't for Zhi being so arrogant and persuasive…they were always together, whispering plans. Zhi and Auntie looked down on us. Not any more."

Jinsong was talking faster, becoming agitated. Who was this cousin May had never mentioned?

"Tell us slowly what happened," said Guan, trying to translate for Ricki at the same time.

Jinsong spat on the ground. "The last I heard of Cousin Zhi was through Benny - him and Zhi had a thing together... He sent a message back from Nanchang that Zhi had been thrown out of the factory and was working on the street."

"A prostitute?" said Jen.

Jinsong nodded. "Not so clever after all. The shame almost killed Auntie. Benny found out Mai Ling wasn't with her, but he didn't know where she was either. The factory burnt down; most of the workers were left to fend for themselves. There was no way of

236

getting in touch with Mai Mai, of bringing her home. We tried, Benny went to the city and stayed there a month, but he never found her. The factory where they worked had been bulldozed. A new block of high-risers took its place."

"So May did work in a factory," Jen said, excited to hear the truth.

She turned the figurine necklace over in her pocket. She'd brought it hoping to find a place, somewhere to return it. He stood in front of her – that place, that man, that home. She held it out to Jinsong. "May would want you to have this."

He took it without looking. "Promise you'll tell her I love her... I miss her...tell her she has a nephew who likes playing in the yard, but who is destined for better things. Tell her he's brave and strong and clever. Don't tell her how pitiful the farm is."

"I won't. I'll say you brought us to your forest."

He placed the figurine necklace on the pine needles. "Xièxiè."

Together, they trudged back down the red dirt track. Jen could see Guan and Ricki already on the road below the farm.

She bent down and scooped up a handful of the red soil. Its colour was not the royal red of blood, but a burnt, rusty orange in her palm. It felt warm as she emptied it into her pocket. She would take the soil to May. A part of Jinsong going home.

A fly buzzed in the moonlit dark that night in Yifan's faded blue bedroom. Jen was brushing her hair at Nǎinai's calligraphy desk.

"What's it like being so clever?" said Ricki in bed.

She turned round. "What are you talking about?"

"I can see why May lied about her scholarship... People admire brains."

"She was clever enough to bullshit us for six years," said Jen.

The fly circled their heads.

"I've decided not to bother applying to uni. My grades aren't good enough," said Ricki.

"I don't know whether to go either."

"But the Milne family honour's at stake if you don't take up a place at Oxford or Cambridge."

"All I ever wanted was your love," said Jen.

Ricki glanced away. "What will you do with that soil?"

Jen hadn't thought it through that far. So many things her supposedly big, brilliant brain didn't know. Only that she needed a hug and that she wanted to go home now. To Manchester.

Ricki folded back the thin sheet and Jen climbed in beside her. The fly found its way out into the night, its path illuminated by the chunky spit-faced moon.

"Ricki," she whispered. "I have a letter you should read; it's addressed to us both. May wrote it a long time ago."

Effects and belongings

Never let you go.

That's what I promised them.

The Bluewater Hotel was a ten minute walk from the welfare institute. In the mornings I served breakfast and washed pots. In the afternoons I cleaned rooms and steamed sheets in the hotel laundry. The hours were easy compared to Forwood and I was even allowed an hour's break, mid-afternoon.

I spent it hanging around the welfare institute; I'd sit on a bench and pretend to read my hotel copy of the *Jiangxi Daily*, when really I watched and waited to see who came for my babies.

Around 4.30 in the afternoon, the welfare workers took the babies out into a small tarmac yard. A high wire fence made it hard to see individual children's faces, and I daren't risk getting any closer, in case the staff reported me. I never saw my babies, not once during all the weeks I sat on that bench, and yet I was sure someone from the institute must have found them on the steps. Somewhere inside that grey, ugly building were my daughters and it killed me every time I had to whisper goodbye and return to work, I feared I'd miss their departure.

The Bluewater Hotel got away with paying me a pittance because I had no work permit. I didn't care, money wasn't the reason I stayed. The guests were my reason – the foreigners who came to The Bluewater to collect their adopted Chinese baby daughters. I saw at least ten baby girls arrived at the hotel in the space of a fortnight. It was only a matter of time and mine would come.

My boss at the hotel was called Suzinne. She'd suggested to the Domestic Manager I start on a trial basis; perhaps she saw something of herself in me. I was eager to do whatever she asked and grafted hard. After a few weeks, the Domestic Manager forgot all about the trial. My foot was in the door and I proved too valuable to lose, especially when a glut of cleaners walked out for better paid jobs at the State Waste Disposal Unit. In gratitude to Suzinne, I kept my gob shut when I caught her stealing from the hotel safe.

One cold December morning, I was cleaning the lobby and emptying ash trays when a pair of westerners checked into The Bluewater. I was in the habit of memorising every foreign face. The woman was typical of many guests – in her mid-forties, with pristine clothes and the nervous demeanour of a first-time parent. Her husband wheeled their matching green cases up to the reception desk. They were booked in for ten days under the name of 'Milne'. He carried a posh camera. She gawped at her surroundings and ran a finger along the reception desk when she thought no-one was looking.

At breakfast the next day, I served their congee. They requested English breakfast tea and cold meats. The husband thanked me in Chinese and introduced himself. He was Iain, his wife's name was Nancy.

I bowed. "*Nín hǎo* Nan-see."

Suzinne told me off for making contact with them. "They're desperate people," she said.

In fact, she wanted their tips. We all knew how to smile sweetly and be polite to get the most out of westerners. Suzinne was one of the best at it, having worked at The Bluewater longest of anyone.

A whole week passed without any baby deliveries from the welfare institute. The babies hadn't been taken out to the yard and I began to panic. Had they run out of babies? Were they poorly? I feared for my girls.

The foreigners at The Bluewater became increasingly edgy. Iain and Nancy were forced to book in for an extra week's stay. Their guide cleared off, leaving them without a translator. Kim, the receptionist, spoke a little English and so did Suzinne – between them they figured out what guests wanted: mainly, to know what the hell was going on with their babies.

One morning, there was an urgent knock on the laundry room door. It was Iain. Suzinne stepped outside and I overheard a flurry of whispered English. I spied Iain as he gave Suzinne some yuan, which she later claimed was a tip, for providing extra bed linen.

She laughed it off. "You know what these foreigners are like? If they don't get clean sheets every single week they think they're going to catch bird flu."

Three days later the hotel lobby reverberated with the sound of crying babies. I was cleaning rooms on the first floor and ran downstairs, my hands tingling. I scanned the lobby full of tightly wrapped bundles. There were ten babies in all. The welfare institute

240

staff carried two each and failed to comfort them. Kim, on reception, was frantically phoning around, telling the couples to "come quickly, your baby has arrived." She worked under the glare of the welfare institute manager, whose job was to ensure the correct matching of kids and foreigners. I hovered by the lifts.

Iain and Nancy were first downstairs. They were instructed to line up and a woman from the institute checked each passport in turn. I watched, rigid, to see if any of the babies would be handed over as twins – the possibility of them being separated was too awful to consider.

One by one the babies were given out. The westerners cradled them so carefully it was as though they were holding their life's worth in gold. No doubt they were. I'd heard a rumour that the average baby cost three thousand in fees to the institute.

I approached the three couples that were left. The two remaining babies didn't look like my girls. But what if I didn't recognise them? It had been three months since I had left them on the steps of the welfare institute. They might have already gone.

Just then a white coat appeared through the revolving door carrying two more babies. I knew it was them. It had to be. In the next instant they were handed over to Iain and Nancy. The noise in the lobby rose to such a level my head felt light.

Iain immediately began taking pictures of Nancy with my girls. He pulled back the hoods of their little jackets and she bounced them, one in either arm, to get them to smile. They didn't want to smile for his stupid camera. Nancy looked to Iain, bewildered and unsure.

Put them on your shoulder, hold them high and whisper you love them so that it tickles their ears.

They weren't her babies, how could she know? I thought foreign mothers planned for these moments, waited and planned, and now she was left unprepared like a fool.

One of my babies screamed and I could see all her gums, angry and inflamed. Her crying set off the other daughter. It was how they used to be.

Sshh, don't cry. Don't cry little girls...

They were scared of this Nancy woman staring down at them with tear-filled eyes and springy grey hair, so unlike their real mother's. Her cloying floral perfume enveloped them, filled their noses; they needed the comfort of my skin, the warming tang of spice, of home.

"Aren't they beautiful?" Nancy beamed at me.

I hadn't realised how close I was, peering around her elbow at the two bundles. I clasped my hands behind my back to stop myself from reaching out and grabbing what belonged to me. Their hair had grown! They had gained weight, their cheeks now plump as cherries.

"Yes, yes, very beautiful," I said and began to hum one of their lullabies.

My youngest, with her dimples, stopped crying for the briefest of moments. Her eyes moved to find my voice.

I watched Nancy kiss them on the top of their heads. *These are mine*, the kiss said. I forced myself to smile and congratulate her.

Iain gestured for me to take a picture on his expensive-looking camera. I had to do it, didn't I? They fit perfectly inside the square viewfinder. A perfect, happy family and I was nowhere in the photo.

"Xièxiè!" they said. "Xièxiè."

How could they know how much there was to thank me for?

I couldn't bear it a second longer and rushed to the toilets, where I fell to my knees inside a cubicle.

My sickness turned out to be a stomach bug. I clutched my belly for twenty four hours. Suzinne took pity on me and let me rest in the laundry room. The warm air and constant whirr of the driers made me drowsy and I found myself dreaming about Manager He; his hands all over me; pleasure exquisite as warm syrup dripping from a spoon. We were in his bureau, he told me he loved me and would never leave me, he even promised to love my babies. He caressed my stomach swollen with pregnancy, kissed the place where the babies kicked and jostled against his cheek.

A tapping sound woke me; it was coming from the small window above the tumble dryers. Someone was throwing bits of gravel against the glass. I opened the window and breathed in the bracing December air. There below me in the yard was Fei Fei, hugging herself warm; her cheeks white with cold.

"Hello Mai Ling."

My immediate reaction was to leave the two-faced cow standing there.

"Please, don't shut the window, I've brought your things," she said.

"What things?"

"Let me in and I'll show you."

I met Fei Fei at the back door and hurried her inside the laundry. She settled beside the radiator and blew her cupped hands warm. Her fingers were bony, her knee caps visible beneath her jeans. Her hair smelled unwashed. Nothing remained of the girl whose ambition was to be beautiful, like a lady who shopped on Women's Street.

"I gathered your belongings from the dorm when I realised you weren't coming back," she said. "They threw me out."

I stopped emptying the tumble dryer and dropped onto a laundry basket. So it was true, the workers had been disposed.

"They tried to fob us off with redundancy pay-outs, but we knew they'd never do it. Crock of bureaucracy shit. It was a rubbish place to work anyway," she laughed bitterly.

I laughed too, comforted to see suffering in someone else's face other than my own. "You want a drink?"

I stole Suzinne's liquor which was hidden behind the washing machine inside a small cavity in the brickwork. The heat of it warmed my throat and settled my aching guts. My eyes returned frequently to the carrier bag containing Yifan's book of traditional tales and my wooden figurines. Fei Fei poured us both another drink and helped herself to some of Suzinne's peanuts while I flicked through Yifan's book.

"To our pride and joy, our dear son..."

I thought of my own family, their faces fading as the months passed, their voices reduced to common phrases, "Husband! Your food is making the chickens fat!" and "Wife, why aren't the chickens making us fat?" The inscription wished Yifan *a happy life, working his hardest for the good people of China.* Gentle Yifan, working hard and loving deeply, he had been a friend when I needed one. His soul was goodness. I couldn't say the same of mine. I couldn't say I was a good woman of China.

I left the other items in the bag. It was too much to go through everything, all those broken pieces of the past.

"I'm sorry," Fei Fei said.

"Don't apologise."

"Not for the bag, I mean I'm sorry for not doing more to help you."

"Maybe you should leave," I said in an attempt to hide our past behind the wall. "My boss will be coming back soon to check up on me."

Fei Fei wiped her nose on the sleeve of her thin and mucky jacket – it was the denim one I'd bought her the night of the ferris wheel.

"It was me who followed you to the abortionist, Mai Ling," she blurted suddenly. "I told Manager He you hadn't gone through with it. I snitched about Yifan, too. I said you were seeing each other... I'm so sorry. I was on my way to warn you the night Manager He came to your dorm and... oh, Mai Ling, I made things worse not better. I didn't realise what I was doing or the consequences... I was so stupid."

"Stop!" I stared at her, numb.

"He said I was beautiful. He gave me extra money to send home to my family. I didn't know he was using us. He told me not to worry. I asked why I was spying on you, he said it was for our own good, for our safety. I followed you into town and all around the factory." Fei Fei shook as she confessed.

"I thought I was going mad," I said, remembering the feeling of being watched wherever I went. I knew someone was there; that day I met Yifan in the Suseng Teahouse, I saw something at the window and then you were gone. And in town, when you bumped into me on your way to buy melons. You insisted I buy the pink shoes; it was him who sent you to bring me back to the factory, wasn't it?"

Fei Fei nodded, her head bowed in shame. "I've come to say sorry...not to be forgiven."

I picked the bag of my belongings off the floor and held them close to my weary heart. "You've said it, so now you can go."

Suzinne appeared at the laundry room door, scowling.

"Who's she?"

"She's just leaving."

Suzinne shouted at me about the state of the breakfast pots, how I hadn't scrubbed them hard enough – another guest had gone down with stomach pains. I felt humiliated being told off in front of Fei Fei. It was like we were back at the factory. Out of the corner of my eye, I noticed Fei Fei cowering.

Suzinne shoved a pile of sheets into my arms. "And make sure you tuck the sheet corners in tightly."

"I can see you have work to do. I'll go."

I felt a twinge of something, perhaps sorrow or maybe an impulse to forgive her. We had all made such terrible mistakes at Forwood.

"Fei Fei –" I called after her.

She kept on walking. Her legs were so thin, unlike the rest of the plump, well-fed guests who sauntered along the hotel corridors. Without my belongings Fei Fei had nothing to carry. I think perhaps they were all she had owned in the world. I closed the laundry door and put the dirty bed linen into the machine. Then I watched the machine fill with water and started to plan.

My first step was to learn English. I began with the McDonald's menu in Kim's drawer, but burgers and milkshakes weren't going to get me to England. At breakfast, I earwigged conversations and managed to pick up the odd word. Sensing Suzinne was in one of her better moods, I asked if she'd teach me the basics.

"Why do you want to know?"

"Isn't everyone learning it these days?"

I thought I'd blown my chances, then later, whilst folding sheets, she said, "Pass me the sheet... the *sheet*," she repeated, pointing to the pile.

"Seat?"

Suzinne laughed and pulled over a chair. "No, this is *seat*." She picked up the linen. "This is *sheet*."

For the rest of that week Suzinne spoke only English. Her mouth pouted like the English Queen as she told me off.

"No, Mai Ling, you're putting too much soap into the washing machine! Clean the sheets! Don't waste expensive powder!"

Most sentences went over my head, but I could tell when she wasn't happy with the way I did my chores.

Meanwhile, the couples showed off their new babies at breakfast, lunch and supper. There was a captive audience of hotel staff and guests, even the odd businessmen who stayed a night at The Bluewater cooed at the sight of so many babies. Nancy and Iain stole the show with my twins. 'Twin eggs,' as Chef nicknamed them. Of course I was jealous. People are such bloody hypocrites. They couldn't see they were the same beloved children whose mother had once begged on the street to afford clean water; and that it was only the arms that held them and the clothes they wore that had changed.

My girls yelled a lot. Their front teeth were cutting early as mine had done. I made their congee especially runny. I wanted to tell Nancy she hadn't wrapped them up warm enough. Our Chinese babies like to feel safe inside plenty of layers, not dressed up in little velvet dresses and bows. These thoughts ate away at me so much that some days I couldn't bear to serve at Nancy and Iain's table.

The hotel made a big effort in December to make the place jolly. Management ordered in a fir tree from Xiangshan Forest Park, but by mid-December it drooped pitifully. It was a nightmare for me, crawling under the tree to sweep up all those pine needles, crying because they reminded me of a brother I might never see again and the babies that were so close but so far from me every day. By then, the westerners had grown friendly with one another and some decided to spend Christmas in Nanchang.

Iain organised a group photo of all the new babies and parents. The children were grouped together on a settee in the lobby; some wore Santa outfits that said, 'My First Christmas'. My girls managed to smile at their new father and, for a brief moment, I persuaded myself I had done the right thing. Iain and Nancy could offer them a much better life, a whole future's worth of *Happy Christmas,* fat turkeys and presents enough to fill a room. I emptied the dustpan full of pine needles into a rubbish sack. What right did I have to chase after them?

On Christmas Eve, Nancy and Iain were late down to breakfast and I started to panic they may have checked out early. I was so relieved to see them that I dropped my tray, some teacups smashed across the tiled floor. Iain rushed over to help me pick them up.

"Thank you, you very kind man," I said in English. He looked impressed because it was the first proper thing I had said in his language.

"We're leaving for England today," he smiled.

His words punched through my chest.

"We'll be home for Christmas."

I wanted to tell him he was wrong, that I was their home. "Mr Milne, I have present. For babies' Christmas." I reached urgently into my apron and offered him the wooden figurine Fei Fei had salvaged from Forwood.

He turned Mrs Nie over in his hand and stroked the new slippers I had stitched in red satin.

"Oh my, she's lovely, did you make this yourself?"

Yes, just as I made your daughters. I nodded.

Nancy was busy settling the twins into their buggy; I gave a polite smile in her direction. It was too hard for me to say goodbye.

Never let you go.

The stairs felt steep as I raced to the third floor. I paused on the stairwell to catch my breath and wait unseen for Nancy and Iain to appear in the street below. They were going to the park, to take photographs before leaving Nanchang. I watched them cross the road with their new double buggy bought from Walmart.

Taking the master key from my apron pocket, I unlocked Room 111. It smelt sweet. They had positioned my babies' travel cot near the window; I dragged it away, cold air was no good for their *qi*. I stroked the tiny indentations their bodies had made in the mattresses. Their blankets were still warm as skin against my cheek. Two bottles, half full, rested on the bedside table. How much Nancy expected them to drink! What was she thinking, feeding my babies like they were giants? Their matching green suitcases were packed and ready by the door; their dirty towels strewn over the bidet for me to collect.

I didn't have much time. Iain had left his wallet out on the dressing table. Silly man, he was far too trusting. I rifled through it in search of his business cards, taking only one, so as not to rouse any suspicions.

Iain Milne, Portrait Photographer.

It even gave me the name and the address of his studio, 'Fleeting Moment,' including a telephone number. His hometown was Manchester. I slipped the card inside my apron and went to collect some of the dirty towels, in case Suzinne caught me out.

The corridor was empty apart from an elderly couple doddering in the opposite direction. I bowed and hurried to the laundry room with the bundle.

Manchester... I said the word quietly under my breath as I raced down the stairs.

Manchester, I go live... The words were like salty food in my Chinese mouth. I thirsted to be there.

Man-chest-er... I loved the way that English city tasted on my tongue.

The nurse at Hope didn't warn Ricki that May looked like modern art: wires strapped to her head, tubes sunk from her nose, tape on her hands, pads on her chest – what the hell were they all for? Ricki perched at the foot of her bed. After a while, she edged closer, checking May's face for any movement.

I see your eyes and nose. I feel your tears…

Ricki had memorised whole sections of May's letter. She didn't need a translator to figure out that May loved her, that she hadn't just dumped her and Jen without giving a shit as she had believed before China, before Jinsong, before everything.

A small grain of goodness in my bitter agony of a life.

This woman in a coma loved her.

I will guard you with my life.

May's choice – no choice at all.

The doctors at Hope had transferred May from Intensive Care to a private room attached to their high dependency ward. The perfect place for a life to slip away unnoticed, without any fuss, without trauma. Ricki gazed at the tube which disappeared into May's nose and wondered what they fed her on – was it the same watery stuff they served in The Bluewater for breakfast? Or full English?

It's true, May: *I think of you all the time, from the start to the end of the day as well as all through the night.*

A voice from behind startled Ricki. "You can stay, we won't be long," said a nurse. She was accompanied by a younger nurse holding fresh sheets. "It's important we keep her moving,"

"It's okay. I'll go buy a Coke," said Ricki.

When she returned, May looked the same, but the clean sheets were smoothed down, the window opened a crack. A box of tissues sat on her bedside cabinet, along with a fresh jug of water.

"May," she whispered. "Can you hear me?"

Thoughts of you burn like a fire over wild plains.

"I read your letter… Jen gave it to me in Hunan. She translated it into English so I could understand. What a brain box, huh? I wanted to come and see you…I wanted to say sorry, for not letting you be part of me…I didn't realise. I pushed you so far away…. I thought my tummy mummy hated us. I didn't believe

Mum and Dad's stories – I thought they only told us you loved us to make us feel wanted... But now I've read your letter."

How long will it be before you arrive and these arms hold you?

"They don't know I'm here – Mum, Jen, the social worker, any of them...I wasn't going to come. I wanted to leave you in China...I even went back to the institute, thinking I could say goodbye to you there. I left your photograph on the steps - the one from the birthday party, do you remember, May? Shit you looked frightened, like you were out of control. I guess you were. What did it feel like seeing me turn sixteen? I thought of you, you know...that day. I thought about my real mum and wondered if... Shit, May, you kept a good secret."

If I cannot keep you here, then I'll find a better place and a way out for us.

"Do you think you found that place, May? Did you do the right thing coming here to find us? I dunno, really I don't...You did what you had to do. You were a shit hot sleuth, May, I'll give you that."

They cannot take you from me.

"Your brother misses you...We went to find him. It was Jen's idea, she talked Guan into going – he's Yifan's son. I'm guessing you don't know about him? He's really cool, his exhibition was awesome, it's given me loads of ideas. I've decided not to bother with the unit at Afflecks, I'm going to use part of Dad's studio instead. I can even sell some of my work...I don't know whether people will get it, but it's a start... I've promised Mum and Dad I'll take up a place at Queen Elizabeth's...It's not Oxford but, hey, they have some pretty good dark rooms and one of the tutors seemed cool, Dad and I went to meet them... It feels right, May. I'm gonna give Afflecks a miss for a while... No point hanging round where you're not wanted. You know what I mean, don't you May? Oh, and something else, Jen got her A*s – nine of them, and one for Chinese...you must have done a good job with her, May. She got all the brains, huh? But then we're not stupid, you and me, are we?"

No harm will ever reach you.

"It's weird, but since coming back from China I feel safer, like I can breathe again. Like a big stone's been rolled away... I had to go back and see it, didn't I? China...couldn't avoid the place forever. Boy, do they like cycling! I nearly got mowed down in Nanchang."

Ricki reached out and nudged May's hand. "May...*pssst*, May, can you hear me beneath all that wire and shit? You do know how weird you look lying there? I keep thinking you're going to wake up and say "Surprise!"...Maybe not, hey...I think somewhere you can hear me though? Maybe I could hear you too, if I'm honest. You were always telling me you were my mum. May...May? You used to look right through me sometimes, like you had x-ray vision...don't think I didn't notice."

May's lips looked dry where they hung slack around the tube. Ricki rubbed them with some of her lip balm. Melon flavour, she would like that, there were loads of melons in Nanchang.

Whatever they say, we'll never be parted – not even for a second.

"I'm shit at goodbyes," Ricki whispered. "So I won't say it...I'm just gonna turn round and walk out that door...but I'll take you with me, May...I'll take you...Shit, Mum, I've got to go now. It's getting late. I've got to go home..."

She waited a second, in case May's eyes opened, her hand twitched, her tongue lapped against the tube in gratitude for the lip balm.

She reached out and laid the bag of red soil from Hunan at May's feet.

The September air felt warm and fresh inside her room, as though it was spring and not the beginning of autumn when everything starts to die. Summer's effects lingered on – perhaps May would feel the sunshine behind her eyelids?

Ricki squeezed one last time on the hand that had rocked her as a baby; then let go gently, sensing the right time would never come.

Portrait of a young woman

Woman at Piccadilly bus stop say, "Typical bloody weather!"

She say it at no-one, so I not answering.

On bus, I check Pocket Collins English Dictionary which tell me *weather* is tiānqì, sky breath. Today weather is white sky, feeble rain. Bones, they ache. March in England not like March in China, where sky sometimes yellow and fierce and rain feel ancient, like is falling for centuries.

Woman from bus stop she sit next to me.

"Chinese?" she ask and lights up cigarette. Her fingers yellow from love of smoking. She want sell me something? I think.

Chance to practise English. "Yes, I'm Chinese."

Simple! Phew! English not so hard after all. Ten years of Suzinne's lessons are not waste.

Then she say, "Student?"

I say, "No. Teacher."

The law is no smoking on English bus. I keep my gob shut. Stranger tell her off anyway.

"Typical bloody buses," she moan. "Typical bloody government, no pleasure in anything these days."

No-one on bus care she insult government. I terrified. Rest of journey I wait for cadre to appear, but only more little English grandmothers get on with bags on wheels. Eventually I take giant breath.

Woman, she talk to herself. She lonely like me? No man at home? She ask where I live. I tell her home no place for me right now, and she offer cheap room in *bedsit*. Woman's name is Mrs Eva.

Mrs Eva bedsit nowhere near middle of Manchester, nowhere near Iain and Nancy. I will hunt *long and hard* for find New Street, where Iain work. For that, I am needing better map.

Cooker in my room it have no fire. I light with switch. Shop on street corner are Indians and I buy 5kg of rice in plastic bag, enough for strangers in bedsit. Then I go big store that smell of bread in some place and sick in other. Spend two hungry hour looking for food, trying to understand label, with English nonsense music sounding in my ears. I buy ginger, chilli, onion, garlic, noodle and some other vegetable called *daffodil* which I not know, but it look like chive. I also buy 'Wide-rule Notebook,' pen and 'A-Z of Greater Manchester'. Manchester, it not seem that great so far, but maybe tomorrow it will be better... the ASDA good place for learning new words. It smell also of dog. Dog belong to man with magazine, *The Big Issue*. He standing on pavement outside. But I walk by, pretend like I invisible magic paintbrush in tale of Ma Liang.

There are five *New Streets* in Greater Manchester: New Street Swinton, New Street Eccles, New Street Droylsden, New Street Radcliffe and New Street Altrincham. In words of Mrs Eva, search for daughters is *piece of cake*. I have Iain's business card, but what if Iain not photographer no more? What if, ten years pass, 'Fleeting Moments Photographic Studio' not exist? Maybe he become ancient and stop working? Maybe so many things... I have to try. I have to look.

Feeble rain all April.

May. I new woman – new woman called May. *Cut and finish* from 'Kayz Cutz,' give me curls for first time my whole life. I wear respectable teacher clothes from BHS. Everything ready. So why not I feel ready? I journey long way to find what belongs me and today sky breath is smiling, good sign. Happiness in the air down New Street Altrincham.

I turn a corner and see 'Fleeting Moment Photographic Studio'!

Relief. It feel like sunshine after storm. I walk past the shop on different side of street: one time, two, three time, I walk by. It definitely Iain shop. I re-born on New Street Altrincham.

Open door and enter. Suddenly Iain, he right there in front of me! He same face of English Prince Charles. Ha! My English go and I say "nǐ hǎo" by mistake. Iain is proud because he know two words in Chinese.

"Nǐ hǎo." He even bow.

I am like shy English raspberry.

He quickly run out of words. His Chinese, not so good. "How can I be of help?" he ask.

I need him to do portrait, a gift for my fiancé back home in China.

He seem very interested in me; it definitely same Iain I remember from Bluewater Hotel. He fussy and polite. Iain also very productive worker – so many happy, foreign faces staring at me from his walls! Like ancestral shrine. All smiles on Iain's photos. All happy families, babies, pretty women and many, many grandparent who should really be dead.

Emotions, they get the better of me. I start to cry, ready for seeing my daughters after all the lost years spent waiting.

He pass me a Kleenex from box on reception desk. "Oh dearie me."

I blow my nose so loud. "Sorry."

"Take a seat. I'll fetch you a glass of water? My name's Iain Milne, by the way."

"Thank you. My name's May."

I sit in the corner where cool airs from fan. It all very nice 'Fleeting Moment,' no wonder photos they all smiling. Even water tasting clean and chilli. I hold my knees still when they are shaking.

Iain say, "Pardon me for asking, but I feel like I know you from somewhere. Have we met before?"

His sentence long and hard for me to understand. I prefer he speak slow.

He repeat, "Do we know each other?"

Best answer I have is, "No, I don't think so." I am good liar after years. Quickly, I tell him about my job as Chinese teacher in Altrincham. He swallow down all my story.

Iain gets his diary and ask me what date would suit me for the portrait. I say Saturday 10 o'clock. Enough time for getting two bus to Altrincham from Mrs Eva bedsit. Altrincham nothing like where I live with Mrs Eva. People here they taste tea in street cafe. Where I live, man he sit outside the ASDA with dog and *Big Issue* and taste tea on street. Easy to believe why man like Iain work in a place like Altrincham where there is happy, smiling, rich.

Portrait, it cost a hundred quid. About 1,000 yuan! I think how much of my daughters that buy me back? One hand? Two eye? Another beautiful black hair to match the one in my pocket?

Three days I wait. I buy new outfit from the ASDA. I choose a dress that make me look and feel more British – but I know my place: a person who not belong. Foreigner. I see myself from outside, like window shopper. Way other see me: getting on the Stagecoach buses and asking direction, walking here and there in town, always a little lost. Is like watching myself in movie. My head, it still in China, thinking different way about how to do things like eat, talk, get up early for work and follow rules.

Iain happy to see me. Maybe he feel relief? I turn up and am not *scamming it*, as Mrs Eva say. He lead me into different room and sit me down. I like British Queen on his stamp. Prince Charles take my photograph, all big ears and greying hair. I laugh without meaning to.

He start taking picture. His camera is new, still posh. "Oh, that's lovely!"

At Forwood, factory photographer say smiling not allowed. He tell me to have "face without expression". With Prince Iain, it impossible not to smile. So much my face has to say that words cannot. Ten years I live without my daughters and nearly I am seeing them – that one hell of a lot to smile about.

Iain say "lovely" again. I like that word. I like the way he say it. *Luv-lee*, through his nose. Feel like long time since I hear such nice word said in such nice way. Last person to speak like that is Yifan. Iain ask me a question about him like he hearing my thought.

He say, "Your fiancé is going to love these pictures. What's his name?"

More *scamming*. Secretly I wish my story is the truth. Yifan, my fake fiancé. "Yifan? Ah yes, he's a doctor." My mouth is excited by the lie and won't stop. "We meet at university. He work in a very large hospital in China."

Iain, he concentrate on my photo. "Ooh, clever chap then. And no talking for a second now, that's it. *Luv-lee*."

Iain he take hundreds of photo of my girls in ten years. Even in The Bluewater Hotel – one second after they are given him and Nancy – Iain snap-snap-snapping. You see, my mind it still in China even when body move to England; it not really matter if I wear British dress from the ASDA.

The past, my past, my girls' past – that not something that can be deleted like bad photo on digital camera.

Next we try a different sort of picture. A 'missing my fiancé' picture. Iain, he take away chair. He say, "Act natural." Impossible! He gets me a flower – a white rose – and asks me to smell it. We stand by open window. Summer light it flood in. Outside church bells are ringing. Shame photo have no sound. If Yifan could see me now! I so glad, at last, standing by this window. Truthful smile appear.

After he finish taking photos, we talk. Chance I am waiting for. I rehearse a thousand times, same way I rehearse Schnelleck. This time, nothing go wrong. I make promise to myself.

I say, "Excuse me, Iain, but can I leave some of my business cards in your shop?" I hold one out for him to see. It say:

May Guo, Chinese Teacher
All ages. GCSE level and beyond.
Competitive Rates.

I not include Mrs Eva's address on card because then everyone would be knowing I live in ungreat part of Greater Manchester.

Iain take one, he look at it carefully. He like me and feel sorry for me, I can tell. *It not easy running a business. Not easy loving fiancé in China.* I know this what he think.

"Usually I'd say no…" He hesitate like he making some big political decision. "But why not? You can leave them on the desk, where people will see."

"You have customers who wanting learn Chinese?"

"Yes, as it happens."

"Oh, really?" I act surprised.

"I have a daughter. She's desperate to learn Mandarin."

Only one? Where my other daughter? I almost blurt out.

"Her name's Jennifer, she's ten."

"Ten… Good age for learning. You take this card and ask Jennifer and then you ring me on this number. I come to your house for lesson… Rates very competitive, Mr Milne."

He smiling again. What he thinking? That I am good little Chinese business woman? He not thinking I his daughters' good little Chinese mother… But what's all this crap about only one daughter, where's my other girl? I know they both living with Iain and Nancy. I see them leave Bluewater Hotel with my own eyes.

"Listen, May, I'll call you when the portrait's ready, you can come and collect it and we can talk more about the lessons then."

"Thank you," I say. "That's very kind; I look forward to seeing photo."

After this I pay huge sum of £100 and leave the 'Fleeting Moment'. A breeze blow at the hem of ASDA dress. I am flying with happiness. My plan, it work.

A week later and phone ring. It Iain.

"Hello, May, your portrait's ready."

I say, "That very good news. What about Jennifer's lesson?"

Line, it go quiet.

"Um, actually May, we've decided not to go ahead with any lessons at the moment. I talked it through with my wife, Nancy, and she felt it was too soon. Jennifer has been quite unsettled at school lately and we… Well, like I say, it's a little premature. But we'll keep your card and perhaps in a year or so… I'm happy for the cards to stay in my shop."

So many words, what this shit he telling me?

"May, are you still there?"

"Jennifer not want lesson?"

"Not at the moment, I'm sorry to get your hopes up."

"I come collect photograph." My heart so swollen it on the floor. I not waiting another whole year until they decide time right for daughter to be learning Chinese. Has to be now!

"Goodbye Mr Milne." I drop phone like it a snake in my hand.

Room feel so lonely all of sudden that I want to scream just to hear some noise. I not sure if I make a sound? I'm on my bed, thumping pillow.

Where my daughters?

Where my daughters?

Where my daughters?

Where my daughters?

I wake up with face like wet sponge. Mouth dry. Heart lumpy. I take little wooden figurine out of wardrobe where I keep all my old Chinese belongings, it all what's left of past. Childish to talk to a doll, I know, but I not feeling like sensible adult. Mr Nie tell me not to give up; he want Mrs Nie. I promise to try again with different plan. Why my life never going way I want it to?

Portrait of me is bigger than I expect! And surprise beautiful. Iain some kind of magician.

"Well, what do you think?"

We sit in reception. Photograph on his walls are like audience to my performance.

"I like it. You done very good job, Mr Milne."

"I must admit, I was pleased with it. The light was just right by the window."

He must know his camera like an old friend. My Chinese face, it look gentle on picture. My skin is silky like *chang-p'ao*. Nothing like Worker 2204, Electronic Circuitry. It is portrait of a young woman, *alive and kicking*. I feel pride to survive all way to England in secret.

"Would you mind if I do a re-print for display?" Iain points at other photo. I even beautiful enough for his walls – for his posh Altrincham customers! This shock me, seriously.

"It would be an honour." Perhaps, with my face stuck on a wall, daughters they have more chance of seeing portrait than real face, I think, miserable.

That very same second door open and in walk Nancy with my twins. It like some big God he hear my thought and decide to lend a hand. I not ready. Not knowing what to do: laugh, cry, be serious?

"Nancy, is everything alright?" Iain say.

She has hurricane face. Her arms they heavy with bags from Sainsbury's supermarket. She look at me like I might try sell her *Big Issue*. I smile polite. It feel like fast river runs between us and we stand either side – but whether she feel this, I doubt.

"Sorry to interrupt," she say, not recognising me. "Jennifer, Ricki, go play with the toys while I talk to Daddy."

I repeat their names in my head. Jennifer. Ricki. What kind of names these are?

What they mean?

Nancy angry about her bank card not working. She *sick and tired* of shops.

Twins they start to squabble over toys. Next thing I know, I'm kneeling at coffee table for make jigsaw. Twins, they stop fighting and watch. Ricki's frown melt. Jennifer, she pass me corner piece. Jigsaw is pony. Jennifer tell me she has pony called Lucy who she share with French girl, Sandrine. I am wondering what French girl doing in Altrincham? I ask if Lucy is good at jumping. She tell me about winning silver medal in *gymkhana*. Jennifer she such a chatter box, she borrow Ricki share of word.

I see Ricki guard final piece of jigsaw under table. "You want to finish pony off?" I ask.

She shake her head. My stubborn baby, she always resist – sleep, food, nappy.

I say, "Poor pony can't see without your piece."

She shrug. I see a tide roaring inside my little girl and a piece missing from her also. She not understanding yet. The piece, she come find her.

"Who are you?" asks Jennifer.

"My name is May. Your Daddy take my picture. Look! What you think?" I show her the enormous portrait.

Jennifer tell me pretty. I want to kiss her forehead.

In the background, I hear Nancy explode in angry whisper. She not half as good as me at hiding feeling.

257

"Are you from China?" asks Jennifer.

"That's right, how you know?"

"Your face is like mine."

She not knowing how right she is – her skin from me, her nose, her eyes. I tell her China is where I grew up, but now I live in England. I wonder how much Nancy has told them about their past. It not easy for Nancy to invent story for telling a little girl who so full of question. Jennifer, she probably grow up to be police officer, she so nosy.

"Girls, put the jigsaw away now. We're going."

"Mummy, can't we stay here. I want to stay and play with May."

Nancy give me a look of question like she want to say, "Who the hell are you?" The look blow over. Perhaps she sense how amazing I am to see my babies again. Amazing and relief. Perhaps not?

"Mummy, you've made May cry," say Jennifer.

Ricki so quiet I am wondering if she speak at all. She still holding tight to the final piece of puzzle under coffee table.

Nancy bend over me. "Excuse me, are you alright?"

I shake my head. Stupid woman, what she expect when I not see my daughters for ten years and suddenly I there making pony jigsaw in the 'Fleeting Moment'.

Iain pass me another Kleenex. I am only customer in his shop to be using a whole box.

"Is it your fiancé?" he ask. "Just think how much he'll appreciate seeing your face again."

I storm into tissue. "It very hard not being with someone you love," I say, "Sorry I fussy."

"You have a fiancé?" ask Nancy.

The kids play some more; they not like seeing adult cry.

"He's in China." Iain tells Nancy my made-up story.

"Well that's a long way away. You must miss him terribly. I'm from the States. I know how hard it is to be so far from your family. Listen, what are you doing next Saturday?"

My ears stand up like ears of mountain dog.

"Why don't you come have lunch with us? Perhaps company might help?"

This is more than I can understand. Nancy, she invite me to her house?

Iain say, "Nancy, sweetheart, this is the lady I told you about – May, the teacher."

"May. Oh, right. Of course. How silly of me not to realise. Would twelve o' clock be okay, May?"

Iain he look confused.

Why Nancy change her mind so quick? First I not good enough for Jennifer, who is not ready to speak her own language and now... now it okay to have Chinese woman to lunch! Then I understand she see herself in me: missing home, missing America.

I say, "Twelve o' clock is perfect. Thank you, thank you. You very kind."

Nancy gathers up my daughters. I see Ricki put eyes in pony and complete jigsaw.

Sweet daughter.

I struggle home with my enormous portrait on bus. There is nowhere on the Stagecoach to put such strange object. I hold it to my chest. I hold it so tight because it so expensive. I feel like Ricki holding piece of jigsaw where she think no-one can see. I think of Grandmother and her jasmine bowls.

Never let you go.

Milne house it big. My feet go *crunchcrunchcrunch* towards front door. It twice as big as me in every direction and it painted postbox-red. I like letter arriving on mat.

"May, come on in. I'm so pleased you made it!" Nancy sing, opening the door.

Her hall is tidy. She also neat. "Let me take your coat. Goodness, aren't you too hot in all those layers?"

There is hook waiting for my coat in shape of flying duck. My coat it sit on duck's feet.

"Thank you, thank you."

I give her the most expensive chocolate I find in the ASDA. Mrs Eva give me advice about what to buy. She surprised when I tell her about friend in Altrincham, about lunch. She jealous, I think, because she has TV for friend. No-one else.

"So, May, how are you doing?"

"Oh, a little better. Sorry."

"No need to be sorry. I know it is tough living away from home."

I follow her into a room full of big soft chairs, too expensive to sit on. I sip her tea but it hard to be relax. I wonder, *where my daughters?* I not like to ask in case she think I nosy little Chinese woman and throws me out her big red door.

"I hope you like soup. I'm afraid it's not homemade."

"Soup very nice."

Nancy disappear into kitchen and I *stick my nose where it isn't wanted*, as Mrs Eva say. The house is not a normal sort of tidy. It like no daughter live here ever. Where all their toys? Where the mess? Few animal books under glass coffee table. But there are more photograph than I ever see in all my life – above Nancy fire, side table, all over window sill. All my twins! So this where she keep them, locked up in photo frame. The pictures are so good they must belong to Iain.

My heart, it stop when I see photo from The Bluewater Hotel. Is really the same one? I stare at reception desk in background and yes, there is Kim looking stressed because she having big baby delivery from welfare. This is picture I take! I remember! Picture, it belong to me.

"So, which part of China are you from May?"

Nancy's voice make me jump and I drop photo.

She rush over for fluffy carpet and pick it up; her question forgot.

"Sorry, very sorry, Mrs Milne."

We both have relief it not broken. Mrs Eva tell me I ask seven years' bad luck when I break hall mirror one day – but seven before they also not lucky for me. Only piece of luck I have is leaving China with fake passport.

Nancy start telling me about photo, her girls they adopted from China and this is moment they are 'born'. She should see the night they really born! The yīshēng who try drowning; the blood, the syringe, running half-dead in rain, Yifan who save me... Birth at Bluewater Hotel no birth at all. But to Nancy I see it mean everything. She have face like wet stone washed over with memory and suddenly I feel different for her in heart.

"You not able to have children?" I ask.

"We tried. We tried everything. IVF just wasn't working. I blame myself, even now, for leaving it too late. I put my career first. I was forty and I still couldn't decide whether I wanted children... All that pain we could have saved ourselves, if only we'd tried sooner. But, I guess you can't beat yourself up about the past. We might never have conceived, even if we'd started trying sooner."

What she meaning 'IVF'? I look it up later in Pocket Collins English Dictionary.

Nancy's face it hard around her eyes, like she struggle to stay young. She look two times my age? I ask her if getting girls from China is hard. I admit, I not knowing much about adoption.

"Oh yes, a great struggle. We were questioned about every part of our lives. The social worker came to our home, checked our finances, our medical records, asked hundreds of questions about our marriage, our families, our friends, our past. They watched us, closely. We went on parenting courses. They wanted to make sure we would make good parents. Then we waited two years for all the paperwork to go through before we could go to China for our girls," she say, holding the photograph like it the most precious day of her life.

"Long time for pregnancy."

A smile warms her face. "Yes. I suppose it is."

We talk more over soup she buy from the Covent Garden. It taste of carrot and something else; not including noodles, but it quite nice. I try not to slurp like a peasant in Milne's ever-so-tidy house. We sit on stools like we in a bar, but with no liquor for taking away nerve. Nancy ask me all sort of question. I never speak so much English in all my life. She want to know if I have family, what job I do in China and about my fiancé, Yifan. I take short answer because it hard keeping up so many lies. Tongue, it tired quick.

"Our daughters are from Nanchang," she say.

"Really?"

"Yes, do you know the city?"

"No."

I ask more about Jennifer and Ricki. I want know what happen after they leave China, what kind of little girls they are.

"They can be quite a handful at times, but they're good girls really. Jennifer is very bright, but is going through a phase of being very independent and stubborn. Ricki tends to be quieter, more like her dad – artistic."

It strange to hear her say 'dad' and mean Iain when I know it Manager He's blood that pump in daughters' veins. Honest, I prefer think of Iain as Dad. He gentle. He also very good portrait photographer. Manager He shit manager.

"They like school? Good grades? Education very important Mrs Milne."

"Jen likes school more than Ricki. She got moved up a year because she was ahead of her classmates. Ricki misses her. I'm not sure it was such a good idea to separate them."

It good Nancy care. Better still if my twins they stay together. That what I always wanting. For them never to part. Not like me who leave. I want them to be family: two parent, two sister. That not possible in China. In England everything possible. Now I here, I wonder if it possible have three parent?

"Ricki – what she like doing?" I ask.

"She's very creative: drawing, colouring, making things… Iain bought her a Polaroid for her tenth birthday and she loves taking pictures then making collages. There was a time when all her pictures were very dark – *yin*? We asked our social worker to take a look. She said it was normal and not to worry, that it would pass. She was working things through in her own way. But we're always watching them and worrying."

I starving for know. "Ricki ever ask about Chinese mum and dad?"

"No, never. We thought she'd have lots of questions. We figure in time she might want to talk more about her past, but for now she's keeping it all inside."

"And Jennifer?"

"Jen's more inquisitive, for sure. She's already said she wants to learn about China and maybe go back there one day."

I feel excited when Nancy say this. I want to see her straight away. "Where they go today?" I ask.

Nancy clear away empty soup bowls. "They've gone to play with friends. There's another set of twins in their class at school. I've got to go pick them up at four."

It three o'clock already. Time, it go too quick. I want stay forever and find lost years. I want make new years together. I want to live in family of two children, three parent.

"Mrs Milne, perhaps Jennifer want to learn Chinese?" I say, short of time.

Nancy she at sink, filling kettle. Her shoulders look tense. I know I say something forbidden. She not stop getting cups from cupboard, keeping hands busy so she not have to look at me.

"We're just not sure it's a good idea, May."

"She like China, no?"

"Yeah, she does."

"Then it good to learn language. Improve understanding of culture."

Nancy rub her head like she rubbing away bad thought. "It's just… I suppose it is the right thing to do," she say to herself. "I can't keep her to myself forever. You're right, Jen should be able to learn Chinese if she wants to. It's only fair that she finds out for herself."

I have no idea the decision is so hard for Nancy. I think it only me who has to make tough choice about whether daughters they stay or go.

"I have very competitive rates!"

Nancy give a broken laugh. I wonder why? Money big consideration; important to know how much lesson cost before she agree. I set careful price. Same as guitar lesson. I check the Indian shop window.

"Where do you live?" asks Nancy.

"No, no, I come to you. It better for student."

"It would have to be a Saturday morning; Sundays are our family days. It's Iain's only day off."

"Saturday good day for me too." I try not to sound like I landing on moon, excited for new discovery.

Nancy take giant breath like she dive under water. Her face very expressive. This why photographer like Iain loving her.

"You know, letting go is a strange thing, May. What is it they say, if you love someone you should let them go? It's not that easy though, is it? This might sound strange, but I suppose I'm scared that if Jennifer learns Chinese she might decide she likes it better...China, that is. Oh dear, that must sound very childish of me."

"Maybe daughters they come back?"

Nancy reach out suddenly and is hugging me. I am surprised to find myself tight against chest of foreign woman. Nancy soft around edge. Why she hold me this way? What I say? I only speaking truth, this time.

My daughters they coming into my life again. I am having need for patience. Next Saturday will be first lesson with Jen. Maybe soon, Ricki also want to meet China and her mother. I leave tidy Milne house like Tom Cruise: *Mission Impossible* complete.

Back at Mrs Eva bedsit I write in 'Wide-Rule Notebook'. I try capture feelings way Iain capture face beside window. Room is dark. I open curtain and it still dark. Tomorrow I buy fresh flowers from market to cheer up room. It not good for a mother to feel like she at her own funeral. Too long I am dead woman. Time for May to live.

But May, who she is? Illegal immigrant, living Greater Manchester, teaching Chinese. She story with new chapter for writing every day. Saturday, new words to add, new pages in book of May. A daughter to meet and lots of possible endings. It important for me to keep learning English to be good teacher. This language still so chewy in my mouth. I not always understanding what they say when they talk through nose, those Mancunians. But I am here!

It like I am sitting on big stone I keep secret – stone is past in China. How long until stone roll away and everyone realise May is Mai Ling? That for future, a different chapter. For now, it only present tense. Present most important tense in Chinese language. Writing feelings down in 'Wide-Rule Notebook' best thing to do.

I write until room turn black and I no longer seeing my writing on page. Right hand, it ache. It forget how to work hard, way it work in China. I turn on lamp, go to wardrobe and find carrier bag. I want to look one more time at old things Fei Fei bring to Bluewater Hotel. One thing stand out from all my belongings: Yifan's book, *Traditional Tales from China.* Good book for teaching Jennifer. She want to know all about where she from, here – old China. Understanding country is about understanding past. Same with people. Why I not know this before now? Yifan know it, but he very wise. That why he's doctor and I little nobody working in factory. I miss him same way plant miss sun in winter.

I climb into bed. Words in Yifan's *Traditional Tales* are lively, they jumping like sparks. Long time, I stare at words on page, at drawings. They brighten dingy bedsit and heart. I like light plugged into socket when I read. This what my twins miss. They also needing spark in their Chinese soul.

My right hand, it hot when I turn page and find story of the 'double happiness'. I not even knowing this in here! It so long since I am hearing this story. Student who fall in love on his way to capital. A picture of the couplet written in beautiful red ink on next page, just like Little Brother and I paint on door at Spring Festival. Two symbols, they join together. Student and his lover. Mother and her babies, I think. It very old story. Today it feel new – like me.

I see Yifan in God's Help Hospital where he work, so brave, so full of good. My heart, it ache a little to think this kind man forget all about me. More than ten years since we are speaking... I close *Traditional Tales*. My eyes, they heavy and ready for sleep. Today big day in life of May. Finally I step inside Milne family house. I talk to Nancy about my girls. Tomorrow feel exciting possible.

Last thing I see before my eyes close is portrait done by Iain. May, she stare at me. If she speak, portrait say she finally okay. May alive and hoping well. Alive in daughters. She even smiling truthful smile. What she thinking, this secret mother? That her babies they be *right as rain*, as Mrs Eva say.

Acknowledgements

I have been greatly blessed by a number of individuals, without whom this book would simply not have been written.

My praying friends: Sarah O'Sullivan, Lucille Toumi, Lucy Dobson and Nicola Allatt. You encouraged me to dream, believe and achieve this book whilst trusting in the Lord.

Steve O'Connor, thanks for your writing exercise on plot which led to a short story that grew into *The Secret Mother*, and Fran Brewin for your warmth and early encouragement. The talented writers on Lancaster University's Creative Writing MA 2007-08 made it one of the best year's of my life – thank you all. Deborah Swift and tutor George Green, your wise and generous insights improved this book and made a lasting impact on my writing.

Special thanks to the families who welcomed me into their homes and allowed me to ask questions about the long road to adopting Chinese daughters. As loving families go, yours are amongst the best.

The enthusiasm of my first readers blew me sideways and I'll always remember our special book feast. Ross Allatt, Sally Bowden and Rachel James I'm so grateful for your shrewd feedback and kind words.

The 'lovely ladies' from my book group: Caroline Mathole, Katie Levell, Jo Wysel and Sarah Boley. For sharing life, as well as great reads. Thanks, also, to the book groups who voted for my novel as part of the Hookline competition and Yvonne Barlow, my editor, who made the novel a published reality.

My family: how can I sum up your massive love and support? Thank you for believing in me at all times. Especially you, Mark, for living and breathing this book, well into the small hours, with such patience and shared joy.

Finally, to the one I call Father - thank you always, from your child.

Discussion Questions For Book Groups

1. May keeps her identity as the twins' birth mother a secret from them for six years. What else does she conceal and from whom?

2. Do you think secrets protect or harm the characters in the novel? Which character's secret made the biggest impression on you and why?

3. May is sixteen when she leaves home. The twins, Jen and Ricki, are sixteen when they realise May is their birth mother. How does the author portray growing up? How are the twins' experiences of adolescence similar to May's? How do they differ?

4. In what ways does May's character evolve? Do your feelings towards her change over the course of the novel?

5. Which character provoked the strongest reaction in you, and why?

6. Different kinds of love are depicted in the novel: parental, sibling, romantic and platonic. Which relationship interested you the most, and why?

7. To what extent do you think May was in control of her own fate, or was she a victim of circumstances?

8. How do the female characters in the novel exert their own will? What limits them?

9. The novel is set in Nanchang and Manchester. How would you describe the sense of place in The Secret Mother? What links the two cities? How does the novel present economic and cultural changes in post-Mao China?

10. What surprised or interested you about Chinese factory life?

11. May's belongings reveal her to be the twins' birth mother. What other objects are important in the novel, and what do they tell us about the secret mother? Which of your own personal effects reveals the most about you?

12. If the story was to continue, what do you think should happen next?

About the author

Victoria Delderfield was born in 1979. She grew up on the edge of the North York Moors, and has also lived in Burgundy, France. She holds a first class honours degree in English and French from The University of Manchester and an MA in Creative Writing from Lancaster University. She has worked in the charitable sector as a Marketing Manager. Victoria is a mother of two boys and lives in Manchester.

The Secret Mother is her first novel and was chosen for publication by book groups from across the UK.

@delderfi
www.victoriadelderfield.com

Lightning Source UK Ltd.
Milton Keynes UK
UKOW04f1344180915

258807UK00002B/10/P